The clockwork be[...]nt, pinioned on the bla[...]g's face. Then it slowly, a[...] its tracks. Whirring noises rose and clattered briefly from its collapsing form, only to die away once more.

Silence descended immediately on a battlefield wreathed in acrid-smelling fog. The king let go of his blade and stood up unsteadily, shoulders trembling. Aunadar, the only man still holding a sword, poked at the glittering body a few times.

It lay still, but Thomdor could barely see it through the swimming tunnel. He staggered forward. He had to tell Azoun to summon aid for Bhereu. . . .

The baron stopped short at the sight of His Majesty. The king's flesh was bone-white and drawn as tightly over his skull as that of any mummy in a tomb. The royal eyes were wide, almost panicked, and Azoun's brow and beard were beaded with dripping sweat.

The king mouthed a few words Thomdor could not catch, then collapsed. . . .

Other FORGOTTEN REALMS® Hardcover Novels from TSR

FANTASY ADVENTURE

CORMYR
A Novel

Ed Greenwood
and Jeff Grubb

CORMYR:
A NOVEL

Copyright ©1996, 1998 TSR, Inc.
All Rights Reserved.

Distributed to the book trade in the United States by Random House, Inc. and in Canada by Random House of Canada Ltd.

Distributed to the hobby, toy, and comic trade in the United States and Canada by regional distributors.

Distributed worldwide by Wizards of the Coast, Inc. and regional distributors.

Cover art by Ciruelo Cabral

First Printing: July 1996
First Paperback Edition: April 1998
Printed in the United States of America
Library of Congress Catalog Card Number: 96-60811

9 8 7 6 5 4 3 2 1

ISBN: 0-7869-0710-X

8572PXXX1501

U.S., CANADA, ASIA,
PACIFIC, & LATIN AMERICA
Wizards of the Coast, Inc.
P.O. Box 707
Renton, WA 98057-0707
+1-206-624-0933

EUROPEAN HEADQUARTERS
Wizards of the Coast, Belgium
P.B. 34
2300 Turnhout
Belgium
+32-14-44-30-44

Visit our website at **www.tsr.com**

This book is dedicated to Jen and Kate,
who showed extreme restraint,
and who did not kill us while we
were writing it. Our love always.

E.G. & J.G

"And in this land I'll proudly stand
Until my dying day, sir;
For whate'er king o'er all command,
I'll still be a Cormyte brave, sir."

The Cormyte's Boast
Master Bard Chanthalas

A NOTE ABOUT CHRONOLOGY

Traditional year names in the Realms were established by Alaundo the Seer, a powerful ancient wizard who is still held in great esteem, since his prophesies continue to come true to this day. Years prior to the time of Alaundo are (generally) unnamed. Those since his time (circa –200 DR) have recognized names in the Realms.

Cormyr has its own form of reckoning years, dating from the crowning of the first Obarskyr king and the official founding of the nation. However, for convenience to the reader, the authors, and the beleaguered editor, we have used Alaundo's original year listing, and the better known (though similar) Dale Reckoning (DR) throughout.

Prologue

The Dragon's Land
A Time Before the
Years Were Named
(–400 DR)

hauglor, King of the Forest Country, turned in a low, banking dive. As the wind's whistle became a tearing, humming drone, the treetops of the vale rose swiftly to meet him. He let out a deep-throated roar, and the small herd of forest buffalo bolted from their hiding place, stumbling and snorting in panic. Most of the shaggy beasts swerved to plunge back into the forest as Thauglor's shadow passed over them.

Not good, thought Thauglor. The dragon banked again and cut across the path of the beasts that were still visible, bellowing a second time. The twenty or so animals that remained wheeled in a confusion of dust and churning hooves and headed in the opposite direction, back toward the clearing where Thauglor intended to meet them.

The great black dragon unfurled his wings and beat down powerfully, cutting the heavy summer air in long, steady strokes, seeking to catch the stampeding beasts just as they broke from the forest cover. For a fleeting moment, he could hear the splintering and thrashing of their frantic passage beneath him. Skimming the treetops, Thauglor had to curl the tips of his wings and

1

swerve to dodge the tallest oaks and duskwoods as he rushed to bring death to the beasts below.

Thauglor the Black and the buffalo herd reached the clearing at the same instant.

The expected updraft at the edge of the trees lifted the great dragon slightly as the first of the shaggy brown forms broke free of the forest cover. Thauglor's great shadow fell across them, the high summer sun shining through his thin wing membranes. The bawling herd tried to turn again, back to the cool protection of the trees, but by then it was too late.

The dragon roared a third time, a roar of triumph, and fell among the tightly packed, frightened animals. They were screaming and bolting in all directions now, but Thauglor swooped among them with ruthless precision.

His great scaled bulk bore down on one luckless beast, snapping the buffalo's spine and smashing the hapless creature flat. Thauglor's claws reached out to tear the bellies of another fleeing pair. Even as they shrieked and struggled, the dragon's jaws closed on a fourth meal and tightened with a splintering of bone.

The dying beast thrashed in the teeth that imprisoned it, not realizing yet that it was dying. It lowed softly, calling for aid and comfort that would not come. The great wyrm shook it as a cat shakes a mouse, then flung it to the ground. The buffalo struck the hard-packed earth with a wet, messy thud, spasmed once, and then sagged into immobility, its struggles done forever.

Thauglor the Black, master of all the forest, looked about in satisfaction. The surviving buffalo had bolted back into the safety of the trees, leaving behind only the four offerings to the dragon's huntsmanship. Three lay like brown-shaded boulders tinged with fresh crimson streaks. The last of the offerings still twitched and spasmed in its final mortal moments.

Thauglor watched its passing with idle interest. The buffalo was lying on its side, staring up at its slayer with a single blood-filled eye. As the ancient black dragon loomed over it, the bleeding eye widened in even greater fear, and its owner attempted to squirm away, its broken back spasming as it tried to rise on shattered legs. Thauglor ripped open the creature's belly with a casual claw, and the light in the forest buffalo's eyes died.

It was time to dine. The great dragon wrapped his jaws around the still-warm body and tilted his head upward. Powerful muscles surged, distending the jaw to widen the passage to Thauglor's throat. The blood-drenched buffalo, small in comparison with the beast devouring it, slid effortlessly down the dragon's gullet. Had any creature dared to tarry in the clearing to watch an elder black dragon feed, it would have seen a small lump slide slowly along the throat, corded muscles halting it for a moment to crush it further before the buffalo disappeared forever into the belly of the wyrm.

The first morsel took the edge off Thauglor's hunger, and he approached the second in a more leisurely manner, taking the time to savor the buffalo's steaming entrails and stomach, rolling the juicy organs around in his mouth with an appreciative tongue before swallowing. He cracked the skull of his prey with the heavy grinding fangs along one side of his jaw, then plucked out the soft contents within with a deft stab of a delicate tongue tip.

The gentle, wet sound of Thauglor's feeding was drowned out by a small nearby screech—more of a draconian cough—and Thauglor raised his head from his midday meal, eyes suddenly narrow and dangerous.

At the edge of the clearing, another black dragon was settling out of the sky—a youngling, a runt no more than ten winters old, his scales still soft and shining as if he were newly emerged from the egg. The lightness of his belly plates marked him as one of Casarial's brood, and he showed all the impetuousness of Thauglor's youngest granddaughter. The newcomer eased forward, seeking to snare one of the remaining corpses from his elder.

Thauglor's eyes narrowed to slits, and he let out a low, throaty growl. There would be no sharing this day, at least not until the great black had had his fill. And definitely not with some youngling who showed so little respect as to try to sneak away a few scraps from Thauglor's buffet.

Thauglor rose on his haunches and spread his wings to their full extent, touching the tips together above his head and eclipsing the youth in his shadow. The young dragon froze in place beneath Thauglor's stare, and the older dragon wondered for a moment if the youngster would be foolish enough to press the issue.

The youngling's eyes told the tale. Pools of fear glimmered at their heart as the youth suddenly realized his peril. Slowly the youngling edged back.

Probably when the runt landed he had been thinking about how easy it would be to steal a scrap from the doddering elder, a creature so old that his scale edges were turning a pale violet. Only now would the youth realize that this was no aged and toothless wyrm. Only now might the youth think of stories told of the great and venerable progenitor of the local black dragons.

"Do you have a name, youngling?" said Thauglor, posing the question in the most archaic and exact tones of Auld Wyrmish. The scent that wafted from Thauglor's scales underscored that this was no polite request, but an imperious demand.

"K-Kreston," said the youth, stammering slightly, handling the ancient tongue with all the discomfort of a schoolboy in grammar class. "Spawn of Casarial out of Miranatol, grandchild of Hesior, blood of the mighty Thauglorimorgorus, the Black Doom. Sir."

"Your mother Casarial was often impetuous," said Thauglor. "Ask her how she gained the scar over her left eye." After a moment, he added levelly, "You should put that question to her carefully and politely."

The young dragon nodded, and Thauglor rumbled, "Wait at the edge of the clearing. You may have the remains. Better next time that you watch the hunt and learn to catch such meals yourself."

Another gulp and nod, and Kreston retreated to the forest's edge. His eyes still held their fear and never left the elder dragon. Though Thauglor never gave his own name—the youth was wise enough not to demand it— the purple-scaled elder was sure the young dragon had recognized his forefather.

Thauglor cut the choicest meats from the forest buffalo's corpse, wielding his dewclaw with the slicing skill of a master butcher, and took them into his mouth with a tongue that curled in indolent ease.

Not bothering to glance at the younger blackscales, Thauglor gnashed his old, yellowing fangs once, yawned, and turned to his other kills. His hunger was sated, but the King of the Forest Country deliberately cracked the skulls and feasted on the entrails of the two remaining bodies, gorging himself. As he did so, he cast an errant eye at the young male who waited like a quivering statue at the clearing's edge, wide eyes recording Thauglor's every move.

There were more like this Kreston every decade— black dragons of his bloodline whom he did not know personally. It had been at least a hundred summers since he'd last visited all of his descendants, children and grandchildren combined. Most of his own brood were properly deferential, as were their children. But these latest pups were almost insulting in their presumption . . . and the cute boldness of youth would be little protection as they moved into gangly adolescence. Thauglor would see to that.

Others would, if he did not. Perhaps another tour of his forest domain was in order, to put a little fear of their elders into foolish and arrogant young draconic skulls.

And he'd best be spreading more than a few tales of the ancient past, and lessons on hunting as well. Thauglor almost sighed aloud. He preferred to hunt, though he knew of blue wyrms and reds who would settle for the scavenger's life. But corpse wings—little more than scaled vultures—descended from his blood? Hmmph. Perhaps Casarial, who as youngest had always been spoiled, was remiss in training her young. Thauglor bore no qualms about eating creatures he hadn't slain, but he'd sired a family of hunters, not corpse buzzards.

5

Yet that was a matter for another day. The summer sun was glimmering brighter in the cloudless blue sky, and already black flies were swarming about the cooling carrion. The young dragon waited his turn at the spoils, shifting no more than one errant talon in his growing impatience. Thauglor thought of carrying off the remains as a lesson or burying them in dust, but relented. A hungry hunter hunts poorly.

Thauglor arched his back and gave a great catlike yawn. Then he spread his wings and, without addressing the youth again, leapt into the sky. The black's old muscles and pinions strained as he scalloped the air beneath his wings in great, heavy beats, seeking the chill heights with a speed no smaller-winged youngling could hope to match. One more warning to the youth, Thauglor thought.

Thauglor circled back over the clearing to find the youngling still crouched in the same spot, a little more eager, perhaps, but unwilling to rush forward until he was sure that Thauglor was finished. And gone. Most definitely gone.

Thauglor suppressed a grin and rolled slightly in a half-mocking salute as he passed over the clearing again, gaining altitude with every stroke. Yes, a grand tour of his domain was in order, on the excuse that recent encounters had made it necessary to ensure that younglings of his line were being properly trained, but in truth just as much to remind Casarial and the others who the true master of the forest was. Obviously she had not taught that one—Kreston?—well enough.

Beneath the great dragon, his forest kingdom stretched out in a great green patchwork. The bulk of the land was closely spaced trees, broken every few miles by a tree-fall clearing, bare patch, or a bald tor. The lighter phandar and silverbarks dominated marshy spots, while the shadowtops and duskwoods rose like spires on the drier hills, and they in turn gave way as the land climbed to the cinnamon hues of gnarled felsul and coppery laspar that ringed the timberline, where the soaring rock began.

Thauglor's land was bounded by mountains on three sides and a narrow inlet of the Inner Sea on the fourth. To the west rose the youngest of the mountain ranges, still sharp-toothed and newly crafted, its peaks sharp and forbidding. To the north was the largest range, a great buttress of stone against the failed and fallen wizard kingdoms beyond, an impassable wall made more hazardous by continual storms, whose flashing lightning lashed its flanks almost daily. Thunder ruled in the eastern mountains as well. Though tall, these peaks were more weathered, splintered by ages of rain and snow. This last range was broken by a number of low passes, where the forest spilled out into flat coastland beyond. Their peaks marked the eastern border of the lands of the Black Doom. All that lay between these mountains was his.

The southern border of his lands was guarded by a slim, silvery arm of star-carved sea, a drowned gulf born in violent skyfall so many eons ago that even Thauglor knew of it only through legends from his grave-gone elders. The shore was twisted and boggy, as if the land were slowly sinking into the island-dotted coast. A few great manyroots rose in their gnarled, defiant glory here, but the shore was more the domain of silverbarks, willows, and other water-loving things. For a dragon, it was a short hop to lands farther south, but these belonged to other wyrms, and the narrow sea made a suitable border.

Within these bounds Thauglor ruled supreme. There were reds and blues in the mountains, some older even than the great black wyrm, but they were sluggish, elderly creatures, driven to slow and vague wakefulness only a few times a millennium by hunger and thirst. Generally they gave the large black with the purple-tinged scales a wide berth. The wyverns that nested around the lake at the heart of Thauglor's domain paid fealty and treasure to him and his brood. All other draconian beasts who came winging over the mountains paid their respects, and their tribute, or were driven off.

Ed Greenwood and Jeff Grubb

Still, Thauglor was getting old. With each passing year, his scales lightened, so much so that now he was more violet than ebony along the sinuous ridge of his spine. His eyes, too, though as unerring as ever, were shifting from yellow to a dusky purple. His naps were now lasting upward of a month, and when he awoke, it was with ravenous hunger. Would he soon become as removed from waking life—from cold reality—as the old wyrms of the mountains, scarcely knowing if some other black claimed his forest kingdom?

The thought of anyone, even his own children or grandchildren, replacing him as the mightiest creature in the forest, its undisputed master, disturbed Thauglor. He pressed such dark concepts into the back of his reptilian mind.

The King of the Forest Country swooped low, disturbing a flock of craw vultures roosting in the skeleton of a lightning-struck oak. Squawking, the carrion birds scattered before him as the buffalo had done earlier, but Thauglor did not bother even to snap at them as they fluttered and squalled. Yes, a tour of his domain was in order before he settled down for a long nap. Best to determine now which of his children was strong enough to challenge him.

Thauglor's nostrils flared at a new scent in the wind, a mere whiff of smoke on the breezes. It was too late in the season for a spring lightning strike. . . . Perhaps one of the younger reds was immolating a corner of the forest to flush out prey, or a pack of hellhounds had come down from the northern range again.

The great dragon banked his huge body and glided toward the sharp western peaks. There was still an hour or so before the sun touched their higher mounts, casting premature nightfall across the land. The smoke scent had come from that direction. . . .

As the ancient black wyrm drifted westward, the scent returned, growing sharper and more pungent. Thauglor saw a thin, lonely wisp of smoke above the trees. With idle grace, the massive dragon glided earthward in the

8

softest of dives, the wind sliding past with nary a whistle.

The ground drew nearer, and nearer. The fire was at the base of an old massive oak, a many-branched giant that should be able to support even a large dragon's weight.

Thauglor backbeat his wings once, curled the tips to steer and brake for one last, deft instant, and landed delicately on the great bole, his talons closing with almost fastidious care. Even so, the great tree groaned in protest as smaller branches were ripped away to crash to the forest floor below. The black spared their cascading fall nary a glance, focusing his eyes instead on the source of the smoke.

It was a cooking fire, smoldering and abandoned within a hearth of loosely packed rocks. It had been burning for some time, but was in little danger of spreading. That made Thauglor a trifle uneasy. A fire made by a lightning strike or a red dragon could be contained, and would often drive game into the open. This was the work of other sentients . . . men, goblins, or dwarves.

The site was abandoned, but Thauglor remained immobile on his perch, waiting. Tribes of northern goblins often hunted in these lands, and occasionally a band of Netherese refugees—gaunt, hungry, and powerless without their magic—would try to cross his territory. Dwarves distrusted the woods from some long-past racial trauma and would only risk crossing through a dragon's domain if there were rich metals to be found. Thauglor gave them little desire to explore.

Thauglor waited. Any humanoid with half a mind would be fleeing for the mountains at full speed or cowering behind some toppled log, waiting for the black-winged death to move on. That was right and proper, and with luck the escapee would live to tell others of his narrow escape and warn them to avoid the forested basin, home of the great black wyrm.

There was movement to Thauglor's right, and he turned his head in that direction. It was gone as soon as he saw it, fading back into the forest. Yet, for an instant, their eyes had locked, and the black dragon knew who was trespassing on his land.

The intruder was an elf, more slender than even the gauntest of humans, taller than the dwarves, more graceful than the goblins and their brutish kin. This one was dressed in green, the better to hide among the surrounding trees. Jade-colored leggings and jerkin, a green cape with a mottled green hood. The only flash of metal came from the guards of a scabbarded blade, undrawn at the elf's belt.

The elf was gone, fading back into the trees, leaving the remains of its fire for Thauglor. The black dragon knew the intruder would not return to this site. The black dragon also knew the elf would be fleeing for safety beyond the mountains.

In the half-breath when their eyes had met, Thauglor had looked into the soul of the elf invader. He saw there wonder and amazement at Thauglor's size, a kindling of new respect for the might of dragons.

What Thauglor had *not* seen was fear. The black dragon felt resolution and strength in the elf's gaze, and in his poise. He fled from dragons not out of terror but from wisdom, choosing to withdraw from Thauglor's might. Were he to return later, he would do so on his own terms.

Thauglor found the brief encounter disquieting. He sat in the great tree for a long time, stirring only when the first shadows from the distant mountains reached their cool claws towards him. Then he rose suddenly, scattering the last fitful embers of the dying fire with a lash of his tail, and paddled the air hard to gain height in the cool evening sky. This time he headed east, toward his lair.

The newcomer would have to be watched. So bold . . .

The elf neither attacked like a warrior nor fled like an animal. If he were alone, so much the better, but Thauglor had heard more than once that in a forest, elves were like vermin—if you saw one, another watchful hundred were waiting behind nearby leaves.

One last reason to visit his family, the King of the Forest Country decided. If they were encountering intruders as well, something would have to be done. For a brief time, refugees from the north might be allowed to find their way into his kingdom . . . before he visited *them*. The survivors would warn others of the perils of intruding into Thauglor's domain. Then it would be time to smile, Thauglor thought, imagining the smell of mortal terror that kept his realm secure.

But there had been no fear in the eyes of the elf.

And that troubled Thauglor more than all the goblins of the northern peaks.

1

The Hunting Party
Year of the Gauntlet
(1369 DR)

he king of all Cormyr raised the bright silver hunting horn to his lips. Three short, sharp blasts floated out through the forest, a small silence following their echoes. A faint creak of saddle leather was the only sound from the other three hunters as they listened to the echoes fading into far places. Then, faint and far off, came the expected response—three short, high notes, followed by a long enthusiastic blast that rose mockingly at the end.

The king grinned, his even teeth flashing briefly beneath his graying mustache, and said, "That's Thundersword's wind work, to be sure. By the sound, they're about a mile and a half east of us . . . with quarry and without any great desire to return yet. We shan't have to worry about them for a while."

Two of King Azoun's three companions, men as old as the man who wore the crown, nodded and chuckled at some shared joke. The third, a younger warrior in stiff, new hunting leathers, nodded solemnly, as if the king had delivered sage words from on high.

"Perhaps they've found the Ghost Stag," came the deep voice of the stouter of the old hunters, accompanied by a sly smile. Baron Thomdor was a massive man even without his protruding stomach. His shoulders were as broad and as muscled as the withers of many a stallion. He was cousin to the king, as was the old hunter on Azoun's far side. Thomdor ran one gloved hand through unruly dark hair that was shot with gray and leaned forward in his saddle to better see his brother, the Lord High Marshal of Cormyr.

Duke Bhereu, the king's other cousin, shook his bald head. "Then know ye they bid fair to be gone for most of the day, my lord," he replied in mock-courtly tones, sketching as much of an elaborate bow as one can in an old and worn hunting saddle, before erupting in easy laughter and continuing, "to return to the lodge with empty hands, tremendous stories—and raging thirsts—this evening."

"Agreed," said His Majesty, "And you, young Aunadar Bleth. What make you of this possible portent?"

The younger man took a ragged, obviously nervous breath, but there was only a slight stammer when he spoke. "If—if they're chasing the legendary Ghost Stag of the King's Forest, I'd not bet against the stag. They've Warden Truesilver among them, true, and Bald Jawn as their guide, but the Ghost Stag has eluded us all for generations. And besides, would even so noble a hunting party seek to bring down the chosen prey of the King of Cormyr?" As an afterthought, he added, "Sire."

The king allowed himself a relaxed smile. "Perhaps that's what's been keeping the stag alive all these years. It's waiting for me, eh?"

He nodded at the younger man and added, "Let's go down toward the river—the ruin you wanted to see is there. And so long as we're out here in the woods, you can drop the 'Sire.' Azoun will do very nicely; it's a name I've heard a time or two before."

"As you wish, Si—er, Azoun," said the youth, and then added "my lord" with a quick smile.

The king matched it as he wheeled his destrier and reined it down a ferny slope toward a trail that led to the riverside. The youth followed, his mount tossing its head at the uncertain footing. The two royal cousins held back, watching their king and the young knight bobbing through the trees.

"What do you make of young Bleth?" asked Thomdor, pointing at the receding back of Aunadar Bleth with his chin.

Duke Bhereu shrugged broad shoulders. "This one has some potential. Courteous without being unctuous. Respectful without overmuch groveling. Has book-learning enough in his head to be interesting and enough wits not to show it off all at once. Filfaeril approves already, you know. He's better than your average pick."

"Not only the queen thinks so," the baron rumbled. "The crown princess likes him, too." As they urged their horses down the loose slope where the king's war-horse had preceded them, letting the massive beasts choose their own leisurely paths, he added, "Did you know the two of them met in the palace library?"

"I've heard the story," Bhereu replied wryly, "though with each retelling, the court gossips adorn it. The strains of harps and songhorns positively swirl about it these days, grown as sweet and syrupy as any minstrelry of the Brokenhearted Knight. The last time I heard it, the tale had their eyes meeting, and without another breath, our bold young Bleth sweeps the Crown Princess up and onto a table, scattering tomes and scrolls in all directions. They *say* he practically kissed the lips—to say nothing of a good court gown—off her before the maids clawed him free of the royal person. Whereupon *she* leapt up, snatched him away to another table, laid him out on it, and bestowed a mighty kiss upon *him*, to return the favor."

The two men shook their heads in amused disbelief, and Thomdor murmured, "The worst of it is, some folk'll believe it when it comes to their ears, half a world away, in a tenday or two."

Duke Bhereu nodded, ducked under a tree limb, and said, "Yet a full glass to it all, and more, if Tanalasta is fond of him. It's better than the king trying out future sons-in-law on her . . . and forcing an unhappy marriage."

"I can't see Azoun playing that game," Thomdor replied, frowning equally at his brother and the offending low tree limb. "Other kings, perhaps, but you know our Purple Dragon dotes on both his daughters. Truly, not mere honeyed words and kisses."

"Aye, but our pet wizard has been going on of late about storied heritage and ancient bloodline and solemn succession. Pointing out none too delicately that age stalks us all, and Azoun'd best get his house in order before it overtakes him. You may guess how successful *that* argument has been."

Baron Thomdor, Warden of the Eastern Marches, whistled air out sharply between wryly curled lips. "Azoun probably smiled, nodded, and serenely ignored the Royal Magician," he judged, hefting a boar spear in his hand. Then he shrugged. "Vangerdahast worries about everything, you know. I swear the Obarskyr bloodline keeps Azoun young just as magic keeps old Vangey alive."

He patted his stomach and added in grand, courtly tones of doom, "Age stalks us all." An errant branch poked at his middle, and he backhanded it aside with a mock scowl, adding darkly, "Some, of course, more than others."

"Some more than others," echoed Duke Bhereu, passing a meaningful hand over his bald pate. "As the royal cousins, we'll always be in Azoun's shadow, growing old while his youth and vigor rides on. The day'll come when we'll both be doddering graybeards, counting our teeth as they fall into our laps by warm firesides—and he'll still be using these hunts to check out suitors for his lasses."

"And grandlasses," said Thomdor with a rueful smile. "And bite your flapping tongue about counting falling teeth. May the watchful gods deliver us both from such a fate!"

"Grandlasses? Well, perhaps, *if* either daughter ever marries," the duke replied, doubt heavy in his voice. "Tanalasta's almost a wizard herself, at least with her ledgers and sums, but no taste for rulership there. You've seen her at court—cool and quiet. Too quiet. Hesitant to speak out, and the words halting when she does . . . a royal wallflower."

The stout war-horse beneath him snorted, as if in dispute, and the duke steered it deftly between two phandar trees before adding, "Can you see her at the head of an army, staring fiercely at the foe as she draws her abacus and account book for the fray? Not your typical Obarskyr, that one."

"Aye, all the family traits bred into young Alusair," Thomdor agreed, scanning the nearby trees with the alert vigilance of a veteran warrior. "Hell on horseback, all ego and fury, with talent to match. Every time she comes home, bets are heavy among the kitchen staff as to how long it'll be before she and her father get into a row about politics that breaks half the goblets and platters!" He leaned low over his mount's neck to pass under another phandar bough and added, "She's all swords and armor right now, and would rather be on the battlefield than on the throne."

"Aye, it boils down to that," Bhereu agreed. "Neither wants to rule, or truly has the aptitude for it. So perhaps a child of Alusair, or more likely of Tanalasta, will be the next king . . . and that's what makes these hunting parties so bleeding important. You think Azoun would pull you from Arabel and me from the High Horn just for a social gathering? You'll notice he asks us and not Vangerdahast, every time."

The baron stuck his forehead in mock woe. "I am crushed under the weight of the responsibility. It smites our shoulders like a falling castle turret!" The heavier of the cousins chuckled, then added in more normal tones, "No doubt the good mage delivered a five-volume report on Aunadar and the entire Bleth clan—every last highnosed noble and illegitimate woodchopper among them, back to the dawn days of the kingdom."

The leather saddle creaked as he reined in his prancing mount and added more quietly, "I say let Tanny choose her own prince consort and be done with it. She was smart enough to see right through that proud flower of the Illance line . . . er, Martin?"

The duke smiled at the name. "Martin Frayault Illance, the most untrustworthy young noble in the kingdom. You know after Tanalasta rejected his entreaties, he got on his horse and rode hard and straight for Alusair? Of course, our elder princess had already told her sister all of Martin's favorite lines."

It was the baron's turn to smile. "I bet she broke both his arms."

"Dislocated a shoulder, actually," said the duke. "With a table that had the misfortune to be standing, all innocent like, outside the window he was hurled through." He snorted. "A month gone, and he was still telling folk he got it in a barroom brawl." His voice took on the brightness of an earnest young courtier who's just grasped one of the king's dry jokes a day or so after hearing it as he added, "Which was true, strictly speaking!"

The baron snorted loudly. "I never liked that Illance boy. He's got teeth like a werewolf—big incisors, the size of my thumb!—and he's always smiling, like he wants to show them off." He leered at the duke, cocked his head to one side, pointed at his teeth, and growled in mock lascivious tones, "Care to see what I ate last?"

As the duke snorted in amusement, Thomdor straightened in his saddle and growled, "Good thing neither lass showed him any favor. I'd hate to be hunting with that one."

"Probably there'd be a 'hunting accident' before long," Bhereu replied. "The sort that plagued the realm in the bad old days when Salember was regent. And if asked, I'd support the king's story about it, whatever the story was."

"I as well," the baron grunted.

The trail to the river narrowed before them, and Baron Thomdor had to fall back behind his brother's mount. Neither man had ceased his habitual, wary glances at the deep, damp, and watchful wood during the banter. They knew the king and Tanalasta's young suitor had already reached the riverbank near the ruins of an old beacon tower.

The king still could pass for a man of forty, if you discounted the gray streaks in his hair and beard. Still, he was as lean and well muscled as ever, and could still best both his cousins at arm-wrestling, fencing, riding, or any other sport either could name.

His riding leathers were his informal set: white leathers trimmed with purple, even the heavy boots and gloves. His court garb had been left at the lodge, a symbol that the general ceremony attendant on the crown should be set aside. Azoun's sword hung in a tattered scabbard on a weathered belt that one of the palace stewards would have consigned to the fire heap at a glance. The king wore a plain circlet on his brow, and an old, tattered brown scarf—a luck token from his queen— hid the hunting horn at his belt. Yet he rode like the great monarch he was, shoulders straight, quietly confident, clearly master of all around him without any need for arrogance or pomposity. As they came down the hill, both Thomdor and Bhereu were struck with the noble bearing of the man who was both their king and cousin.

The youth who rode beside Azoun seemed dim by comparison, as did any mortal next to the King of Cormyr. On a crowded dance floor, young Aunadar probably cut a dashing figure, his boyish charm and gallant looks leavened with a serious, almost bookish demeanor. The youth wore dark ebon leathers trimmed with gold, accented by a short golden riding cape. It was rather somber wear. Even so, in another hunting party, he would have been the center of attention, but here he was subdued by His Most Radiant Majesty.

The youth could have dressed more grandly, Thomdor thought, but at the risk, of course, of competing with his possible future father-in-law. Was such a diminished appearance cold calculation on the young man's part, or merely common sense? The baron wanted to believe that it was the latter, not the former.

As they watched, Azoun raised a hand to point at the wreckage of the beacon tower. Such turrets bristled all over Cormyr, their summits used to relay messages quickly from one side of the realm to the other. Thomdor remembered when Azoun returned from Thesk and his triumph against the Tuigan horde. Every beacon tower was alight with bonfires that night, their red, leaping glow outshining the stars themselves.

This tower hadn't been part of that celebration; it had been abandoned long before there were human kings of Cormyr. The faded but fluid script over its door proclaimed elven builders now gone and forgotten. Their slender handiwork had once been three floors in height, but passing centuries had taken their toll, until it had collapsed into a small shell reached by broad, vine-covered steps.

Thomdor knew by heart the history lesson it told. He had heard it from Rhigaerd, Azoun's father, just as Azoun had gotten it several years later. The king would be telling it to young Bleth now, speaking of the dragons that once ruled this land and the elves who followed them. And the men who followed thereafter. The moral was clear to any man of noble station and clear thoughts: "We do not own this land. It was here before us and will be here after we are gone. We are but guardians. Make the best of the time given to us here."

If Aunadar was getting the history lesson, Thomdor thought, Azoun must have decided about young Bleth. Vangey, Bhereu, and, yes, the overweight Baron Thomdor as well would be consulted, but it was clear Azoun had already made up his mind. Had he not seen it so many times before, the baron's ego would have been bruised. But how can one bruise a stone, one of the two pillars who held up the realm under the king? They had been called that, Bhereu and he, and as his brother duke had said, they were always to remain in the shadows.

Thomdor smiled and shrugged. What knight of the realm wouldn't die to win the places they held? He looked at Bhereu, and they traded half-smiles of easy contentment, slowing their mounts in silent accord as they approached the king, so as to avoid having to hear the history lesson yet again.

The thought of shadows brought Thomdor's eyes to the wreckage of the elven tower and the darkness beyond its carved lintel. Someone had been to the ruin since the last time they'd visited, for its broad steps were bare of heavy vines, and the stones that could be seen inside the door were no longer heaped with old rubble.

In that darkness something glinted, like a gold coin. Or a suit of armor.

Thomdor pointed and opened his mouth to say something about poachers to the duke—and the glittering thing moved.

And raging doom broke loose and came down on Cormyr.

"Aye?" Bhereu's puzzled query burst from his lips as something sprang out of the tower like a stallion bursting from its stall. A golden flash and glimmer, the creature from the tower charged at them without hesitation.

The four hunters goggled, frozen for a moment by the sight. The creature was golden and bull-shaped, but its mirror-polished hide was covered with sinuous overlaid scales, much like a lizard's. As it surged forward, sunlight danced on its scales, reflecting the light scattershot. Its forward-swept horns were impossibly long and curved so that their tips were mere inches from its faceted amber eyes. Steam billowed from its flaring nostrils and fang-ridged maw as it roared, deep and triumphant. The beast clattered down the broad steps and closed swiftly with the four mounted men.

The two mounts closest to the beast, Azoun's and Aunadar's, reared at the sight, turned about, and bolted. The king sprang deftly clear of his horse, drawing his sword while he was still in midleap. Aunadar Bleth was less successful, sprawling awkwardly to the ground but rolling hastily and managing to come up with his own blade bare. His free hand had tangled in his short cape, which partially covered his face in a confused tangle.

The golden beast was coming on too swiftly for much thought or plan for attack. As the fleeing horses rushed past, Thomdor and Bhereu fought to keep their own warhorses from bolting, snarling and hauling on the reins like madmen. Then, in unison, the royal cousins roared a challenge and spurred their mounts forward, hauling out their own blades. Neither had seen such a monster before, but there was no time for speculation as to what it was or how it had come to be here. Perhaps Vangerdahast or the sage Alaphondar could puzzle out its origins after they killed it.

The royal cousins met the golden creature in a flurry of slashing steel and golden horns. One man went to either side of the snorting beast, their blades gleaming in the dappled sunlight, and as one, they slashed at the glittering flanks of the golden bull.

Such an assault would normally take down a wild ox, but the blades bit into no flesh. They sparked as if they were smiting armor and squealed harmlessly along the creature, dragging along as if scoring metal.

The two brothers scarcely had time to curse before the golden creature bellowed, turned with lightning speed, and tossed its massive head. Wickedly sharp horns tore open the belly of Bhereu's mount, spraying hot blood over the fray. The horse had time for one horrible scream before it collapsed in a rush of steaming innards, tumbling the duke out of his saddle.

Thomdor reined in his own mount in a pounding of hooves and threw his boar spear. It struck with a ringing sound, metal on metal, and sprang away, unable to sink home. "The luck of bloody Beshaba!" he snarled, rolling hastily out of his own saddle. The horses were little more than moving targets to the creature. The bull turned and rushed after Thomdor's mount but gave up the pursuit when the horse plunged into the river.

Thomdor cast a look back at his fellows as the golden monster turned, crashing through shrubbery and saplings, and added a few more curses at the goddess of ill fortune. Most of the royal bodyguards were off in another part of the King's Forest, with Thundersword's hunting party. Everyone's armor was minimal, and each bore weapons more suited to gutting boars than battling a magical juggernaut.

The golden ox must be an enchanted machine; it clanked and squeaked as it moved. To take it down, they'd have to aim for the thing's clockwork joints. Thomdor cast a glance back at the ruined tower, but there was no activity in the dark doorway or beyond. There was no sign of other golden creatures, nor was there any sign of someone who might be guiding this one.

Bhereu was slow to rise, and Thomdor saw that the duke's face was pale and already streaked with sweat. We're both getting too old for this, Thomdor thought as he raised his heavy blade and charged.

Aunadar and Azoun had split up and taken their stances, His Majesty to the creature's right and the Bleth lad, his face still partially covered with his cape, to the left. The youth was obviously trying to make himself as small a target as possible, crouched and wary, ready to spring, but the king stood upright, chest out and feet planted firmly, bellowing a challenge.

The beast had been lumbering straight at Thomdor, but at the king's shout, it swerved to charge at Azoun, leaving the baron with a chance to strike it as it passed. He kept his eyes on the mirror-bright beast, danced carefully in to just the right spot, and swung—hard.

The impact shook Thomdor to his very teeth, but his stout blade sheared deep into the bull's left leg just below the knee, digging into the joint with a satisfactory thunk.

As the man spun helplessly away, struggling to keep hold of his notched and bent blade with numbed hands, the glittering monster stumbled, breaking its charge. As the baron's world stopped whirling and turning, he saw the bull regain its footing and turn his way. It had acquired a limp.

Thomdor's satisfaction was short-lived, however, for the beast's great, doleful eyes were settled on him, staring steadily into the baron's own hot gaze. The steam from the bull's maw wreathed its face, and Thomdor smelled a bitter, acrid odor, like burnt oranges.

The smell was strong and pungent, seeming somehow *oily* in his mouth, and the baron stumbled back a few paces, wondering if this could be some transformed, renegade mage with a grudge against the crown.

Aunadar took advantage of the bull's menacing advance on the baron to launch his own attack. Charging forward, he repeated the mistake the royal cousins had made earlier, trying to drive his sword into the beast's flank. The tip of the blade skittered across the bright scales, leaving only a thin scratch. The bull thrashed its head, and young Bleth sprang back, lost his footing, and sprawled backward into the trampled ferns.

Bhereu and the king were both closing in on the beast now. Thomdor inwardly cursed Azoun for risking himself, but the king had always been like that, even as a lad. To ask him to stay out of a battle while others fought was unthinkable. The baron set his jaw, strode forward, and took another hack at a leg joint. His aim was true, but the blade dug less deeply than before.

Something was terribly wrong. The air around Thomdor felt stifling, the thick oiliness was curling and moving in his throat, and the forest seemed to close in on all sides.

The baron snarled a curse and staggered backward. His vision was collapsing into a small tunnel around the massive, steaming golden beast. Once more the creature's doleful eyes stared tirelessly into his, and Thomdor could feel sweat pouring out of his body. He was starting to tremble and feel numb all over. This was more than the ravages of too many years spent gorging at the board; this was magic . . . deadly magic.

Thomdor looked at Bhereu. His brother's face looked like a death mask and wore a look of grim realization that must mirror his own. The duke nodded in unspoken answer to Thomdor's look as he came around the bull, hacking at its legs as vigorously as Azoun was doing on the beast's other flank, then opened his mouth to speak.

What came out was a weak cough, and Bhereu's eyes turned an odd green color. Then the beast lunged in their direction, and the world became a place of stabbing horns, hacking blades, and desperate dives for safety clear of plunging hooves. Both royal cousins fell and rolled, then rose to topple backward again. Thomdor struck the ground hard more than once, but the pain felt distant, as if the world were slipping away into numbing mists.

The tunnel that the world had become heaved and rolled, and Thomdor knew he was rising very slowly, pushing at the stubborn ground with his hands. Beside him, Bhereu rolled over, but did not try to rise. Somewhere the bull roared again as the Warden of the Eastern Marches staggered over to his brother, using his sword to support himself.

The duke was laboring to breathe, his face taut with pain, his eyes bright and wide.

"Poison!" Bhereu gasped. He was shaking under Thomdor's hands, his burly body streaming with sweat. He tried to rise once, scrambling to gather himself in the baron's firm grasp, and then collapsed, head lolling and limbs jouncing loosely.

Thomdor laid him back down. Poison, not magic. Yes, that would make sense, particularly with a clockwork creation. To have any hope of surviving, he and Bhereu would both have to get back to the Royal Chirurgeons in Suzail as soon as the battle was over.

Aye, the battle. Where was that bull, anyway?

Head buzzing from the effects of the poison, Thomdor looked around, the tunnel shifting and flowing crazily until he spotted a golden flash.

Aunadar was up and hacking ineffectually again, but the beast seemed intent on slaying Azoun, trying to smash the ever-dodging king down with its golden hooves. As Thomdor watched, Azoun danced away from a lashing hoof and struck out backhanded with his blade, sweeping his sword's tip neatly into the beast's right eye. There was a flash of spraying sparks, and the eyeball—a faceted gemstone!—bounced to the ground.

The bull stiffened and let out a tremendous roar. Internal bellows whined, and the burnt-orange smoke billowed from the monster's maw and empty eye socket with renewed vigor.

Poison, Thomdor reminded himself grimly as he lumbered forward on rubbery legs. Horns slashed, but he drove them aside with his battered blade and then lifted it and drove it weakly into the gaping eye socket amid the flowing smoke.

The bull shook its head, and Thomdor's blade was wrenched from his grasp. He stumbled again, the tunnel before him becoming smaller, the beast receding in the distance. . . .

Azoun struck at the monster's other eye, and the clockwork golden head swung around again. The bull stamped once and then charged, trying to impale the king on its wicked horns. Its maw was open, and the acrid smoke wreathed its head, trailing behind it in oily wisps.

To dodge left or right was to be gored on those glittering horns. Azoun dropped to one knee, raising his blade in front of him. As the creature bore down on him, the king made a desperate lunge, striking into the bull's open maw, driving his blade in to the hilt.

Sparks sprayed and metal skirled as the blade bounced from one unseen innard to another. There was a metallic singing and snapping, and the blade burst out the back of the bull's skull, spraying a thick purple-black fluid.

The clockwork beast hung motionless for a moment, pinioned on the blade, its horns inches from the king's face. Then it slowly, almost gracefully, dropped in its tracks. Whirring noises rose and clattered briefly from its collapsing form, only to die away once more.

Silence descended immediately on a battlefield wreathed in acrid-smelling fog. The king let go his blade and stood up unsteadily, shoulders trembling. Aunadar, the only man still holding a sword, poked at the glittering body a few times.

It lay still, but Thomdor could barely see it through

the swimming tunnel. He staggered forward. He had to tell Azoun to summon aid for Bhereu. . . .

The baron stopped short at the sight of His Majesty. The king's flesh was bone-white and drawn as tightly over his skull as that of any mummy in a tomb. The royal eyes were wide, almost panicked, and Azoun's brow and beard were beaded with dripping sweat.

The king mouthed a few words Thomdor could not catch, then collapsed in front of the golden bull's horns.

Thomdor stared down at him, feeling his own knees going weak, but Aunadar was at his elbow in an instant, holding him up, voice shrill with fear. "What happened? What's wrong with the king—and the duke? Are they ill? The bull didn't strike him. What's wrong?"

The tunnel of his vision was growing smaller; Thomdor sagged against an arm that seemed afraid to hold him. He had to get this boy to summon help, or House Obarskyr was lost.

"Right . . . boot," the baron gasped. The words felt like acid in his throat; he could barely speak. "King's . . . right boot," he rasped. "Wand."

Aunadar looked at him blankly for a moment, as if trying to translate Thomdor's wheezing words, then knelt down beside the king and peered into his right boot. His fingers closed on something, and he looked questioningly back at Thomdor as he drew it forth: a slender ivory wand, sheathed just inside the royal boot top.

Thomdor set his teeth and managed a nod, mentally snarling at the young man to get on with it. The tunnel had closed almost to nothing, and the darkness around it was crawling with dark, monstrous serpents and spiders, waiting for the Warden of the Eastern Marches to falter so they could claim all three of the royals.

Aunadar turned to the baron with the wand flat across his palms. There was a shocked, questioning look on his young face.

Thomdor licked lips that were suddenly thick and numb. "Break it," he tried to roar, but it came out as a husking whisper.

The youth remained motionless. Either Bleth could no longer understand his words, or too little of the world was left for the baron to know what he was saying.

He repeated his command, but the young puppy remained still, the wand in his hands and that shocked, waiting look on his face.

With the last of his fading energy, Baron Thomdor of Arabel, Warden of the Eastern Marches and Royal Right Hand to King Azoun IV of Cormyr, lunged forward and grabbed the boy's hands, forcing them to close over the wand and pressing them up and together. The wand snapped like a brittle bone.

A humming familiar to the baron filled the glade, and a small silver coin appeared in midair, tumbled once, flashed, and quickly widened to form a hoop. The hoop stretched swiftly into a great circular doorway, and out of that entry to otherwhere poured royal guards in white and purple, priests of Tymora in their blue and silver, and war wizards in their violet robes. Last came Vangerdahast, the fat old mage in his familiar red-brown robes, rolling slightly as he walked, bellowing orders right and left.

The Royal Magician knelt next to the king, then looked up sharply and yelled something. Thomdor could no longer understand what was being said, and his vision had faded to a mere pinprick of light, the russet-robed wizard kneeling in a vast void of slithering darkness.

It had been enough. They had summoned aid. Whatever was wrong, the Royal Magician would see to the matter and set things right. Vangerdahast would fix everything. The crown was saved.

And with that thought, Thomdor let go of the last of his crumbling, once iron-strong grip on life and said farewell to the tiny light. . . .

2

The Passing of Power
A Year of Good Hunting
(–205 DR)

The elf stood on the lowest step, waiting as impassively as a statue. Behind him, the broad flagstone steps led up to the horn tower—a tower that in turn soared up above the surrounding bare trees, stabbing proudly into the cloud-studded sky. Its peak was a huge, glowing crystal carved into the shape of a leaping flame. The crystal, glowing a brilliant blue against the riot of autumn color, was lit in expectation of the guest.

The elf did not turn to look at it; he needed no reminder of the power of his people. Nor had he looked again at the words above the tower's door since the day his spell had carved them out of the smooth stone. He knew the traditional warning to goblins well enough not to have to be reminded of it each time he passed, like some forgetful child.

Key'anna de Cormyr, read the runes: "We guard this wooded land." Or, to put it more bluntly, "Beware: this land is ours." Soon those words would hold truth at last.

A deep shadow passed quickly across the tower steps, followed by two more. Had he not been expecting it, the elf would have flinched or fled for the security of the

28

tower. He did neither. He was accustomed to the manner of his guests by now, and for once welcomed it. Red and ocher leaves whirled and danced in the great wind that followed the shadow, scuttering around the elf's ankles. He did not spare them a glance.

The three guests made a low, banking turn over the forest and pulled up sharply, beating their wings and tails to bring them to a halt. More dead leaves swirled up as all three alit gracefully and in unison, on coiled hind legs. The largest of the elf lord's guests, his ancient black scales fading to a violet shade, swept his wings back once to steady himself, in the process blowing the elf lord's cassock and cope about with a sharp snap.

The elf permitted himself a small half-smile. It was just like the dragon to use even his entrance as a display of dominance and power. The intent was to make the elf flinch, step back, or raise an arm to ward off the swirling leaves and buffeting wings.

A game for children, he reflected. Neither of them were children any longer.

With slow, deliberate grace, the elf came down from the step, raising his arms in welcome. His face remained impassive as he strode forward. His green garments billowed out behind him like a sail, the soft cassock and the long, slightly darker cope, flared so that it was almost a full cape. Threads of spun gold entwined and circled along the cope's front and hem, and here and there among their warm splendor gleamed delicate carvings of amber. Long, silver-blond hair drifted behind the elf in the false wind the dragon had wrought. The hair was held from wild and tangled ruin by a thin circlet marked by three spikes in the front and a purple amethyst at the center of his brow.

In one hand the elf bore a golden staff, its haft twisted to resemble a heavy rope, its tip adorned with another purple stone, this one carved into the shape of a soaring bird. The sash that gathered in the cassock at his slim waist bristled with wands along one hip, each wand in its own sheath. These battle wands had made the warrior-mage famous among elves even before he rose to power. On his other hip the mage wore a thin elven sword, a long, narrow blade with a graceful haft and pommel.

Faint glowing auras surrounded some of the wands, seeping through their sheaths. They were the reason the best warriors of the elven House of Amaratharr bowed to this slender, still young wearer of green. His was the power that had brought them victory in battle after battle with the strongest foe they'd ever faced, the dragonkin of dread Thauglor, and his fellow warriors all knew it. That was why he'd been chosen for this meeting, as well as for his fearless demeanor and quick wit.

The dragon, for his part, was well aware of the elf's lack of fear, but dignity demanded a fitting entrance. He had met this one before, and it would not do for the lord and master of the forest to come crawling like a lizard to any humanoid, regardless of what power the small creature might wield. Even—or especially—this small one, so mighty in his magic. The dragon towered over the one who strode to meet him, the elf appearing like nothing more than a small green dot against a living wall of black and purple.

The two smaller dragons, one red, one blue, flanked the great black-scaled beast a respectable few yards behind their liege. They were younglings, newly out of their shell, their colors as bright as the forest around them. That, too, was a sign of power from the dragon. He confidently chose inexperienced youths as his seconds.

"Iliphar Nelnueve," said the largest dragon in a booming voice, "who is called Lord of the Scepters."

"Thauglorimorgorus," replied the elf, bowing slightly, "who is called Thauglor the Mighty and Thauglor the Black Doom."

The dragon beckoned with one wing, then the other. "Gloriankithsanus." The blue made a solemn bob of his neck. "Mistinarperadnacles." The red made a jerky, coltish nod as well, her eyes already scouting the surrounding woods for elven ambushers. "Did you bring your witnesses?"

30

Not seconds, thought the elf lord, but witnesses. "They are within the tower and await my command."

"You have good cause to summon me to this parley?" asked Thauglor, a warning rumble behind his precise and polite words.

"Ask, not summon," Iliphar returned calmly. "I appreciate your coming, for we have need to discuss matters of our two peoples. I trust you are well."

"As well as can be expected," said the dragon as calmly, "given the continual battles between our two kindreds. I trust the wounds you acquired at our last meeting have fully healed."

Despite himself, the elf touched the jagged scar that crossed his face from temple to chin, the only mark that marred his otherwise smooth skin. It was a souvenir of his last encounter with Thauglor, a reminder that even proud elf lords should think twice before entering into battle with the Black Doom.

The elf ran a finger along the scar, hesitated when he saw the slow, toothy spread of the dragon's smile. The elf lord had flinched first, after all.

"Our healing spells are sufficient," Iliphar said steadily. "I trust that draconian curative spells have similarly undone the damage inflicted on you?"

The dragon's fang-studded smile grew broader. "Damage? Oh, a few scales lost, and a bit of blood, but little in the way of major harm. Thank you for asking, but I doubt such concern was the reason for your summons."

"I wish to talk about the difficulties between our peoples. The strife that ends not, between dragons and elves," said the Lord of Scepters. "Our battles must come to an end."

"Battles?" said Thauglor, mock indignation coloring his tone. "Do you mean our little games of hunter and prey? Or the valiant attempts of pointed-ear sneak thieves to steal into our homes? Or the red fires and black bile of our brethren burning out nests of the invading elven vermin? Are these the battles you speak of?"

"I mean the battles in which elf and dragon perish needlessly," said the elf lord.

"You are ready to surrender to my authority, then?" asked the dragon in tones of quiet triumph.

"I am prepared to show you that you have no such authority," Iliphar replied as quietly.

"Then this discussion has ended before it has begun," said Thauglor silkily, spreading his wings and flexing his lower haunches, preparing to leap into the air. "This was not," he added warningly, "worth rousing me from my slumber." The other, lesser dragons spread their wings and lowered their necks, ready to leap into the sky.

Iliphar raised a hand. "Hold a moment. This is our last chance to speak."

The dragon drew in his wings again, brow quizzical. "Speak then, little intruder," he said, cocking his massive head to fix Iliphar with one cold eye.

"There are more of my people coming. Already elf and dragon have been fighting in this beautiful woods, my kin to defend themselves, yours to destroy what we have built. Neither race is as numerous as humans or goblins; any loss is felt."

"Your people are the invaders," Thauglor corrected coldly. "My families, and those of other dragons, seek to defend our hunting grounds. We must live and hunt as we have always lived, free and unfettered."

"There is still a chance for us to live in this place together," the Lord of the Scepters told the ancient wyrm. "You have merely to respect those areas that elves have claimed."

"And *what*," snarled the dragon, "avoid them? Restrict ourselves in where we hunt? Little humanoid, know you that this land has belonged to dragons before the hatching of my eldest known ancestor, and I have hunted here for a time that is long even to the proudest elf. For almost all of those passing years, I have defended these great forests against the depredations of other wyrmkin, and through hard battle have come to dominate them—the redscales, the mighty blues, and the greenwings—such that now, and for a thousand years before now, my word is and has been law from the eastern peaks to the western and from the northern range to the narrow sea. And if, as you oh so subtly threaten, there are more of your kind coming, will the lot of you not soon force us from our hunting grounds *entirely?*"

As the thunder of his roar echoed back from the horn tower, the dragon rose to his full height and added almost casually, "We should stop you elves now, before you take any more of our domains as your own."

"Very well, then," Iliphar replied. "Stop us now."

Thauglor the Black regarded the slender elf at his feet in surprise, wondering just what the small one with the raised and ready scepter was planning this time. He had not long to wait.

"You speak for all the dragons in this forested basin?" said Iliphar. It was more confirmation than question.

"By blood and by Feint of Honor, I am master," snarled the dragon. "My words are those of every bog-dwelling black, mountain-hunting red, and forest-lairing green. That is my authority, and I demand you recognize it."

"I recognize it as authority over dragons, not elves," replied Iliphar. "And I represent my people as well." He pulled a small golden scroll from inside his cope. "This is a document of my people, from mighty Myth Drannor to the north. It gives me hegemony over the elves of this land."

"The elves, but not the land itself," sniffed Thauglor. "You are invaders, and like the human wanderers and orc barbarians, you will recognize my sovereignty or be destroyed."

"We recognize no sovereignty of yours," said the elf, "but at my command, I can empty this region of elves. We can abandon this place and set our borders at the northern range."

"For your people's sakes, I hope you do," said Thauglor, a small reptilian smile tugging the corner of his jaw. "Though they do make tasty treats."

"I said 'can,' old wyrm." Iliphar kept his face solemn, not rising to the dragon's baiting tone. "Not will. Not unless you can convince me."

"Convince?" replied the dragon, suddenly sterner. "How may I convince you of anything, if you are not wise enough to see that your people court their own deaths by opposing us? Your kind are not welcome here. Not welcome to hunt, not welcome to farm, not welcome to stay. Use your authority over your fellow creatures and leave us to our land."

"You say you represent all of your people," said Iliphar, drawing himself up to his full height. "If you tell them to leave us in peace, will they do so?"

The dragon's eyes narrowed to mere slits. "What are you proposing?"

"I propose a Feint of Honor," said Iliphar.

The dragon made a harsh, barking noise that might have been a laugh. "A Feint of Honor with a mammal? How droll. Feints are between dragons, to settle their differences without killing one or both parties."

"A battle until one is subdued and surrenders to the other," the elf went on, nodding. "You represent your people, and I represent mine. The winner takes the forest country." Iliphar stopped there, holding his tongue and waiting to see if the dragon would take the bait.

A silence descended on the forest, broken only by the rustle of leaves in the autumn breeze. The red wyrmling was still skittish and kept craning her neck around, looking for attackers. Her blue cousin seemed deep in thought.

Thauglor rumbled, "When I win, you will pull your people back beyond the northern passes."

"Should you win," said the elf lord. "And should I triumph, you agree to leave the forests of this land to my people?"

The dragon's eyes narrowed, then opened wide again, showing milky violet orbs beneath a curtain of black scales. "Why should I agree?"

Iliphar motioned with his golden staff, and his retainers poured out of the horn tower. There were twenty elves in all, carrying five great reptilian skulls. The skulls were set with amethysts along their brows. One had as few as three stones, one as many as twenty. The skulls had massive fangs in their upper jaws, but no horns. They were the remains of green dragons.

Stone-faced and impassive, the bearers laid their prizes on the steps behind Iliphar and retreated silently back into the tower. One remained in the doorway, the elven witness to the proposed duel.

Iliphar kept his eyes on the dragons throughout the proceedings. Thauglor remained motionless, but the muscles bunched beneath his jaws. Two sacs inflated along his neck, just behind the head, where, the elf lord knew, the black acidic bile of the dragon was stored. The blue tried to mime his master's determination, but his eyes were wide. The red looked as if she were ready to bolt, and only fear and respect was keeping her in her place. To both the younger dragons, the message was clear: Their skulls could be added to this collection.

Iliphar spoke flatly, seeking to draw out the dragon but not to goad him immediately into battle. "These greens were slain within the past month. The gems on their foreheads represent the elves who lost their lives fighting the creatures, one for each elf."

Thauglor's lips tightened in a snarl, but only for a moment, and the dragon's response was as flat and mannered as the elf's. "It would seem your people got the short end of the bargain."

"Aye," the elf replied, "but there are more of us. And if it costs a hundred elves to take down a creature of your power, there would be a hundred elves afterward who would remember their deed and honor their memory. Can you say the same for your people? How many dragons are there in the forested land?

Thauglor was silent a long time, considering. "Feint of Honor?" he said at last.

Iliphar managed a small smile. "With the winner getting the forests, and the loser promising not to hunt the

Ed Greenwood and Jeff Grubb

winner's race. I challenge you, O Thauglorimorgorus, by
the ancient rites of your people."

The black dragon looked at the gem-encrusted skulls
of his subjects. "Agreed. Neither side uses his spells or
wands, and neither uses his, eh, breath weapons. Are you
prepared?"

The elf lord took a deep breath, as if the difficult part
of his task had been completed. "I am as prepared as I
ever shall be." He began to take off his flowing cope and
cumbersome cassock, to reveal a fine mesh of silvery
mail beneath them.

The dragon leapt upon him immediately, like a fox
leaping on a field mouse. Yet Iliphar was ready for the
sudden attack, and in midleap, Thauglor realized his
error. The elf whipped the capelike covering upward
across the outstretched claws of the black beast.

Thauglor roared and pulled his claws back. The hem
of the elf's cope was studded with some impossibly sharp
crystals that cut into the thick, fleshy pads of the
dragon's claws. The crystals were coated with something
else as well, for the shallow wounds stung. It was akin to
grabbing a giant porcupine.

Iliphar made use of the dragon's momentary distraction to divest himself of his robes and toss aside his belt
of wands. Now he stood on the steps, facing the dragon.
His entire body, from neck to ankles, was encased in the
thinly spun chain of the elves. Iliphar drew his sword as
well, a slender, whiplike blade, perfect for digging beneath the dragon scales into the tender flesh beneath
them. In his other hand, he still bore his golden staff.

"You did not tell me your coat was a weapon," said the
dragon, now crouching low. The other two dragons
backed to the edge of the clearing to give their liege room
to engage in battle.

"You did not tell me you would not allow me time to
remove it," replied the elf, gracing Thauglor with a wide,
calculated smile. The smile was taunting, but the dragon
saw that the eyes above the smile were cold and hard.

The elf took two steps forward and lunged with his

36

staff. Thauglor easily beat aside the blow with a swipe of his taloned claw, but again Iliphar had thought beyond the dragon's reaction. As the staff's blow was caught and struck aside, he stabbed hard with his slender blade, driving it deep into the shallow wounds carved earlier.

It felt as if a hot sliver had been driven into the dragon's flesh. Thauglor bellowed and convulsed. Iliphar cursed as the blade was ripped from his grip, clanged once on the stone, and went skittering down the steps to stop at the feet of the dragon.

Almost immediately Thauglor reacted with a sharp blow from his other paw. The blow was weak and clumsy, but it still knocked the elven lord sprawling from his feet. His mail made a serpentlike whisper as he slid across the flagstones, dropping the staff as well.

The dragon snaked his head forward and grasped Iliphar by one leg in his heavy jaws. Iliphar felt the ragged daggers of fangs cut through the mail and into his soft flesh. He held back a scream beneath tight lips.

The dragon then whipsawed his neck upward and let go, flinging the elf in a short arc that ended back on the steps. Iliphar bounced against the flagstones and felt something sharp give along the muscles of his ribs. His head was ringing from the force of the landing. It would clear if he had a moment's rest. . . .

But Thauglor gave him no rest, instead repeating the maneuver, grasping the elf tightly in his jaws and flinging him up in the air once more. This time something snapped in Iliphar's leg, and he screamed from the sudden stabbing pain.

A third time the dragon's jaws flung him aside, and Iliphar landed on his shoulder, enough to dislocate it but not enough to strike him senseless. His sword was beneath the dragon's claws, but his ornate staff lay just a few feet away.

The dragon was now playing for the crowd, Iliphar realized, both for his own two young minions and for the elves in the tower. See how easy it is! See how inconsequential and weak these elves are! See what happens to those foolish enough to challenge the might of Thauglor!

The dragon's head came close again, his jaws gaping wide. Thauglor could swallow him easily, the elf lord realized, but then who would enforce the agreement? Iliphar shoved that thought to the back of his mind and rolled sharply toward the staff. The dragon's jaws closed on air.

Iliphar's entire body was wracked with pain. He clutched the staff, but could not rise. His legs, lying at odd angles to his torso, would no longer obey his mind's commands.

The dragon's head snaked down once more, jaws agape.

Drawing on the last of his strength, Iliphar surged upward, using the staff as a crutch, and leapt forward into the jaws of the great creature. He shoved the staff upright, into the dragon's mouth, the wide nob of its base jammed into the lower inside gum. The delicately carved bird at the top shattered as it scraped the roof of the purplish beast's mouth and dug into tender flesh.

Thauglor reared back in pain, giving the elf lord the moment's respite he needed to roll free of his attacker's maw. The pain was returning to his legs, but Iliphar managed to rise unsteadily to one knee.

The dragon thrashed, trying to dislodge the staff crammed into his mouth. Thauglor tried to pull it out with a taloned finger, but only succeeded in driving the shattered tip farther into the roof of his mouth. His tongue lolled to one side, and great tears dribbled down the black dragon's cheeks.

The great acid pouches in his throat swelled, and Iliphar realized that the creature was going to melt the obstruction loose. Knowing the nature of his staff, he dropped to the ground and flattened himself there.

The dragon spat a great gout of watery blackness from his throat, bathing the golden staff in its hot sludge. The staff began to glow, then, weakened, slowly bent under the pressure of the dragon's jaws. Finally the elf lord's staff snapped.

And the dragon's throat exploded. The enchantments within the staff were discharged in a single great fireball. For the first and only time in his long life, Thauglor the Black breathed flames.

The force of the blast drove the dragon backward, and the Black Doom thrashed on the ground, smoke spilling from his mouth and nostrils. The sight was too much for the red, and she bolted, rising from the forest like a frightened pheasant, then wheeling and barreling northward toward the distant peaks. The blue held his ground but seemed to pull in on himself, as if he, too, expected a sudden and merciless attack.

Iliphar pulled himself slowly to his feet. He heard movement behind him and tried to wave off the elves from the tower. Somebody pressed another staff, this one gnarled and wooden, into his hands. He did not refuse it, but used the gnarled staff as a crutch. He looked down involuntarily. One leg was hopelessly mangled beyond all but magical remedy, and the other felt as if it had been shattered in a dozen places. He staggered down the steps to where Thauglor lay, belly up, smoke streaming from his burned jaws. The dragon's eyes were wide and wreathed by the smoke.

The elf lord did not even make for his sword, for fear that the effort would be too much. Instead, he put the tip of the wooden staff against the dragon's head and asked, "Give up?"

The dragon hacked a great cloud of black smoke up from his gut. "You weren't supposed to use magic, technically."

"You weren't supposed to use your breath weapon. Technically." He did not move the staff. Let the dragon think this was another magical staff, as deadly as the first.

The dragon responded with another great cough, and Iliphar added, "It was your own breath that caused the magical damage. You know that. We elves have honor. Do you dragons?"

Thauglor, the Black Doom, gave a weak nod and

barked for the remaining blue. Iliphar took a half-step back as the two conversed briefly in the Auld Wyrmish tongue of the dragons. Then the dragon turned to Iliphar again.

"We dragons have honor," said the black, the last tendrils of smoke wreathing his head. "And we honor our agreement. You have the forests of this land, and the dragons who swear fealty to me will not trouble the elves who swear fealty to you. Glor, here, will carry the word and reassure those that Mist encounters that I survived this battle.

"But know this," the dragon added. "We honor the letter of the law. Our agreement is with your elves and only applies to the forests. The swamps are mine, and the mountains and bare hills belong to my people as well. The day will come, elf lord, when you will regret winning this battle as much I resent losing it."

And with that, the young blue dragon, Glor, leapt into the air with a majestic beating of wings and flew to the north, hoping to catch up with the cowardly red. Thauglor himself coughed one last time, folded his wings, and slunk off, half crawling, into the forest.

The dragon had surrendered, thought Iliphar, at the cost of one elf's shattered body. Still, it was not a bad price for a kingdom. Thauglor was ancient and would have to sleep a long time to recover from the wounds inflicted today.

The other elves streamed from the tower and surrounded him now, the priests intoning the healing enchantments and the retainers shifting back and forth between fearful worry and jubilation.

Iliphar waited until the last of the dragon's black tail vanished into the multihued forest before surrendering to the inner darkness of oblivion. He put his trust in the gods and his shattered frame in the hands of the priests.

And in the blackness, Iliphar Nelnueve, the Lord of the Scepters, dreamed a singular dream. He saw in his dreams the battle he had just fought, but with himself as the dragon, tormented by a multitude of smaller, frailer creatures. And though he did not speak of it upon his awakening, he carried that dream with him for the rest of his long elvish life.

3

A Death in Suzail
Year of the Gauntlet
(1369 DR)

hey lost Duke Bhereu, Lord High Marshal of
Cormyr, in the first few moments after the
hunting party had been brought to the palace.
Before they could even move him to a sickbed,
he lapsed into convulsions, vomiting streams of thick,
black blood. High Priest Manarech Eskwuin of Tymora
was bent over the duke, in midword of a powerful curative spell, when this befell, and was coated over face,
chest, arms, and hands with the warm, viscous bile.

The priest's nerve broke at that point, and he gasped
out some very unholy words and fled from Satharwood
Hall, abandoning his lesser curates and bishops and
leaving them to deal with the disaster. Behind him, the
duke twisted, shook, and with a final, rattling breath,
died.

Vangerdahast cursed, in part because of the duke's ig-
noble passing and in part because of the priest's flight. A
blood-covered Lord High Priest Most Favored of the Luck
Goddess, running through the palace halls, frightening
the staff, and spreading this day's ill tidings further was
just what he needed right now.

A few other clergy, wearing frightened, pale faces,

42

scuttled from the room. The Royal Magician scowled at them, and a few visibly flinched from his gaze as they bolted. He spared them no more attention than that; right now the realm had even less time than usual to spare for overweening fools. Most of the remaining priests were all staring back at him like so many cornered rabbits.

Vangerdahast could almost read their thoughts as they regarded him. The wizard was not an imposing man physically, being of average height and greater than normal girth, but because of carefully placed spells, the very air crackled around him. His eyes could be as sharp as any sword, and his glare as piercing as any spear. The wizard used his glare to keep the remaining priests at their tasks. He took care not to let his eyes fall to the sprawled bulk of Bhereu on the floor and thus spawn another exodus.

The ranking cleric remaining in the chamber ignored the wizard. She was an adventuress, a young bishop of Tymora, bedecked in sapphire-shaded robes, whose flaxen hair was wrapped in a severe bun. She wore a severe expression as well. While Vangerdahast was regarding the other priests, she had dropped to her knees beside Bhereu, determinedly pulling a scroll from her satchel. Vangerdahast laid two restraining fingers on her arm.

"I have an incantation here that can raise the dead," she said, her voice low with urgency. Her face was calm, but her eyes were wide and nervous.

"Concentrate on the living now," said the wizard, indicating the other two recumbent forms. The king was lying as still and serene as a tomb effigy, but a murmuring Thomdor was thrashing, hands clenching and clutching at imaginary foes, just as his brother had done a few breaths ago when Bhereu had yet lived. Expressionlessly Vangerdahast watched three guards struggle to hold the baron down.

"But, Lord Wizard," the young priestess protested, "I can bring his lordship back with this single spell!"

"And two more lords may die while you're about it,"

43

Vangerdahast said sternly. "Your duty is to the king and the baron, who still live—at least for now. The duke won't leap anywhere to elude your ministrations; he'll keep for the moment."

The young woman opened her mouth to protest, brows darkening, then swallowed and shut it quickly. It opened again, like a trap in a dungeon door, to snap, "Yes, sir." There was a swirl of sapphire-hued robes as their owner turned to where Thomdor was thrashing.

Reaching in over the struggling guards, she laid her palm on the baron's forehead and muttered a few words. Instantly his thrashing subsided to mere twitchings. Vangerdahast dismissed the soldiers, telling them to bear the remains of the clockwork monster to the castle. The present crisis was a matter for priests and wizards.

Both of the living royals were then lifted from the floor and gently laid on makeshift biers. They looked like wax statues of their former selves. Their skin was translucent, and seemed to be melting. Their eyes were opened wide but clouded, staring at nothing through milky orbs. Thomdor twitched and spasmed slightly, even under the effects of the bishop's spell. Azoun lay still but taut. Vangerdahast could see that every sinew in his body was tensed.

With no more bodies being carried here and there or expiring spectacularly, a babble of voices arose in the room. An argument had broken out between a priest of Deneir and one of the Tymorans over whether or not the bodies should be moved immediately to "a more suitable resting place for men of their station." Other men, including the two belarjacks, or door butlers, assigned to the room, looked to the Royal Magician to still the wrangling, but he said nothing, standing statuelike, face grim.

The dispute ended with the arrival of Loremaster Thaun Khelbor of Deneir, who curtly agreed with the Tymoran priest. For her part, the adventuring priestess of Tymora offered no argument to the decision, nor to the high priest of the rune-god assuming ministrations over the king while she worked on Thomdor.

Vangerdahast was still standing with his best scowl on his face, thinking furiously, but as fine-robed shoulders pushed past him and cultured voices lazily demanded to know "what was befalling, by the Purple Dragon," he roused himself enough to note that there were twice as many people in the room as needed to be. His hand went to his belt pouches, which carried a variety of magical baubles, spell ingredients, flash stones and light stones, and other sundry devices. He fished out a small silver whistle.

A high-pitched blast of the whistle gained everyone's immediate attention. The Royal Magician issued orders in cold tones that meant instant obedience for those who desired a few further moments of life. Unless, perhaps, they favored a long, damp career as a toadstool. . . .

He spoke, and half a dozen minor priests and more than twice that number of peering courtiers were ushered out by hard-faced men-at-arms. From among the best guards in the room, Vangerdahast dispatched a runner to find Queen Filfaeril and ordered all but two of the others to clear the entire floor. The last thing they needed was gawkers and kitchen staff crammed in every doorway of Satharwood Hall trying to snare a look at the grievously injured royals. Vangerdahast bade the last guard stay by him in case something else was needed and sent the only other guard out to find Eskwuin and hose the terrified priest off before he fled into the city and started a full-fledged panic.

At about that time, the shoulders of the guards streaming out the door parted to disclose Alaphondar and Dimswart, the leading sages of Suzail. They were rivals of sorts, but at the moment, brushing shoulders as they peered across the chaos of moving people looking back over their shoulders at the king, they more closely resembled two weary prisoners caught in the same cell.

Alaphondar looked as if he'd been up the entire previous night researching some genealogical question in the library. He was followed by an argil, a page boy in palace livery. The young lad was frowning under the weight of a large box of tomes. Dimswart seemed to have been interrupted in midmeal and was servantless, bearing his own oversized black satchel with silver latches in one hand and a dripping leg of roast sarn fowl in the other. Both sages nodded to the Royal Magician and immediately asked the priests for a full report on "the stricken."

Thaun Khelbor spoke first. "No change here. I've thrown every curative I know of to drive the toxin out, tried every preventive against disease, even used a charm against possession by tanar'ri. Nothing seems to catch hold." He spread his hands in a gesture of frustrated futility. Khelbor was a balding man with patches of thick gray hair above his ears. He usually looked kindly and slightly comical, but right now his face was as white and tightly drawn as those of the two men who lay beside him on the trestle tables.

"Dispel magic?" asked Dimswart, gesturing with his leg of fowl.

"When I first arrived on the scene," Vangerdahast replied, "and a spell to slow the spread of poison. Neither had any effect."

"No improvement here, either," said the young bishop of Tymora, "though I did calm him with a spell to remove fear."

Vangerdahast stroked his beard. "That may just be a symptom, like night sweats or palsy."

"If you can't halt the disease," quoted Alaphondar, "at least arrest the symptoms."

Vangerdahast nodded. "We don't know if it *is* a disease, or a poison, or a combination of curses, or what. But you are correct, at any rate."

He turned to the priests and ordered, "Concentrate on lowering their temperatures, and perform a remove fear spell on His Majesty as well. That may ease the rictus in his frame. Make sure their breathing passages are unblocked and their hearts remain beating. Leech them if you have to—but only if you have to." He looked around. "Where's the one who was with them? Where's Aunadar Bleth?"

The priests and sages ignored the question as they bent over their charges. Azoun's breathing had become ragged and short, but as the calming spell took hold, Vangerdahast watched it lengthen and deepen, becoming more regular and measured. For the moment, at least, it seemed unlikely that the king and the baron would find their gods and leave Faerûn behind this day.

Vangerdahast looked around the temporary sickroom. The two sages passed from one stricken man to the other, pausing only to confer and compare notes. Khelbor of Deneir and the young bishop tended to their individual charges. Lesser priests bustled back and forth, bringing clean cloths and ewers of fresh water. The page boy had sat down on his master's box of tomes, excitement sharp on his young face.

Of Aunadar Bleth, there was no sign.

The Royal Magician looked to the guard beside him and the door butlers, including them all in his question. "Where did young Bleth go? Did you see him?" he asked both the guard and the belarjacks.

When mute, reluctant head shakings came as the only reply, Vangerdahast frowned again and sent one of the belarjacks to find out what had happened to the young noble, with instructions to contact the Royal Magician in his private library when the noble youth had been found. He then gave the lone guard orders to let no noble of the realm or stranger come near the two royals, then left the impromptu sickroom.

His private library—the one the folk of the court knew about, at least—was little more than a large anteroom whose three full walls were covered by bookcases. Vangerdahast skirted the pedestal with its guardian watchskull and pulled down three volumes from the shelves: one on toxins, one on diseases, and a treatise on mechanical creatures.

He sat in his favorite chair, the one upholstered in sahuagin flesh, and set the books on the small duskwood table next it, placing the topmost tome in a book holder fashioned to resemble a silvery human hand. The hand immediately shifted to open the book to the title page and held it there, propping the pages open with its smallest finger and thumb.

Vangerdahast thanked the magical contrivance gravely—the book bobbed a trifle in reply—and reached out to touch the helm of a staring knight carved into the decorative column of one bookcase. The helm slid inward with the faintest of clicks, and the spines of three massive, immovable tomes on a nearby shelf folded outward, revealing a small—and almost full—hiding place.

The wizard pulled a flat plate from a stack in the hiding place, a circular, mirrored disk with runes around its periphery, and tapped his finger on the door of the secret place, which rose smoothly to conceal the storage niche again. Vangerdahast paid it no attention; he was muttering a spell over the message plate, quickly committing words to it for later retrieval.

A chime only he could hear sounded. Vangerdahast laid one hand on the little sylph statuette that could spit lightning if need be and said sharply, an instant before a cautious knock fell upon the door, "Come!"

The door opened to reveal the anxious face and shoulders of the door guardian, with the news that Lord Bleth the Younger was in Princess Tanalasta's quarters. Vangerdahast delivered a mild curse to the ceiling and gave the message plate to the page, with instructions as to whom to deliver it to among the war wizards and what he was to do about it. The young boy nodded and scampered off, his face stern and serious.

Vangerdahast's features were equally stern and serious as he stalked through the halls of the royal wing of the palace. His grim face and stride, and the half-heard curses he was muttering under his breath as he trod the purple carpets, confirmed to the servants he passed that something terrible had happened to the king.

The Royal Magician put a hand to his lips for silence, swept past the belarjacks and the knights of the chamber, and walked into Princess Tanalasta's sitting room unannounced. The room had been young Azoun's when

Rhigaerd was on the throne, but the princess had brought her own delicate hand to its furnishings since then. Gone were the heavy, stained oak armchairs and tables, and the maps of the realm that had looked down on them. Vangerdahast threaded his way through filigreed chairs of white-painted bow wood and gilded lounges covered with floral print cushions. The maps were gone, too. The old wizard thought, as he always did, that there were too many mirrors in these chambers now. As a mage, he thought of mirrors as things from which unbidden horrors could emerge, not as something to admire oneself in.

Princess Tanalasta was seated on her favorite divan, wearing a dark blue high-throated, swept-shouldered gown that made her look like a mature, no-nonsense priestess instead of a high-ranking noble. Her dark brown hair was pulled back into a half-coil, from which it flowed freely down her back—and inevitably strayed over her face when she was distraught. Now, for instance.

Aunadar Bleth was on one knee before her, stroking her hand. Tanalasta looked as white as a ghost and much older than her thirty-six summers. Tears glistened on her cheeks and chin. A damp and crumpled anathlace in her hand told the tale that these were not the first tears she'd shed this morn. Bleth looked up, then hastily stood as Vangerdahast strode up to them.

"His Majesty and the others . . . ?" began the young noble.

"Duke Bhereu is dead," said Vangerdahast without preamble, his eyes on the princess. She gasped and flinched away, as if his words were blows, but she seemed in no imminent danger of swooning. "His Majesty and the baron are out of immediate peril, but still lie senseless under the effects of whatever killed the duke." Without a pause, his gaze turned to Bleth and sharpened. "Why did you leave us?"

Aunadar looked at Vangerdahast and blinked, as if he did not understand the question. The Royal Magician

Ed Greenwood and Jeff Grubb

seemed to exude crisp, commanding power, but the slender noble stood like a stone that ignores the wind of a raging storm. Bewilderment flickered across his face for a moment before he said hesitantly, "I'm sorry. Was I needed?"

"You are the only conscious survivor of an attack on the king," said Vangerdahast flatly, only barely concealing his irritation. "Furthermore, all of you may have been touched by some malady, which might be poison, or spell, or a virulent and contagious disease. And the first thing you do upon returning to the palace is spread that potential disease to the heir apparent."

Bleth's face went dark red, and he sputtered, his eyes beginning to blaze. One of Tanalasta's slim hands reached up to squeeze his own. He looked down at it, put his other hand over her soft fingers, and seemed to remember both his own station and who he was addressing. He shook his head as if to clear it and said with dignity, "I'm sorry, Lord Wizard. I felt my place and duty was near my beloved. I wanted to be the one to tell her—"

"Tell me, then," said Vangerdahast, lowering his bulk into one of the thin-legged chairs that usually held the more petite derrieres of one of the princess's ladies-of-chamber. It creaked alarmingly. "And tell me everything."

Aunadar sat down next to the princess, pressed his hands together in his lap, frowned, and haltingly began to relate the tale he'd just told Tanalasta. Vangerdahast leapt on every other sentence or so, distressing the young noble and making him flush and stammer. Twice the old wizard demanded Aunadar recount once more the sequence of who attacked the golden beast when, and in what order it struck at them.

"Bhereu went down first, then His Majesty, then the baron," Bleth said at last, exasperation sharp and shrill in his voice.

"But if what you say is true, Baron Thomdor attacked the beast first," Vangerdahast said heavily.

"Both cousins did—one from each side!" Aunadar said,

50

almost protesting. He looked to Tanalasta, as if hoping
that she might end this interrogation by decree, but she
was looking sadly from wizard to noble and back again,
eyes wide and red-rimmed, lips set in a silent line. Aunadar sighed unhappily and added, "It was Bhereu who
seemed affected first by the beast's breath."

The Royal Magician nodded as if he didn't believe a
word and asked, "When the baron returned to the fray,
did he seem affected?"

"Yes, I suppose he was . . . that is, he was pale and per-
spiring."

"You say you attacked with your cape held up over
your face. Why did you do this?"

Aunadar blinked. "I thought it was a gorgon—a metallic beast with steaming breath that turns one to
stone. . . ."

"It wasn't," the wizard said flatly, "and it doesn't. It
was an abraxus, a magical creation similar to a golem or
automaton."

The younger noble started, eyes flaring in shock—and
then narrowing to slits of suspicion. "So you've seen one
of these before?"

"I have, or rather, my mentor told me of them,"
Vangerdahast said simply, and shut his mouth, letting
the noble's unspoken question hang unanswered in the
air between them. They stared at each other in silence,
gazes locked in mute challenge, for two long breaths as
the princess looked from one face to the other. Then, eyes
still locked with Aunadar's, the Royal Magician whispered, "And after the royals fell, you snapped the wand
and summoned the rescue party."

"I—" The noble tore his gaze free from the old wizard's
and looked at Tanalasta, eyes almost pleading. Then he
dragged his gaze reluctantly back to the wizard. "I pulled
the wand out, but . . . I didn't know how to activate it.
Baron Thomdor showed me how."

"Fortunate," said the Royal Magician, "that the good
baron remained coherent long enough to give instruc-
tion."

"Fortunate indeed," said the young Bleth almost tone-lessly, slumping his shoulders in exhaustion. Tanalasta put a comforting arm around him.

Vangerdahast nodded. No doubt the youth had glossed over this last detail when he'd told the princess his tale.

"I'm—I'm very sorry for all of this," Aunadar offered wearily to the room in general, slowly bowing his head.

The three sat in silence for a long moment. Tanalasta kept her arm around Bleth, who looked at the floor. Her hand tightened on his shoulders and shook him a little; he looked up at his beloved then and managed a weak smile.

His elbows resting on the arms of the chair, fingers steepled in front of him, the wizard studied the pair on the divan. His eyes never left the face of the young noble.

At length, Vangerdahast spoke. "In the future, young Bleth, when you are involved in *any* serious matter in-volving peril to a member of the royal family, you will re-main around long enough to inform others who need to know what befell. I think you know who those others are."

Aunadar raised his head and their eyes locked, noble and wizard, brief fire passing between them. The youth nodded slowly. "Of course. I thought the others were in your capable hands." His words held no hint of bitter-ness.

Tanalasta leaned forward and captured Vangerda-hast's gaze with her own reddened, pleading eyes. "My father . . . will he be . . . ?" Her voice trailed away into silence.

The Royal Magician inclined his head to her. "I know only what I told you earlier, Lady Highness," he said carefully. "The tremors he and the baron experienced have subsided. However, neither has roused nor re-sponded to any curative power we have brought to bear."

The eldest princess of Cormyr went even paler at his words, her skin becoming almost as pale as milk. Now it was Bleth's turn to put his arm about her. He whispered soft words in her ear, but his eyes, flaring the sharp light of an unmistakable challenge, never left those of the High Wizard.

"Your Majesty," said Vangerdahast to the princess, returning Bleth's look with a steady, steely gaze of his own as he spoke. "I am sure this matter will be swiftly resolved. The Lords Alaphondar and Dimswart are already in attendance on . . . the stricken, and I will be returning to them to render whatever aid I can. However, if the worst comes to pass . . ."

Tanalasta raised her hands in front of her and spread her fingers, as if warding off a blow. "No," she said quietly.

"Your Majesty," Vangerdahast pressed, his voice softening, "it would be most wise to prepare for every possibility. . . ."

"No," she said again, louder, and raised her head to regard the Royal Magician. She was crying again, but fire burned in those sapphire eyes.

"Even so," the wizard began softly, "the realm—"

"I said *no*," she said, steel creeping into her voice for the first time. "I refuse to even consider that until . . . until all other possibilities have been excluded. Am I clear?"

"But, Your Majesty . . ." Vangerdahast said mildly, raising his brows.

Tanalasta stood, taller than most men and as imperious as Azoun at his most fierce. "*Am . . . I . . . clear?*" she repeated, biting off each word. Aunadar rose behind her and placed a supportive hand on her shoulder. He had to reach up to do it. As he looked at the Royal Magician, his other hand went slowly and deliberately to the hilt of his sword.

"As always," the wizard replied calmly, also rising, "I will send word as we know more."

"Do so," said the princess coolly. "You have my faith, as my father and the baron have my prayers. You are dismissed."

Expressionlessly Vangerdahast turned his head to regard Aunadar Bleth. The young noble treated him to a short, serious nod—a warrior's farewell to an equal—but made no motion to depart. Nor did the princess make any motion that might have been interpreted as a dismissal of her suitor. The High Wizard bowed slightly from the waist, then strode to the door.

Before leaving, he looked back at the pair. Already Tanalasta's moment of strength had passed; she was slowly collapsing back onto the divan, her face in her hands. Her slender shoulders were shaking. At her side, Aunadar Bleth stroked her shoulder and her hair and spoke words the wizard could not hear, his face close to hers. It was as if Vangerdahast, the palace, and all the court had become invisible, leaving the pair alone together.

Vangerdahast heard the heavy outer door of the princess's chambers close behind him—and, ominously, the sound of a lock being thrown. The wizard raised his head as if to take in badly needed fresh air, letting his gaze stray up at the hallway's ceiling. Warriors, witch lords, elves, and dragons battled in the yellowing plaster. Their eternal struggle ran all along the ceiling of the hall, in silent contrast to the tumult stirred up by this day's disaster.

Vangerdahast lowered his gaze to see a figure running along the carpets toward him, a figure dressed in sapphire-hued robes. He gave her a raised hand of greeting and asked, "What are you called, lady priestess?"

She blinked at him, and then said, "Gwennath of Tymora, lord wizard, sometimes called the Bishop of the Black Blades Adventurers." And then, without pause—a swiftness which Vangerdahast admired greatly—she plunged into what she had been going to say to him. "The convulsions have stopped for both men, and their breathing is weak but steady. Neither has roused, and both are extremely pale. They are hot to the touch, but cold compresses seem to moderate this condition somewhat. Loremaster Khelbor argued against leeching, but the sages are taking just a bit of blood for their own divinations." She paused for breath, brushing a stray hair out her face with an impatient thumb.

The wizard nodded approvingly. "Any idea yet as to the cause?"

Gwennath shook her head. "None. They're bringing the clockwork thing into Belnshor's Chamber, next to the Satharw—but you know where that is. I'm sorry, lord . . . I assume you'll want to look at it. Its very presence at the fray suggests poison, but whatever afflicts the king and his cousin continues to resist every purgative, curative, and medication we can call to mind." Her confused frown deepened. "And, lord . . . ?"

"Yes, blessed lady?"

"I tried that incantation to raise the dead on his lordship the duke. It didn't work."

"Given everything else, I'm not surprised," Vangerdahast told her, the barest hint of bitter weariness in his voice.

"It's not supposed to happen like this," she added, shaking her head in exasperation.

"Just what is *supposed* to happen when a royal duke dies and your king's life is endangered?" asked the Royal Magician in the mildest of tones, raising his eyebrows slightly.

"I'm sorry, lord wizard," stammered the young priestess. "I was thinking aloud and meant no disrespect. It's just that . . . when one of the royals falls ill, cost means naught, and no power need be spared. There are a score or more things one can do to give aid. We've tried them *all* . . . with no result. There's more spell power in that banquet hall than anywhere else shy of Waterdeep and, I suppose, Shadowdale—and we cannot get either man even *awake!*"

"And frustration eats at us all," the wizard murmured, eyes no longer seeing the earnest young priestess before him but looking instead at the distant room where priests and sages were fighting for the king's life.

"Yes," Gwennath sighed, then pursed her lips. "Lord wizard?"

"Yes?"

"Should King Azoun . . . I mean, if we can't bring them back . . . what happens then?"

"Indeed," Vangerdahast echoed softly, looking at the closed door of Tanalasta's chambers. "What happens then?"

4

The Raid
Year of Leather Shields
(–75 DR)

lea Dahast crept along the edge of the clearing, the dappled green and burnt orange hues of her hunting cape making her almost invisible in the long shadows of the Cormanthor sunset. All around her moved companions who were just as well concealed. The only sounds of their passing were occasional wolf whines in the brambles, each followed by a soft shushing noise, and then silence again.

They came down from the low hills, using the trees for cover. Ahead was the clearing: a scar carved out of the forest, which had once run unbroken to the rocky lakeshore beyond. Its edge was a rough pile of uprooted, close-tangled trees and brush. Alea was still amazed that these humans were so stupid as to think that this unguarded rampart of tumbled, ravaged forest would be enough to keep out a determined predator.

And she and the other elves in her hunting band were determined predators. They had carefully scouted, and easily found, passages through the maze of woody detritus, both the intentional routes and the ways left by carelessness. These humans aped the brambled fortifications of her people, but their work had none of the

Ed Greenwood and Jeff Grubb

beauty of elven creations—and none of the security.

Another wolf whine, and another soft shush; the beasts were getting restless. Alea wondered about the wisdom of bringing them along, but they would undeniably be useful both for their speed and their ability to terrorize the humans.

Despite their growing restlessness, she gave the signal for a halt and heard the faint noises of the sign being passed among her people. She wanted to watch the humans for a moment. She wanted to be sure.

Inwardly she heard Iliphar's voice. The old Lord of the Scepters always recommended calm, always recommended accommodation . . . always recommended negotiation. When the furry brutes had attacked the first elves they encountered, he'd recommended containment and observation.

Iliphar was letting the weight of his years rule him. There were more and more of these humans wandering through elven lands now, wreaking havoc as they went.

Typical humans were like orcs come down from the mountains—hunters seeking prey, refugees seeking settlement, merchants seeking stability. The great forest held no long-term lure for them, and when they saw that the land of trees was held by the elves, they drifted on, to . . . wherever humans drifted on to. But these men were different. This breed of human cleared the forest, killing nearly all the trees. They piled the rent corpses of forest giants—and their own wastes—around their clearings and chased off the animals. And when they had done all this, they moved on to do it all again, in another part of the forest. Someday, if they were allowed to go on, there might *be* no forest.

Alea watched the human camp from her hiding place. The houses were little more than camp hovels, consisting of nothing more than bent saplings lashed together and topped with animal hides. Elves put together such flimsy quarters only for a evening's housing against a stormy night, to be dismantled the following day. These humans made such crude sheds their permanent homes, to be

58

used until the land was despoiled and sucked dry.

The largest of the huts was a common feast hall and sleeping quarters, and likely the home of the reigning petty lord. There was a scattering of smaller buildings, including one low hut with bars that Alea thought was for tamed beasts, but she'd seen no sign of goats, chickens, or the like.

The humans looked little better than beasts themselves. They were frightening parodies of the elven form, with too much skin, hair, and fat hung on oversized frames. They dressed in the same hides as wrapped their houses, with only slightly better tailoring. They were hairy and coarse and never seemed to have bathed since the last drenching rainfall. Alea had heard that they rolled around in the dirt to keep fleas at bay. Looking at these humans, she believed it. The elves had approached downwind from the campsite, since she was unsure if the humans could smell anything beyond their own pungent selves. The stench was strong; humans lived in their own waste . . . which was why the wolves were whining.

Most of this group was male. There were a few tough-looking women, their hair as matted and rough garb as stained as that of their mates. She'd seen no cubs; perhaps they were kept in the low, barred hut . . . or been abandoned early in life to fend for themselves.

The last of the camp dwellers were returning now, dragging a large buck behind them—more game poached from forests that belonged to the elves and wolves!

Two deer were already turning on rude spits over the fire, and another pair, badly dressed, hung amid buzzing flies nearby. Alea cursed. They didn't even need the food, yet they continued to despoil the forest!

Two days ago she'd come across the site of a human kill. Something large, perhaps a bear, had been brought down. Both human and elf arrows were at the site, and from it led the trail of something heavy dragged off in this direction—passing the corpse of an elf of the Elian clan, who lay bristling with crude human arrows, his ears lopped off.

Alea had no doubt the elf had brought down the game, then been attacked by the humans afterward. She'd tracked the downed prey through the forest to this camp before gathering her hunting companions for the raid. Most of the elves around her had seen fewer than a hundred summers. The elders were discussing and mourning the dead Elian. While the elders talked, Alea's hunters would do something about this outrage!

But a good hunter makes sure of his prey . . . and they had to be sure of these reeking humans. As the buck was brought into camp, the humans all shouted and waved, jabbering at each other in their mongrel tongue. So much like real speech, thought Alea, but all twisted, like the humans themselves. The buck's slayers made big, sweeping hand signs, indicating the bulk of the stag that had escaped them. The others laughed and hooted, outlining with gestures their own rival escaped beasts, of even more impossibly large proportions.

Alea growled deep in her throat just as the wolves did. These human vermin poached on elven lands! Their clumsy butcherings were beginning to drive the game away; they didn't even have the sense to move on and let the land recover from their depredations. Alea growled more loudly and almost rose to signal the attack, but Lord Iliphar's admonitions held her in place. Were she wrong, she'd be little better than these rightly despised savages.

The door of the largest hut in the camp scraped open, and out strode the petty lord. Apparently he'd been waiting for the last hunters to return before making his own entrance. This one had leathers of a finer cut than most and was bedecked with polished gemstones on leather thongs. He was flanked by two equally tough-looking women. Consorts? Bodyguards? Both?

On one of the lordling's thongs hung two pale slivers of meat, just starting to wrinkle and yellow with age. The ears of an elf.

Alea gave the signal to prepare for battle.

The hairy human lord strode to the fire pit at the center of the gathered humans and jabbered at them. They made assenting sounds. He jabbered at them some more. They grunted another assent. He pointed in Alea's direction, and the elf froze for a moment. Did they know of her presence? But then the lordling marked off the other cardinal points, and Alea realized what he was doing.

He was staking his claim, like a cooshee marking its territory: all this land was his. A fire began to burn within her, rising up into her chest. How dare the savages claim elven hunting lands!

She was about to give the signal to attack when the human lord grunted and waved, and the two muscular bodyguard wives went to the low barricaded hut. One stood outside while the other entered and then dragged out some sort of prisoner.

At first Alea thought the prisoner was an elf, for he was thin and pale compared to the barbarians. But on closer examination, it was clear the prisoner was another human, tall and lean, with a ratty reddish beard. Half his face was puffy with a monstrous bruise, and he hobbled forward on an equally swollen ankle. His wrists were crossed before him and secured together with a single iron cuff. He wore loose, tattered trousers and a shirt of similar stuff, all worn and filthy but still of finer cut than the garb of the humans of the camp. He didn't look much like his captors.

The women dragged the frail human forward and forced him to his knees in front of the hairy lord. His lordship puffed out his chest and smiled. He was missing his front teeth, upper and lower.

His lordship barked a question in the mangled human language. Alea did not catch the wispy human's response, but it was apparently insufficient. The lord cuffed him, hard, on the bruised side of his face. The captive's eye on that side was swollen shut, and he did not see the blow coming. He went sprawling backward for his lack of awareness.

The crowd of watching humans shouted its approval. One of the muscular consorts dragged the thin human back to the barbarian lord's feet. Again the question was jabbered. Again the damaged human said something. Again the local lord cuffed him, he sprawled, and the crowd hooted.

This apparently passed for human entertainment, and the crowd looked as if it could enjoy it all night. The local lord boasted of his accomplishments, pointed in all directions, and pulled the elven ears on the thong at his side, dancing them in front of the other human. And again he asked the question.

Alea raised her hand, and in the semicircle concealed around the camp other elves raised theirs as well, preparing to leap forward. Safety wedges were carefully unclipped from crossbows, and wolves were slipped silently from their harnesses.

The predictability of humans did not disappoint them. Once more the lord slapped his frail prisoner down and the crowd hooted their approval. Alea dropped her hand and charged forward.

It took more than a moment for the humans to react, to realize that the shouts they heard were not their own. By that time, the elves were fully free of the brambles. The wolves bounded in front of their masters but were beaten to the foe by elven crossbow quarrels, which hummed into the crowd of humans from both sides of the clearing. More than half a dozen human warriors toppled, clutching at transfixed stomachs and necks, and the beaten ground tasted barbarian blood.

Then the wolves struck as most of the humans were still grabbing for their blades. Alea had managed to gather only a dozen, but they were well trained, as responsive as an elven hound in the court of Myth Drannor. They knew to go for an arm holding a weapon, or if no weapon was obvious, bite at the crotch. Nine or ten humans crumpled under their assault as the rest scrambled to stand and fight.

Alea led the main charge, about twenty elves in all, with those who'd fired crossbows dropping their weapons and joining the assault in a second wave. The elves ran through the confusion of wolf-savaged warriors into the heart of the shouting, hurrying humans. Any chance of the hairy folk of the camp forming a battle line, if they even knew what one was, was gone in the space of a few breaths as the battle became a series of single combats.

As straight and unswerving as a leaping arrow, Alea made for the human lordling. He was the one most responsible for what these stinking folk did, the one who wore the ears of an elf of the Elian clan. He would pay the price for the crimes of his people.

The lordling was ready for her. He'd used the time bought in blood by his dying comrades to pull his own weapon from his scabbard. It was a heavy black sword, little more than a cold iron bar with a single rough edge. He snarled and jabbered something in barbarian-speak. Alea's only reply was to draw back her lips in a grin that promised swift death.

The human lunged, and Alea dodged nimbly out of the way, her own narrow blade a mere ribbon of steel. As she glided past, she brought her blade up smoothly and was rewarded with the wet, tearing sound of leather and flesh parting. She danced back to face her foe and saw that the human was bleeding along his sword arm.

Bright rage flared in the human's eyes, and he snarled, but then calmed visibly and went into a crouch. This was no battle-mad beast that would charge conveniently onto her sword. Instead, the human held his blade out, its point tracing a small circle in the air, waiting for her to come to him.

She took a step forward, and he lunged again. This time she brought her steel up against the human's iron blade. The cold-wrought iron grated roughly against her own smooth-edged sword, and she caught the lordling's blade against the guards of her own weapon. Straining, she turned it aside, stripping the weapon from her opponent's hand. As it clattered to the ground, she danced back, and then darted in, blade sweeping up to gut the man from belly to throat.

Something large and furry thundered into her ribs from the right, and Alea was suddenly falling to the ground herself, rolling clear as she fell. The large furry thing was one of the female bodyguards, who loomed large above her—and then disappeared under the leap of another fur-covered streak, this time a wolf. The barbarian woman toppled backward with a scream that ended in a bloody gurgle.

Then Alea was on her feet again, shaking her head to clear her vision. The lordling had disappeared in the dust and confusion of the fray. Was he hunting for another weapon, or had he decided the surrounding woods would be a safer place for him than an encampment overrun by elves?

The frail human captive with the ragged red beard was stumbling up to her, holding his manacled wrists forward. In elvish, the rail-thin mortal said politely, "Unlock these, if you please."

The words hit Alea with the force of a blow. She hadn't expected any of these ground apes to know the True Tongue, and this one spoke it with only the barest hint of an accent. Who was he? And if she let him go, would he help or flee into the woods?

Across the dusty clearing, she spotted the hairy human lordling.

"Later," she said, pushing past the manacled one. He bellowed something else at her back that she did not catch.

The lordling saw her about the same time and swatted aside an elven hunter to reach her. He hadn't found another sword but instead wielded a long chain topped by a metal ball bristling with spikes.

He swung it at her when she was still out of range, the ball moaning an arc through the air. Alea lunged in behind it, hoping to skewer the shaggy human before he could react.

She'd misjudged; even as she moved, the human stepped forward, pulling his shoulders around, quickly reversing the direction of his swing. The chain wrapped tightly around her lower arm, the spikes at its end grabbing at her flesh.

Alea snarled, caught off-balance, as the human braced himself with both feet and pulled hard.

She was quicker and more nimble than the barbarian, but the human had the edge in height, weight, and strength. As she was hauled forward, she dropped her blade and toppled helplessly at the lordling's feet. A boot stamped cruelly down; she twisted and took it on her shoulder rather than her throat.

He smiled, the last rays of the setting sun setting the scars on his face ablaze and highlighting the gap in his teeth. One hand firmly gripping the chain that held her braced against his planted boot, he used the other to draw a steel dagger the size of a dragon's tooth from his belt.

Then a pair of frail hands reached up on either side of the lordling's head, and Alea heard someone shout an ancient archaic word, a magical word, one that would trip a memorized spell.

The hands glowed a fierce blue, and the barbarian chieftain's head disappeared in the radiance. When the glow vanished, the head was gone as well. Slowly, like a boat with a slow leak, the barbarian's reeling body settled to the earth.

Behind the corpse stood the red-bearded wizard, who'd apparently gotten his manacles off after all. He offered a hand to Alea.

Alea grabbed her own blade and stood up, looking around the encampment. The fight was over. There was a snarling cluster of wolves atop one still-struggling human, but the other foes were now nothing but inanimate, shaggy lumps strewn on the ground.

Many of the elves had shed some blood, but none had fallen. There was not a human standing except for the pale, bearded one in the ragged finery. "You're welcome," he said quietly in the True Tongue.

Alea frowned. "You're not with this lot, are you?" she asked gruffly, pulling the ear-laden thong from what was left of the human lord.

"Observant as well as strong," murmured the human.

"No, I am not with them. These savages caught me, thought me an evil wizard, and were about to use me for the evening's entertainment when you made your . . . timely arrival."

Alea put the elven ears into her pouch, to be returned to the Elian family and entombed with the rest of the elf's body.

"So vengeance was your motivation," said the pale human, still trying to strike up a conversation. "A pity. I thought it was concern about my impending doom."

She looked hard at the human, as if seeing him for the first time. "You're Netherese?"

The human moved his head in a half shake, half-nod. "Netheril is no more."

"You can go your way then, human," Alea declared, turning back to where the rest of her hunting group was gathering. The huts had been looted for what little treasure could be found, and one of the elves moved from hut to hut, setting fire to the buildings with a burning log. Thick smoke began to curl, and the elves started to toss human bodies into the huts, to be consumed in the blaze to come. Many had already had their ears removed.

"That won't stop them, you know," said the pale human.

Alea stopped again and looked hard at the human. She sighed. "*What* won't stop *who?*"

"Killing. Humans. Well, *these* humans, at any rate." He nudged a mauled corpse with one toe. "If you kill a human, you have to worry about his children coming after you. And grandchildren. And sister-kin, and distant kin, and friends and all—until whole peoples are arming against you. No, killing just encourages them."

Alea's upper lip curled back from her teeth. "The matter is more simple, you-who-love-to-talk. This is land is ours. We are its guardians. It is our hunting ground."

The human nodded. "And other humans know this: the Dalesmen spilling across the Dragon Reach, and the greedy or desperate from the wealthy merchant nations of the south. They know of this land of forests now—a rich, untamed hunting ground, with only a few elves to defend it. Ripe for the taking."

"A fair warning," Alea said grudgingly, eyebrows lifting. "And yet I wonder why you make it. You *are* human, you know," she said, curiosity twisting her voice as the last of the huts were set ablaze.

"Sometimes I wish I weren't," said the frail form, extending a hand. "Baerauble Etharr."

Alea looked at the man's outstretched hand. He disdains humans, she thought, yet the pressing of palms was a very human action.

She looked back up the arm to its owner, his beard wild in the last fading light. He looked almost comical, though at the back of her mind, she was thinking his looks hardly mattered. He'd probably die out here in a matter of nights without elven protection.

And looking into his eyes, she realized that he knew it as well.

She took the offered hand and shook it warily. "Alea Dahast," she replied. "Are you . . . ?"

"Am I what?"

"An evil wizard?" she prompted calmly.

"Wizard, yes; evil, no," Baerauble Etharr replied, and Alea saw a gleam in the human's eye. "But as a mage, I find the boorish company of humans to be rather a strain at best."

Alea turned and started walking back to her people again. The human kept pace alongside her, matching her smooth stride. After a few moments of ignoring him, she turned her head and asked, "So if we don't kill human poachers, what do we do? Give them this land?"

"You can scare them."

She stopped and looked questioningly at the mage. Facing her, he smiled slightly and added, "You have wolves here."

"Observant as well as magical," she murmured, making her words sound like his slight accent. It had to be northern. It resembled the chimelike speech of the Netherese.

67

"Many?" he asked, acknowledging her sally with the merest ghost of a smile.

"Some."

"Get more. Feral ones, like dire wolves. And some owl-bears, bugbears, and whatever other wood-dwelling horrors you can find. Not enough to burden the forest or make the hunting too perilous for your folk. Put them along the borders . . . particularly the eastern verges, near the human settlements."

She stood there, thinking. "If humans see that there are dangerous creatures on the edges of the forest . . ."

". . . they'll think worse beasts lurk in its depths. To some, this might be a peril to eradicate at all costs, but any man going near the forest will be so busy fighting the roaming beasts that very few humans will venture far inside the woods. And so you have—again—your un-spoiled hunting preserve. One can't possibly kill all the humans, but one can steer them aside."

Alea managed a half-smile as she looked at the burning wreckage of the human camp. She felt the truth in his words warm her inwardly as much as the flaring flames heated her face.

Yes, Iliphar would raise bloody tumult over this when he found out, but this simple strategy, plus the returned ears, might buy her a little grace with the elders. And if she brought along the human mage as a prize . . .

"You'll come with us," she said flatly, then turned her head and shouted a command at her hunters, bidding them make ready to travel.

"Of course I shall," said the lanky human. Alea did not see the gleam in his eye and the widening smile on his lips, but she knew it was there.

5

The Abraxus
Year of the Gauntlet
(1369 DR)

ou sent for me, lord wizard?" The fur-cloaked high priest's tones were barely respectful. Augrathar Buruin, High Huntmaster of Vaunted Malar for all Cormyr, wasn't used to answering any summons that did not come from the crown itself.

"I did," Vangerdahast told him gravely, "and I count your presence in Suzail at this time as a stroke of good fortune for the realm."

The huntmaster merely grunted, a sound of mingled disdain and disbelief, and swaggered past Vangerdahast, the many dangling claws on the pelts he wore dancing with the weight of his stride. He headed straight to a platter on a sideboard, where he tore a leg deftly from a roast mountain bustard and asked, "So where's the blood you want spilled? And in the meantime, what's happened to the wine cellars?"

The Royal Magician's eyes silently answered the query of the nearest belarjack, and the man scurried over to the cleric with a jack of wine and a goblet. The priest snatched the jack, leaving the startled servant holding the empty goblet, and Vangerdahast turned away before anyone could see him smile.

Ed Greenwood and Jeff Grubb

His movement brought him face to face with the next arrival: the battered old warrior Aldeth Ironsar, Faithful Hammer of Tyr, whose face was stiff with disapproval at the priest of Malar's manners and presence. The Royal Magician greeted Ironsar warmly; even as they clasped each other's upper arms, the Chamber of Crossed Dogs began to fill up rapidly. High Priest Manarech of Tymora, resplendent in vestments so new they seared the eye, nodded to Vangerdahast. Manarech smiled, seemingly bearing the High Wizard and the palace in general no ill will for being bathed in Bhereu's last breaths, and drifted to the sideboard. Junstal Halarn, ranking Visiting Songmaster at Suzail's shrine to Milil, was not far behind.

All of these good clerics were accompanied by their personal scribes, consecrated pages, and watchpriests. With glances and finger gestures rather than words, Vangerdahast saw to it that all of them were given wine and the small savory pastries that the kitchens of the court were justly famous for. Then he smiled and nodded, listening to their self-important chatter with every evidence of deep interest, hoping that the three men he was waiting for would not be too much longer.

As it happened, they arrived together. The sage Alaphondar and Erdreth Halansalim, a gaunt, no-nonsense senior war wizard, crept in unobtrusively through a side door, while Runelord Thaun Khelbor, Loremaster of Deneir, swept in through the main door. The loremaster bore a tall rune-graven staff of darkest ebony, and small lightning bolts crackled around the staff's tip.

Vangerdahast fought the urge to smile again at the sight of the loremaster and his portable lightning storm, and he was careful not to raise his eyes in a patronizing glance. The loremaster was the oldest and most gentle of the assembled holy men. Why not allow him a moment of pride? Alaphondar, always calm and graceful, led the tardy cleric over to the sideboard as the Royal Magician stepped forward. Now was the time to take control of these proud men, before their mutual patience was stretched further and disputes could break out.

In a back corner, Vangerdahast saw the grim, white-bearded face of Erdreth start to turn, beginning to ceaselessly scrutinize the gathering from a back corner. The Royal Magician smiled in approval. Erdreth was checking for all manner of magical devices and potential dangers. The priests, of course, took Vangerdahast's approving grin as a smile of welcome to them and made various gracious nods of superiority.

"Respectful greetings, your hallowed graces," Vangerdahast said loudly and pleasantly. "The Crown of Cormyr requires your services in an important matter involving the very safety of the state, of your persons, and of the health of every man, woman, and child in Suzail." *That* got their attention.

"There is a man in the chambers of Crown Princess Tanalasta," he went on, not giving them any time to interject any speeches about their willingness, loyalty, and the like, "who may bear a disease, or a poison, or even fell magic. A nobleman. He must be examined without delay, lest he spread a plague—or worse—throughout the palace. And what afflicts the palace touches the court, fair Suzail, and eventually all the realm. I need you to make that examination."

"Us?" The huntmaster demanded, waving the jack of wine without shame. "Why can't you—or your precious war wizards—do it?"

Vangerdahast spread his hands in a gesture of helplessness. "My skills are insufficient, and my presence has been for the moment judged undesirable by the princess." He fell silent, giving them the opportunity to ask the questions he knew they would.

"Forgive me if this verges on the indelicate," Manarech of Tymora said tentatively, "but am I to understand that we are being asked to force our way into the *bedchambers* of the princess? And interrupt her, perhaps, in the company of a man who may be her . . . ?" He fell silent, making a meaningful circling gesture with his hand. No one present lacked the imagination to supply the word that had been omitted: *lover*.

"And just who is this man?" the high priest of Tyr asked, brows drawn together in a frown of consideration.

"The man is Aunadar Bleth," Vangerdahast told them, "and he may be the paramour of the princess, for all I know . . . or have bothered to ask." He made the last few words almost a rebuke, looking around the room as he uttered them so that no man could feel personally singled out and slighted. Gods, he thought inwardly, priests are as bad as wizards—a keg full of pride crammed into a tankard of wits, the lot of them! Including, no doubt, he reflected ruefully, this wizard as well.

"Is the matter as urgent as all that?" the songmaster of Milil asked pettishly. "Could it not be brought to the holy place of—ah, one of us—and dealt with in the usual manner?"

"The fate of the realm does hang in the balance," Vangerdahast told them gently. "And for once, that is no empty tale teller's phrase, but the bare truth."

He turned with slow, tragic grandeur to regard High Priest Manarech Eskwuin. "Do you not agree, holy lord? Was what you witnessed earlier not grave enough to threaten the peace of all Cormyr?"

The high priest of Tymora nodded, drawing himself up to his full height and flinging his arms wide dramatically to make the most of his moment. "It was indeed, and you did right to summon me then, as you do well to call on the holy skills of all of us now. Any time the king of any realm is laid low, and his senior blood nobles with him, is a time when the peace of that realm may well be said to be threatened."

"*What?*" A general confusion of shouted questions broke out, and Vangerdahast held up his hands for silence. Thankfully he did not have to use the silver whistle, for they quieted at once. Interest made them reach eagerly for his next words.

"Yesterday afternoon," he said gravely, "the king, Duke Bhereu, Baron Thomdor, and young Bleth were in the King's Forest on a hunt. They encountered some sort of metal beast, which used some sort of breath weapon on them. Through magic, we were able to swiftly transport them back here, but all of the royals had collapsed. Duke Bhereu died almost immediately, and Thomdor and the king at this moment are fighting for their lives. Aunadar Bleth slipped away and went straight to the princess. I need to know why he did not collapse, if he carries any taint of anything that may afflict him, the princess, or anyone else he comes into contact with in the future, and how he feels right now."

The priest of Malar spat. "Bah! I deal in hunting and slaying, not nursemaiding the sick! See to your own duty, court wizard!"

Vangerdahast did his best not to smile grimly. This is what he'd expected and been waiting for. Indeed, such anticipated response by the huntmaster was the sole reason Vangerdahast had invited him in the first place.

The Royal Magician made a far more grand gesture than he needed to and looked straight at the huntmaster as—with a flash and sparkle of light motes and drifting smoke—the staff of the High Wizard of Cormyr appeared in his hand. He raised it as high as his arm would stretch and willed it to hum and crackle with power. As it burst into life, glowing impressively above their heads, he said regretfully, "I regret having to inconvenience you in any way, holy lords, but it is imperative that you aid Cormyr in this problem without delay."

"And if we do not?" Surprisingly, the cool question came from the loremaster of Deneir.

Vangerdahast silently revised his kindly opinion of the runelord and said sternly, "As Regent Royal of Cormyr, I expect your cooperation in this—or your heads." He caused his upraised staff to wink slightly but meaningfully.

" 'Regent Royal'?" Huntmaster Buruin's voice was loud with derision. "You think this nonsense title gives you any authority over *me*?"

"Good and holy lord, it does—and yet, respected servant of Malar, it is authority I should not need."

"Oh? How so?"

The Royal Magician smiled a crooked wolflike smile. "Hearken to the decree of Garmos Saernclaws, one of the most respected servants of the lord of beasts—a holy decree that still applies to all priests of Malar, as it has for nigh a thousand years: 'The Hunt must be clean. If disease or affliction is visited on hunters by a beast, clergy of Malar must do all they can to root out and exterminate the taint, that bloodlines and beasts in the wild remain always strong.'"

The huntmaster gaped at him in pale-faced astonishment. He hadn't expected a layman, even a wizard, to know the gospel of Saernclaws. They both knew Garmos had said just that, and Agrathar Buruin was bound by it.

The Royal Magician dropped his eyes from the stunned gaze of the Malarite and looked around at the faces of the other priests. There was no more fight in any of them; it remained only to gesture toward the door and add gently, "Lord Alaphondar and Palace Mage Halansalim will accompany you to the chambers of the princess and be your escort therein and when you examine and bring out Bleth."

The priests tumbled out of the room like adventurers fleeing a dragon, the sage and the war wizard in the lead. Vangerdahast imagined the turmoil that would result when the gaggle of holy men arrived at Tanalasta's quarters and dragged off her suitor for laborious tests, examinations, and divinations. The Royal Magician labored to keep a broadening inner smile from spreading across his face.

Instead, he merely made the gesture that caused his staff of state to disappear, then turned away, to leave the Chamber of Crossed Dogs by another, smaller door, passing the gigantic wall carving of leaping hounds that had given the room its curious name.

The door opened onto a small, dark passage that gave onto a step halfway up Halantaver's Stair. Ascending, he passed through the echoing stateliness of Endevanor's Hall into the Salon of Six Scepters, nodding to the belarjacks who sprang to open doors before him. Across a hall from the eastern door of the salon was the Upper Eastern, or Satharwood, Banqueting Hall, the way to its closed doors barred by a solid line of grim Purple Dragons in full armor.

Vangerdahast stepped inside to find himself facing a watchful ring of tired war wizards, who raised wands to menace him out of habit. "For the realm," he said to them wearily; the watch phrase should have been unnecessary. They lowered their wands, but four or more continued to watch him expressionlessly. The others turned back to what was going on inside their ring.

Above the tables where the royals lay, both still motionless and silent, hung a globe of radiant air, its soft glow illuminating the weary faces of the priests who were working on the baron—experimenting with vigorous massaging of his arms and legs, it appeared—under the direction of a weary-eyed Dimswart. Vangerdahast gave him a silent wave when he looked up to see which fresh face had joined the circle, and he replied with a silent negative shake of his head. No change.

The Royal Magician turned grimly away, trying for an instant to recall what pressing business he'd been attending to when the breaking of the summoning wand had dragged the realm into chaos. Thus occupied, he almost ran into the Bishop of the Black Blades. Gwennath was slumped against the wall, silent tears of grim failure and exhaustion running down her face. Vangerdahast took her gently by the shoulders, and as she looked up in weary wonder, he said merely, "Come."

The belarjack by the door had fallen asleep; there was fear in his fluttering eyes when he saw that he'd been sleepily cursing the High Wizard for pinching him awake, but Vangerdahast simply said, "Go and get someone to relieve you and your fellow priests—*after* you bring Matron Maglanna to me."

"Have I—done wrong?" Gwennath asked sleepily.

Vangerdahast kept his hands under her elbows to keep her from sliding to the floor and said, "No. By my decree, however, you are now to go with the matron of this floor of the palace and get some sleep in whatever chamber she puts you."

Maglanna, doughty and dependable, though looking as worn as Gwennath, was at his side before he'd finished speaking. Vangerdahast merely added a gentle "By my command" to her, watched her nod and gather the exhausted priestess into her guiding arms, and turned away again.

Sleep might soon be a good idea as well for certain High Wizards, he reminded himself as he passed grimly on through another set of wary guards—backed up by war wizards this time—into Belnshor's Chamber, where the clockwork beast had been stored.

Usually used to store whatever furniture wasn't in use at the moment, the high-vaulted room was largely bare at the present time. It was lit by moving radiances, the fey lights of working magic.

They gleamed on the golden curves of what had been the bull in the forest, lying in glittering pieces on trestles at the center of the room. Light spells hovered over it, and other magic spells were lifting plates and rings of metal with invisible hands as two women leaned forward to examine them. They wore identical frowns of intense concentration.

One woman was familiar to the Royal Magician. Laspeera Inthré was warden of the war wizards, his deputy in the command of that vital fellowship. Still beautiful, she was beginning to show her years of strain in service to Cormyr. Lines flanked her pursed mouth, and a tiny pair of exquisitely crafted clear crystal spectacles, held aloft by magic, floated in front of her sharp nose as she stared at the intricate assembly of metal objects that lurked behind one of the bull's nostrils. Without looking away from what she was studying, she raised her fingers in a salute. In all his years of working magic, Vangerdahast had met very few mages who could concentrate on as many things at once as this one. She was murmuring another spell now; the deft manipulation of metal plates and coils must be her work.

He'd seen the other buxom, beautiful woman before, too, but never expected to find her here in the depths of the palace, in chambers normally closed to the public. She tossed her head to shake long, honey-hued hair out of her face and favor him with a smile as he approached. The High Wizard knew he'd last laid eyes on that pert, mysterious, rather catlike smile in The Laughing Lass, a Suzailan establishment that often transformed itself from tavern into festhall when the nights grew warm. The woman been dancing on a table at the time, wearing very little more than a smile and a few strings of coins. She smiled now as if she knew him, but Vangerdahast was sure such was not the case. The web of disguise spells he habitually wore to the Lass was impenetrable. Wherefore his challenge, when it came, was a trifle sharper than he'd intended. "And you are—?"

She raised eyes like warm flames to meet his and replied, "I am called Emthrara Undril, and I can show you something that means more. Pray stay your spells and mistake not my intent, lord wizard, which is peaceful. I but open my locket." Slim fingers went slowly up to the ribbon she wore at her throat and the oval of chased silver there, to push a tiny catch and swing the locket open. She lifted her chin to let Vangerdahast get a good look inside.

Within was more black silk, and on it a tiny silver harp. She was a Harper.

The Royal Magician's eyes narrowed. A tavern dancer, aye, that fit with the way Those Who Harp liked to operate . . . but how came she here to this room at such a time?

"Is this more of Elminster's meddling?" he asked suspiciously.

Emthrara frowned slightly. "The Great Oversorcerer, Favored of Mystra? Nay—I doubt he even knows I am here."

She tossed her head almost challengingly, eyes on his, and said excitedly, "I met him once! He was very kind. He

77

said I danced as well as they once did in Myth Drannor, if you can credit that!"

"Harrumph," Vangerdahast growled and turned away.

From behind him came Laspeera's low, level voice; the wizard could tell she was amused. "I brought Emthrara here, lord, because I knew she'd once fought, disabled, and then taken apart a giant spider of metal, called by some a 'clockwork horror.' Is she not, therefore, the best person in all Cormyr to learn the secrets of this beast?"

"Harrumph," Vangerdahast said again, striding toward the door. A pace away from it, he spun around and said heavily, "Accept my apologies, please, for my churlish manner. I am overtired and no great friend to surprises at the best of times."

Emthrara smiled easily. "I'll look for you again in the Lass, High Wizard," she said cheerfully, and Laspeera laughed at the way Vangerdahast winced and put his hand to his forehead.

Still shading his eyes, he asked in pained tones, "The abraxus, ladies. Have you found any traps yet, or reservoirs where more of its breath gas might be waiting?"

"No, lord," they said in chorus, and Emthrara added, "We did find a small metal tray inserted beneath the beast's chin. It might have held the venom, but it was empty, its poison spent. And a switch along the spine, which appears connected to a set of bellows within."

"Is the creature newly fashioned?"

The two women exchanged glances, and then Emthrara said, "We think not. In places where no royal blades penetrated, we believe, the metal is bright from wear and use. Some plates and pieces seem newer than others, as if replacements have been made."

"And can you put it back to how you found it?"

There was some hesitation in Laspeera's voice as she said, "We think so . . . if you hold that such a reassembly would be wise, lord."

Vangerdahast waved one hand. "I was inquiring as to your abilities and the condition of the components, not ordering that such a process be undertaken." He hummed absently for a moment or two, lost in thought, and then asked, "What powers the magic that gives this beast life? Can you tell?"

Laspeera shrugged. "I cannot be sure, but I am almost certain that life-force must be drained from a beast or a man to make this construct move."

"And would this be an unwilling sacrifice or an unaware victim? A summoning, perhaps? And does it function according to its own will, or is it directed from afar?"

Laspeera spread her hands in mute demonstration of her ignorance. Emthrara followed suit, but added, "There are devices in the South that use a victim's life-force for power. These sometimes require a victim of particular ability or appearance to make them function. In such cases, the life-force is sucked from the body as a great green flame. This may or may not be related."

The Royal Magician sighed and turned back to the door. "Answers, as usual, are all too few and speculations all too many. Nonetheless, both of you have done well. My thanks." He laid a hand on the door, then turned once more and asked, "So who, in your opinion, might be able to direct such a thing against Cormyr?"

Laspeera spread her hands again, but the Harper dancer smiled thinly and said, "Ah, now, lord wizard, you ask us to venture forth upon the seas of pure speculation."

Vangerdahast gestured for her to do so.

She shrugged. "Leaving aside the always present but slim possibility that arcane magic has been sent to beset us by liches, lone mad mages, or cabals of ambitious powers from the world below who want our land as their surface playground—illithids, the Phaerimm, and others we know too little of to even list—leaving all these aside, we can easily name the Zhentarim, the Red Wizards of Thay, perhaps even the Arcane Brotherhood of Luskan, or individual archwizards of Calimshan or Halruaa. Such folk have the necessary mastery of the arcane. As to why, we must open a far greater sphere of speculation. The folk who might hire such fell magic could be descendants of the Tuigan Khahan seeking revenge, elements of Sembia, the Zhentarim, or even Archendale seeking to weaken the realm—or even a rival noble house here at home, desiring to exterminate the Obarskyr line."

The Royal Magician lifted an eyebrow, but the Harper added softly, "That is where I would look first, lord. Outlanders rarely manage to strike with swords or beasts at a specific person, in the heart of the realm, without knowing the ground . . . and their target . . . fairly well."

Vangerdahast nodded slowly. "I have had similar thoughts. If this crisis passes, we must talk again, Lady Emthrara."

She lifted her shoulders in a shrug. "I am no lady."

"Then you'll not find a flagon of fine wine too much of an effrontery," the wizard returned, "will you?"

She laughed. "Later, then—and be sure that it's good wine."

"The best," Vangerdahast promised.

Laspeera rolled her eyes as the Lord High Wizard opened the door, then asked Emthrara loudly, "Do you know how many times he promises that?"

The Royal Magician of the Realm, Court Wizard of Cormyr, Chairman Emeritus of the College of War Wizards, Lord High Wizard of Suzail, Scepter of the Stonelands, and Master of the Council of Mages paused at the doorway and turned, his eyebrows arched in mock surprise. Both ladies laughed merrily and waved farewell.

Vangerdahast pointed at the abraxus on the table and growled, "Leave that not unguarded!" as the door swung closed. Turning from it, he found himself grinning and shook his head. He *must* be overtired. . . .

"So tell me," Emthrara said calmly as the door closed on the mage, "now that the free entertainment is gone, just how does one guard such a thing?"

Laspeera winked at her. "First, be aware that he loves to listen at doors. Our Royal Magician is seldom truly gone when you're in the palace. Secondly, *I* don't know. I'm going to raise a shell of antimagic around it, and then surround that with several spherical force barriers of various sorts."

The Harper eyed her steadily. "And will all that work?"

Laspeera spread her hands. "With magic—as always—who knows?"

* * * * *

Vangerdahast managed six steps along the quiet hall toward the back stair that led down to, among other things, the kitchens, where there *might* be some still-warm sage-and-pheasant soup in a pot somewhere, before a breathless palace page whirled around a corner and gasped, "Lord wizard! Lord wizard! The Sage Lord Alaphondar sends me to tell you that the priests have done their work—and adequate work, he terms it—and have pronounced Aunadar Bleth free from hurt or contagion!"

Vangerdahast nodded and smiled. "And—?"

"He and Sir Wizard Halansalim have Lord Bleth in their care now, in the Redpetal Room, and await your earliest pleasure there."

"Well," the Royal Magician demanded, "what are you waiting for?" And he plucked up his robes at the knees like a servingmaid and ran. The winded page could barely keep up.

* * * * *

"Untouched, all the high holy men agree. Untouched when the three you were riding with lie stricken, one dead . . . and yet you," Vangerdahast said, spacing his words with menacing gentleness, "are . . . entirely . . . untouched by the beast's breath. I find that most curious. Would *you* not find that curious, Aunadar Bleth, if a man under your command came back unscathed from a fray with a poison-breathing beast that laid *all* of his companions low?"

"What are you saying?" the young noble snapped coldly, his face red with anger. He had been poked, prodded, and enspelled for the past several hours, and the strain and irritation shone on his face.

Alaphondar and the gaunt old war wizard across the room regarded him impassively. There were wands in both of their hands, and when Aunadar's hand moved unconsciously toward the hilt of his sword, the tips of both wands lifted, to catch his eye, and twitched warningly.

The young man's lips thinned as he set his mouth in a hard line, but his hand fell back to his side.

"What am I saying?" Vangerdahast's voice was bitingly mild as he strolled back and forth, hands clasped behind his back. Aunadar's eyes followed his progress. "I have, so far, said nothing. I merely ask. I ask you for your opinion, knowing my own already. But then, fat old men in robes never seem to have a high regard for the bravery and sword skills of swaggering youths, do they?"

Aunadar turned to face the wizard and snarled, "Enough of your insults, old man! I am a Bleth, not a lowborn dotard who happens to have a few wands and a title at court! I may not have taught the king everything he knows, but my father and his forebears have walked this land as long as the Obarskyrs! Few throughout all those long years ever dared to impugn *their* bravery!"

Aunadar's blustering was met with only silence . . . cold silence. When he, too, fell silent, his last shouted words fell like stones into an abyss, past eyes that were very gray with age this night, but as calm as if they belonged to a painting.

They belonged, in fact, to the Royal Magician of the realm, who said mildly, "As I recall, the Bleths have always been strong on old history and bearing grudges until full-fledged feuds are born. Since you mention longevity, let me inform you that I, lowborn commoner that I am, am descended from someone your tutors just may have acquainted you with: Baerauble Etharr. That means my ancestors have been treading the dirt of

Cormyr longer than the noble sod has known the weight of either Obarskyr feet . . . or Bleth boots. Longevity, it seems, grants no special status."

His tone changed from sadness to something with a little more thunder as he added, "Nor, as seems increasingly clear, does it have anything to do with loyalty."

"Just what are you saying?" the young noble demanded, his rising voice making the challenge almost a plea.

The old wizard spread his hands. "I need to know—the crown needs to know—your loyalties in this affair."

Their eyes locked in silence, and Vangerdahast added, "I need to know if I can trust the man who may be our next king or prince consort, depending on the decisions of Queen Filfaeril and the crown princess. I need to know if I should be aiding the man who can give true love and support to the heir apparent—or blasting him to ashes, that he have no more chance to bring the fair realm down into ruin."

Aunadar Bleth licked suddenly dry lips and asked, "So what would you have me do?" His eyes were drawn to the moving hands and lips of the war wizard across the room. Halansalim was murmuring a spell . . . a magic that would, no doubt, tell him if a certain young noble was trifling with the truth.

There were suddenly beads of sweat on Aunadar's handsome forehead. Vangerdahast eyed them but said nothing. Is there a noble in any realm lacking a few dire secrets best kept hidden?

"Swear fealty to the crown," the court wizard said. "Oh, I know you knelt before Azoun and laid your sword at his feet. That holds, if our great king sits on the throne once more, and I shall then see that you are honored for this minor humiliation. But I need to know what is in your heart now."

"I suppose the alternative," Lord Bleth the Younger said with a trace of bitterness, his eyes darting to the watchful war wizard, "is to have my wits probed until they are torn apart by the loyal wizards of Cormyr?"

Ed Greenwood and Jeff Grubb

The Royal Magician nodded slowly in silence. Bleth went to one knee and said hoarsely, "I swear, then. By whatever words you want, and on anything you desire. I will be loyal to the crown of fair Cormyr, upon my life."

The wizard raised one hand, and suddenly, without fanfare, there was a blade in it. The blade was a relic of days gone by, its broad and heavy blade incised with deep, angular runes. Bleth had never been so close to it before. He drew in his breath involuntarily at its power and beauty as Vangerdahast lowered the sword to his lips, hilt first.

"The blade I hold is Symylazarr, the Fount of Honor, upon which every leader of every noble house swears his or her fealty to the king. Kiss the dragon's-head pommel and repeat the last sentence you uttered," the old wizard said, and the other two men in the room took a single step forward in unison.

The young noble did as he was bade and added firmly, "Moreover, I pledge upon my honor to do whatever I can to help the Princess Tanalasta."

Vangerdahast nodded gravely. "Well said." With a wave, the ancient blade was gone again, as suddenly and as silently as it had appeared.

As he rose, the young noble seemed calm, composed, and almost regal, as if he'd been touched by some magic of the blade or the ritual itself. For the first time, he spoke to the wizard as an equal and an ally. "For my part," he said anxiously, catching at Vangerdahast's sleeve, "I am worried about Tanalasta and the future of the realm. Will she see what she should do? Will she rule well, or is it truly a challenge for someone else? And if—the good gods forbid—Azoun should die now, who will rule if the princess hesitates?"

"Who indeed?" the court wizard agreed gravely, studying the ornately tiled floor. He had already overheard whisperings in the halls, among both courtiers and palace servants: Who *will* rule?

The Royal Magician shrugged, not even raising his head. "We shall see," he said absently and added, "You have our thanks, Aunadar Bleth. You may go."

The young noble stiffened, fresh color washing across his features. "A royal dismissal? Who crowned *you* king?" he asked angrily. "My oath is to the crown! By what right do *you* dismiss or summon or order about any highborn man or maid of Cormyr?"

"I have the legal right, if you want to look up the dusty rulings of Rhigaerd and see for yourself Azoun's signature upon them, giving me the authority to act in defense of the realm should he ever be unfit or unable to rule," Vangerdahast replied softly, blinking at the young noble in mild surprise.

Bleth's features twisted in a sneer. "That was a power given to the adult tutor of Azoun as a young boy, not to an old dotard once the boy has become a man and been crowned king and has a queen and daughters of his own."

Vangerdahast shrugged. "None of this truly matters now, does it, young Bleth? You waste my time while the realm crumbles. If you seek to test my authority, go out that door and bring a guard back. Order him to do one thing, and I shall countermand the order. See which of us he obeys, and you have your answer."

"Pah—a guard! They know where their next coin comes from! What if I—or any noble—refuse to obey?"

"Ah, well," Vangerdahast said mildly, "a stellar career as a toadstool always awaits."

At that moment, the doors of the Redpetal Room swung wide, and as they all looked up in surprise, a white-faced, wild-haired woman rushed in, flanked by men-at-arms. Gwennath of Tymora looked as if she'd foregone a much-needed sleep to bring important news, as indeed she had.

"Noble lords, the sage Dimswart has discerned—I know not how—that the beast's breath carried a venom," she gasped without salutation, her eyes meeting those of the court wizard. "The venom spreads a blood disease resistant to conventional magic. That is why my spell had no effect on the late duke. This magic-resistant blood disease in the venom eats at internal organs and destroys the body from within! And once the body is slain, the resistant nature of the disease prevents any restoration of the victim!"

She swayed as if about to faint, and Vangerdahast absently caught her shoulders to keep her upright. "Death will come to them both, then, and none can stop it," he murmured, letting Alaphondar take charge of the exhausted priestess.

He straightened, stepped forward briskly, and said, "Come, Aunadar Bleth! 'Tis time you learned some of the secrets of the realm, to give you something to be loyal to. Besides, even arrogant young nobles should be able to learn a thing or two."

As the Royal Magician moved toward the door, the Bishop of the Black Blades shook herself free of the sage's grasp and said fiercely, "I will accompany you!"

Vangerdahast gave her a surprised look, but nodded and waved a welcoming hand. "Come, then."

The court sage asked quietly, "Where go you, lord wizard? Should you not return—or should there be a change with the stricken royals—I must know."

Vangerdahast did not pause on his way to the door. "Use your stone to summon me. We're bound for the depths, to see that there are still spells in the world that can create new kings from bits of the old." He nodded farewell to the sage, the war wizard, and the guards and set off at a quick pace down a narrow servants' passage. Bleth and the lady bishop followed.

He led them through a ready room and on along another passage, stopping suddenly partway along it. They almost bumped into him as he did something to a section of wall that looked no different than any other. It swung inward to reveal darkness, the smell of damp stone, and cobwebs. One of the glowstones at the court wizard's belt roused into life, its green radiance stabbing out in a beam that illuminated a narrow passage running down into darkness.

"Where are we going?" Gwennath asked, wide-eyed with wonder.

"To where secrets sleep," the Royal Magician said shortly.

"Prisoners hanging in chains?" Aunadar asked, lifting a sardonic eyebrow.

"To where things of magic are kept safely away from prying eyes and adventurous hands," Vangerdahast replied sourly, not looking at Bleth. "*Noble* hands, for instance."

The passage took them down a steep, almost breakneck flight of steps to a cross passage. The Royal Magician turned left, took two long strides, and then turned to the right-hand wall and did something swift and deft again. The wall swung open to reveal more darkness—and a curious, high-pitched singing sound. Vangerdahast held up one sleeve of his robes, and something winked there.

The singing died away, and the mage stepped forward. The young noble gestured with acidic courtesy for the priestess to precede him, then followed her through the opening. "Keep your sword in its sheath," the wizard said softly to Bleth without looking back, "or the guardians ahead will surely separate your head from its accustomed place on your shoulders."

Aunadar made no reply, even when niches began to occur on either side of the narrow passage, each one filled by a dark, silent armored figure. Something scraped ahead, and Vangerdahast muttered something low-voiced but hasty.

There was a soundless flash, and then a spreading purple radiance as an oval opening occurred in a hitherto-invisible barrier. It fell away before them, followed by a white radiance flickering with green around the edges, to reveal a closed stone door whose smooth surface was broken only by a pull ring and a keyhole.

"Was that a teleport ward?" Bleth asked curiously.

"Partly," the wizard replied calmly. He drew something—a tiny pierced, hollow metal sphere—from his belt. Holding it out at arm's length, he muttered something else they could not quite hear, and it twisted and grew, to become . . . a key.

Holding it, Vangerdahast turned to them. "Only the king, the queen, and the princesses have one of these—besides myself, of course."

"Of course," Bleth responded sarcastically. The court wizard eyed him expressionlessly for a moment, then slide the key into the lock. The door grated inward.

The room within held several ornate, ancient-looking suits of bejeweled armor, three massive chests, and a great deal of dust. Along one wall hung a number of dragon skulls, each set with small purplish gems along the brow. A preserved minotaur, tattered and leaking stuffing at the seams, reared over a line of crowns. The crowns ranged from a simple circlet topped with a ruby held in a golden dragon's maw to a heavy ornate helm crested with another dragon and encrusted with gems and filigree over its entire surface. Blades and other weapons hung along the opposite wall, including, in a small glass case, the head of an ancient sledgehammer, scorched by heat.

Against the far wall stood an armoire of tarnished electrum, surrounded by the pulsing blue glow of strong magic. Its double doors had no latch or lock but were sealed with a medallion of wax, as large as a man's head, bearing the impression of the royal arms of Cormyr.

"Before you break that seal, mage," Aunadar Bleth said softly, his blade suddenly in his hand, "suppose you tell me what's in there. I have no wish to be trapped into fighting some sort of family guardian beast."

Vangerdahast made a gesture and muttered a word, and the noble shrieked. The sword in his hand was suddenly a tangle of spitting lightning, steel shards, and acrid smoke. Bleth dropped the blade and wrung his hand, hissing curses of pain, as the priestess of Tymora backed away to where she could see both men, her hand moving to the slender mace sheathed on one thigh.

The court wizard lifted a reassuring hand. "If young Bleth is quite finished demonstrating his bravery," he said, "know you both that in this cupboard are kept samples of flesh, preserved by special magic, from all members of the royal family. From these samples, I may, through my arts, recreate one who is otherwise lost. Brave Duke Bhereu, and if need be his brother and the king as well, can be reconstituted through these bits of flesh and the proper spell. At most, they will lose the memory of the last few months of their lives. We'll have to stop them from going hunting for a while, I suppose."

His hand came down, and in front of his fingers, the wax parted, drawing back as if seared, breaking the seal with a flash of discharged magic. Then he glanced back at Bleth, to make sure of his location and activities, ignored the noble's glare of hatred, and gently swung the doors wide.

The interior of the armoire was empty of all but ashes—ashes that were slowly growing mold. Fire had melted a row of glass vials into now-hardened puddles and ravaged their contents, leaving no mark on the shelf or walls. A very precise, magical fire, cast some time ago.

The second chances of all the Obarskyrs had been wiped out. Bhereu was forever dead . . . and should Thomdor and Azoun succumb as well, they would follow him into eternal oblivion.

6

Settlers
Year of the Firestars
(6 DR)

ndeth Obarskyr was being watched, of that he had no doubt. Throughout the morning, he had felt someone's eyes following his every move— an ever-present gaze that came not from the stockade or the houses, but from the forest itself.

It made him slightly anxious—an unseen watcher could mean no good—but there was nothing to be done about it, so Ondeth continued his tasks. For this day, that meant splitting the last large trees.

When they'd first arrived in this glen, it had been strewn with piles of uprooted trees and overgrown brush. Some of this tangle had rotted where it lay, and the Obarskyrs mixed it with the rich, crumbling earth to feed their crops. The larger chunks of hardwood that withstood the weather were used for building or burning, depending on their size and condition. The evening hearth and the firepit, it seemed, would have ample fuel for as many as four years.

Ondeth had already used the most suitable wood to erect the small stockade and the low houses within it— mean, small huts, unlike those his wife Suzara was used to back east. She bore up to the harsh conditions as best she could, but their evenings together often held hushed, whispered arguments in which Suzara spoke most, and about the same things: the dangers here, and how things would be so much safer on the eastern side of the sea, back in Impiltur.

Ondeth chose his next victim from the woodpile, a good-sized piece that young Rhiiman and Faerlthann had sawn into a thick, drum-shaped slice. The original tree had been scorched and apparently felled by lightning, and as such would be unsuitable for building. Everyone knew that using a lightning-struck tree in your home merely attracted more bolts from the blue. Ondeth grunted and hefted the thick chunk onto the chopping block, a stump of iron oak not worth the work needed to uproot it or carve it apart.

Whoever was spying on him, thought Ondeth, could at least be civil and introduce himself. Ondeth could definitely use some help.

The boys were out tending their snares. Ondeth's younger brother Villiam was hurrying to finish his own house. Two days from now, the younger Obarskyr would begin the slow hike eastward to the rough-hewn, swampy port of Marsember, where the rest of his family would arrive. Perhaps Suzara would be happier with a few more women about.

Suzara wasn't the mysterious watcher, of that he was certain. She had enough to do at the moment. Their last argument, hissed in urgent whispers in the depths of the night before, had been the worst so far.

"At least we could go back to Marsember!" she'd implored him, her head resting on his massive, hairy chest. She wouldn't argue in front of the boys, so Ondeth lost sleep as they fought in whispers so as not to wake the others.

"When you first saw Marsember, you called it a poisoned swamp town," he'd replied wearily.

"It *is*," she said harshly, "but at least there are *people* there! Real people—not ghosts and goblins waiting beyond the trees."

"There are no ghosts here," said Ondeth, recognizing where this argument was going. Their disputes had begun to travel well-worn paths. "We are the first men and women here. It's a chance for a new beginning."

"I *know* there are ghosts. They're watching from the woods." Fear pervaded her tone, as it always did when she spoke of eyes in the trees.

"There's no one out there," Ondeth reassured her. "Well, perhaps some elves out hunting, but nothing else. Give it a full year, then we'll decide."

"I *have* already decided," said Suzara. "I'm only waiting for you to agree."

"We are staying," said Ondeth firmly, in the iron tone of voice that signaled an end to the conversation. He had used that tone overmuch in recent days.

"So *you* say," his wife hissed coldly, and he felt her jaw clench against his chest.

He curled one arm up to touch her shoulder and stroke the curving flesh there. She grasped his wrist tenderly, but held to it firmly. She'd not let him work his charms on her this evening, to cozen and calm her and convince her to stay. She would not let him reassure her that there were no strangers lurking in the forest waiting to slay them, that the crops they'd planted would bear rich yields, and that the vast stretches of land were better than the cramped city warrens they'd come from.

And when her ragged, angry breathing had at last grown long and measured, Ondeth Obarskyr looked into the darkness and wondered if he had been right in dragging Suzara and the boys all this way, to a small hold hedged by dark woods in the wild heart of the Realms.

He needed the boys to help him build, and he couldn't leave Suzara behind alone, as Villiam had done with his Karsha. Yet she might wither and die here. Marsember was no more than a muddy straggle of ramshackle houses clustered around a few piers, but at least there were people for her to talk to there. They might have stayed there—or go back there now. Or perhaps further east, to Sembia. Southerners from Chondath held those towns, but it was said there were some eastern folk as well.

Or north. He'd heard the men up there had made their peace with the elves and agreed to settle the empty lands. A realm full of folk—even a rough, young place with little to buy or share, and no fine clothes or wine or idle company to enjoy—might well soothe Suzara's concerns. Perhaps they had come too far, outstripping the support of town and farm and fellow human beings.

Perhaps when Karsha and Villiam's eldest daughter Medaly arrived, things would be better. Perhaps in the morning, he told the darkness silently, things would be better.

But morning came, and Suzara remained distant and nervous, not sparing any of them more than a dozen words.

And now, as the last of the morning fog pulled away from the trees in tatters, Ondeth as well had gained the feeling of being watched. He thought with bitter mirth about how well wives could convince their mates of all manner of things. Perhaps it was a sort of magic women shared. . . .

He examined the block of wood, turning it with his hardened hands. It was solid, free of fungus and rot, and its slow drying had opened a series of cracks radiating from the center. He chose the longest of them and set one of the thin iron wedges along the break.

The iron tools—wedge, hammer, and axe—were the most important things Ondeth had carried with him from Impiltur. He had his skinning knife, of course, and had bought the boys short, heavy-bladed swords of Chondathan design, but if they were going to survive here, he'd have to do more than just hunt. He'd thought of getting a steel blade for the plow, but until the first crop came in, there was nothing to sell, and therefore nothing to buy with.

He tapped a second wedge along the crack, wielding the sledge in one hand. Then he stepped back a few paces, shaking his shoulders to loosen them.

Ed Greenwood and Jeff Grubb

Wheeling the heavy-headed hammer in a great arc over his shoulders, Ondeth brought it down squarely on the wedge. Half its length disappeared into the wood, which jumped and quivered, and there was a satisfying crack.

Ondeth dealt another mighty blow to the first, inner wedge, and a third swing to the outer wedge again, forcing it deep into the wood. One more ought to do it. . . .

He swung one last hammerblow, and the great chunk of hardwood split with a sound like sharp thunder. Two roughly even pieces rocked on the block; the last splinters fell away as he pulled them apart. Each could be comfortably carried. The exposed inner wood was solid, unaffected by decay. It would burn well.

The stranger was there when Ondeth looked up again. Ondeth would have started, but he wasn't the sort of man to start.

"Morning," he said instead, as if they both stood on a boggy street in Marsember.

"Good day," the other man replied. He was certainly a beanpole of a fellow, slender to the point of emaciation. Yet this was no starveling; he was well groomed and wore a jacket and leggings of green linen. Elven make.

Ondeth looked into his eyes, and then back to his work. Framed by a well-clipped red beard, the stranger's mouth was a thin line, for all the syrupy, mannered nature of his voice.

"Help you?" asked Ondeth in level tones, hauling the larger of the two halves onto the stump.

"Perhaps," replied the stranger. "Can I ask why you're here?"

"Have to split the logs," said Ondeth. "They won't do it by themselves."

The stranger gave the burly Obarskyr farmer a brief, amused smile and said, "I mean, it looks like you're settling here in the wolf woods."

"Aye," said Ondeth. "Is there a problem with that?"

"The elves claim this land for their hunting."

"I've heard that. And I intend to leave them to it. I'm a

94

horrible shot with a bow. I lost an older brother to a boar hunt back in Impiltur. Let the elves have their hunting; I'm a farmer."

"So they've noticed. Other men have come into these lands, and when they chased off the deer, the elves had to act. You haven't taken any of their prey, but you are on their land."

Ondeth's brow rose. "You are not an elf," he said flatly.

The lean man shrugged and held out a hand. "I am Baerauble Etharr, a friend to the elves."

Ondeth returned his own name and shook Baerauble's hand. The man's grip was limp and unpracticed, as if it had been some time since he'd last used it. A small silence fell between the two men.

"May I ask why you settled here?" asked the thin man, his voice still pleasant. "I mean, both in the wolf woods and in this particular place?"

Ondeth shrugged. "Some bad times have come down on the land we came from. Plagues. Tyrants. Bad kings. The usual. When it becomes easier for a man to face goblin attacks than pay his taxes, then it's time to take his chances with the goblins."

"There are few goblins, and they keep well to the north of here," said Baerauble.

"I take it your elves keep them at bay," said Ondeth.

"We guard this land," said Baerauble simply. "That is one reason I'm here."

Ondeth thought of his wife's talk of ghosts and watchers. How long had this rail-thin stranger been watching them?

"As for settling in this particular place," said Ondeth, "we struck west from Marsember, following the hunting and game trails along the coast, looking for enough open space to farm. We found this spot, open to the sky, with some ancient trees already felled. It's easier than cutting timber on our own."

He swung one muscular arm south. "The shoreline is close . . . nothing but sharp-toothed rocks, but we can build a small dock if need be . . . eventually. The soil's rich here, and it should bring in a good crop. Have you claimed this land already?"

The farmer hefted his hammer, as if to indicate he would contest any such claim.

The newcomer surprised Ondeth. He gave a thin, worried smile. "No, I was a . . . guest of the original inhabitants."

"Your elves killed those original inhabitants." It was a statement, not a question.

The lean man started. "You know?"

"I've found bits of bone and broken swords when I was plowing. You don't have to be Sage Alaundo to figure out there were other inhabitants here earlier. Haven't told Suzara; she'd just worry."

Another pause between the two. Ondeth broke it finally with a direct look up from his hammer and the gruff question, "So—are you here to kill us as well?"

Baerauble started again. Ondeth wondered if he was being too hard-tongued with the stranger, but this one had called himself a friend of the elves and had probably not been near humans for a decade.

Baerauble blinked and then said slowly, "Perhaps. They sent me to determine your intentions."

Ondeth nodded. "I intend to farm. My sons do a little snaring. Brother's going down to Marsember tomorrow to fetch his wife and family. If you want to kill us, I'd appreciate your doing it before the younger folk arrive."

The stranger did not—quite—smile. "How many folk do you intend to have here in this settlement?"

Ondeth shrugged. "I know of a dozen, maybe two dozen folk who'd trade Marsember for some dry land." After a moment, he asked, "Your elves aren't going to destroy Marsember as well?"

The lean man shook his head. "The elves claim the wild forest, this part of the great forest known as Cormanthir—what you call the wolf woods, or Cormyr. Marsember is, as you may have noticed, a swamp. Two dozen, eh? Farmers like yourself?"

"Some are. Some will hunt, likely. There may be more.

I can't very well speak for every human along the western shores."

"Leave the rothé—the forest buffalo. You can take enough deer for your settlement, but if you drive out the native herds, the elves will take their own measures. Take deadfall branches, not live wood for your fires and buildings . . . and I think they will let you stay."

"Extremely generous of them," said Ondeth sharply. "And where *are* these elven masters who we're being so gracious to?"

Baerauble looked at the large man, brows drawing down, as Ondeth continued. "I've been here with my family for four months now, and you're the first thinking creature we've seen since we left Marsember. Now you tell me this is elven land, and if I want to remain I have to tailor my life and that of my family to the dictates of these elves. I'll need a good reason to do that . . . a very good reason. So my question is—where are these elves?"

The thin man was still for a moment. Looking at him, Ondeth thought a stiff wind would uproot him. Then he said, "I will take you to them."

With both hands, the lean newcomer traced out a large circle in the air, indicating an area of the trodden ground around them as if he were one of the women back home telling Suzara how big her next gown was going to be. As he did so, he spat out a cascade of harsh words. Neither elvish nor the trade tongue, the words rolled out, rich and sinuous with power, and Ondeth almost shivered. These words were deep; they'd been old when the legendary dragons were young. As the bearded man moved his hands, they trailed scars of light in the air, lines of radiance that continued to glow and spread outward.

Ondeth took a step back and brought up his hammer, more to ward off the magic than attack the newcomer. The glow rose all around him; it was blinding for a moment.

And when it subsided, they were somewhere else.

"You're a wizard!" exclaimed Ondeth, realizing how

stupid that sounded even as he said it. "You could have warned me," he added, and after another pause, "Suzara is going to be peeved if she finds me gone."

The mage stood stock-still. "You wanted to see the elves of Cormanthir. Watch."

They were standing somewhere deep in the forest, in cool, green shade. The woods were relatively free of ground cover. It felt to Ondeth as if he were in a green hall, the huge, moss-girt trees its pillars and the leaves above a roof of jade-colored glass. There was a sharpness to everything around him, as if the rest of the world had been wrapped in fog.

They were scattered around the two men in a rough line that curved like welcoming arms—or waiting claws. At first the elves were indistinguishable from the forest itself. Then Ondeth realized that they were dressed in tunics made of solid shades of green and yellow, and their trappings and accoutrements were gold.

The nearest elf was a female, her features clear and sharp enough to etch glass. She was dressed like the others. Ondeth saw that her tunic was really a chain mail shirt, its links so small that they appeared as no more than loops of fabric. She held a thin ivory spear, its barbed tip of beaten gold.

She shifted her head to regard the two humans. Ondeth suddenly felt as rough and uncouth as a dung-smeared hobgoblin in his worn linen jacket and heavy pants.

Then she smiled, a thin flash of pure white between her lips, and it was as if daylight had broken through the forest canopy. A small smile, but enough to lift Ondeth's heart above the trees.

The smile was not for him. Baerauble the wizard bowed with stiff formality back at the elf, but his face was wide with a grin. Ondeth felt a flash of jealousy.

"What . . ." he began, but the mage raised a hand, stilling his question before it could be asked.

"It's beginning," Baerauble said. "The Hunt."

The elves were all facing the same way, and from that

direction came the blast of a great horn. A second horn call joined it, and then another, each in perfect thirds to form a single swelling, melodious chord. The elves along the line shifted positions and readied their spears.

Then lights shone out beneath the forest canopy. Soft blue and green glows, like the radiant fungus found on rotting wood. Yellow and orange balls of lightning sang in and out of the trees, joined now by red spheres as bright as an angry dragon's eye.

To Ondeth, they looked like lanterns held aloft in a procession. But as they bobbed and weaved through the trees, the farmer knew they were magical, controlled by approaching elves, no doubt.

Beaters. These lights and horns were intended to drive prey forward, toward the line of waiting elves. But what beast was so powerful it needed such effort?

The answer was quick in coming. Ondeth heard a crashing in the forest depths, a crunching of brambles and trees in several places, that soon grew so loud and frantic that it overwhelmed the cacophony of blasting horns.

Trees swayed and shed their leaves in clouds as great, shaggy beasts burst past them, bounding through the forest, wild-eyed and snorting. Their hooves shook the earth and made a sound like thunder as they rushed toward the elves. These were the small buffalo of the forest, surging in a flight as wild and fleet as a herd of deer. Ondeth saw red-rimmed eyes shining with fear, and he swallowed in spite of himself as the huge beasts rushed down upon the line of elves, who stood calmly waiting, spears ready . . .

. . . and passed through unimpeded. A few elves stepped deftly aside to let a snorting buffalo pass. Ondeth watched the monstrous creatures race past, as tall as the huts he'd been building. The ground shook under their charge, and the farmer hefted his sledge, his breath quickening, but then the beasts were gone in a cloud of drifting dust and fading thunder, running hard into the distance.

The elves had let them go. The forest buffalo were not the prey they were hunting.

Ondeth started to form a question over the tumult, but he got no further than opening his mouth before there was a greater crashing from the forest. In the dim distance, as the earth beneath his boots trembled, an old, massive shadowtop tree toppled slowly over. Then the cause of its fall burst into view, and Ondeth's words died in his throat.

It was an owlbear, that dangerous predator of the woods all over Faerûn, but this one was larger than any owlbear he'd ever seen, looming as tall as two men or more as it lumbered along. Its fur was scorched in places, and it snapped its birdlike beak as it came nearer, slashing and raking the trees as it passed. Its claws were like rows of daggers, each as long as Ondeth's forearm, and it shredded the leaves around it in sheer rage as it advanced.

The farmer watched it, fascinated. The creature's fur became longer and finer toward its head, resembling brown feathers, which framed wide, watery eyes, golden orbs filled with a deep and mighty fury.

The great owlbear checked its rush only for a moment when it saw the line of hunters ahead. It reared fully erect, its triangular head grazing the spreading branches of the largest trees, and wheeled around to glare at the lights bobbing behind it.

Then it snarled, made its decision—and charged.

There was a slight gap in the elven line, between the human farmer and the elven maiden who had smiled at Baerauble. The owlbear went for it as fast as it could move.

The wizard took a step nearer Ondeth, raised his hands, and barked a string of twisted, clacking syllables that should not have been possible for a human mouth to form. Radiances burst into being around his hands, flared to a blinding brightness, and left his fingers as a crackling, crawling arc of lightning.

The wizard's bolt seared its way along the great owlbear's flank, then died away. Smoke curled up, and the air suddenly smelled of summer storms and burning fur. The owlbear did not slow down.

The elves were running from both ends of the line now, but they'd spaced themselves out too far. The owlbear would be on top of the two men before the hunters could bar its path. Ondeth swallowed.

This forest monster would likely kill them unless the mage had another lightning bolt up his sleeve. Kill them—or slay the elf maiden with the radiant smile.

Ondeth's imagination offered him a brief, vivid scene of her being torn apart by those great claws, blood spraying in all directions, and he roared out a denial, hefted his sledge, and stepped in front of the elf maiden. The owlbear swerved, not to pass through the gap he'd opened up but to attack, claws glittering, and Ondeth Obarskyr brought the heavy hammer around in a single, solid blow, smashing into the beast just below its shoulder.

The owlbear howled, a keening wail that drowned out the blaring horns, then lowered its head in pain—and slammed into Ondeth, butting him with its fur-covered head. It felt like a pillow wrapped around a building stone.

Ondeth was aware he was flying through the air, flung backward to land hard, dropping his sledge as he bounced bruisingly and fought to find air. Tears of pain stung his eyes, but through their blur, he saw the owlbear break through the elven line.

The elf maiden was there. She'd driven her spear into the monster's other shoulder and used it to pull herself onto the beast's back. She shouted something in the elvish tongue and brandished a long bone-colored knife. The owlbear roared as she drove the blade into the back of its neck, but still the creature did not slow down. Coming to his knees, Ondeth saw it charge on into the forest beyond, the elf maiden whooping and shouting as she clung to her spear, riding the owlbear as it disappeared.

Baerauble reached down a hand, helped the farmer to his feet, and handed him his hammer. Ondeth started to say something, but the wizard shushed him with the words, "One more thing to be seen first," and turned back to face the trees whence the owlbear had come. Ondeth looked in that direction, too.

The beaters were appearing through the trees. Without question, they were the most radiant beings of beauty Ondeth had ever seen. Without saddle or bridle, they rode the sleek backs of deer, graceful beasts that sprang along lightly and effortlessly. Most of their riders wore the same fine chain as the hunters, but some were clad only in diaphanous robes that trailed behind them like smoke. Their battle horns curled about in large, sweeping circles, and were tipped with huge-mouthed bronze bells.

The riders were surrounded by the flying lights, spheres that bobbed and darted playfully around them, casting half a hundred shadows. Ondeth could see these strange, beautiful radiances rippling with energy across their otherwise featureless surfaces.

Then came the elf nobles; Ondeth knew their exalted rank at a glance. Their mounts were huge stags whose gilded antlers were laced with silver filigree and flew more than bounded. Proud riders bestrode them, lords and ladies of the forests in fine, flowing outfits of silklike finery, their silver and corn-colored hair streaming behind them in long braids.

The most ornately robed figure, obviously the leader of the elves, passed close by the two humans. Baerauble bowed low and tapped Ondeth's shoulder, indicating he should do the same.

Ondeth stayed on his feet, hammer in hand, and regarded the lordly elf with calm admiration.

Elf and man locked eyes for a moment. The elf lord had a long, ragged scar down one cheek and carried an ornate golden scepter topped with a glossy-polished amethyst. He wore a simple crown of some silvery metal. It consisted of a circlet with three spikes along the brow, each spike topped with another purple gem.

The elf lord held the man's eyes for a measured

moment, then smiled, a great, toothy smile that dimmed even that of the elf maiden.

And then he was gone, his stag bounding away through the underbrush, and the elven hunters on foot were sprinting away after the nobles, spears held high, racing off into the forest after the echoing, fading wail of the gigantic owlbear.

Ondeth watched them pass out of sight, staring after them in wonder. He started when the mage touched his shoulder.

"I think Lord Iliphar approves," Baerauble said gently.

"Approves?" asked Ondeth, not understanding. Then he turned to face the wizard and said slowly, "You brought me here not to show your elves to me . . . but to show me to your elves."

A half-smile touched the wizard's lips. "First meetings are important. If Iliphar's Hunting Court first saw you as a human intruder disputing some forest kill with an elven hunter, your dealings with elves would probably follow the trail of most humans—a long, descending spiral of testings that would end in the destruction of your homestead. This time, they'll remember a brave human who helped in the taking down of one of the last giant owlbears in the eastern reaches."

"That woman . . ." Ondeth said slowly. "She didn't need my help, did she?"

"My lady Dahast is a show-off," said Baerauble with a smile, stressing the word 'my' ever so slightly but clearly. "No, she did not. I can tell you she appreciated it, however."

Ondeth nodded. "It was so—" he searched for the right word—"beautiful."

The mage arched his eyebrows in surprise.

"Beautiful," repeated the farmer. "The lights in the trees, the horns, the elves themselves." He spread his hands out in the direction the elves had gone. "Beautiful."

Ondeth turned to Baerauble. "This is a wondrous land . . . a land of startling beauty. It is better even than

Ed Greenwood and Jeff Grubb

Impiltur, and a palace compared to swampy Marsember or the other rough holds of men on these shores. If the elves seek to keep this as their hunting place, I will respect that and see to it that any who settle with me respect it as well . . . if they'll allow us to remain."

The wizard replied, "I think they will after your actions today. But you surprise me, Ondeth Obarskyr. I did not think you had such resolution and poetry in your heart."

Ondeth smiled. "I've many surprises yet. I come from a family of many poets, heroes . . . and scoundrels as well. Come, we've been gone too long, and Suzara will be worried about me. You must come for dinner."

The mage nodded and then paused. "I really should return you, then return to the Hunt."

"Dinner!" said Ondeth, placing a hand on the mage's shoulder. The wizard jumped slightly at the touch, but only slightly. "You've shown your hospitality, and I must show mine. Besides, you have a great task ahead of you this evening."

Baerauble blinked. "Oh?"

"You have convinced me to live with your elves," said Ondeth. "Now you must convince my dear Suzara to stay here with me. This shall be our home—forevermore."

104

7

Alusair
Year of the Gauntlet
(1369 DR)

sh-blonde hair swirled as its dark-eyed owner looked up sharply. "Something's wrong," she murmured. "Take over, Beldred."

The bearded nobleman in plate armor turned his head. "Of course, Lady Highness . . . are you unwell?"

His commander shook her head without replying and spurred her mount away to the left, across rising ground. Beldred watched her go with worried eyes, then said, "Brace . . . Threldryn? Follow her and see that she comes to no harm."

"Aye," they replied in unison, drawing blades and turning their mounts. Just before they sprang away in pursuit, Brace murmured, "But will you see that we come to no harm from *her?*"

"Aye," Threldryn said, grasping for words. "What if she just wants to, uh, perform some, ah, private business?"

Beldred gave them both a tight, wordless smile in return and urged his mount onward.

They were deep in the Stonelands, on one of the high meadows north of Startop Crag, a score and four knights under the command of a lady. No common Purple Dragon knights were these, but the youngest sons of the proudest noble houses in the land, all with titles and wealth of their own. And they rode under no common commander, for the lady riding hard to the west under the watch of Brace Skatterhawk and Threldryn Imbranneth was Alusair Nacacia Obarskyr, Mithril Princess of Cormyr.

Beldred Truesilver could spare no more thought for her right now, however. Alusair's knights were hot on the proverbial heels of an orc band. The twisted humanoids had been so bold as to raid a caravan on the road east of Eveningstar six days back, and they had almost caught the sweating, snorting beasts twice. Each time a handy ravine had allowed the swine-snouts to scramble free of fair battle and climb higher into the Stonelands hills. And so they chased the goblinoids deeper into this perilous region that Cormyr claimed but could not rule except by sword point.

Over dying fires of night, the folk of northern Cormyr traded fearsome tales of flying fanged things, wolves, trolls, and orcs, and even dragons and evil wizards slithering down out of the Stonelands to strike at honest folk. Beldred could well believe such tales now. He'd never seen a hydra before this venture, nor a fire lizard, but in the last few days he'd had a hand in slaying both, plus a trio of chimeras as well. He knew now why retired Purple Dragons stood proud when royals rode past, but wanted no part of present glory. Even slight wounds hurt too much for anyone to feel valorous.

Now the orcs were running for broken ground again, and Beldred Truesilver—like most of his fellows, he had no doubt—would be damned and blasted by all the battle gods before he'd let these bestial humanoids slip away again. Well ahead in the distance, over trampled grass, he saw a flash of armor as someone—Dagh Illance, probably, as hot and eager for blood as ever—threw a spear.

An inhuman wail arose, and Beldred smiled. They had found the orcs. This time they had them! The knights were going to be able to block the orcs from scurrying flight, forcing them against where the rocks rose ahead.

There was a bowl-shaped valley ahead, if Alusair's description of the region was right. Then there would be no more riding. The orcs could climb out of the valley, but at least they'd also have to fight at last. Beldred thought of calling to the princess and the two men he left behind for her. Then he swallowed and frowned. They could watch out for themselves, and the rest of the company would not want to wait for the attack, princess or not. He touched the reassuringly hard, smooth pommel of his sword and spurred his mount on, shouting for the other horsemen to follow.

* * * * *

The vision—and Vangerdahast's mind-touch—had been faint but unmistakable. Get to a place of privacy and wait for a falcon that looked—thus.

Alusair's mouth tightened. Blasted matters of state again, no doubt. She rode around to the other side of a rise of rocks, watching warily for orcs. It must be something the Royal Magician needed kept secret, or he'd simply have farspoken to her. What would it be *this* time?

At least she'd not be kept waiting long, to be inwardly branded a shirking coward by the young brightblades riding with her for the first time. Already she could see a dot high in the blue skies, a darkness that fell like a bolt toward her. To spare the horse a fright, she dismounted, walked a little way across a dell, and stood waiting, the dagger from her left boot in one hand and her sword bare in the other—just in case. In the Stonelands, one could never be too careful.

The falcon was in her vision, and in its claws was a flat, circular silver plate, its heart a mirror, its edges crawling with running runes. A message plate.

Half the height of a man from the ground, the falcon pulled up, wings braking deftly, and began to swell. Feathers melted into rippling, expanding flesh that flowed and bulged in a sickening manner. This was the flowshift, which meant the being would take its own form only temporarily and had no desire to break the spell that made it a falcon. The transformation spun with blurring speed now, then coalesced suddenly into the robed, barefoot form of a sharp-nosed woman in a plain maroon robe, with fresh lines of care on her face. She was older now, Alusair noted, but was still as beautiful and as graceful as ever. The wizardess knelt, holding out the plate.

"Laspeera!" Alusair exclaimed in recognition, letting her weapons fall, shaking off her gauntlets, and striding forward with arms outstretched for an embrace.

The warden of the war wizards gave her a wan smile but said formally, "Well met, Lady Highness. I bring this in urgent haste."

Alusair frowned. Laspeera's formality could only mean bad news. She took the plate, set it carefully on the turf, swept the sorceress into her arms, and kissed her cheek. "I'm pleased to see you anyway, 'Speera. What news of father?"

The mage returned her kiss but said nothing, nodding sadly at the plate.

Oh. Oh, damn, thought the warrior-princess. Blast and damn.

Alusair took up the plate and touched the runes meant for her with her bare fingertips. The runes shimmered, then faded away. It was a once-only message; grave news indeed, then.

A moment later, the familiar voice of her father came to her from the disk, quiet but unmistakable.

"Alusair, the realm is in dire peril. Bhereu is dead, and Thomdor and I may have joined him by the time you receive this. We do not know who is responsible. Stay in the Stonelands. Keep out of sight of those who may come to search for you. If you hear word of my death, trust it not unless it comes to you from those few we both trust. Take the crown if you feel it best, but follow your own heart—don't rule just because you believe I wanted it so. Know, little one, that I love you. I have always loved you, and if the gods will, I shall always love you, watching over you and the realm even if you see and hear me no more. Gods keep you, Alusair."

Alusair swallowed; forgotten, the plate almost fell from her hands. Laspeera took it and murmured, "The luck of all the gods be upon you, Lady Highness. I fear I have other matters to attend to now."

The war wizard kissed the princess's forehead, became a falcon again, and soared aloft, climbing hard into the sun.

Numbly the princess watched her go. Then she drew in a deep, trembling breath and shook her head, fighting back sudden tears.

Biting her lip, she stared out over the harsh grandeur of the Stonelands. She no more wanted to be queen than shy Tanalasta. And as long as Tanalasta lived, she would be spared that responsibility. Poor Tana!

Poor Father. Gods! She'd always know this day might come, but . . .

The gods. Yes, it was time—past time. There would be time for grieving later, but first, driven by duty, as always . . .

She went to her knees on the hard rocks in prayer, pouring out a silent supplication. When she was done, she did not open her eyes but concentrated instead on calling to mind the Royal Magician of the realm. She attempted to initiate the farspeaking that allowed the wizard to converse at great distances with the Obarskyr battle maiden.

She thought of Vangerdahast. Those dark brown eyes—red when he grew testy, which was often—around jowls and a close-trimmed beard . . . white, and his hair, too, though both still had a few reddish-brown hairs. Kindly, stern, a paunch beginning to show through those plain robes. . . .

Her mental picture seemed to move for a moment and acquired flickering candelabra and an impression of hurried movement along a hall. A hall in the palace? Or . . .

"Lady Highness?" Brace's voice was anxious. Alusair shook her head in exasperation as she knelt amid the stones, eyes closed. The contact, brief and hurried, was broken, the vision was slipping away. . . .

"Lady Alusair?"

It was gone. She sighed and fought down a surge of grief-driven rage. Couldn't these men see needed to be alone? No, they couldn't. They did not know of her father, and Bhereu—poor Uncle Bhereu! Instead, she slowly rose, tossing her hair back over her shoulder again. She replied levelly to the interruption. "Yes, gentle sirs? Or should I say 'trail hounds'?"

"Beldred sent us," a deeper voice said sourly. "I thought you'd not want us. . . ." He trailed off. Alusair was fairly certain the guards had not seen Laspeera, or her using the message plate.

"Beldred Truesilver's orders are wise, Threldryn," the princess replied, giving them both of them a quick smile as she vaulted a rock and plucked her reins from around the dead sapling where she'd wound them.

When she looked up, two sets of concerned eyes were looking a silent question at her. Neither man was going to ask a princess of the realm if a need of nature was all that had brought her here, but they had already sensed it was something more.

Alusair sighed. They were riding into battle; this was something her men needed to know. "I had something of a . . . vision," she said carefully, "from the Royal Magician. You know he laid tracing spells on both my sister and me when we were babes."

"To prevent kidnappings," Brace said, nodding.

"To let my mother find us when we wandered off," she offered, quoting the official reason with derisive amusement clear in her tone.

"Aye. So we've heard," Threldryn prompted.

She gave him a brief glare and continued. "Something of a link remains . . . unreliable, and weak, but . . . something. Through it, he contacted me—unintentionally, I believe."

"And in this vision, you saw . . . ?" Brace asked hesitantly.

"Something that might be a secret of the realm or might not. I'd know which right now if two overinquisitive noblemen hadn't interrupted me at precisely the wrong moment!" she snapped.

"My apologies, Lady Highness," the two men mumbled in unison, holding out her gauntlets and blades.

Their commander took them and waved a dismissive hand as she swung into her saddle. "I shan't slap your wrists for doing your duty. You had your orders, and the one who gave them was thinking of the safety of Cormyr, no doubt. The fault's not w—"

As she spoke they rounded the rocks, and the noise of the war cries reached them. She broke off speaking to stare, at first puzzled, then angry. Below the three riders, a small band of orcs was fleeing into a steep-valed wash, the cream of Cormyr's young nobles pouring after them in a headlong rush, shouting enthusiastic cries. Alusair and her "trail hounds" could see movement along the sides of the vale. More orcs, waiting for the humans to come surging into their waiting and weapon-laden arms.

Alusair bellowed, "Beldred, you *fool!* It's a trap!" and raked the flanks of her mount in frantic haste, screaming at it for speed.

The two noblemen, Threldryn and Brace, found themselves galloping hard after her, hearts in their throats, before they quite knew what had happened.

The trap was sprung before Alusair was halfway to the charging nobles. From the walls of valley magical lightning flashed, the thunderous boom rolling along the steep walls. Bright-armored figures danced in their saddles at the stroke of the bolt, their arms and legs jerking spasmodically, their weapons flying from hands that could no longer grip anything. Those men who survived the assault shouted in alarm and fought to control their rearing or bolting horses. The retreating orcs turned, practically under those flying hooves, and began to inflict vicious slaughter with their blades. More horses screamed and went down.

111

Ed Greenwood and Jeff Grubb

A furious Alusair snatched out her saddle horn and blew. The high, clear call rang back off the rocky heights: the retreat. Heads turned as the proud young knights of Cormyr heard their commander's signal and pulled back on their reins in disbelief . . . or relief, depending on their wisdom. Those whose horses would respond turned and streamed back out of the valley, followed by the hoarse jeers of triumphant orcs.

Alusair roared like Azoun himself as she rode to meet them. "Is charging all you dolts know how to do? Beldred, couldn't you *tell* the valley had all the makings of a trap?"

"I couldn't have stopped them if I'd tried, Lady Highness," the bloodied Beldred Truesilver replied wearily, "but I must admit, I did *not* try. Who could expect a few orcs to be able to hurl a lightning bolt?"

Alusair flung up her hands in exasperation. "No wonder they don't let you handsome swashcloaks out unchaperoned! You all seem to keep your brains in your sword scabbards!"

Alusair looked at the valley mouth and muttered a curse. "I'd tell you to regroup back at those hillocks, but the orcs will slaughter anyone downed by the bolt if we do. We have to go after our fallen comrades. Form a wedge behind me, *now!*"

In a chaos of thudding hooves, snorting horses, and shouting men, she swiftly got the formation in place. "Is anyone known to be dead?" Alusair called, not taking her eyes from the mouth of the valley.

"Dagh Illance," someone in scorched armor muttered. His helm was gone, and his hair was mostly ashes. He rode past her almost in a daze. "Perhaps one or two others that caught the brunt of the blast."

"Good riddance to Illance, the idiot. Foolishness must run in the family," Alusair replied, her voice low enough that none but she could hear. She drew a dagger from her left boot and reversed it, so that the large blue-green gem in its pommel pointed foremost, and called, "Go in fast, split up, and ride around each side of the valley;

don't trample our fallen comrades! Throw daggers and spears at orcs on the upper flanks of the vale, and knock them to our level—we can ride them down at that point! If there's any cave or cleft at the back, keep clear of it! Ye hear? Right, then—*ride!*"

And with her shrill bellow echoing in their ears, the noble knights broke into a gallop. The cheerful hooting and war cries of their earlier ride were absent now. They were injured and angry at their foe, and every man rode with the fresh, chill jolt of seeing comrades fall in death. If the princess had not been the warrior she was, half of them would be riding for the lowlands now, leaving the other half dying on the battlefield. As it was, they rode grimly, wondering what would prevent another lightning bolt from snapping down their throats as they rode into the valley.

They thundered on, fear rising in their mouths. They were close enough now to see orcs, looking up with tusked snarls as they went about the grisly business of slitting the throats of their fallen friends. The humanoids hadn't expected the mage-blasted knights to return.

Then the Cormyrean knights were between the rocks and into the vale itself. There was a sudden flash of light near where Alusair's unbound hair streamed back over her shoulders, followed by a roar of flame.

A huge burst of red, roiling fire blazed up in front of them, and someone in the wedge of horsemen gave a frightened shout, but Alusair did not hesitate. The fire flared, then melted away as if it were a wisp of illusion, parted by their commander as she rode. She still held the jewel-pommeled dagger out in front of her, and a few of the men saw smoke streaming away from the gem. Doubtless it was some enchantment to fight the magical power of the enemy and turn aside its energies.

Then there was no time for such thoughts, for orcs were everywhere, and there was something to strike out at, at last! The knights parted to ride along the sides of the vale, cutting down everything in their path.

Brace Skatterhawk caught a glimpse of a snarling,

gray-green face. He slashed out with his blade, struck something thick and soft, and rode on, never knowing whether he'd felled his foe. Short grunts and screams rose all around them amid the thunder of the hooves, and then fresh fire blossomed ahead.

The princess had been right. There was a cavern at the back of the vale, and from it was rolling an angry red sphere of flames, cartwheeling toward them. Alusair barked a command directing the knights to move to either side of the rolling fire. Then she charged the rolling fireball. Again the ball of flame evaporated at the touch of Alusair's bejeweled dagger.

With new respect, her warriors obeyed and reined in along both sides of the valley, watching a few surviving orcs cowering out in the open. Others of their goblinoid foes moaned and twisted feebly where they fell. The rest lay still and quiet. There was no further resistance save from the cavern itself.

"What's in the cave, Princess?" Brace asked. Threldryn Imbranneth was close behind him.

Alusair was winded and gasping, and the noblemen, romantics both, thought they'd never seen her look more beautiful than now, helmless in her armor. She shot them a quick glance and then swung her gaze back to the cavern.

"A dark naga, unless I miss my guess," she said. "Beldred's over on the other side of the vale. Let's hope he can convince the hotheads not to charge *this* time."

"A naga?" Threldryn asked. "I mean no disrespect, Princess, but how can you—or anyone else—know that?"

Brown eyes blazed into his. "When you go to war, do you merely ride, Lord Imbranneth? Try thinking, just once—you may find things go much better!" Some of the fire in her gaze ebbed, and she added, "So far on this campaign, we've fought hydras and fire lizards and orcs bold enough to come down into our lowland farms not once, but thrice. Where are all these creatures coming from?"

"Well, uh—the—the Stonelands, Princess," offered Threldryn, floundering. "Where else?"

"Don't you think it just a trifle odd, my lord, that three chimeras would line up to do battle with us one after the other? Beasts that should be fighting each other when drawn so close together?"

"Zhentarim," Brace murmured. "The Black Network. Using their magical gates and monstrous charms again!"

"Precisely," Alusair said in fierce agreement. "And that suggests these orcs were fleeing to their master, in that cave, one of those dark nagas the Black Network set up as mentors to their bands of orcs. We took a lightning bolt, and then a fireball; my spellshield dagger took care of the latter. If it had been a mage in yonder cave, he'd have hit us with something more potent by now, or else fled. Instead, we got a flaming sphere!"

"Therefore, a naga, now mystically spent and down to its lesser spells!" Threldryn said triumphantly. Alusair allowed herself a smile. There was hope for the young nobles of Cormyr yet.

Beldred rode up now, and the princess said, "There's a naga in there, and I'm going in after it. I want two volunteers to go with me—and only two. If I don't come out by sundown, my orders are that you decide on the best attack you can think of and follow us in."

Brace, Beldred, and Threldryn volunteered, of course. The princess left Beldred behind in command of the surviving nobles. The Truesilver captain immediately set out scouts to look for surviving orcs or other surprises of the Zhentarim.

Alusair took the other two nobles with her, striding steadily along the rocks on one side of the vale toward the dark cleft ahead. When some rocks provided a bit of cover close to their goal, the princess motioned them to halt behind her and took the time to glance back to see if her companions were ready.

Then she cast a long look at the rest of her company, pulled into defensive positions in case the cavern held any more surprises. This section of the Stonelands afforded a great view of the lands of the south, and Alusair could see at the horizon a thin line of green, the distant woods of

Cormyr. Farther south would be Suzail, where Uncle Bhereu lay cold and Thomdor and her father lay dying.

Brace and Threldryn saw sudden tears glimmer in the princess's eyes. She drew in a deep, shuddering breath and turned away from them, tossing her head in fresh resolve.

"Princess? What's happened?" Brace asked hesitantly.

Ash-blonde hair danced as his commander's head snapped around to face him again. "Nothing any Purple Dragon shouldn't always be prepared for," she said curtly, and slowly drew her blade, silently daring them to say more about her tears.

Silently they followed suit, and she seemed to almost smile.

"Now, gentle sirs," she said crisply, "are you with me? For Cormyr?"

"For Cormyr!" they echoed, and this time she did smile. "Then let us take the battle to our foe." And she eased toward the waiting darkness of the cave.

Brace Skatterhawk never forgot what followed. To his dying day, he could call to mind the frantic fight in the cavern with the serpentine naga, with spells blazing all around, and Alusair's fearlessness through it all. Their foe coiled and hissed as they slashed and sprang and hacked at it again. Its venomous tail loomed above them repeatedly, stabbing down with frightening speed. Alusair was the one who braved its jaws to blind the beast, of course, crying, "For Azoun and Cormyr!"

All three warriors had a blade in the creature's death, thrusting like madmen as the naga screamed and eventually died. It sounded chillingly like a woman sobbing as its lifeblood flowed out of it.

As the serpent-thing lay dying, thrashing about in oily, spreading black gore, Alusair leapt over it in frantic haste. Brace saw her snatch another gem, some last gewgaw of magic, from her belt as she leapt.

She threw the gem at what stood, flickering, behind the naga. Her target was an upright oval of blue magical fire cradled in the depths of the cavern. It was the magical gate she had spoken of, a door created by the Zhentarim. The gate collapsed with a roar, just as a red creature like a gigantic upright crab lurched through it. The magical radiance of the gate winked out as the gem struck it, and the crablike monster tumbled forward, cut in half.

Brace allowed himself to exhale, then heard a general roar of approval from behind them. The impatient nobles had flooded into the cavern. Apparently they had been unable to wait until sundown, particularly once they heard the naga's screams.

"Hurrah! Our work's done, then, Princess!" Ulnder Huntcrown, one of the young hotspurs, bellowed exultantly.

"No, Ulnder," the warrior princess told him grimly, hands on her hips. "Our work is just beginning. We have to hunt down and close all the other gates like this one."

"Huh," the noble growled in exasperation. "Why are victories never so clear and final as when the minstrels sing?"

"Because singers don't clean up after themselves. Warriors do," Alusair told him tartly.

"Or they soon die," Harandil Thundersword murmured from nearby. The princess looked at the soft-spoken nobleman sharply, then nodded in agreement. The warrior princess regarded the others, and they, too, nodded, slightly embarrassed.

Alusair allowed a smile, teeth flashing white, and shouted, "That's enough of great battles for today, lads! Let's find a good guardable place to camp and get some rest. We'll be in the saddle scouring the Stonelands on the morrow!"

There was a general sigh of breath let out as the nobles relaxed. A chorus of good-natured groans answered her words, but she saw more than one man raise his blade to his forehead in salute. She smiled in genuine pleasure. "That's my bold band! Gods, I'm proud to think of Cormyr in the years ahead, with all of you sitting in your halls as the lords and barons of the realm!"

* * * * *

The watch fires crackled and spat sparks as their flames reached orange fingers for the stars. As Alusair walked softly among them, a dark night cloak thrown around her shoulders, she could hear laughter and even some less than tuneful singing. The men were happy this night. The deaths of Dagh Illance and the others had already become tales of renown and heroics, in which each survivor had a story of his own legendary ability in the face of the orcish hordes.

The six men at the southernmost watch fire didn't see the warrior princess approach, or they'd surely never have said what they did.

"Damn you, Brace Skatterhawk, you always take the other man's side in any argument! How many sides d'you want?"

"Just like the king at that, he is!"

"And why not? He's a son of Azoun, after all. Haven't you heard the tales?"

Threldryn spoke up now. "We all have, Kortyl, but most of us have the wits not to say such things when we're riding with Azoun's daughter!"

"Aye, Kortyl. What if she heard you?"

"Bah! I don't fear her! Why, if I . . ." Kortyl's voice trailed away suddenly, and the others around the fire looked up, feeling a sudden tension. The princess stood over them like some dark shadow of the night, the firelight gleaming in her eyes.

"Yes, Kortyl?" she asked softly. "What would you do?"

"Uh . . . well, I . . . that is, I . . ." The young knight looked away.

She knelt down by the suddenly abashed nobleman, took hold of his ear, and said into it, "Well, if I were you, Kortyl Rowanmantle, I'd have the basic wits to look all around to see if someone's listening before I talked about them!"

The princess playfully shoved the kneeling Kortyl backward onto a pile of kindling. Whatever apology the

118

youth tried to stammer was lost in the general roar of mirth.

The roar was cut off abruptly by Alusair's next, soft words: "Brace Skatterhawk, I'll see you at my fire, once you've eaten. Don't forget."

* * * * *

Overhead, the stars were bright tonight; there were few clouds to dim their sparkling beauty. Alusair lay on her back, her own personal fire warm at her feet, and stared up at them, remembering the many tales she'd overheard of her father's . . . excesses. Nay, lass, she thought, call it what it was: philandering. Most such tales stemmed from before he was even married, and some were mere boasts, to be sure, but . . .

She closed her eyes and was back in the Grand Chamber on a bright morning when she was still in her teens, when many young noblemen who'd come of age together were being presented at court. One after another came in to kneel—and one after another resembled Azoun. Finally old Vangey murmured from behind the throne, "Moderation, my liege?"

She remembered her father's solemn frown and her mother's tight, amused smile, and she remembered pestering Uncle Bhereu about it until the kindly warrior, red-faced and stammering, explained the situation in gentle terms.

"You and your sister are the heirs to the Obarskyr throne," he had said, finally surrendering to the inevitable task of explaining the complex nature of life to the young. "Yet there are others who share your bloodline, though not officially noted as such. Unrecognized, these half-siblings stand no more chance at the throne than a chimney sweep, yet they are there and cannot be ignored."

She sighed and opened her eyes to the stars again, wondering with a sudden chill just how many of these half-siblings shared Bhereu's assessment. How many thought they were justified, by their unrecognized blood, to rule Cormyr? How many of those men with something of her father in their faces would she have to fight, should her father perish?

She sat up and drew her sword. So it was that Brace Skatterhawk found her, still in full armor all misted with night dew, her naked sword across her knees. His eyes widened, but he said merely, "I am here, Lady Highness. You sent for me."

Alusair turned her head and wordlessly beckoned him nearer.

When he stood over her, she looked up at him and asked softly, "So, are you my brother . . . as they say?"

"Princess!" he said reproachfully, "Does it matter? *Should* it matter?" He raised a hand to wave away his own irritation at the question, only to find her sword tip at his throat. His commander had come to her feet faster than any night-hunting hill cat.

"As I grow older and more and more of a hag," Alusair murmured, looking into his eyes, "I grow less and less patient. It may have something to do with the ever-decreasing time left to me before that last step into the waiting grave."

She let out a deep, ragged breath, and Brace realized she was a good deal less calm than she was pretending to be.

"I am also, as I grow older," Alusair continued, "falling more and more in love . . . with the truth. So let me have some of thine, young Skatterhawk. By your oath upon the Crown: Is my father Azoun also your father?"

Brace swallowed, feeling the sharp point of her war blade at his throat and the even sharper points of her eyes, gleaming at him in the gloom. He breathed deeply and said, "So—so I've been told, Lady Highness."

And the blade was gone, bouncing on the turf, as Alusair flung her arms around him and said, "Damn! That means I can't rightly do more than this!" And she grabbed the startled Skatterhawk by the forehead and placed a solid, sisterly kiss upon it. Such was the force of

her action, however, that her breastplate bruised Brace's
ribs.

Then she spun away, to kneel by the fire and draw
forth from it her other blade, the slim court sword she
kept at her saddle. Brown things were shriveling on its
smoking blade. "Care for some fried mushrooms,
Brother?"

He stared at her for a moment in amazement, then
burst into shouts of helpless laughter.

"You find mushrooms funny?" she asked in mock ag-
grieved tones and slid the hot blade between his lips.
Hastily he took a toasted mushroom, moaning at its heat
as he gabbled and chewed. He managed to get it down at
last, tears coming to his eyes from the burning. A glass
was steered into his hand, and he downed its contents in
one long, thankful swallow. Then he nearly choked in
fresh amazement.

"Elverquisst! Gods, Lady Highness, but this is a gift
fit for . . . kings." His voice trailed off slowly, his eyes on
hers.

Alusair shrugged. "I like you. I must admit I want you.
You fight well, better than most of the citified nobles I've
had to command. And if I can't have you as husband—or
openly, as brother—well, I need a friend at the moment."

"Aye," Brace said softly. "I have noticed that." He gently took her arms and looked steadily into her eyes. "Do
you mean this?" he asked. "I mean, needing a friend? The
gulf between noble and royal is as deep at times as that
between noble and farmer. You and your elder sister
Tanalasta have always occupied another sphere of existence, removed from even the rarefied intrigues of the
nobility. Can Alusair the Firetongue trust a mere member of the nobility?"

Oak-brown eyes blazed into his with a leaping, amber
fury like a brushfire for a moment, and the arms in his
grasp trembled. "You *dare?*" she gasped.

Brace held her gaze steadily and said, "I do."

They held gazes for a long time, during which neither
drew breath, and then he added softly, "Forgive my

blunt words, High Lady, but it had to be said. I have been raised to respect the Obarskyr line, and though I have been told my heritage, I and . . . others like me have been taught not to dream of the crown. That belongs only to one truly Obarskyr born and Obarskyr raised. Yet, even given all this, can you trust me—or anyone—enough?"

She looked down and away for a moment, biting at her lip. Then her head came up again, proudly, and she met his eyes again with all the fire gone. She nodded. "It was fairly asked," she murmured, "and—I can trust. I will trust. For you. And as a friend, I will tell you we will be on patrol out here longer than we had planned, until we have found all of those Black Network gates."

Brace Skatterhawk let go of her arms and trailed his left hand down to her right hand. He grasped her hand and raised it slowly to his lips. "Then I should be honored to be your friend."

Then he reached for the buckles that held her armor along one shapely flank. "I can think of one way to celebrate this friendship. Brothers daren't do such things, or people talk. And lovers are always in too much of a hurry to get to—other matters. But friends, now . . ."

"Keep your hands on the buckles, 'Friend' Brace," Alusair said warningly, turning to let the firelight fall on her side so that he could see what he was undoing. He gently laid aside the plates that covered her torso and gestured to her to sit. She obeyed.

"As I was saying," Brace continued in dignified tones, "friends have the only hands suitable for the removal of chafing armor . . . and the rubbing of tired feet."

"Ahhh," Alusair moaned, lying back and closing her eyes in genuine ecstasy. "I've made the correct choice! I should have surmised you were as good with your hands as you were with your blade. It's good to have a championship foot rub, particularly when the realm is in dire peril." An errant thought crossed her mind as she spoke, and she stiffened involuntarily.

"Princess?" he asked anxiously.

She waved a dismissive hand. "No . . . I just remembered something, that's all. . . ."

"A secret, or something to share?" he asked, and she shook her head absently.

"A secret," was all she said, but the thought was blazing through her brain over and over again. She knew she was right. In all her life, she'd never heard her father say, "the realm is in dire peril," but it had always been one of Vangerdahast's favorite phrases. She frowned and thought of the message plate. Why would the old wizard be impersonating her father?

What was Vangerdahast up to now?

8

Massacre
Year of Distant Thunder
(16 DR)

ndeth and the others picked their way carefully through the smoking remains of the Bleth farmstead. The eldest Obarskyr's face was like stone, and he said nothing as he stared around at the devastation. Not a single building had been spared . . . and not a single creature was alive.

The farm was only a mile from Suzail, a small glade that Mondar Bleth had cleared to twice its original size. Three main buildings, one with a stone foundation, had stood here, and in this place Mondar had reared a prodigious supply of goats. Now those buildings were smoking husks, and the riven corpses of the goats lay strewn around the camp, along with the human bodies.

Ten men and women had been slain here for no good reason. Mondar himself had been found at the entrance to the farmhouse, his battered body supported by a tripod of thin ivory pikes tipped with gold. Elven weapons. Their bloody points had stood up out of his chest and belly, holding his huge, bearlike body clear of the ground. Mondar's eyes were open and accusing.

Faerlthann came up to his father with Mondar's sword, a huge, heavy-hafted blade that had always hung

124

at the large man's side. Mondar had never been shy about drawing that sword to make a point. The blade was sticky and dark with drying blood. Though there were no elven bodies among the dead, it seemed Mondar had held out well against his attackers.

The eyes of the older and younger Obarskyrs met, and Ondeth saw accusation in his son's eyes. Two of the Bleths had survived this slaughter by being in Suzail at the time. Minda, Mondar's sister, had been a guest for dinner the previous night and had brought Arphoind, Bleth's youngest son, a strapling of all of eight winters, with her.

The visiting Bleths had come for dinner and stayed the night, Arphoind in the loft and Minda ... well, Minda was in Ondeth's quarters. No one should have known of their tryst, and the Bleths would have left with the morning sun, the rest of Suzail none the wiser. But in the dawn there was smoke rising from the northwest, and panic in the household, and not a few eyes noted that the raven-tressed beauty of the Bleths had emerged from Ondeth's private room.

They had left Minda and her nephew behind when they went to investigate, which was just as well. Ondeth did not want the woman to see her brother pinioned like a goose held over a fire. And the elves who did this might still be nearby.

Upon seeing the devastation, Ondeth's first thought had been, "What will I tell Minda?" Yet looking into his own son's eyes, he was faced with another question: What do I tell Faerlthann? His son was among those who'd noted Minda's emergence in the morning. His face was pale with anger—not anger for elves, but rather for Ondeth Obarskyr, who had betrayed his mother's memory.

As they'd hastened out of Suzail, Faerlthann had said but one thing, a short, barely heard whisper as they pulled their swords from the wall and gathered their light suits of armor. "How could you do it? How could you do that to Mother?" But then he had turned to join the others and there was no time to talk.

Ondeth should have spoken out, and spoken out then. It had been four years since Suzara had left them, tired of the wolves and the mosquitoes and, most of all, the endless work. He should have replied that Mother had already done unto him. Nor had this tryst been the first time, only the first time they'd been caught at it. If Minda had not been at Suzail, she would be dead, here among the flies, and young Arphoind, Faerlthann's friend, as well.

Ondeth should have said something then, but there'd been no time. And now his son looked at him over the bloody edge of Mondar's blade, and his eyes were as accusing as Mondar's own.

Perhaps later they would talk, father and son. Perhaps later he could explain, but now they had to cut down Bleth's body and give him and the others a decent cremation. The Silver brothers were already gathering the dead into a pile, goats on the bottom and humans on the top. Another column of smoke, thick and oily, would rise here this day.

Ondeth looked at Bleth's suspended form, pitched slightly forward, as if taking flight. Mondar's jaw hung loose, as if he were passing on some drunken secret to those below. Yet there was no secret to be found here, only a warning from a people who had for the past decade been Ondeth's allies.

"Why now?" asked Ondeth. Faerlthann started at the dreadful quiet in his father's voice. "After all these years, why did the elves attack now?"

* * * * *

The center of the settlers' universe was Suzail, and the center of the Suzail was Ondeth's manor.

The town, named after Ondeth Obarskyr's now departed wife, had slowly crept its way up the low hillside behind the original glade. The lumbering had been carefully supervised by Baerauble Elf-friend, with the felled trees being used immediately for housing. Most of the original homesteads had been given over to farming, the buildings Ondeth and Villiam had erected now home to tools and coops and shearing floors. Newly arriving families moved upward, inside the sprawling wooden wall that embraced the entire hill. Its height was claimed by the Obarskyrs by right of first arrival, and none argued with that. Three hundred and fifty or so folk called Suzail home, a muster that could live in a single block of a packed city in Chondath or Impiltur, or even in the mercantile outposts of nearby Sembia.

Yet they were prospering. A dock had been built four seasons ago, allowing ships safe moorings along the rocky coast. Previously waterborne visitors had to make landfall at Marsember, then trek along the coast to Suzara's City, Suzail. Merchants were now bypassing the swampy town in favor of the Obarskyr settlement. Baerauble's contacts with the elves made it possible for the port to ship out elven cloth, nuts, and beast hides, receiving in return tools, weapons, and various fine mongery from the human cities on more southerly shores of the Sea of Fallen Stars.

Ondeth's manor looked out over the city. Despite its two floors, it was a low, solid rampart of rough-cut stone and gray slate shingles, set partially into the hillside behind. Its stone foundation had been the first in Suzail, and envy of it had spurred the other families to build likewise.

Ondeth had talked of raising some towers at the ends of his home, but had been too busy to commit time enough to do so. When he built the manor, most of it was a single great hall, and here most of the populace of Suzail was wont to gather in the early evenings around the great fire pit in the center of the chamber. The families would come to cook their evening meals, gossip, and trade tales, lies, and legends. With the rising popularity of Suzail, even an occasional bard or minstrel would join those at the fireside, to swap sweet tales in exchange for a roof to sleep under.

And from a great chair close to the fire, Ondeth

Obarskyr was the center of his own universe. He, too, had grown in the past decade, the heaviness of advancing years settling firmly around his waist. And though there were plenty of young and unattached women in town, particularly the daughters of the Silver brothers, he never stepped beyond mild flirtation with any of them. At least not at first.

Knowledge held him in check—the knowledge held by the folk of Suzail. Most knew Suzara, and knew about the heated rows she and her husband had shared. Ondeth had never convinced his wife that this was a place worth staying in, and all the stone foundations and swelling population in Faerûn would not keep her here. Once, early on, there'd been a chance Ondeth might change his mind about carving a home from the wilderness, but that chance had died in one afternoon of elven horns and lights in the trees . . . and with it, their relationship.

Suzara took the youngest lad and returned to Impiltur, sailing away on the first boat to moor at the new dock. Ondeth did not see her off, but Faerlthann did. In the new settlement, he'd grown to be taller than his father, his muscles hardened by work, his face tanned by the sun, and his eyes keen. And there was something else in those eyes from time to time: a faraway misty look the young man would get when Baerauble would visit, with his tales of elven kingdoms and their wild hunts.

Yet in the four years since Suzara's sailing, father and son had settled into their roles. Faerlthann was the dutiful son, Ondeth the desolate father, and both seemed comfortable in their parts. The young women of the Silver households respected old Ondeth, but their eyes lit up for young Faerlthann.

So things had gone until Minda Bleth arrived, after Mondar her brother. Mondar had shown up six years ago, hard behind Jaquor and Tristan, the Silver brothers. But while the twin Silvers had agreed to settle within the confines of the already cleared area, Mondar would have none of that. There was a glade a mile northwest of the main settlement, little more than a clearing burnt bare by some elder wyrm or lightning strike. It had water and wood close at hand, and the place was far enough away from Suzail to allow privacy and close enough to afford protection.

Or at least that was Mondar's opinion in the matter, voiced loudly enough to ring from the rafters of Ondeth's first house. Mondar was as massive as a thundercloud, with a temper to match. He was already balding, but he kept a thick beard that reached nearly to his belt. His forehead was plowed with deep lines, and when he was in full fury, which was often, he could outbellow, outshout, and outargue any man in the colony, including Ondeth. It was generally agreed that by allowing Mondar to settle elsewhere, Ondeth was keeping a potential rival at a safe distance.

Oddly enough, the two had eventually become friends and allies, sharing a love of both the land and of homebrewed ale. Ondeth was at the bedside when Mondar's wife died giving birth to Arphoind. The night that Suzara left the town named for her, Mondar and Ondeth had gone on a roaring drunk, wandering in the night together bellowing out rude, impromptu lyrics to all the elven tunes they could recall.

Mondar and Baerauble hated each other instantly, of course, and the elder Bleth did not miss an opportunity to goad the elf-friend. Yet despite this and Mondar's rapid clearing of the glade, the sky did not fall, the elves did not attack, and the world did not end. Suzail continued to grow, and others besides Mondar began to say that perhaps the elven restrictions were just grand old words, that perhaps by now the elves had come to terms with humans moving into their lands.

Ondeth held to the limits set down by Baerauble, for there was still more than enough land within the rambling town wall. Still, a distance had grown between the old farmer and the wizard, and when Baerauble came to visit, he spent more time with Faerlthann and the youngsters than with his old friend.

The arrival of Mondar's sister, Minda, strained the new friendship between Mondar and Ondeth. She'd come to Suzail a year ago, as fair as her brother was rough-hewn. Her hair was the color of the darkest night, and her eyes glowed like bits of silver. Her face was unmarked and had a golden sheen to it. She was as tall as her brother and Ondeth and, like her brother, wouldn't take no for an answer. Even if Mondar disliked the attention Minda paid to the older farmer, he could do little to dissuade her.

Minda spent more and more time in the manor hall. She brought gossip and tales from old Impiltur and told them with colorful flourishes. In a private moment, she told Ondeth that Suzara had officially dissolved the marriage and remarried a Theskan merchant. Ondeth never told Faerlthann, but afterward Minda's presence in the Obarskyr manor became more frequent.

Until one day when she didn't go home at all, and the morning brought spirals of black smoke rising from Mondar's homestead.

* * * * *

The wizard appeared as they were laying Mondar's corpse atop the others. Suddenly he was there, at the corner of the glade, as if he had just stepped out of the woods. For years Ondeth had thought that the spell hurler walked through the woods, until finally he noticed the bending of light around the wizard when he first appeared. The mage arrived by wizardry and probably did not walk anywhere.

The passing decade had changed Baerauble not a whit; he was still lanky and emaciated, his hair and beard unbroken auburn. He carried a heavy, gnarled staff now, but Ondeth never saw him use it for support.

As the elf-friend approached, the Silvers and others pulled back. Several laid hands on their blades, ready to draw them if the wizard showed any sign of menace.

Ondeth and Faerlthann held their ground. The older Obarskyr nodded to the mage and spoke quietly. "Were you involved in this?"

"Not directly," Baerauble replied, his face haggard and worn. Faerlthann noted that no shock chased across the wizard's features as he glanced at the heap of corpses. "You need fire?"

Ondeth shrugged and turned to the carrion pile. He offered a prayer to Lathander and Tyche and all the old gods for the safe passage of those slain "to their fitting final fates."

Baerauble bowed his head along with everyone else, muttered a few quiet phrases, and stretched out his hands. A gout of fire burst from his outstretched palms.

The wood beneath the bodies caught in an instant, and in the space of a few breaths, the entire pyre was ablaze. A new column of smoke rose into the Cormyrean sky.

The settlers and the wizard watched the flames catch hold of Mondar's shirt and flesh, then crackle along his beard. "What do you mean, 'not directly'?" asked Ondeth at last.

"Iliphar's court has been debating the fate of this farm for some time," said Baerauble.

"This farm has been here for six years," said Ondeth sharply.

"A pleasant day for an elf," said Baerauble calmly. "The briefest slumber for a dragon. Elves decide things slowly."

"And act quickly," said Ondeth. "So quickly you had no chance to warn us?"

Ondeth expected a denial, one that would have shattered the last remains of their friendship. Instead Baerauble sighed. "Would a warning have helped? Would it have been better for you to have died here, sword in hand, helping an ally who was clearly in the wrong?"

" 'Twas six *years*, man!" said Ondeth hotly, his brows coming together in a fierce line.

"Aye, and I would have thought you could talk some

sense into the man in that time," Baerauble replied. "You know the elves only allow slow growth, and only where we have permitted it. Now the rest of the human settlers will stay closer to Suzara's town and leave the elves to their hunting."

"You think that?" said Ondeth. "You honestly think that my people will not seek revenge? You honestly think they'll agree to protect your precious forests out of *fear?*"

The two older men, with young Faerlthann beside them, watched the flames dance among the dead. Mondar and his family were little more than black lumps among leaping red and orange fiery tendrils now, only vaguely human in form.

"No, I do not," said the mage at length. "But my voice does not carry the weight it once did in Iliphar's court. There are those who point to my human blood and call me your puppet and spy. Some were expecting me to ride with a warning to you, and so betray myself." He looked at the grim, watching men with their hands on their swords, and then back to Ondeth. "Tell me, are these men loyal?"

Ondeth looked at the mage and said nothing.

"Are these men loyal to you?" Baerauble asked again. "Will they do as you ask?"

Ondeth looked at the others. The Silver brothers, Rayburton, Jolias Smye the smith. Faerlthann. Without thought to the choosing in his haste, he'd chosen them to ride here with him.

"Yes, they are loyal," he said slowly, eyes narrowing as he looked at the wizard.

"Loyal enough to kill for you?" pressed Baerauble, "Or, more importantly, *not* to kill?"

"What are you getting at, wizard?" snapped Ondeth.

"I could not stop this attack, but we *can* stop the war," said the elf-friend. "The elves have no argument with you and your settlement in general, though it now grows large enough to worry some in the court. Only Mondar, who broke the covenant, was punished. If you and your men tell your people that elves did this, they'll attack the court and their hunters, and this—" he waved one hand around the smoldering battlefield, ending at the pyre— "will befall Suzail and all of you. Do you want that?"

Ondeth was silent.

"But if orcs did this," the mage continued, "If the pig faces were responsible, then your settlement continues. Will your men tell that lie to save your people?"

Ondeth's brows did not rise. "Why would they want to lie?"

Baerauble ignored the question. "If you told them to, would they obey you?"

Ondeth thought about it for a moment, looking at the others. The Silvers already had a large and growing brood in the settlement, Rayburton a daughter, and Smye a wife heavy with their first child. They had all argued with Mondar about the wisdom of settling beyond the walls. Yes, they would—reluctantly—agree, if the alternative was explained to them.

"Aye," said Ondeth. "They would obey."

"Let this be the work of the goblin-kin, then," said Baerauble. "I will go back and work peace among the discontented elves. But there is another matter: Why will these men obey you?"

Ondeth blinked. "Because they choose to. They're reasonable men, and they know they cannot take on the elves themselves and have any hope of victory." Yet, he added to himself.

Baerauble shook his head. "They follow you because they choose to, but also because you choose to lead. You are the founder of your town, and the strongest voice in it. Were I to ask them to do this thing, regardless of the soundness of my arguments, they would ignore me, even though it would mean their own deaths. You they will listen to."

"What are you saying, mage?" Faerlthann asked, looking from his father to the elf-friend and back.

"You are their leader in truth," said Baerauble. "I want you to be leader in name as well. Declare yourself king, or duke, or whatever rank you so choose. I can offer the support of Iliphar and the court in this matter. With Mondar dead now, there is no other strong voice. Marry your Minda if you want to seal the matter." He ignored the younger Obarskyr's sharp intake of breath at the mention of Minda's name.

Ondeth did not look at his son, but instead regarded the wizard. The elven attack had come when Minda was not present and had silenced the only man in a hundred miles who could challenge Ondeth's tacit leadership of Suzail. If it were blamed on orcs or goblins, the peaceful lives of Suzailans could continue alongside the elves . . . with the threat of death under elven arrows helping the town elders keep the secret of the assault.

How much *did* Baerauble know of this massacre?

Ondeth watched the crackling flames, aware of the scrutiny of both the mage and his own son. If he were to agree, that would mean Faerlthann would gain everything upon his death. More than a farm, more than a name, Faerlthann would have a kingdom. Would that be enough for the young man to forgive him his affair with Mondar's sister?

At length, Ondeth opened his mouth and said deliberately, "No."

The mage protested, "But—"

"No," repeated the farmer. "Many of us have seen kings, and in general they are a bad lot. If I command these men, it is by their choice, not mine. If they obey the strictures you and the elves have laid down, it is through loyalty to me, not fear of you. If they hide this foul deed, it will be through their own desire to remain, not any order I enforce upon them."

He looked at the pyre, where the Bleths were barely recognizable as things that had been human. "No, I cannot be your puppet king, dancing to elven tunes," Ondeth continued. "You have no authority to offer me such a title. These men do, and they have had their fill of monarchs and official leaders. I will see that your secret is kept, because it is in all our best interests to keep it secret. But I will not take a crown born out of a massacre."

The flames were beginning to die now, thick smoke pouring from the pyre. The smell of burned flesh hung heavily in the air.

At length, Baerauble spoke. "I will convey your refusal back to Iliphar's court. Know, Ondeth Obarskyr, that the elves are concerned about the growth of your little settlement. If you will not take the reigns of leadership in an official form, they will have to decide what to do about the humans in their wolf woods."

With that, he turned away from the pyre.

Ondeth shouted after him, "And how long will this decision take?"

Baerauble paused, then turned. "Ten years. Perhaps twenty. The elves are slow to decide. . . ."

"And swift to act," finished the farmer. "And will you warn us when they choose to eliminate us as they did this farmstead?"

Baerauble Etharr, the elf-friend mage, said something, followed by a jumble of syllables in a strange tongue. The light shivered, flowed like water, bent around him, and he was gone.

Gone back to his elven masters to report his failure.

Ondeth caught the mage's last mumbled words and thought the wizard said, "Prepare yourselves."

Faerlthann heard those same words but thought the mage had said, "I shall try."

9

Cordials
Year of the Gauntlet
(1369 DR)

rincess Alusair? My dear, she's probably gallivanting around the realm with all the handsome young men she can grab with both hands! Gone to fight beasts at the borders of the realm, indeed! More likely she's off to one of the king's secluded hunting lodges for a weekend of dalliance. *That* one wants to try out all the nobles in Cormyr before she marries one!"

The prawn-and-cress sandwiches were all gone, and the dove tarts as well. The servants had been dismissed—Darlutheene had bidden them to leave the cordial decanters behind—and the two ladies had settled down in the parlor window seats with the drinks between them for their favorite post-highsun pastime: a good old gossip.

Darlutheene Ambershields was in fine form today. To look at her—something few men cared to do for overlong—you'd never think she'd been born to a family of longtime palace servants. Her gown of royal blue musterdelvys was alive with cut gems—glass, a jeweler would have said at a glance—that glistened like tears, and her formidable bodice was a masterwork of upswept filigree

136

adorned with peacock plumes. The red silk of a fitted chemise flared through her slashed and puffed sleeves, and in half a dozen daring cutouts upon her breast and belly. Huge rings flashed and glistened on every finger as she waved expressive hands, and a small silver ship was under full sail across the raised billows of her blonde hair.

In truth, her companion, Blaerla Roaringhorn, considered this bellow-sailed vessel in very poor taste, but it was after all Darlutheene's parlor, and her cordials, too, so Blaerla held her peace.

"She doesn't matter at any rate," Darlutheene confided in a whisper that set the crystal ringing several rooms away. "They say Azoun has three sons—that's right, no fewer than three!—shut up in dungeons at High Horn and Arabel and even right here in Suzail, their wits stolen away by those wicked war wizards, waiting to step onto the throne should anything happen to him. The other nobles are simply *furious*, of course, and have spent quite a respectable amount of money over the years trying to get to these idiot princes. If they *grabbed* one, you see, they could kill everyone in the Palace at once with magic and still have a recognized blood heir to put on the throne!"

The earrings at Darlutheene's green- and pink-dyed temples shook with the excitement of her words, tinkling almost like the diamonds they were cut to resemble, rather than the glass that they truly were.

Blaerla leaned forward, jewel-topped toothpick busily at work, to look out over what they could see of the royal gardens, just in case armies of men hired by the nobles were charging the palace to get at one of those chained princes right now, but the shrubs and flower beds were empty of rushing men in armor; perhaps they'd chosen another route. "You speak truth indeed about my mistress, the princess," she said, putting her glass to her full, very red lips, "but I've seen her with a sword in her hand, love, and I tell you if anyone sits on the throne that she doesn't agree with, we'll have *war!*"

"War? Why, Blaerla, you do say such dramatic things sometimes! Why, who would want to ruin all this"—Darlutheene waved a languid hand out the window, fluttering the long, green lashes she'd had glued to her own mousy brown ones that morning—"by attacking and fighting and burning and . . . all that sort of thing?" To underscore her question, she opened her striking violet eyes very wide.

"Half a hundred ambitious nobles!" Blaerla replied excitedly, her own brown eyes flashing in response, color coming into her cheeks. Her companion's cheeks always sported a blush—and several beauty spots—thanks to her capable crew of six maids-of-adornment, who also powdered her several chins. "At least twenty noble families consider the crown is as rightfully theirs as it is the Obarskyrs'!" She drained her glass to underscore the gravity of her words.

"You exaggerate, dear," Darlutheene said indulgently, pouring more of her fourth-best bitter orange generously. Blaerla licked her lips appreciatively, unaware that she wasn't actually getting the finest amberfly the bottle proclaimed it held. "Azoun is poorly, yes, but he still lives, and everyone, simply *every*one, is looking to Tanalasta. It seems our silent miss is to have her chance at last!"

"Is she strong enough to seize it?" Blaerla asked eagerly, eyes snapping with excitement. "Or having taken the throne, to hold it?"

"Ah, but you must be unaware, my dear, that our weak, frail princess of books and sighs has—a man!"

"No!"

"Yes!"

"Tell!" Blaerla demanded, almost upsetting a tall glass with her chin in her forward-leaning eagerness. "Who is this next king of ours? Taldeth Truesilver? That leering one who gives her all the flowers—what is his name . . . Hundilav . . . Hundilavatar Huntsilver? Surely not that popinjay, Martin Illance?"

"No, no . . . you'll never guess, dear; *I* didn't!" Madam Ambershields made the most of her moment, pausing to leisurely sip her current glass of cordial while her companion almost bounced and squealed with impatience. She settled for stroking Darlutheene's hand fondly, several dozen times.

"Well?" Blaerla demanded at last, unable to wait any longer. "*Tell* me!"

"His name," Darlutheene said slowly, refilling her glass, "is Aunadar Bleth, a hitherto overlooked young blade of the old and respected Bleth family."

"Respected, my dear? By whom?" Blaerla was a Roaringhorn, and the Roaringhorns did not think well of the Bleths as a matter of principle. The reasons went back several centuries, and by now the particulars were quite forgotten, but were thought to have been very good at the time.

"By—by, ah, all sorts of highly placed people at court, dear! They say he's quick with a blade, and handsome enough, and, well . . . has stayed at her side. A true young gallant!"

"Of the sort that rushes about waving his sword and his jaws nonstop and falling off his horse every tenday?" Blaerla asked dryly, and they chuckled together over their glasses.

"Well, whatever happens," Madam Ambershields said with satisfaction when she could speak again, "Princess Tanalasta has labored too long in her father's shadow, supporting him with her every word and act! It's high time she built a life of her own."

"Well, yes, she needs to chart her own voyage . . . but is she *ready?*"

"Are any of us, dear? It's true she's led a sheltered life, and all this may have come rather suddenly, sooner than she might have wished . . . but she should be happy now that she has a man!"

"Hah! Men!" Blaerla's passing acquaintance with men had not left her with all that high an opinion of the creatures; dogs barked more frugally and got into less mischief, on the whole. "What do we know about this Bleth boy, really?"

"Well, that *is* a matter of some spirited dispute, I may say," Darlutheene allowed. "Some say he has an impeccable character, but it must be said that none speaking so are women. He *is* rather obscure. . . ."

"But they were saying in the palace yestereve that Tanalasta—delicate rose that she is!—quite lost her wits when the duke died, and though she's recovered enough to speak and recognize folk and feed herself, she's still a shattered thing!"

"No, no, my dear. Your sources are quite mistaken. The shattered one is *Filfaeril*. The queen is quite mad with grief. She's been shrieking so, and pulling the hair of courtiers, and rushing about half dressed, howling at guards to plunge their swords into her bosom, and I don't know quite what all else . . . that they've put her away."

"No!"

"Yes! Locked her in a coach and spirited her away by night, into seclusion clear up in quaint little Eveningstar, at a temple there called the Spires of the Morning or something like that. They say she won't recover, so there's no thought of the Dragon Queen ruling on alone, even if such a thing were possible. The crown goes to one Obarskyr-born. Marriage grants you a title but not the throne."

"All the worse for poor, poor Tanalasta." Blaerla sighed. "What are the nobles here at court saying? They won't let us in the palace speak to them, you know!"

"Ah, that's the master hand of the Royal Magician at work! Always trying to run things, that one—spells enough to turn the realm upside down apparently aren't enough for some people! He's got them in a proper frolic at court, you know. The old nobles are furious that anyone's doing anything until Azoun's actually dead, of course. The older patriarchs insist that the king will recover and that we do blasphemous treason if we prepare for, or talk about, anything else! Yet I notice not a few of them have sent their sons home to their estates and mustered all the family armsmen—*and* all the swords they can hire in Marsember—around them!"

"I thought the lower orders would be crying out for Alusair to come riding in and take the throne," Blaerla said thoughtfully. "They love her, you know."

"All Cormyr loves our Mithril Princess—but wouldn't living under her rule be like trying to hold the leash of an angry dog when it sees foes on all sides? And she *did* vanish off north *just* when her country needed her most!"

Darlutheene's closing sniff consigned Alusair to the no-longer-need-be-discussed category, and Blaerla abandoned championing her absent royal mistress in favor of a sigh and a murmured, "So I suppose it's to be Tanalasta—with all the court nobles hungry to see her on the throne, so that they can tell her what to do."

"Of course! There're even some of them who want Filfaeril to rule alone, even if she's barking mad, so that they can speak for her and do just as they please with the realm."

Blaerla rolled her eyes. "Is there anyone else seeking the throne?"

Darlutheene laughed heartily, spraying raspberry cordial all over the table and herself. "Of *course*, my dear. All the timid mice among both merchants and nobles are skulking about the corridors, suggesting that it's time to install a merchant—or a noble, depending on whose tongue is flapping—council to run the kingdom and put whatever powerless puppy seems most convenient on the throne. One man with little taste and less sense than most actually suggested having Azoun's corpse stuffed and putting it on the throne to entertain the flies, while everyone else got on with the task of running Cormyr!"

"Gods above!" Blaerla was scandalized. "It'd be just like the regency all over again! If there isn't one crowned head to spew the orders, everyone spends his time looking over his shoulder in fear, or burying daggers in the bellies of rivals, and *nothing* good gets done!"

"And that," Darlutheene said triumphantly, "is where our favorite fat old mage comes in. Vangerdahast, the Lord High Court Wizard, Royal Magician, and Chamberpot Watcher, is being friendly with all of the factions,

whispering this here and that there, egging them all on
. . . to each others' throats! Whenever anyone accuses
him of double-dealing or speaking falsely, he goes all
grim and grand and talks about 'doing what he must for
the safety of the realm.' You should hear him!"

"What does he truly want, I wonder?" Blaerla mused,
suddenly very serious. The palace was all too uncomfortably close to be ruled by madmen, or feuding butcherers
. . . or mad wizards. "He could be the most dangerous
man in the kingdom."

"He *is* the most dangerous man in the kingdom, dear,"
said Darlutheene darkly, leaning forward to snatch the
last bottle of cordial—lime, her favorite—practically out
from under Blaerla's nose. "The gods help us if he
changes."

"Changes?"

"He's always *been* loyal to crown. Still, he is a wizard,
and they are tricky in the extreme."

"Yes, tricky . . ." Blaerla echoed, and they frowned in
unison and shook their heads disapprovingly. One could
never tell with wizards.

10

Coronation
Year of Opening Doors
(26 DR)

Ondeth's smoke clung to Faerlthann Obarskyr as he stormed into the elven court, the wizard Baerauble trailing a short and respectable distance behind him. Even so, the mage had to lengthen his strides and hasten to keep up with the young man.

The Court of Iliphar, Lord of the Scepters, had set up a great pavilion on the site of Mondar's Massacre, now nearly a decade ago. The reason for their appearance here was as obvious as it was threatening. Few humans knew that the massacre had been more than a goblin raid, and it had become a cautionary tale against farming beyond the comfortable wooden palisade of Suzail. But around late fires, tongues wag, and more than a few folk had been told by their fathers in confidence to beware of the elves and not "be the fool that Mondar was."

The timing of the elven arrival was obvious as well. Ondeth had died yestereve, his great heart finally giving out after a life of hard work and harder revels. He was struck down while trying to help Smye the smithmaster unmire his cart on a muddy road. Ondeth lingered a single day, weakly making his final farewells to friends

143

and family. When the gods finally came for him, Faerlthann was there, beside Minda and Arphoind. Minda and Ondeth had married, and Faerlthann had come at last to accept her as his father's love, if not as his rightful mother. Arphoind, now sixteen, had been taken into the household but kept his family name in honor of Mondar.

Baerauble wasn't present when Ondeth died, but that didn't surprise Faerlthann. He'd seen the mage only a dozen times since the day they burned Mondar, and each time the wizard had gone behind firmly closed doors with Ondeth to deal with some matter of Suzailan import. Faerlthann recalled the old mage telling tales by the fireside when Faerlthann was a boy and wondered if he avoided the town out of shame or guilt for his knowledge of the massacre.

Ondeth's passing came at midnight. Wood was gathered and laid in a towering pyre at the foot of the Obarskyr hills, below the expanded manor house. The old farmer's body was dressed in a saffron gown, and his ancient hammer and sledge were laid on his chest. When the first rays of the sun struck Suzail, the wood was set ablaze, and Ondeth's spirit was sent to join his brothers' and Mondar's in the halls of the gods.

It was then that word spread that the elves were here. Not one or two, as sometimes wandered into town, or even a party of hunters like the dozen who'd commandeered a tavern five years back. This time it was more, much more: The elven court had arrived.

North and west of the town, their huge tents of diaphanous green and yellow broke smoothly above the green shadowtop leaves like the shoulders of some great draconian beast.

'Twas a strange coincidence, folk said, their arrival so soon after Ondeth's passing. Faerlthann no longer believed in coincidences, and he believed in them even less when Baerauble, green-robed and as lean as ever, finally appeared.

The mage pulled him away from the feast hall while

the pyre was still blazing strong. Faerlthann set his jaw. The cheek of the man! If the wizard was still a man, truly . . .

The wizard made a few mumbled apologies to Minda and young Arphoind and said that matters of utmost urgency demanded that the scion of the Obarskyrs accompany him. Lord Iliphar wished to have words with Faerlthann Obarskyr.

Faerlthann protested, but there was a look on the mage's face that stopped his words as surely as any spell. He looked at his family. Minda nodded for him to go. Arphoind's face was creased with a deep frown, and his nod was slower to come—but come it did.

Still in the hall, in front of all the leading families, Baerauble grasped young Obarskyr's shoulders firmly. He muttered his inhuman words and the two were bathed in a brilliant glow. From his father's tales, Faerlthann knew what to expect and stood calmly under Baerauble's hands. When the radiance faded, they were standing at the cavernous entrance to the elves' pavilion.

The structure had been raised, and was kept aloft, by elven magic. A series of spires curved out like horns from a floating dragon's head to shelter huge open spaces beneath. Diaphanous fabrics hung from those spires, shimmering in the morning sun, to make the vast walls of the pavilion. The air smelled of warm summer earth. Butterflies, whose season had not yet come beyond this place, fluttered to and fro on soft breezes. From ahead came the soft, liquid chords of a lute played with more skill than the Obarskyr heir had ever heard before. As he shook off Baerauble's hands and strode forward, a singer's voice rose to join the music—an almost sobbing voice of velvet, clearer and higher than that of any human woman.

Faerlthann had no time or patience for the wonders of the elves; he was too busy charging forward. The dratted wizard and these damnably imperious elves hadn't even given him a chance to change! He still wore mourning white, the tabard and hood covering most of the rest of his garb. At his hip swung Mondar's heavy-hafted sword, now his own, which had gained a name in the past decade: Ansrivarr, the elvish word for "memory." The smoke of the pyre still clung to him, and Faerlthann saw several delicate elf women hold sleeves to their nostrils as he passed. That small slight fed his fury even more.

He burst into the main chamber unannounced, the wizard doing nothing to impede his progress. Faerlthann catapulted into the place beneath the highest spire, a space larger than any human church on this side of the Sea of Fallen Stars.

The voice and the lute stopped immediately, and a there was a soft, sibilant drawing of breath from a hundred elven throats. Clusters of courtiers in Faerlthann's way parted as if split by a blade, clearing a path for the young Obarskyr. The last to get clear of his route was the elven troubadour herself, who paused only to give a small bow as she ceded the floor to the newcomer.

A tripartite throne stood on the far side of the pavilion. It did not look crafted so much as grown there, for it seemed rooted firmly in the earth itself, the high seats reached by a set of low, broad crystalline steps that glistened like pools of melted ice. The right-hand seat was occupied by a stern-looking elf in full armor, the fine links of his silver mail flowing to match his lean body. In the left-hand seat was an elven woman, her flowing gown the same shade of green as Baerauble's robes.

In the center sat the tallest and eldest of the elves. He was a wan, thin creature, to Faerlthann's eyes as ancient as the forest itself . . . or more. This elf's eyes gleamed like bright gems at the bottom of great, sunken pits, and his skin possessed a sallow luminescence, strengthened by the light filtering through the fabric of the pavilion. The ancient elf was not unmarked; down one side of his face ran a single great scar. On his brow, the elf wore a circlet of gold, its three tall spires set with purple amethysts.

"Greetings, Faerlthann Obarskyr, son of Ondeth," said the eldest elf calmly, his voice a rich symphony of pleasantry. "I bring you the greetings of Iliphar Nelnueve,

Lord of the Scepters, and all the elven peoples. Our condolences on the passing of your father."

"You did not summon me from my father's funeral for mere condolences, elf lord," said Faerlthann flatly. "What is so important that I could not finish honoring my father's memory?"

The stern armored elf on the right stiffened, and Faerlthann saw him grip the arms of his seat firmly. The female on the left-hand seat, on the other hand, merely raised her eyebrows and gave young Faerlthann a small smile.

If the centermost elf was stung by the human's words, he did not show it. "It is your father we need to discuss with you. More importantly, the legacy of your father, to you and to the humans who remain in Cormyr."

Baerauble came forward and placed himself to one side, between Faerlthann and the elven triumvirate. He was choosing his side in this fight, Faerlthann thought. In the middle. Faerlthann felt abandoned and alone, but did not let his worry cloud his face or his judgment.

The elf continued, ignoring the human mage. "There have been humans who came into the wolf woods before Ondeth's people. Some passed through. Some sought to despoil our lands. The former we allowed to pass. The latter . . . we destroyed. Your father, and those he brought with him, did not pass through. Nor did they despoil our hunting grounds. They kept to their first glade and rarely harmed the land beyond it. Ondeth's people served as adequate caretakers of the land under your father's leadership."

"My father was not . . ." began Faerlthann, but Baerauble raised a warning hand. Interrupting a lord among the elves simply was not done.

"Your father was the leader of your people, regardless of his own denials. When those of Suzail needed direction, they turned to him. When they needed strength, to him. When they needed wisdom, to him. He may not have carried the title of king or prince or duke, but he was your people's leader, and now he is no more. And he left no one ready to take his place. Typically short-sighted. Typically human."

Faerlthann started to growl another protest, but Baer-auble raised his hand once more, this time adding a sharp glare. Let the elf speak, he seemed to say, and *listen*. Faerlthann nodded and held his tongue.

"So now we have a town full of humans, not the few dozen he told us of a mere twenty years back. A town almost in our midst, full of humans without a leader, without a master, without written law. Held together for the shortest period by one honest human. And now that human is no more." He raised a hand in what might almost have been a salute—or a gesture of resignation.

"We few of the elven court have become divided, even as your kind multiply," the elf lord continued, the smallest of smiles flickering across his face. He motioned to the armored elf on his right. "Othorion Keove, here, believes that with Ondeth's passing, our agreement is null and void, and Ondeth's people should be driven into the sea."

He motioned to his left. "Alea Dahast, who once hunted men in this forest, now believes you should be allowed to remain, but confined to your current warren. Were you to spread farther or increase your numbers beyond reasonable bounds, you would have to be destroyed, or else we would be destroyed."

Faerlthann put his rage aside and started to listen to the elf—not just to the words, heavy with foreboding, but to the tone. Iliphar sounded old and tired, like Faerlthann's father after an evening of arguing with his mother.

Others have pressured him into this, Faerlthann thought. Probably the chain-clad one on the right. That one had a hungry hunter's look to him. He appeared to be looking for any excuse to put Suzail to the torch.

Yet the choices they spoke of were abhorrent. Even if Faerlthann had wanted to, he could not abandon Suzail, nor could he prevent it from growing. More people were arriving each month. Now there were tales of plague and lurking sea monsters in Marsember, and boats were passing that city by, to moor at smaller but cleaner Suzail. Deciding not to grow might be an elven solution, but it could not be a human one.

"There is another possibility," announced Baerauble. "You could recognize the sovereignty of Lord Iliphar in all things and allow appointment of a minister to oversee your community. You could therefore remain in the Land of the Purple Dragon."

Baerauble turned his head briefly to the trifold throne. The woman on the left favored him with a radiant smile. Faerlthann saw what was going on here. Baerauble would be that minister and would run things as the elves saw the world and as these forest folk desired. No Suzailan townsman would stand for that.

Faerlthann was about to speak when there was a disturbance behind him, outside the pavilion. Ondeth's son considered the time it would take for a band of men to organize and ride out to the elven pavilion. He almost let a grim smile creep onto his face. Even the densest Suzailan would be able to figure out where Baerauble Elffriend had disappeared to with Ondeth's only son and heir.

They charged into the main area, men in leathers with swords already drawn. The elven nobles fell back without argument or threat. Faerlthann saw some of them smiling indulgently at the humans, as a man might smile at the antics of a yapping puppy.

The humans came in a tight group, Arphoind in the lead. He was flanked by the two elder Silvers, each with his oldest boy, and several Turcassans and Merendils brought up the rear. These latter were recent arrivals from the south, where folk held low opinions of both elves and wizards.

Upon seeing Faerlthann, Arphoind raised a shout, echoed by the others. The young Obarskyr held up both hands for silence. The group quieted and slowly sheathed their blades. None re-tied the peace bonds that would prevent their swords from being swiftly drawn again.

Turning back to the throne, Faerlthann saw that the warrior-elf was on his feet with his sword drawn. As he glared over it at the intruding humans, the elven blade shimmered with its own light, and small arcs of lightning sizzled along its blade. Iliphar put a hand on Othorion's shoulder, and the armored elf slowly sheathed his weapon and sank back into his seat. The fury in his sky-blue eyes remained.

"Gentlemen," said Baerauble, "we were discussing the fate of this land, called by some Cormyr, by others the Wolf Woods, and by still others the Land of the Purple Dragon. So far the following suggestions have been put forth: a purge of all humans; a containment of all humans; or a recognition of elvish sovereignty under a minister."

The gathered humans started shouting at once, primarily to reject all the offered options. Faerlthann held up a hand, and once more they grew quiet. "I have heard two options from elves and one from an elf-friend. What of a human solution? Did not Ondeth agree to care for this land placed in his trust?"

"He did so," admitted Baerauble, speaking for the elves.

"And how long have we been in this land?"

"Twenty summers," said the mage.

"My father saw sixty ere he died," said Faerlthann, "so he spent a third of his life here, farming and helping other farmers. True?"

Baerauble made an exaggerated nod.

"Lord Iliphar," Faerlthann asked calmly, "may I ask your age?"

The elf lord permitted himself the briefest of smiles. "I see your point. No, this land is not as it was a third of my lifetime ago. In many ways it is tamer, with many of the more dangerous beasts hunted out, never to return. The forest buffalo were diminished before you even arrived, and Ondeth himself proved his mettle against one of the last giant owlbears. Even the dragons are not what they were; the greatest sleep their lives away far from contact with any of us. And we, too, grow fewer, as more elves travel north to rejoin our cousins of Cormanthor. The wolves survive, of course, and the deer and the great cats, but, no, the land is not as it was. It would be folly to deny that."

"So we have been suitable caretakers of the small patch of land entrusted to us?"

"Ondeth was, but Ondeth is no more."

"Ondeth lives on in me," said Faerlthann firmly. "And I am prepared to take on his responsibilities."

"We offered a crown to your father, human," spat the warrior-elf Othorion. "He threw it back in our faces."

There was muttering behind Faerlthann. The young Obarskyr knew of the offer, as did the Silvers, but they had kept much of what had occurred that day quiet. "He rejected an offer of the elves to be the keeper of humans. He did not want to be a puppet dancing to an elven tune. Did I quote him correctly, mage?"

"Sufficiently closely," the lean wizard agreed. Baerauble had an anxious, excited expression on his face. Faerlthann took that as a good sign.

"A rulership demanded from the elves is as weak as a rulership offered by the elves," Iliphar responded calmly.

"I am not demanding this of you," said Faerlthann, turning to the other assembled men. "Good gentles, these elves will not deal with us seriously unless I hold some sort of power in our community. You've known me almost all my life. If you must have an official leader, is there any better available, any you'd rather serve than I?"

Arphoind was the first to reply. The youth strode forward and stood before Faerlthann. He drew his sword as he did so, and drove it into the soft earth before him point first. Kneeling by the blade, he said, "I pledge my loyalty to House Obarskyr, to the memory of Ondeth, and the blood that runs in your veins." His thin voice cracked and quaked, but the words rang clearly throughout the pavilion.

Faerlthann pulled Mondar's blade free of the earth and gently tapped the youth on the shoulder. "Arise, Sir

Bleth, first of those who serve me."

Arphoind's kneeling pledge was followed by those of the Silver brothers and their sons. Then the Turcassans and the Merendils knelt, and one of the Rayburtons. All swore their fealty to House Obarskyr and named Faerlthann their lord.

Faerlthann turned back to the throne, a lump in his throat, and saw that Iliphar had left his throne and was now gliding down the wide steps toward him. The elder elf moved effortlessly, his robes billowing like the sails of a great sailing ship as he drifted down to earth.

At last the ancient elf stood face-to-face with the young human. Iliphar towered over Faerlthann. His sallow, hollow-cheeked face was stern as he gazed down upon the younger man. Faerlthann tried to keep awe from his face as their gazes met. The elf lord's deep old eyes danced with . . . mischief?

"We meet now as equals," Faerlthann said, rousing himself with an effort. "As leaders of our people. Let us come to terms now."

"If you would be king, you must have a crown," said the elf, raising his slender hands to the circlet that banded his own brow. Behind Iliphar, the warrior-elf spat a protest, but the old elf took off his crown and held it aloft over Faerlthann's head.

"I cannot make you king, for your own people have done that," said Iliphar, and though his voice seemed quiet, it called forth echoes from trees outside the pavilion. "I only recognize that fact in granting you this crown, Faerlthann Obarskyr, son of Ondeth, lord of Suzail, master of the humans within it, and King of Cormyr, the Wolf Woods . . . the Forest Kingdom. I call upon you to protect this land as the elves have protected it, to recognize the rights of the elves to hunt within its domains, and for you and your heirs to show wisdom and compassion in the dispatch of your duties. Your father ruled for twenty years while rejecting any title. You will have the harder job, for much will be expected of you."

With that, the elder elf laid the circlet on Faerlthann's

head. Jaquor Silver led a shout of acclaim from the watching humans.

Othorion, the warrior-elf, let out a cry of rage as his radiant blade slid out of its scabbard once more. "Has age finally addled you, my lord," he snarled, "that you invest such children—such rough, uncultured, unfeeling, *unwashed* cubs—to protect our forest? I say we should drive them like the rothé before us and make this land truly ours again, washing free the stain they've left upon it with their own blood! Let us be masters of this forest once more!"

There was a murmur of assent, small but definitely present, from the watching elves. The men drew together, hands straying to their blades. Arphoind Bleth strode to Faerlthann's side, his blade half drawn.

Baerauble broke in. "Your first challenge, O Lord of the Land of the Purple Dragon. How do you respond to this?" There was a trace of mockery in his tone.

No, not mockery, thought Faerlthann, putting out a hand to stay Arphoind. The wizard was stressing the title of the land. The fledgling King of Cormyr looked at Baerauble, seeing if the mage's tone meant sarcasm. No, the wizard was nervous now . . . more anxious than before. What did he mean, then? And why did he keep mentioning the mythical purple dragon?

Suddenly it dawned on Faerlthann Obarskyr what the wizard meant and whose side Baerauble was on, after all.

"When I was but a child," he began, nodding toward Baerauble, "a venerable and wise elf-friend betimes would sit by our fire and tell stories. His tales were wondrous and great, and chief among them was the saga of an elven king who bested in single combat a great dragon whose black scales had turned purple with age. This elven king's battle skill was mighty, but his words were mightier still. He showed the dragon that twenty elves might fall to slay a dragon, but twenty more elves would come to replace them—to face no dragon, for the loss of a dragon is a harder thing to recover from than the loss of a band of elves."

The young man looked at Iliphar. Yes, the lights of mischief were dancing in the elf lord's eyes, and something else, too. Respect.

"So I offer you the same hard lesson, Othorion. You may step down from your high throne and slay me, and perhaps kill all my companions. You might even burn Suzail as other human camps have been burned. But that will not be the end of things, for more humans will come. And these may not be as friendly or as kind as we of Ondeth's people. If they find our bones, they will know peril awaits in the woods. They may be armed with fire, with steel, and with magic. They may choose to destroy your woods to take the land for themselves. And even in our graves, we will have won, if only in bringing your world to ruin. Is that what you choose, warrior-elf?"

Othorion opened his mouth, then closed it. He looked at Lord Iliphar. The elder elf raised an eyebrow, daring the elf to speak. Slowly, and very reluctantly, Othorion sheathed his blade once more.

"You take on a heavy mantle," said Iliphar, turning back to Faerlthann. "Your father's work and lands and these woods of the elves are great and carry a great weight. There will be more humans, and you and your kindred must teach them, as Ondeth was taught, to use the land but to respect it. It is a daunting job."

Faerlthann nodded.

"For that reason, I think you need an advisor," said the elf lord, "one who will remain with you and aid you and your descendants. One vested in the knowledge of the elves and in the passions of humans." He turned toward Baerauble.

For the first time, the mage was surprised. "Me? I cannot! Lord, I have served you well these many years!"

"And you shall serve us well again," said Iliphar, "for humans have short memories and short lives, and you must guide them."

"But I have a life among the elves!" the wizard protested, motioning to the elf woman on the throne. "I

have my love and children here . . . and my grandchildren!"

"And they shall be cared for as well," said Iliphar, stepping before the mage. "I know you well, Baerauble
Etharr. You calculated that these other humans would
follow young Faerlthann here, and you contrived to make
them search their hearts and honor Ondeth's memory
and his son with a crown. And you aided this young king
in finding the perfect tale to cool hot Othorion. You prodded, poked, and manipulated us all. And all—I trust—
because you desired to protect this land."

The elder elf smiled. "And now you *will* protect this
land and its rulers. You will advise, and calculate, and
teach now among humans. I charge you with protecting
the crown of Cormyr."

Baerauble sputtered a few protests but trailed off into
silence. Looking into Iliphar's eyes, he nodded in surrender and acceptance.

The elder elf muttered a few words in a tongue
Faerlthann did not recognize, then placed his hands on
either side of the wizard's brow, as if he, too, were being
crowned with an invisible helm. There was a brief, soft
glow where the elf's hands touched Baerauble's face.

The elf lord stepped back. He looked older now, but his
eyes still danced. "We will go now. You shall see less and
less of us with each passing generation. Perhaps we will
become legends like Thauglor the Black, the great purple
dragon. But know that we lived, as did he, and remember
that old legend you spoke of as well, for it holds both a
promise . . . and a warning."

It was then that Faerlthann realized that the elves
were disappearing. One at a time, they were turning
translucent and fading from view like fog on a sunny summer morning. The elven court held some powerful magic,
it seemed. As the men gaped around, knuckles white on
the hilts of their blades, the elves simply vanished, in ones
and twos, like wisps of smoke. As Iliphar spoke, more disappeared, until at last all that remained were the humans
and the three elves who had sat on the thrones.

The warrior-elf Othorion nodded grimly to the humans as he faded away, and as he did so, the voluminous tent began to fade as well.

Alea Dahast rose and gently descended the steps, standing at last before Baerauble. Under her feet, the steps melted away into smoke, and as the throne dwindled into drifting shadows, the elf lady parted the human wizard's reaching hands and reached up her hands to his face.

The mage looked devastated as she took his head in her hands and kissed him, gently and yet deeply . . . almost hungrily. For two breaths and more, the kiss went on, and everyone heard Jaquor Silver shift and swallow at the sight. And then suddenly Alea was gone, leaving Baerauble staring at nothing, with tears running down his cheeks, holding only empty air.

Iliphar placed a hand on Faerlthann's shoulder. "Rule well, child," he said gently.

And then he, too, was gone, and with him the great pavilion. King Faerlthann and the nobles of Cormyr were alone in the smoky dawn of their first day.

11

In the Shadow of the King
Year of the Gauntlet
(1369 DR)

f you should . . . ever cross into Sembia . . . there's a little place called Yuthgalaunt, on the road from Ordulin to Yhaunn," Baron Thomdor whispered, gasping with effort. Eyes bright with sudden resolve, the stout noble was lying on his curtained, guarded bed trying to grip Vangerdahast's arm firmly, but lacking the strength. "There's a lady in a cottage by the well there—over forty winters old, she'd be now, and a beauty. . . ."

Vangerdahast looked across the sickbed at Gwennath. The Tymoran priestess had remained by the baron's bedside since the first day. She had gotten some badly needed sleep, but she still looked haggard and red-eyed. The old wizard did not quite manage to suppress a sigh.

The baron ignored the wizard's glance and added fiercely, "Hear me! I wronged her years ago; said I'd come back to wed her when I had made something of myself . . . and I . . . never have. Will you take her coin enough to see her through her shadowed years? And send my apology? It's . . . one of my few regrets. . . ."

"Of course I will, Thom," the Royal Magician said, "if ever I have to. But you need not worry yourself about things undone before death yet—you've years left. You can ride over and marry the wench yourself!"

The tired gray-blue eyes of the Warden of the Eastern Marches blazed up into his. "Don't toss courtiers' lies at me, wizard! I know what happened to Bhereu. This gaudy tent here is my deathbed. Azoun's lying near death somewhere *that* way—"

He waved one large and hairy hand eastward, toward the next chamber. The hand trembled and quickly fell back to the bed furs. He growled, "And so here I am, with none of my men clanking in to tell me jokes. No pretty lasses coming to bring me flowers and wish me better—"

"Huh!" Gwennath, the Bishop of the Black Blades, said indignantly from across the bed. "What am I if not a pretty lass?"

Thomdor turned his head to face her with visible effort and said, "Oh, gods, don't start! Ye're an honest sword maid, not a perfumed court wench!"

Gwennath winked at Vangerdahast, and the wizard hid a smile, watching the baron rouse himself in embarrassment. "I meant no slight!" the old warrior protested, and then the color went out of his face and he fell back onto the pillows and gasped. "So here I am . . . waiting in the king's shadow to die . . . just as I've been waiting, come to think of it, all my life."

He managed a wry smile as he turned to look at the Royal Magician, and he was still smiling when the light in his eyes went out, a grayness came over his cheeks, and his head lolled sideways. His eyelids slammed down like shudders, and the chamber was filled with his ragged breathing.

Vangerdahast bent forward with a swiftness born of fear and almost bumped noses with the priestess, who was making the same lunge from her side of the bed. Thomdor still lived, his breathing slow but even. He'd fallen into the deepest of slumbers. "This could go on for years," the old wizard murmured.

"Both he and the king roused this morning for the first time. Yet after knowing the world and their wits this morn, both he and His Majesty have failed fast," Gwennath said softly, looking down at the deepening lines on the baron's face. "I wanted him to pass, if he pass he must, in peace . . . but to rouse him to fight on if he could be roused."

The High Wizard of Cormyr looked into her eyes from only inches away and said gently, "You did well to summon me, Bishop of the Black Blades. You have my thanks. You continue to do Cormyr great service. Know that I, at least, take notice and am grateful."

Gwennath of Tymora gave him a wan smile, then reached out to squeeze his arm. Vangerdahast was careful to still his automatic reactions of stiffening warily and reaching for a belt wand, allowing himself—for once—the trust to merely reach out and return the gesture.

"I'll stay with him, whatever befalls," the priestess said, indicating a cot on the far side of the canopied bed.

Vangerdahast smiled, glanced at the four motionless, full-armored Purple Dragons standing with grounded swords at the four corners of the bed, and replied, "And I'll be sure that some of the men he commands come up to slip him wine and sweets and a little rough cheer."

"Do so," the priestess agreed, sitting down on the edge of her cot, where she could watch the baron's face. She lifted a hand in farewell.

Vangerdahast waved to her, feeling the weariness of too little sleep as a bone-deep ache in his shoulders and at the back of his head, and strode to the guarded door. He waited for the guards to open it and reveal the wary faces of still more guards, parted them with a gesture, and passed on into Gryphonsblade Hall, where the king lay.

Watchful Purple Dragons with naked swords in their hands were everywhere, peering grimly at the priests and war wizards flanking the high bed and warily escorting the excitedly murmuring nobles one by one up to the pale figure that lay on it. Like Thomdor, His Majesty had awakened that morning as well but remained stricken by the affliction that was slowly killing them both.

An eagerness gnawed at the air in the sapphire-domed room . . . a tension of waiting. The nobles of half the realm, and as many rich merchants of Suzail as cared to bribe a minor noble to serve as escort through the court bureaucracy, had gathered to see Azoun's passing. They were there to see the king close up—closer than most had ever gotten in their lives—and to whisper prayers and wishes of encouragement to His Majesty, in hopes of being remembered in the royal will and so they could say to neighbors and descendants, "Azoun conferred with me on his deathbed, you know, and I told him . . ." But mostly they were here to see the king die.

If you gave not a thought to civil war or invaders rushing down to ravage the realm, it was thrilling to be right on the spot when something that would shake all Faerûn was happening right before your eyes!

Those who knew what it would *really* take to shake all Faerûn, Vangerdahast thought, were busily arming and patrolling their holds or hiding what they valued, not standing gossiping in the long lines that wound up from the palace gates, waiting to get in here. The catch-phrase "The king is dying!" had spread from one end of Suzail to the other in a matter of hours after the return of the hunting party, of course, and the court had been jammed—was still jammed—with folk demanding, pleading, insisting, and bribing their way in to see their king . . . while he still was their king. There was always a chance that someone with a knife or a suicide spell would try to make sure of what the abraxus hadn't—yet—and so layer after layer of spells had been laid and the king put under heavy guard.

Huh, thought the court wizard sourly, we should *all* be under heavy guard, with this many nobles flitting in and out. Or should that more properly be *crawling* in and out?

That thought carried him almost into the long, pointed nose of the noble who was badgering the king right now, some popinjay who wasn't going to let a comatose ruler get in the way of seeking personal favors. Blundebel Eldroon, from the minor so-called nobility of Marsember, if memory served right . . .

"Your Majesty," Eldroon was saying earnestly, "if you could just see your way clear to signing—"

"The king won't be signing anything today," Vangerdahast said firmly. "Today is cloudy."

The noble straightened up with a frown. "Go away, old man! This is the king I'm talking with, and I'm a very important—"

"And widely praised buffoon known to one and all as Blundebel Eldroon, among ruder things," the Royal Magician interrupted. "Go away. Come back when the weather is clear."

" 'Weather is clear'? Guards—take away this madman!"

A Purple Dragon as tall and muscular as the front end of a horse grinned, sheathed his sword, and obediently took Blundebel Eldroon by the elbow and forearm, lifted him off the ground, and trotted to a side door.

"What— Hey! Ho! What're you doing?" the Marsembian noble shouted.

"Taking the madman away, as you requested," was the gruff reply. An instant before a door banged open, Blundebel had a dizzying glimpse of several more grinning guards swinging wide another door onto a vista of descending marble steps, and the painful grip on his arm was released. He barely had time to grasp the fact that he was sailing through the air, down a flight of stairs that looked very solid and hard indeed, when he wasn't anymore. His roar of pain was lost in the laughter from above.

Back in Gryphonsblade Hall, the next noble in line, smiling uneasily at the greatest mage in the realm, wisely decided to keep silent and await a later moment to speak with the king.

"Old friend! Your match hat is a werebeast, I see!" Azoun smiled weakly, then frowned as he himself heard what he had said. "Your match-hat . . ." he began again, "is a were-beast," then shook his head. Whatever fever raged in his brain prevented him from communicating his ideas fully. The King tried to wave an arm, but the limb wouldn't do more than twitch on the silken sheets and then fall still again.

"Yes," the Royal Magician agreed gravely, "My match hat *is* indeed a werebeast. I've thought that for some time. But how are *you*, my liege?"

"Several bottles of strong drink rage in my gut," Azoun said slowly, forcing each word and dropping one eyelid in a slow, deliberate wink. "All I *can* feel. Fingers . . . feet . . . nothing. A little dagger point of pain here, there. That's all."

He closed his eyes for a moment, and the wizard thought sleep had captured the king as it had the baron. Then Azoun's brows furrowed, and he opened his eyes again, spearing Vangerdahast with their intensity. "I am dying, am I not?" asked the king.

The wizard bent down to mutter in his ear, "We don't think so, but these vultures we call nobles do. Try to disappoint them for me, will you?"

Azoun tried to laugh, coughed with an alarming catch and a weak, sobbing breath, and shook his head. "They . . . just might be right . . . this once," he managed to wheeze.

Vangerdahast frowned. "Mounds of bull droppings to that! Majesty, there doesn't seem to be anything that can halt the poison yet, but we've barely begun to try—"

"The whole range of tortures on me. I know," the king replied, his voice growing stronger as he concentrated on his words. "Worse than the nobles, in their way."

"Your condition may be due to something found in warmer climes or even on another plane of existence," the court wizard said, still muttering. "All of our sages—and the Harpers, too, I'm told—are consulting with their brethren in other cities."

The king caught his eye. " 'Consulting with their brethren'? Is that not the phrase we used for a quick trip to Arabel—drinks to toast our arrival there, ladies to share them with? Back when we were young and healthy?"

The joke was as weak as its teller, but Vangerdahast laughed in relief. A flash, at least, of Azoun's true spirit meant the king hadn't given up on life just yet.

But the king was looking oddly green about the eyes, and his head had fallen back on the pillow again. "So . . . gods-blasted . . . tired," he gasped, his voice trailing away. A breath later he was asleep, eyes closed, head turned to one side.

"He needs to sleep, doesn't he?" the wizard asked the priests who were hastily gathering around the king's head, feeling at his hands and brow and neck.

One of them, a short man whose face was almost hidden by a bristling mustache, looked up. "Of course," he snapped. "Who can heal in peace with *this* going on?" He indicated the long line of waiting, chattering nobles with an angry wave of his hand.

Another turned from Azoun to say, "In general terms, I agree. Yet from time to time 'tis probably best if the king speaks with folk, as he did with you. The converse forces him to use his wits, especially if matters new to him, or which he's not considered in some time, are raised."

"Nonsense!" The first priest snarled. "He's not fallen on his head or been smitten with a mace! It's rest he needs, not a lot of chatter! I—"

"Your understanding of the king's condition is hardly—"

"I dispute what both of ye say! We of—"

Vangerdahast's hand went to his pocket belt, but instead of pulling out the whistle, he instead pulled out a milky flashstone. He held the magical stone up, and it issued a sharp, brilliant strobe of light, startling more than one holy man into a fall and shocking them all into silence.

The source of the blinding burst of radiance stood with his hands on his hips and looked grimly at them all. "If the king wakes and wants to talk to you or any of these nobles, let him. If he wants them to leave his side, see that they do. If any noble tries to rouse the king or complains about having to wait for his awakening, throw him out."

One of the priests blinked. "Throw a noble of the realm out of this chamber? Lord wizard, that's hardly—"

Vangerdahast held up an imperious hand. "I know. That's why these good Knights of the Purple Dragon around us here will enforce my command and bring chamberpots and pillows to any nobles who want to spend the night defending their precious place in line." He turned slowly, to catch the eyes of the men-at-arms, and collected many nods of grim satisfaction and a few open grins.

"If any noble has a formal complaint to make or tries to countermand my orders, refer him—personally—to me." He turned back to the priests and added darkly, "They should settle any matters pertaining to titular or property succession with their kindred first."

He looked slowly at each of the priests in turn, meeting their gazes, and asked, "Is there anything unclear in what I've just said? Does anyone find the slightest room for misunderstanding or speculation as to my will? Speak if so!"

Silence was his only reply. The Royal Magician smiled coldly and said to one of the guards, "Thanorbert, send pages down the line of nobles to repeat the orders I've given and send men enough after them to see that they aren't manhandled. A noble who lays an unfriendly finger on any page is to be thrown to the ground, lashed on the behind just once with a swordbelt—but make it a good blow—and thrown out, losing his place in line. All right?"

"More than all right, lord," the Purple Dragon veteran said from behind him. "It shall—enthusiastically—be done just as you have said."

"Good," the Royal Magician said and strode out of the hall without looking back. He passed through the Hornbow Bower, one of a number of small sitting rooms that littered the palace, marked by potted plants and ornate screens. He did not speak to the cooks and servants assembling there to prepare food for the war wizards, men-at-arms, and priests attending the king. Face set, the old wizard ignored greetings and queries alike and hurried out through the Mirror Bower, down the statue-lined Hall of Heroes. The normally silent, deserted hall was crammed with waiting nobles and a stolid trio of Purple Dragons, who moved up and down the line quelling fights and restoring queue jumpers to their former places. Many nobles called out to the wizard, and the armsmen quickly moved to hold back the few nobles headstrong enough to try to bar the court wizard's way.

Vangerdahast shook his head sadly at the chaos of sneering and declaiming and posturing—was *this* the best the realm could muster from its noble bloodlines?—but did not slow his stride. Soon he reached the end of the royal purple carpet, where the last pair of white marble statues guarded three doors that led from the hall.

The wizard took the door on the left, into the Argent Robing Room, and reached for a fine chain on his belt that held a certain key. His hand fell away again when he saw that a man he did not know was waiting for him, bareheaded but in battered and stained battle armor, flanked by two Purple Dragons. "Yes?" he asked shortly, his tone almost a challenge.

The man in armor bowed stiffly, metal plates shifting, and laid a hand on his breast, saying, "Eregar Abanther, servant of Tempus."

Vangerdahast nodded his head, and the priest continued. "We have prepared the duke's body for resting in state, Lord Wizard." He raised a hand and waved at the walls around him, asking delicately, "Where . . . ?"

"Our thanks, sword brother," the Royal Magician said gravely. "Let it be done fittingly. Algus of the Keys will give you the duke's sword. Take it and four of your brethren of good strength and shared size to carry the duke. Let there be four more holy men of Tempus with lit torches to serve as escort. Bid the carriers take down Bhereu's shield of honor from the Gallant Gallery—

Algus will show you where—and bear it in solemn procession to where the duke now lies, his sheathed sword upon it. Let such holy prayers as please Tempus be said then, and the duke taken up."

"Forthwith?"

Vangerdahast nodded. "Lead them yourself from that place. Bear him slowly, with dirge and tolling bell, through the palace, so the Purple Dragons you pass can give him sword salute, and take the fallen to the court, and to the Marble Forehall there. A bier awaits in that chamber. Lay him down there with the Warrior's Farewell."

The priest of Tempus bowed his head. "Lord, it shall be so."

Vangerdahast took a ring from his belt pouch and pressed it into Abanther's hand. It bore a device shaped like a golden lion and inscribed with the numeral 3.

"Redeem this at the treasury after the solemnities are done," he murmured. "They will have instructions to render unto you nine thousand golden lions, one thousand for each priest of Tempus who walks with the duke."

The priest bowed his head. "Tempus thanks you, lord."

"And I thank Tempus," the wizard said, startling Abanther with the ritual response known only to faithful followers of the god of battles. Then he inclined his head in dismissal and gestured to the guards to depart. They and the priest went out together, leaving Vangerdahast alone. He looked around, noted the two belarjacks, the unarmed servants guarding the door he'd come in by. The wizard nodded at them, then murmured a word he'd not used in a long time.

Utter darkness came down, darkness only he could see through. One of the servants cried out in alarm, but the Royal Magician spoke no word of explanation or reassurance as he drew forth the key he'd been reaching for earlier, went to a wall panel that very few living folk knew was a door, and unlocked it with the key while murmuring a spell to keep the enchanted guardian of the portal at bay.

There was a moment of swirling, fairylike chiming, a stirring of the air, and he was through the ward. In the room he'd left, the darkness should be clearing already. Ahead down a long passage stood a row of motionless guards in full armor. Vangerdahast strode right up to them and on past, and they stood like statues. "Helmed horrors" some called them; in truth, they were little more than empty suits of armor animated by his own spells. They guarded a door that the touch of his palm opened— a door that led into the Hidden Chambers.

Bright sun spilled down from a vaulting skylight into the comfortably furnished room before him. Bookshelves lined the walls, and on a huge table gleamed colorful maps of the Dragonreach lands, from Tunland as far east as the Vast. At the heart of the room, comfortable high-backed chairs and lounges surrounded a dragonhide rug. It yielded under his feet, soft and warm, as the Royal Magician strode from where his door opened, in the wall beside the fireplace, to face the two folk who sat waiting for him: Alaphondar, Sage Royal of Cormyr, and Filfaeril, the Dragon Queen. There were few people in the realm that the stout old court wizard knelt to, but he did so now, in true reverence.

Queen Filfaeril Selzair Obarskyr was blessed by the gods and her breeding with ice-blue eyes, golden blonde hair, exquisite carriage—so that she drew the eyes of all men and most women whenever she moved—a slender figure, and alabaster skin. What had attracted the interest of the young Azoun—for whom there was no shortage of available, even eager, stunningly beautiful women— however, was less her looks than her mind. Filfaeril was brilliant. She noticed everything that befell around her and understood people and implications better than many widely respected sages.

Her once exceptional beauty had begun its slow fade, but to men who respected intellect and stubborn bravery—and Vangerdahast was one of those—she was more beautiful than ever. Her poise and dignity still bewitched eyes that saw only external beauty; all that betrayed her

167

deep grief at the probable death of her husband now was the deep blue rings around her eyes. They gave Filfaeril an air of vulnerability, and Lord Alaphondar was obviously smitten with her, but Vangerdahast reminded himself of how often the queen bested the Dragon of Cormyr over the chessboard.

"Rise, old and faithful friend," she said quietly. "You of all men *are* the realm Azoun and I serve. I need your counsel and strength now, not your courtesy."

Vangerdahast rose and said gently, "Great lady, my courtesy *is* my strength."

She nodded, eyes flashing briefly in acknowledgment of, and agreement with, his words, then asked, "What news?"

"All Suzail—and probably most of the realm by now, for I know word has reached both Arabel and Marsember—has heard of Your Majesty's madness of grief and retreat to seclusion in Eveningstar. In the early hours of this morning, someone unleashed a flight of flying daggers and over a dozen helmed horrors into the temple of Lathander where you were supposedly staying. They made straight for the private apartments given over to the war wizardess posing as you, my queen, and took the lives of several underpriests and all of the openly posted Purple Dragon garrison. A full sword of additional knights—veterans ennobled by the king, not drawn from the established noble families of the realm—were stationed in the private apartments and did their utmost to protect the lady they thought was their queen. Four gave their lives; the others are all of the opinion that the attacking constructs they fought, and were forced to destroy in order to prevail, were directed by someone able to observe the fray at all times."

"In these days of magic for hire," Filfaeril said with a shrug, "almost anyone in the realm beyond a simple woodcutter or yeoman farmer could be involved in such an attack."

Both men nodded. "What is clear, great queen," Alaphondar said bluntly, "is that someone is willing to pay much to see the Obarskyr line broken, or at least a young, easily wed or easily swayed daughter on the throne."

"Safety demands that you disappear for a time," Vangerdahast added. Filfaeril looked at him for a long moment, her eyes locked with his.

"I see the wisdom in that," she said at last, "and yet, my lords, I must warn you that if Alaphondar's words are true—a most likely conclusion, I agree—you yourselves both stand in as great peril as I. If one is to sway my Tanalasta or Alusair, one will want all her trusted sources of support and advice permanently removed from the scene."

The Royal Magician shrugged. "For me to flee now would be to leave the realm unattended, surrendering the throne to anyone who wants it. We would thereby thrust the realm into chaos as every greedy hand grabs for the crown and inevitably battles other claimants. Moreover, if we all disappear, an observer can reach no other conclusion than that we have all gone into hiding—and a long and devastating hunt will begin." He shook his head and strode forward. "It would be Tethyr all over again.

"Nay, Highness," he continued, "our only hope lies in spreading the tale that more than one attack was made upon you in Eveningstar, and that the second succeeded, taking the lives of yourself and Lord Alaphondar here in a fireball or something else that left no bodies behind."

"While you remain behind to face the storm almost alone, in the greatest danger of all of us," Filfaeril said quietly, eyes troubled.

Vangerdahast smiled grimly and corrected her. "While I remain behind to enjoy the lion's share of the fun, watching the disloyal in our realm fall all over themselves and each other trying to take the Dragon Throne."

Something that was almost a smile rose to touch the queen's lips for just a moment, and she murmured, "I do almost envy you, my lord. I would dearly love to see some of the things that will unfold in fair Cormyr in the days ahead."

"So you accept, Your Majesty, that you must 'disappear' for a time?"

Filfaeril nodded slowly. "Know you both that my greatest desire is to remain with Azoun—in life and in death. Were the realm strong and a clear and rightful heir ready to take the crown, I would command you and all in the court, by your oaths, to make my husband's passing as painless as possible."

"It is a pity that you cannot take the throne yourself," said the wizard.

"It is a pity indeed," said the queen, "but only one born into the Obarskyr line may rule. I may wear a crown, but I cannot rule without my husband."

She rose and took two restless steps toward the fire. "The realm is not ready for smooth passage to the rule of an unchallenged heir . . . so I accede to your wise scheme, for crown and country, for king and Cormyr." She stared into the distance for a moment more, then turned to face Vangerdahast and Alaphondar. Next she took the slim everyday circlet of her rank from her head and held it out before her. The sapphires on its two brow spires flashed. "Do what you must do."

Vangerdahast bowed. "Lady Queen, my intent is to send you and the Sage Royal to Waterdeep, your shapes disguised by magic, to a household where certain loyal war wizards of the realm have already been installed to watch over you." The eyes of the Royal Magician and Lord Alaphondar met briefly; behind the queen's back, the sage nodded almost imperceptibly.

"If you lay your hand upon the bowl on yonder plinth and then put your crown in it, the circlet will sink into the metal and lie hidden, cloaked from all by the bowl's magic. Only your hand upon the bowl again can make it rise up and reappear."

Without hesitation, the queen did as he directed. When she turned around again, Alaphondar was gone. In his place stood the stooped, pox-marked figure of a stout, aged merchant in food-stained robes. The merchant bowed to her and grinned, displaying a smile that was missing rather more teeth than the Sage Royal had ever lost.

She smiled thinly. "And what am I to call you now, Alaphondar?"

"Ah, 'sluggard,' 'good-for-nothing husband,' and 'old fool' are all handy phrases," the old merchant told her, "but my name is Flammos Galdekund, and yours is Aglarra, my queen."

Filfaeril's eyebrows rose. "Won't the neighbors be a trifle surprised to see new inhabitants of whatever house or apartments you've chosen for us?"

"Nay, lady," Vangerdahast said. "Both Flammos and Aglarra really exist, and since their luggage has preceded them from the docks, they're expected back this very day from a long vacation in southern Amn, where they went to take healing waters at Iritue's Firesprings, because you fell so ill that your memories left you and your manner and even your voice changed."

The queen's smiled broadened, and she asked, "Yet I suppose I look as dumpy and shrewish as ever?"

The Royal Magician bowed. "Your Majesty is as quick and as wise as ever."

Filfaeril laughed, looking briefly like a much younger woman, and held out her arms. "Change me, then. I've a feeling I'm going to enjoy this!" Then she frowned. "Are there servants, or is Flammos going to grow very sick of partridge, hocks, onions, and mushroom stew? They're the only things I could ever make really well."

Both men snorted in amusement and said more or less in unison, "There are servants, great lady."

Flammos scratched himself and added, "But, O queen of my heart, you could tell them how to make your stew as often as you like. They might never get it just right, you know."

Unexpectedly she giggled. "Change me, Vangey," she said almost pleadingly.

"You'll lose something of your height and grace," the wizard warned, "and almost all of your great beauty."

"Understood," she said firmly. "Must I wait longer?

Change me and let us go, before I start to want this and that from my chambers and my resolve starts to go. . . ."

Vangerdahast touched her hand, her foot, her breast, and her forehead, stepped back, and carefully cast a long and rather involved spell. There was a brief flicker of light, and the Dragon Queen was gone.

A shorter, almost mannish woman with a pot belly, bodice to match, and large, pimpled chin glared at him from where the queen stood. "Well?" she rasped. "Is it a good idea to ask you for a mirror?"

Vangerdahast shook his head. The queen nodded ruefully, took a few experimental steps, wiggled her hips as she looked down to watch her heavy midsection sway, and stamped her feet. "Right," she announced gruffly. "I'm ready."

She ran an exploratory hand over her chin as Flammos stumped up to take her arm, and said, "Hmm . . . tell me, husband mine, do I need a shave as badly as I think I do?"

Both men hooted with laughter, and Vangerdahast reached to take her hand and kiss it. "You're itching to be the terror of the young men of Waterdeep, I see," he said, "so I'll bid you farewell for now, and—"

Aglarra Galdekund snatched her hand away from him, growled fiercely, *"Well!"* and then seized his ears firmly with both hands, dragged the wizard's face down to where she could kiss it firmly on the lips. After she had done so, she said, eyes inches from his, "Guard the realm for us, lord wizard, as our thoughts guard you. Guard it and keep it safe for us all."

"Lady," Vangerdahast replied, feeling suddenly humble again, "I shall." He stepped back, murmured, "Keep still now," waved to them both, and cast the spell.

A glow grew about the Galdekunds as they stood there on the warm dragonhide before the fire. The glow blazed with sudden brilliance, then faded—and when it was gone, they were gone, too.

The Royal Magician shook his head wearily and went to the nearest chair, sinking down into it thankfully to discover that Filfaeril had left behind a dainty little glass and her silver-mounted bodice flask on the table beside it. He picked it up, finding it still warm from her body, and brought it to his nose to smell . . . yes, the last faint wisps of her perfume. He smiled and opened it. Gods, but he was tired.

Spiced wine—Tethyrian tanagluth, his favorite!

"Thank you, great lady," he murmured, pouring the ruby-hued liquid into the tiny glass with slow, deliberate care.

Raising it to his lips, Vangerdahast sipped gently at the welcome fire and thought about the days ahead. Azoun had been—nay, at this moment still *was*—a great king . . . perhaps too great. Even in the crusade there had been little thought he would ever die. Very few plans had been made . . . plans that should have been made.

The glass had somehow become empty. Vangerdahast reached for the flask again. Had there ever been a change of power so precipitous and dangerous as this one?

And would a certain Royal Magician be strong enough to do what he would have to do?

12

The Insufficient King
Year of the Dun Dragon
(245 DR)

agrast Dracohorn, nobleman of Cormyr and steward of the Royal House of Obarskyr, fidgeted in his duskwood chair, wondering if he were strong enough to do what needed to be done. An upstairs room in the Ram and Duck would not have been his first choice for a meeting of traitors. Indeed, Sagrast would prefer not to be a traitor at all, but the reigns of mad Boldovar and now poor, inept Iltharl had given him little choice.

The room itself was rough-hewn and ill-kept, a memory of Suzail's early days. There were fewer and fewer of these rough inns in the city itself these days, though they were common enough beyond the city's walls, in the countryside and in distant Arabel. The timbers were exposed, with muddy patches of dried wattle crumbling between them. Most of the furniture had been broken and inexpertly repaired several times. None of the line of peg-hung mugs on the wall matched. Every tread on the floor reverberated through the loose floorboards of the building.

There was one advantage to this place, Sagrast thought. There was little chance of meeting any of the aristocracy here. That's probably why the wizard had suggested it.

The window shutters, mostly wooden slats set with broken bottle bottoms, had been swung fully open, allowing the sounds and smells of the street below to waft into the room. It was the first hot spell of the summer, and the rot of meat and smell of bodies and offal and horses rose to Sagrast's nostrils. The stench almost took away the bitter taste of the dark, grainy ale that clung tenaciously to the sides of the nobleman's mug.

Sagrast hung back from the open window, knowing on one hand the chance of being seen was minimal, but fearing such a discovery nonetheless. Even if this meeting should prove innocuous, being seen in this place would raise questions in King Iltharl's delicate court.

From his viewpoint, he could see a small part of the city. Most of the buildings were wood-and-wattle, with rough thatched roofs. A few builders on the hillside had taken to using stone for the foundation and lower floors. Only after several goblin raids on the city and complaints from the soldiers about trying to fight in the thick smoke of a wall set alight by brush-carrying foes had Iltharl approved replacement of the wooden palisade with a real stone wall.

Faerlthann's Keep was stone, of course, from shallow dungeon to highest battlement. The great tower, seat of the Obarskyr power, rose from the hillside like a stake from a vampire's chest and seemed to accuse Sagrast of his intended crimes. The keep's windows were barred slits, a memory of Boldovar's time, and Sagrast wondered if anyone stood behind those slits, scanning the city . . . watching for traitors. Watching for him.

The wizard was there when Sagrast turned back to the room. The nobleman hadn't heard him enter, but then again, he never did. Despite himself, Sagrast started at the sight of the mage sprawling like an ancient spider in the chair on the opposite side of the table.

Baerauble the Venerable, High Wizard of Cormyr, sprawled across the chair like a discarded child's doll, all elbows and knees. The mage had always been thin—nay, emaciated, a scarecrow of a wizard. His beard showed only the slightest streaks of its original red, and his hairline had retreated to the crown of his head. His eyes were as cold and ancient as a dragon's. He was dressed, as ever, in the forest green that had become known as "his" color, but the cut of his robes was archaic, harking back—like this tavern—to older and better times in Cormyr.

"Good of you to come," he said simply.

"When a wizard calls, you cannot pretend to not be at home," said Sagrast, bowing slightly. The High Wizard was the most powerful man from Suzail to Arabel, and with the death of Boldovar three winters back, the most dangerous.

"How are matters with Iltharl, the young king?" asked the mage.

Sagrast blew the air out of his cheeks, taking the seat opposite the mage. "As bad as before. He makes no decisions and allows no one else to make any, either. He prefers to be among his sculptures and paintings or listening to lutes and poems, or hosting his parties and feasts. Elvish is becoming the court language, for any who speak it gain his attention first."

"There have been studious kings before," noted Baerauble. "Rhiiman the Glorious, who first pushed back the borders of the forest, and Elder Tharyann, Boldovar's father, who saw the leave-taking of the last great elven families."

"Aye, and Rhiiman slew the last great red dragon of the Wyvernwater, and Tharyann put down the first rebellion of Arabel. This Iltharl is a wan, pale king, moved by his courtiers and consorts. The people are growing very restive, and those of us charged with maintaining the realm have become . . . extremely concerned."

"Convince me," the wizard said softly. "Why are things so bad?"

Sagrast licked his lips. There was still a chance the wizard would turn on him and his allies. "There are goblins and orcs on the road. Bandits and thieves join them, and they grow bolder by the day, while the king's guards hug the tower like children afraid of shadows. Arabel is in rebellion once more, and Iltharl has let it go its own way. There are shortages now in the markets. Some matrons are now wearing daggers openly at their belts to walk the streets and shop in safety. And the Purple Dragon has been seen in the ruins of abandoned Marsember."

The mage made a harrumphing noise. "Every time someone needs an ill omen, the Purple Dragon seems to appear. Usually it is a red dragon espied in moonlight or a small black seen at a distance. And people see all sort of things in plague-ridden Marsember. All else you say is true; do not muddle it with fantasy."

"Many of the lesser nobles are taking greater liberties, and some are now refusing to pay their taxes and raising militias of their own. The trio of Silver families— Huntsilver, Crownsilver, and Truesilver, all the traditional eyes and long arms of the king—are too close to the throne to see the danger. Mewling toadies, they play to Iltharl's ego for his favor and spend their time thanking the gods that Iltharl is not Boldovar the Mad. But even the Mad King held the reins of state firmly when he was in his right mind. The Silvers cannot see that the realm is crumbling around them!"

"And you do."

"I represent a small group of nobles of . . . middling power," said Sagrast, "mostly families who have arisen since the days of Faerlthann himself. We have come to see things the same way, because what we see, however bleak, is the truth of things. The kingdom has been wounded by a mad king, and now it may be destroyed by a weak king. The elder nobles serve out of tradition, but some seek to break up the kingdom and seize their own territories. Our small houses would be swallowed in such strife, yet we cannot convince the crown of the dangers."

"And your solution is regicide," said the mage, his voice as cold as a steel blade.

Sagrast spread his hands in front of him, as if to ward

off a blow. "No, lord wizard—not if it can be helped! I have served Iltharl well, and he is not a bad man. He is only a bad king. We mean him no harm. We just need a decisive leader."

"And you have one in mind," said the mage, looking at the young noble stonily. Sagrast wished that the wizard would blink, and not for the first time he found himself wondering if the mage was merely sounding him out, only to wave a hand and magically transport him to a dungeon cell.

Sagrast took a deep breath. "Iltharl has a sister . . . Gantharla."

"A fine, strong young woman," Baerauble agreed, nodding. "The blood of the Obarskyrs runs strong in that one. And some fear she is truly Boldovar's daughter, brash and impulsive. She has done well in patrolling the Western Marches with her foresters, and I noticed that the marches were noticeably absent in your list of woes. But the Dragon Throne is held through primogeniture. The Crown of Cormyr has always passed to the eldest surviving son."

Sagrast held out one hand to emphasize his point. "Yes, but she is Obarskyr blood, and were she to marry and produce an heir, there would at least be a chance for the monarchy! Iltharl has been barren—with his wife, and among his consorts. If Gantharla could whelp a male child, then Iltharl could step down in favor of a legitimate successor."

"I don't remember Gantharla mentioning being interested in 'whelping' anything at the moment," said Baerauble dryly.

"Well, we were thinking . . . um, that Kallimar Bleth would be a suitable husband."

"*You* were thinking, or Kallimar?" asked the wizard. "Or does Bleth even know of your plots?"

"Well, I . . . " Sagrast thought of the dungeons. He would not choose to share them with another angry co-plotter. "I'm not comfortable talking about who else knows of this."

The wizard favored Sagrast with a smile. "Kallimar is Mondar reborn—large, dark-haired, and proud. And like Mondar, he is crude, violent, bad-tempered, and vicious. Remember, I knew the first Bleth to walk Cormyr two and half centuries ago. Do you really think that Gantharla, who's at home in the saddle and a leader of border foresters, would be interested in such a man?"

Sagrast cleared his throat. "Well, we were thinking . . . or I was thinking . . ."

"That I would wave my hands and work some enchantment over her, eh?" said the wizard. "No, you weren't—but you were hoping I thought you were." His eyes were like two blades, boring deep into Sagrast's own. "You've survived Boldovar and even served Iltharl well, Dracohorn. What were you really hoping for?"

"I was hoping . . . *we* were hoping . . . that we could convince you to stay out of this matter." Sagrast winced, knowing he could have phrased it better and hoping the powerful mage would not take offense.

Baerauble simply nodded. "And by doing nothing, I take it you mean just let you pitch Kallimar's case to Gantharla, perhaps even convince her that it would be good for the kingdom itself, arrange a marriage, and work subtly on His Majesty to convince him he would be better off in private life?"

Sagrast agreed fervently. "It's not as if we would not appreciate any support you could—" His excited rush of words were stopped by the surprising thing the wizard did then. Baerauble laughed.

It was a dry, macabre laugh, the sort puppeteers used when portraying a ghost or lich. It was a rattling of bones that shook the wizard's empty form. Sagrast had never heard it before and hoped he would not hear it again.

"Well, yours is the first proposal I've heard that did not involve poisoning the king immediately or smuggling a dagger-wielding Thayvian maiden in among his personal favorites. Perhaps the nobility is on the verge of attaining civilization after all."

179

Baerauble leaned forward over the table, and Sagrast felt himself being drawn forward in response. "Do you think," the mage asked, his voice suddenly fierce, "that if I could honestly replace the King of Cormyr I would have not done so when the realm had to contend with mad old Boldovar?"

Sagrast stammered a hasty reply, but Baerauble ignored him. "I have been charged with protecting the head that wears the Cormyrian crown, even if the mind within that head is evil, mad, or ineffectual. The elves charged me so and laid their geas upon me to enforce that charge. Typical elven narrow vision, really. A great people, but unable to see beyond their own long life spans."

"So when Tharyann outlived most of his own spawn and left only poor, mad Boldovar as his heir, I protected the new king and sought to treat his madness as best I could with spells and poultices. And he lasted longer than he had any right to, until he fell victim to his own rages and passions."

Sagrast nodded. Boldovar had perished three summers ago, after gutting one of his consorts. Clutching vainly at her slayer, the dying woman had dragged him over the battlements of Faerlthann's Keep. Baerauble had been abroad at the time.

The ancient wizard continued. "Boldovar left behind Iltharl, a spindly child, and Gantharla, who has redeemed the Obarskyr bloodline in many eyes and caused others to worry that she is truly her father's daughter. I know she's more popular in the western settlements than the king himself. I believe all the, ah, great thinkers among our nobles were hoping that Iltharl would see fit to spawn an heir and then conveniently perish of Marsember Pox before he had to rule. The fates did not allow it, and my own binding does not allow me to act against him."

The old man's face clouded. "As you say, Iltharl is not a bad man. Not bad in the same way as Boldovar was. If anything, Boldovar was too much a descendant of

Ondeth and Faerlthann, and Iltharl was too little. Perhaps some of us, myself included, saw too much of Boldovar's madness and sought overly hard to protect his son from it. And protected him so well he's proved to be ineffective as a leader. We ourselves have crafted an insufficient king."

The mage sighed deeply. "I find it amusing that so many people, particularly those of noble blood, respect Boldovar more than his son. Boldovar was murderous, ravenous, rapacious, and insane, yet he was strong and forceful, and his faults are forgiven for this. Iltharl is thoughtful and mild and caring, probably the most learned of any of the Kings of Cormyr, but he is reviled for his weakness and timidity. I had to foil five plots against Boldovar's life in his entire reign. I've had to thwart that many attempts against Iltharl's life this year alone."

The wizard transfixed the young nobleman with his dragon-sharp eyes. "But yours is the first that has not involved killing the king outright. Were you to hang yourself with your own tongue, I would have that tongue, and I would have the priests speak to your eternal essence and tear from it who your conspirators were. You may have figured on this . . . and if so, my opinion of Cormyrian nobles rises."

Sagrast went the color of old cheese. "We only want what's best for the kingdom. . . ."

"You want what's best for yourself," barked Baerauble, eyes glinting across the table with sudden fire. "I see none of the tripartite Silvers here, who nestle so closely to the king's robes. And none of the Rayburtons or Muscalians sit in this meeting. Oh, yes, I know which nobles are hiring mercenaries and drilling militia and buying swords of Impilturian steel. What good end do they serve? And who, if they grow dissatisfied with whomever they install as Iltharl's successor and seek to plunge the realm into war, will rule them? A young noble of a middling house, whose reputation was built on serving the crown if not the head that wears it?"

Sagrast was silent. After what seemed like a very long time, he swallowed noisily. Baerauble smiled at him. "You get your wish, youngling. I will stand aside and not interfere in your attempts to find a 'suitable' king for Cormyr. And how long do you think such a labor will take?"

"I think it will take a year to get Gantharla and Lord Bleth together, with all of us pushing," Sagrast ventured, almost shuddering with relief that his life wasn't going to end horribly right then and there.

"You are young and an optimist," the wizard replied, and Sagrast was afraid he would be treated to another bout of bone-dry laughter. "And if those two individuals notice each other, what then? What does Sagrast Dracohorn oversee then?"

"A suitable courtship," answered Sagrast, his voice gaining strength, "a decent period after the wedding, assuming the first child is male, and then ensuring the heir survives the battery of childhood illnesses and has a basic training in government."

"From such caring nobles as the friends of Lord Bleth," the wizard interjected.

"*And* the trustworthy family wizard," added Sagrast. "I figure twelve years."

Baerauble smiled very thinly. "Do you think Cormyr can stand twelve more years of kind, hapless Iltharl?"

"I think," Sagrast said slowly, licking his lips in nervousness, "that it would if we had the promise of an heir on the way."

The mage was silent for a long moment, and in the city beyond the shutters, Sagrast heard a distant disturbance: shouts and the clashing of steel. Adventurers on a brawl? Or had rebellion finally come to Suzail?

The wizard was apparently deaf to the sounds of battle. "Then we'd best start as soon as possible, shouldn't we?" He reached out a skeletal hand to the young noble.

Sagrast reached out, but before grasping the extended hand, he asked, "Why did you have me meet you here? With all your resources and power—"

"I could have met with you anywhere," finished the mage. "But if I had to kill a traitor, I thought I might as well burn down an ugly eyesore of a building in the process."

Sagrast's eyes widened a split instant before their hands touched—and blinding light exploded around them.

* * * * *

When the light faded, they were standing on the front steps of the keep. Sagrast felt as if his internal organs were still back in the upper room of the Ram and Duck. His insides felt weak and swimming; only after he felt the blood return to his stomach and heart did he notice that there was an uproar around them.

Courtiers and bureaucrats were streaming in and out of the building, some shouting orders, some clutching scrolls and account books. The king's guards were at the base of the stairs, arrayed for combat in their red-leather jerkins and carrying long metal-shod pikes. They were facing outward toward the city below.

The wizard snaked out a hand and reeled in a passing page, one of the young Truesilvers. "What is going on?"

The Truesilver began to curse but swallowed the profanity when he saw who had him by the collar. "Gantharla is back," he gasped.

Sagrast Dracohorn shook his head, frowning. "She was supposed to still be in the Western Marches."

The Truesilver boy nodded. "She was, but the king sent her a message relieving her of command and summoning her here. She came, but she brought her loyal foresters with her! They're in the city now, and she went inside with His Highness." The boy jerked his head at the Keep, and then gulped and added, "I hear that His Highness was wearing armor and everything when she went in."

Baerauble dropped the boy and took the steps two at a time, Sagrast following in his wake.

"Of all the times to finally make a royal decision," muttered the mage, and Sagrast saw that this was as much a surprise to Baerauble as anyone else. He also realized what the shouts were that he'd heard in the city—Gantharla's foresters. But had they been cheers or shouts of fury and anger?

Most of the courtiers were emptying their offices and adding to the panic. They were obviously convinced that Gantharla's loyal foresters would lay siege to the keep at any moment. Fortunately, their quarters were in the outer ring of the keep, and once the mage and noble had waded through the frantically scurrying throng, they encountered little resistance. Deeper within the keep was the Great Hall, and beyond that a small antechamber leading into the official throne room. That would be where Iltharl would meet Gantharla.

The entrance to the antechamber of the throne room was guarded by four of Iltharl's best soldiers. Solid men in red leather jerkins as tall and as broad as some doorways, they stood grim and watchful, with heavy swords in their hands, determined to prevent anyone from passing.

The wizard strode toward them without slowing. The soldiers made a halfhearted attempt to block Baerauble's path, but the wizard ignored them as if they were smoke until a blade actually menaced him. Then he looked straight into the eyes of its owner, and a careful look was exchanged. The man lowered his head, muttered something apologetic, and stepped back. The mage looked at the next guard, and then strode through the gap they'd left him, Sagrast drifting along at his heels. Behind the two, the guards closed ranks again, determined to prevent anyone *else* from passing.

The smooth flagstones of the antechamber thundered under Sagrast's heavy boots. Baerauble glided soundlessly to the great double doors leading to the throne room itself. He pulled at a door handle, but it did not budge. The wizard said something that at first Sagrast thought was a spell but then realized was an elven curse.

Then Baerauble waved at him to stand back, took a deep breath, and began weaving a real spell. From his throat issued strange, twisted vowels and strings of consonants, and from his palm, laid flat against the door, issued a pale blue glow. Strands of the blue radiance streamed between the mage's fingers and lanced out, like the strands of a spider's web, to the edges of the doorframe. There was a series of snaps from the other side of the door, and one large *thunk* that could only be a bolt being released.

The doors swung open inward.

The throne room had been part of the original house built on this site; over the long years, the rest of the stonework had grown up around it and consumed it. Along the walls hung tapestries and a few battle banners. Along one side of the hall, a small series of broad steps led up to a single throne. Iltharl was standing on the top step, Gantharla at the bottom. Both were in armor, with their swords drawn.

Iltharl was decked in gold and white, his normally immaculate robes covered with a bronze breastplate and leg guards. The plate and guards were chased and sculpted into images of fantastic beasts and stood out in bold relief. Ceremonial, thought Sagrast, and the thought struck him that Iltharl had probably never owned a real suit of armor or had any cause to use it. On his head he wore the Crown of Faerlthann, the elven circlet that commemorated the origin of the realm.

Gantharla was in her foresters' leathers, a mottled green from neck to foot, with a hood of the same material thrown back from her head. A shirt of elven chain, fine-linked and tinted green, tightly hugged her torso. Her hair, a brilliant red, was short and mannish. Her eyes gleamed, and Sagrast thought of Boldovar's madness.

Baerauble apparently thought the same, for he raised his hands to work a spell.

Iltharl raised a hand that held the heavy, broad-bladed sword of his father and shouted, "Hold!"

The wizard broke off in midword, but he strode on

toward the pair at the dais. Uncertainly, Sagrast followed.

"I am glad you could make it, old teacher," said the king. "My sister and I were discussing affairs of state."

"My lord, I heard that you—" began Baerauble, but the king cut him off.

"Relieved my sister of command and summoned her here," said Iltharl. "You heard correctly. Had I thought it would cause this much consternation, I would have consulted you in advance. I did not think Gantharla would respond by marching her entire unit here with her."

"What was I to think upon receiving your letter?" Gantharla said, ice water in her words. "We had one of the better-marshaled areas among the western settlements, so naturally you would want to stop that. It makes the rest of the nation look bad."

"And is our kingdom in desperate straits?" asked Iltharl softly, looking down on his sibling.

"I have told you," spat Gantharla. "It is ill, but all it needs is a good king."

"And am I a good king?" asked Iltharl in that same gentle voice, smiling.

Gantharla frowned and chose her words carefully. "You are my brother. You are thoughtful and sweet. But, no, you are not a good king." The words echoed around a room that was suddenly very still. The woman in green drew in a deep breath, threw back her head, and continued. "But you are *my* king, and I will remain loyal, regardless of the foolishness of your decisions."

"I thank you for your loyalty," said Iltharl, "and I agree with your judgment. I am good at many things, but not at being a king. Therefore I now serve my country as best as I know how."

And with that, the young king reached his free hand to his brow and doffed his circlet. "Kneel, my sister."

Gantharla dropped to one knee and Sagrast saw what was about to happen. The young noble stepped forward, but Baerauble reached out and took him by the shoulder. Sagrast winced as he came to a dead stop. Now he knew why the Truesilver page had gasped; the old man had a grip like iron.

Iltharl laid his weapon aside and held the crown in both hands. "I have given this much thought," he said. "I love Cormyr as much as any who have worn this crown, but I know that it needs one worthier than I." His voice wavered on the last words but steadied again as he added, "Let me prove that love by abdicating for one worthier."

He placed the crown firmly on Gantharla's head, the gold shining against her red locks. "Arise, Queen Gantharla, first Queen of Cormyr."

The new queen rose unsteadily. "Brother, when you summoned me here and I saw you in armor, I thought . . ." she began.

"There has been a good deal of foolishness in the past two reigns," Iltharl replied. "Now comes a time for wisdom and strength. I hope you can do better than I."

Gantharla looked into her brother's eyes and slowly nodded.

Iltharl stepped down from the dais to the wizard and Sagrast. "Thank you for not stopping me, old teacher," he told the wizard, "I'm not sure if I could go through that twice. I hope Gantharla will be easier to protect than I was."

Baerauble looked into the Obarskyr eyes and nodded, but said nothing.

Iltharl turned to Sagrast. "And thank you, young Dracohorn. I caught wind of your plot, and I realized if I could not command the loyalty of my own steward, how could I hope to rule? As surely as any assassin's strike, you convinced me to think again, and in doing so I found the best path out. Now I will need your help in convincing the other nobles to follow a woman as their ruler."

Sagrast's mouth was as dry as flax. He managed to choke out, "What will you do, my lord?"

Iltharl smiled. "I think I wish to go north to Cormanthor to join the elves. They will take in a hapless king and leave me to my studies and my art. That way no one will be tempted to put me back on the throne. Can you arrange that, wizard?"

Baerauble bowed low. "As you wish, my lord."

Sagrast looked at the new queen. The young woman was adjusting the crown, setting it firmly on her brow. Looking up, she smiled at Sagrast, and the steward hastily bowed low. How had he missed the obvious? All the planning, all the scheming . . . and all it took was ignoring two and a half centuries of tradition to choose the best king!

Sagrast smiled to himself. Let Kallimar Bleth pledge his own troth to the new queen. Sagrast wished him luck. He flashed the queen a heartfelt smile and unbuckled his court sword, laying it at her feet so that there would be no misunderstanding as he drew it and offered it to her.

The steel grated out. As he drew it, on his knees and using only one hand, Sagrast was aware of Baerauble moving to one side and raising a hand. Ready to blast him with a spell, no doubt, if he tried any treachery now.

Sagrast smiled openly and laid his sword at the feet of his queen. "I offer you my life," he said faintly, "though I want so much more to build a bright Cormyr in service to you."

Gantharla touched his brow with her fingertips, and he looked up.

"Will you, Sagrast Dracohorn, be my loyal man and remain as diligent a steward of the realm as you have been?" she asked, eyes stern, yet dancing with excitement.

"Your Majesty, I will," Sagrast said. She extended her hand, and he kissed it and knelt.

Gantharla sighed. "Ah, yes . . . the kneeling part. Get up and take up your sword. Rise as Royal Steward and loyal subject, and may you bear both duties as long as the gods give you just strength to do so."

She turned her head to look at Baerauble. "Lord wizard—if that is indeed what I should call you—the Royal Steward has knelt to me. What will I say to those who refuse to kneel to a queen and insist that only a man can rightfully sit on the Dragon Throne?"

The old, gaunt wizard smiled at her. "Two things, lady. First tell them that I, Baerauble, have stood by the realm since its founding. I was there when Faerlthann was crowned, and I swore then to serve the Crown of Cormyr, not the King of Cormyr. So long as the crown rests on a head Obarskyr-born, Cormyr endures."

Gantharla closed her eyes and shuddered as if in relief. "I may live to see this year end, then," she said quietly, and then opened her eyes and asked, "And the second thing?"

Slowly, and in evident discomfort, the old wizard sagged toward the flagstones. "You may tell them that the Royal Steward of the Realm *and* the Lord Wizard of Cormyr knelt to you and kissed your hand in fealty."

There were tears in the queen's eyes as the old wizard went to his knees. "Rise, rise," she said swiftly, extending her hand to him.

As he kissed it, Iltharl said quietly, "There is one thing more."

They all turned to look at him, and he said, "Tell them I named you my heir and bade those who dispute my just right to do this to set forth their arguments in writing. They may bring them to the elven court of Cormanthor. I shall refute such entreaties in writing, for I have *some* small talent that can still serve the realm."

Gantharla laughed until she wept, and Iltharl laughed with her. Shaking her head, the queen asked, "Brother, how did you ever find it in you to do this?"

Iltharl looked at his sister and sighed deeply. "It took little time to see I was not serving Cormyr well. It took a little longer to see what I must do. It took a very long time to find the . . . stomach to do it, especially with all the schemers plotting treason. It was fascinating to watch them work." He turned his head and added, "And I mean that, Sagrast, with no ill will or sarcasm." Looking back at his sister, he said, "I wish you luck. I really wanted to be a hero . . . but it was just . . . beyond me."

Baerauble put a hand on Iltharl's shoulder. "The gods do not grant to all of us the shining mantle of the hero," he said softly. "Do what you can, and that will be enough."

The former King of Cormyr managed a weak smile. "Words that should go on my headstone. Come, we should present the new queen to her people before they hurt themselves worrying."

The four walked out of the throne room and stunned the red-jerkined guards, who were the first common citizens to look upon their new queen. Their swords clattered down in unison, making a crash that brought the whole assemblage gathered in the Great Hall to a halt. People gaped at them in silence for a long moment—and then, from across the chamber, a forester in mottled green cried out, "Long live the queen! Long prosper Cormyr and us all—and long live Queen Gantharla!"

Others took up the cry, and the keep shook with the shouts as Iltharl shook his head ruefully and Gantharla beamed.

In a voice that was thick with emotion, the new queen said, "I—I think I'm going to enjoy this!"

Baerauble smiled. "Ah, well, you're young yet. There'll be time enough to discover what it's truly like."

But in the swelling cheering, as folk streamed into the keep from Suzail and someone started wildly ringing the signal bells, no one but Sagrast heard the wizard's words. He opened his mouth to say something, but Baerauble winked at him, and he shut his mouth again and kept silence for many long years.

13

Affairs of State
Year of the Gauntlet
(1369 DR)

he morning sun reached through the window to tinge his beard with gold as Vangerdahast went slowly down on knees that protested every inch of the descent and said formally, "The gods watch over thee, Lady Highness."

The crown princess frowned down at him. "Get up, Lord Vangerdahast. There's hardly need for that—or for this oh-so-private meeting!" She cast an annoyed look at the closed door on the west wall of Brightsun Bower, where she knew a war wizard stood keeping her Aunadar at bay. "You know I've little liking for secrets, lord wizard, so . . ."

She made a gesture—as imperious as her father's—indicating that he should speak. Now.

Vangerdahast rose. "This must be said in private, High Lady, for both our sakes and the sake of the realm. I am sworn, upon my oath and signature, to serve Cormyr. I will do so in whatever way the realm needs me, but wherever possible I shall continue to obey the Obarskyr king . . . or the Obarskyr heir."

Tanalasta frowned but said nothing, waving at him to continue.

"If, High Lady, you feel you're not yet ready to take the throne," the Royal Magician said gently, "and the unfortunate event of your father's going to the gods does come to pass, I want you to know—more than that, I'm obligated to inform you—that you can call on me. I am both willing and capable of serving Cormyr as regent."

Tanalasta's face went as white as new-fallen snow, and her eyes blazed. Vangerdahast saw bright tears well up in her eyes, but she bit her quivering lip and visibly summoned her self-control, drawing in a deep breath and putting her hand out to clasp the back of a nearby chair. In an instant, her slim fingers went white on its gilded curves.

"Loyal sir," she said shortly, "our deep thanks for this news. I'll . . . consider the matter." Her eyes burned into him as if she heartily wished he'd fall to the floor, blazing, and be gone forever.

Vangerdahast stood unflinching in the face of her royal rage. So the lass *did* have her father's fire, after all. That was good! He said softly, " 'Twould be best for the realm, lady, if you consider not overlong."

"You may go, lord wizard," she replied coldly and flung out her arm to point at the door in the west wall. "And take your war wizard with you."

Vangerdahast bowed. "Bright morning shine upon you, Lady Highness."

Her only reply was a curt nod, her eyes two hard points. The Royal Magician turned and strode toward the door.

"My father still lives, wizard," she growled under her breath behind him, just loud enough for him to hear. "You'd do well to remember that."

"I never presume overmuch, High Lady," he told the door pleasantly as he laid his hand upon it. "The realm can ill afford such presumption." And he went out.

He gave the same pleasant smile to the curious frown that Aunadar Bleth sent his way, then signaled the war wizard Halansalim to accompany him.

Three chambers away, he halted abruptly and told the

war wizard, "The crown princess is furious with me just now. Take yourself into yonder robing room and hold this!" And he put an ivory dove figurine into Halansalim's hand.

"I hear voices," the bearded old mage told him.

"Listen to them, and this evening tell me what orders concerning me, the war wizards, or any court officials or changes in rulership the princess utters. The magic will last until highsun, so long as she doesn't remove the ring she's now wearing."

Halansalim bowed silently and made for the door of the robing room. Vangerdahast strode on, heading for the Roaring Dragon Stair at a fast, rolling pace. He had an important appointment to keep.

The broad, sunlit stair led down to the Trumpet Gate of the palace, which faced the sprawling court at the base of the hill, and gave onto the road between them hard by the Crown Bridge. Ahead lay the court stables, and beyond the stables, all along the southern shore of Lake Azoun, sprawled the vast, many-towered bulk of the court. Bhereu had been taken this way already, to lie in state in the busy Marble Forehall, passed by folk crossing and crisscrossing the mirror-polished pavement between the Inner Ward, the Duskene Chamber, the Retiring Rooms, the Rooms of State, no fewer than four grand staircases that all descended into the forehall, and the Sword Portal.

It was the Sword Portal he was heading for now. Most folk in Suzail had stood before those massive double doors at least once in their lives, gaping at the armor plate that sheathed the thick timbers. Everyone in the city knew that the door was as thick as a brawny man's forearm, and everyone in the realm knew what the thick tangle of welded-on swords that covered both doors were: the captured blades of "foes of the Crown." The doors of the Sword Portal opened into the Processional, a long, red-carpeted hallway that led straight to the Approach Chamber, a guardpost of ornate gates and wall-mounted crossbows that in turn opened into the throne room.

What very few folk indeed knew about the Sword Portal was that when it was swung open, the narrow, man-high openings revealed in the thickness of its frame were not only guard niches, though a guard in full armor usually stood in each of them, but also passages that led into a warren of secret ways and closets in the heart of the court.

The Purple Dragon standing guard in the more westerly niche, a usually loyal man named Perglyn, was engaged in a pleasant mental calculation. Namely, how much he'd win if his wager—that Baron Thomdor would join his brother the duke in death before another two sunrises, but the king would hold on a day longer—came good. Of course, for his coin belt to be sixty-two gold lions heavier, the realm would lose its king, but—he shrugged—someone was always dying, and some must lose for others to gain. Of course, the nobles would never stand for that chit of a crown princess on the throne . . . at least, not unmarried. He'd just agreed on another wager about that: the fat old court wizard would call a council, and the nobles would draw lots—or compete in paying him bribes, more likely—to see which of them would get to wed the princess and take the throne. Aye, then old Vangerdahast had best snatch his loot and vanish from the realm before the new king decided to make sure no true tale of how much the crown had cost him ev—

The guard blinked, choked, then blinked again. The Royal Magician himself stood not a pace away, raising an eyebrow. "Pray stand aside, Perglyn," the old wizard said pleasantly, raising his other eyebrow to match the first, for all the world as if he could hear every thought that had just rushed through Perglyn Trusttower's head. Perglyn gulped, tried to salute and move aside at the same time, dropped his halberd with a loud clang, bent with fervent apologies to pluck it up, straightened, and . . .

The wizard was gone, as if he'd never been there. Perglyn blinked, but young Angalaz, across the portal, was grinning from ear to ear. "Ho, most valiant Perg!" he whispered all too loudly. "Aging so fast you've forgotten how to hold a halberd? The Royal Magician gave you a proper pitying look as he went into the passage!"

Perglyn stopped glaring at his fellow guard—young thrust-nose!—long enough to wheel around and peer into the darkness behind him. He saw nothing, of course. When a court wizard wants to stay hidden, there is nothing to see.

The Blue Maiden Room took its name from the life-sized sculpture that stood on a plinth in its center. A modest maiden sculpted of smooth-polished blue glass sat gazing up at the sky—looking for a dragon coming to devour her, legend had it—and in the meantime holding a cloak fortuitously fetched from somewhere over strategic areas of her beauty. The maiden's hands, feet, and breasts were much too large for the rest of her, and the overall effect was one of bold, gaudy, and surpassing ugliness.

Azoun's father, Rhigaerd, had hated it, and his feelings of distaste were mild compared to the opinions held by several Obarskyr queens prior to his reign, but several sages swore that the maiden was somehow connected with the good fortune of House Obarskyr and should never be broken up, defaced, or lost.

So when a careless court sage dabbled overmuch in forbidden sorceries and managed to blow up himself and the topmost room of a tower in the court, Rhigaerd had the maiden raised into the room while it was being rebuilt and walled in there. A narrow ladder shaft was the only way into the lofty, enclosed turret room, and the steep climb to get to it, up through the hidden heart of the court, made the maiden a favorite place for disgusted sword captains to send bumbling soldiers. "Go up and polish the maiden" was still heard on the streets of Suzail as a slightly more polite alternative to saying, "Lose yourself—far away, and *now!*" But only slightly . . .

Nevertheless, it was relatively unusual for the dusty maiden to have visitors in her dark, lofty chamber, but two men stood leaning on either side of her now, in poses that suggested they were overly familiar with the lass. A drifting globe of soft mage light hovered above them, making the maiden glow eerily, but neither man noticed. They were too busy remaking Cormyr.

"I never thought I'd see the day," Ondrin Dracohorn was saying in a harsh whisper, "when the Royal Magician of the realm would have the time—and desire—to hear my dreams for Cormyr."

Vangerdahast shrugged. "The day has come, so say on . . . and you need not whisper. My spells have shielded this place against prying magic and people coming up from below. No one can hear us."

"Aye, good," Ondrin said with an excited smile. "Then I'll not waste overmuch time."

In truth, Vangerdahast hadn't heard that the man had ever wasted so much as the time it took to blink; in fewer than thirty winters, he'd bought his way from obscurity to prominence among the eastern nobles. Not a tenday passed that Ondrin Dracohorn didn't—quietly, mind you—buy this farm or that warehouse with the coins that poured into his lap, it seemed, from his busy fleets based in Marsember and Saerloon. There were the usual whispers of smuggling, piracy, slaving, and running provisions out to the Pirate Isles, and in truth, it was hard to think of any honest shipping bringing quite so many coins. But on the other hand, it was hard to think of Ondrin Dracohorn as a competent slaver.

Or pirate, or just about anything else. His short stature, ordinary looks, and pale, watery blue eyes didn't invite men to do business with him or maids to go to revels with him, but he seemed to suffer no shortage of either. Perhaps, Vangerdahast conjectured, the prevalence of folk greedy for power and easy money explained it.

Ondrin was as exultant as a small boy to be "in the know" and at the heart of deals and important events, but he seemed not to see that he stood outside most real intrigues in the court of Suzail, because—as everyone knew—he was one of the biggest loose tongues in the kingdom. Something in his inner being compelled him to tell secrets to just about everyone he met.

Ondrin liked to drink—he was fumbling with a belt flask now—and watch dancing girls, and impress folk with his wealth. He dressed in the height of fashion. Right now he was wearing a violent flame-orange cross-sash secured with a metal brooch as large a man's face. The brooch depicted a two-headed serpent transfixed on three swords, but the sash clashed horribly with the blood-purple ornamental half-cloak he'd clipped to it. Vangerdahast was thankful for the brooch, however. Keeping his eyes on that scene of serpent and swords was enabling him to keep his face straight as the excited whispers went on.

Ondrin took a pull of cordial, coughed, exhaled noisily—by the gods, cherryfire mixed with . . . with . . . mint wine? Vangerdahast glided a step back. The noble said, *"Well.* Listen, then: I see a Cormyr free of the uncertainty of today, with a king lying near death and the realm stirred up like bees when a hive is broken open. I see a Cormyr where the poor are richer, and the Dragon Throne less decadent. I see a Cormyr—"

Gods, but the man had good eyes, thought Vangerdahast. He was careful to let nothing of his thoughts show on his face; he was going to need this man.

"—in which the laws are more just, and the gauntlet of authority lighter!"

"Good, good," the Royal Magician said encouragingly, leaning forward to put a hand on the Blue Maiden's knee in quickening excitement. "And how will we reach this better, brighter realm?"

" 'Tis a swift and simple thing," Ondrin said, watery eyes alight. "You, as regent, turn over control of the local Purple Dragon detachments all across the realm to the nobles whose lands they patrol. Then name a king—get someone to marry Tanalasta; I'll put myself forward if she hasn't been promised to someone already—and call the first true council in Cormyr's history. The king can only rule as far as the nobles—by vote, one vote per holding—say he shall, so that we, the nobility, will hold the true power in Cormyr."

"You interest me," Vangerdahast said, dropping his own voice to an excited murmur and glancing around to be sure the maiden hadn't lowered her head to watch them, "but say on. You know how hidebound the old families are. I'll need to speak strongly to persuade them to do anything that so weakens the crown. How does Cormyr profit by a council of nobles having a say over the king?"

Ondrin leaned forward until his ornate pin clanked against the maiden's plinth. "Nobles, new and old, are always short of money. However much one has, there's never enough—do you know how much servants *eat?*—and so no noble, once his pride is set at rest by knowing his votes are just as good as those of any other noble, with the old royalblood pecking order swept away and no king hurling absolute decrees about, is going to act in any way that hurts his coffers. We'll govern to enrich ourselves, and so enrich everyone, as they do in Sembia, except that we'll have some control over our realm and can act together to keep Cormyr strong!"

Vangerdahast was nodding like an old man over one tankard too many. "Your words are fair indeed, Lord Dracohorn. I think we can ride together on this, taking Cormyr to brighter days, indeed. But I'll need your help to do it."

"Yes?"

"You are the only man in the realm with broad enough influence to give me the support I need. The princesses—both of them, but in particular Crown Princess Tanalasta—are violently opposed to any regency, and in particular to me. They view me as some sort of spider who tugged their father this way and that, and they want me in my tomb, not standing beside the Dragon Throne. The only folk standing between the Purple Dragons they can hurl at me and my paltry spells—oh, I can topple a tower or two, but not whole armies!—are the nobles. The nobles listen to you, from one end of this realm to another. So I need you. *Cormyr* needs you."

"Say on!" Ondrin Dracohorn had practically climbed

up onto the maiden's lap in his eagerness.

"Well," Vangerdahast said slowly, "you and all the realm have heard tales about the scheming Royal Magician . . . about how I manipulate the king to do this and his courtiers to do that, using my war wizards when I have to. Everyone talks about the way I run Cormyr from the shadows behind the throne . . . and mostly they grumble about it." He leaned forward until his nose was almost touching Ondrin's and added, "So, knowing that about me, would you consider supporting me for the regency, to win a brighter future for Cormyr, free of the ever-present Obarskyr philandering? We've seen Azoun in half the bedchambers of the land, and he's not the first, let me tell you. Do we *really* want to see his daughters doing the same and have to dance to their every amorous whim?"

Ondrin's face grew serious. "Openly support you as regent against the wishes of the princesses?"

"Yes," the wizard said. "I need you to do that, or I'll have to flee the realm soon, and without me, your dream of a council of nobles can never be more than that: a splendid but windblown fancy."

"I—I ache to say yes," Ondrin whispered, drawing himself up. "And yet I dare not do so yet. First I must sound out some of my noble friends—in strict confidence, of course, and saying nothing of our meeting or your personal feelings at all—to be sure that enough of us are ready for such a brave change . . . or our necks may be on the block before our behinds ever find a council seat."

"Well said," Vangerdahast agreed, stroking his beard. "Go and see where the nobles stand, then, and we'll meet again when you send word to me." He grinned and shook his head. "Gods, Dracohorn, but this plan of yours shines brightly!"

"Doesn't it, though!" Ondrin almost shouted, then shrank down and clapped a hand over his mouth, looking scared.

"Have no fear," the Royal Magician said swiftly. "Nothing has disturbed my wards, but you'd best go while they

199

still last. I can keep you cloaked until you reach the Lion Cellar. Go through the back of the *third* cask, mind; the fourth leads straight into a guardpost!"

"Yes," Dracohorn agreed, eyes ablaze again. "Away now, to rescue Cormyr on a bright day soon!"

"Indeed," Vangerdahast agreed, lifting the lid that covered the top of the shaft. Ondrin sketched a dramatic salute—which the wizard matched, moving his hands grandly—and hurriedly started down the ladder.

The Royal Magician watched him descend, hoping the fool wouldn't miss his grip on a rung and fall. When the noble was safely out of sight, he let his mage light fade and patted the Blue Maiden affectionately. "Good girl! Thanks for the loan of your parlor again." Smiling grimly, he started down the shaft himself. As sure as the sun would set this night, Ondrin was one of the biggest loose tongues in the kingdom; word of this oh-so-secret meeting was sure to spread rapidly.

14

The Pupil
Year of the Leaping Hare
(376 DR)

oriann, Tharyann, Boldovar the Mad, Gantharla, Iltharl . . ."

The elder wizard clicked his tongue at her.

"Moriann, Tharyann, Boldovar the Mad, *Iltharl*, Gantharla, Roderin the Bastard, Thargreve . . ."

"Which Thargreve?" interrupted Baerauble.

"Thargreve *the Lesser*," spat Amedahast, and the older wizard nodded, allowing her to continue through the catechism of royal heads of Cormyr.

Baerauble was a teacher of the rote-and-repetition school, whether the subject was history or spell theory. Amedahast hated it. The crowned heads. The noble families. The lands about the Sea of Fallen Stars, past and present. The dead and dry tales of the Cormyrean legend. All the detritus that must be learned for her to serve as his scribe and apprentice in the court of King Anglond.

Baerauble needed a scribe these days. The wizard was skeleton-thin now, and his head was as smooth as glass. The only hair he had left consisted of a few long, white strands that marked where his beard and eyebrows had once been. He needed a gnarled staff to walk, had to be carried by chair from place to place, and was severely taxed by spellcastings. He needed at least an assistant, and at best an heir. Cormyr had always had its High Wizard and would need a new one in days not long to come.

That would be Amedahast, summoned from distant Myth Drannor at Baerauble's request. The young woman had Baerauble's blood in her, that much was certain. She was lean in form and sharp-featured in face, her light red-blonde hair gathered in an ornate, ordered braid halfway down her back.

She claimed Baerauble's mantle through his mating with the elven ancestor of the family line, Alea Dahast. *There* would be a tale she'd want to hear, of elf and human falling in love on first sight, and a life of adventures during which they'd saved each other's lives time after time. Not this droning repetition of facts and lists.

"To serve Cormyr, you must understand Cormyr," said the elder wizard hoarsely. "Facts are merely tools and must be familiar to be utilized effectively."

Amedahast was fully human, the result of many years of mortal blood watering down her elven ancestry. Even so, she had a fey, dangerous look about her, a look that she hoped would make her look even more dangerous among these rustics than she truly was. One lesson that Baerauble did not have to teach her was that if you looked like a tough fight, you did not have to be a tough fighter.

The lesson continued through most of the afternoon. Great battles. The legendary blades of the kingdom, starting with Faerlthann First-King's legendary sword, Ansrivarr. How many times Arabel has seceded from the kingdom (three) and how many times rival Marsember has been abandoned (twice). The legend of the Purple Dragon and his reported sightings in recent times.

There was magical training as well. Visualization and meditation. Schools of spells and theories. Spell ingredients and suitable substitutions. Personal runes and godly interference. Amedahast wondered if she were ever going to see the country that she was supposedly being trained to defend.

In midafternoon a summons came for Baerauble from the king. With much grumbling and cursing, the ancient wizard hobbled to the waiting chair and, snarling at the bearers, set off for the reception hall. His last words to Amedahast, before he was borne around a corner, were that she should study her geography until he returned. His pupil nodded obediently and watched him disappear behind a wall. His now incoherent shouts at the bearers continued for another minute.

Amedahast pulled down the appropriate scrolls and stared at them for all of twenty minutes before she blinked, shook herself, and realized she had not absorbed the least whit of information. The words and descriptions registered through her eyes, but some goblin intercepted the knowledge before it reached her mind and memory. She sighed deeply and looked out the window. It was an early spring afternoon, and the apple trees in the orchard beyond were just starting to bloom.

Amedahast closed the scrolls and looked out the window for another twenty minutes. Baerauble had said to study the geography scrolls. He had not said where she should study them.

She gathered the scrolls up and put them in a small satchel, along with a pair of rolls from the larder and a small bottle of port, then left the wizard's quarters in the royal castle.

The original keep had sprawled in a more or less haphazard fashion along the rolling hillock that dominated Cormyr. Most of the aristocrats, courtiers, and bureaucrats had been banished a hundred years ago for some rebellion or scheme or *faux pas* and now occupied a sprawling tumbledown chaos of stone buildings at the base of the hill called the Noble Court, or simply the court. The keep was home to the royal family, the important offices of state, the treasury and mint, and the court wizard. The Obarskyr castle loomed over the surrounding countryside, much like the Obarskyrs themselves.

Amedahast ignored the sprawling city and headed in the opposite direction, down the other side of the hill. This side had been left more pastoral, much of it a well-mannered garden. Orchards of apple, pear, and peach trees marched in neat rows along one side, and there were wide, stepped banks of primroses, marigolds, and stunted lilies. There was also a low garden hedge maze, a whitewashed gazebo, and a sprinkling of statuary, some of it imported from Myth Drannor itself. In the distance, rising above the trees, she saw roofs of colored slate, the homes of some of the highest-ranking nobles. There lived the Truesilvers, Crownsilvers, and Hunt-silvers, surrounded by a sprinkling of lesser lights: Turcassans, Bleths, and the upstart Cormaerils and Dheolurs.

Amedahast chose the gazebo as her destination. It had a good view of the surrounding area and should provide sufficient warning of Baerauble's return. As she approached, she made a face at the thought of *more* interminable study and pulled one of the scrolls out of the satchel.

And that's when she struck him as she rounded a corner with her head down, her satchel swinging around in front of her, one hand pawing through the scrolls. He rounded an epic piece of statuary from the other direction, and the two collided solidly.

Amedahast teetered back three steps, as if she had struck a massive wall. She would have fallen, but strong, quick hands took her firmly by the shoulders.

"I'm sorry . . . are you all right, good lady?" asked the young man.

Amedahast regained her footing, and the youth removed his hands from her shoulders. He was as tall as she, and broad-shouldered. His face was open and smiling, his smile framed by the well-trimmed silkiness of a first beard. He was dressed in simple riding pants and a voluminous white shirt and bore a short, broad blade on his right hip. On his forehead, he wore a simple circlet, a gold band unadorned by ornament.

"You could look where you're going," she snapped as her brain slowly yielded information about the significance of the coronet. Worn by the lesser royals in Cormyr, the tomes had said, such as the princesses and princes. And Cormyr had but one prince at the moment. "If you would be so kind, Your Majesty," she added, realizing whom she must be addressing.

"I'll try," said the young prince, and his smile deepened. Amedahast felt herself reddening. Her first encounter with one of the royal family, and she had chewed the man out. Though from the tales Baerauble had told her, yelling at the king seemed to be a required duty of the court wizard.

The youth did not move away. "May I ask why you've come to the royal garden?" he asked, and the young mage was struck with the softness of his voice. She had thought a man so muscular would have a deep, booming voice, but these tones were soft and cultured.

"I—I was studying some scrolls for my master, Baerauble, and thought I'd do better in the open air," Amedahast began, then stopped as the young man's face lit with surprise and glee.

"So *you're* the old scarecrow's secret project!" he shouted. "The servants've been wondering about you for two weeks now. You're the mysterious figure Baerauble smuggled into the castle in the dead of night and kept imprisoned in his quarters! Some said you were a creature from the pits and the old wizard was going to trade the realm for eternal life. Others said you were a goddess he'd rescued from the Purple Dragon himself. I see that the rumors were closer to the latter than the former."

Amedahast felt her reddening become a full-fledged blush. This one could give the silver-tongued courtiers of elven Myth Drannor some competition. "I am neither," she said firmly. "Only an apprentice Lord Baerauble has chosen to take on. It was the middle of the night when I arrived, but that was mere happenstance."

"Ah," said the youth with a smile and intoned grandly, "Hearken ye to the First Law of Baerauble: Nothing is coincidence when it involves wizards, and the Royal Wizard in particular!"

"I've hardly been imprisoned, though it does feel like it sometimes," continued Amedahast. "He has been busy teaching me the history and customs of this land before presenting me to the court."

She held out her hand. "I am Amedahast, a middling mage of Myth Drannor, apprentice to Lord Baerauble, High Mage of Cormyr."

The youth dropped to one knee, and Amedahast nearly jumped at the suddenness of his movement. He cradled her hand gently and kissed the back of her wrist. His breath was warm and his lips soft.

Yes, she thought, this one could definitely give the elven courtiers competition.

The smoothness of his manner was broken by the lop-sided grin that spread across his face as he stood up again. A happy, puppy-dog sort of smile. She almost expected his tongue to hang out of his mouth. Instead, he said, "They call me Azoun. I mean, Prince Azoun, son of Anglond and descendant of fifty other kings going back to Faerlthann himself, young lord of Cormyr and scion of House Obarskyr. Azoun the First, since I assume there will be others."

"I know," said Amedahast, bowing slightly but formally. "The circlet gave it away."

Azoun touched the circlet on his head as if he had noticed it for the first time. Then he gave her another grin. "Comes with the title, I understand. Baerauble has trained the Obarskyrs to always make sure that whatever other fashion crimes they may commit, they always wear the proper hat."

Amedahast found herself smiling at the image of Baerauble picking out the royal wardrobe. "Otherwise, you'd look like one of the castle's hirelings."

"This?" Azoun raised his arms to show off the blousey billows of his shirt. "I ride every morning around this time. I was taking a shortcut from the stables back to the castle."

"I see," said Amedahast. A small silence fell between the two. Then she said, "Well, I came out here to study. Baerauble is a cruel taskmaster."

Azoun did not move away. "History?"

"Geography," said Amedahast, taking two steps up the gazebo stairs. "Local geography."

The young prince gave an exaggerated shrug. "Let me help. I know a good deal about the area, given that it is the family business."

Amedahast flashed a hint of a smile and climbed the steps, taking a place at the back where she could watch the castle and keep an eye out for Baerauble's eventual return. Azoun sprawled a respectable distance away. She sat sideways on the bench, with her knees up on the seat, and unraveled the scroll in her lap. "Soldier's Green," she said.

"Small chunk of land north and west of here," Azoun replied.

She nodded. "Used for marshaling the militia and drilling the palace guards in large-scale maneuvers."

"It was originally the site of an old settlement, wiped out by goblins, back before there was a Cormyr. That was where Keolan Dracohorn of Arabel gained the family name killing a blue dragon, and where Gantharla stationed her foresters when she marched on Suzail and seized the throne from her brother."

Amedahast blinked. The blue dragon had been mentioned in the texts, but not the other two. "What about Arabel itself?"

"Almost as old as Suzail," said Azoun. "Originally a logging encampment of folk who moved in when the elves moved out. It's been part of Cormyr, off and on, for about three hundred years. It would petition to join, or be conquered, or be absorbed in one generation, then grow restive and break away the next. It's officially part of the nation right now, but it has always been—and remains—very independent. The saying in court is 'A rabid kobold could start a rebellion in Arabel.' Of course, we don't say that around folk from Arabel. They're a

207

little touchy about it, to say the least."

And so the afternoon passed. The young prince was a
font of knowledge, picked up from a lifetime of listening
to the tales of Anglond's court. It turned out that Baerauble had taught the young king his letters, and Azoun
was amused to hear that the old scarecrow was as demanding and boring now as he was then.

Amedahast shared the bread she'd brought, and they
passed the bottle of port back and forth. The shadows of
the afternoon grew longer, and the young wizardess realized that she was no longer watching for Baerauble's return. The old mage was probably back by now, wondering
where in the Seven Heavens she had disappeared to and
planning a suitable punishment for her return.

She jumped up at the thought, rousing young Azoun,
who had moved himself to sprawl on the bench next to
her. "I should get back!" she said, stuffing the scrolls into
the satchel. "The old . . . that is, Master Baerauble will
have me flayed if he thinks I was lollygagging around all
afternoon." She bolted down the steps two at a time
while the young prince was still pulling himself up.

"Will I see you again tomorrow?" he shouted after her.
"I'll be here after my ride."

Amedahast turned and waved. "If I'm not slain or
locked in a tower room, I'll be here." And with that, she
ran back to the wizard's quarters, her long robes billowing behind her.

Baerauble was indeed there when she returned, bent
over his workbench and examining some detailed clockwork through a huge lens. Without looking up, he asked,
"Have you been studying?"

Amedahast gasped to recover her breath and gulped,
"Yes, Lord Baerauble."

"So tell me something about geography," he responded.

Amedahast took a deep breath. "Soldier's Green was
originally the site of an orcish massacre. It was also
where the Dracohorn family gained its name. Keolan Dracohorn killed a blue dragon there. The ruins of Marsember are regularly used by pirates, and periodically

adventuring groups are secretly hired to clear them out. The High Horn was the first fortification among the Storm Horns and remains the largest, with dwarves emigrating from Anauria being hired to hollow out the mountain itself."

She paused to take a breath, and the old wizard interrupted, still without looking up. "Good enough, but slightly inaccurate. Keolan Dracohorn found a dead young blue dragon there, drove his sword into the cooling body, and told his version of the tale so often that it became the family legend. Not everything that is claimed as history is true. Remember that. Now go prepare for dinner. We'll be discussing Lathanderian philosophy."

Amedahast bowed formally and retired to her quarters, taking the steps two at a time. She couldn't see the old wizard's face as he crouched over the clockwork nor see the wide smile on Baerauble's lips.

* * * * *

Amedahast and Azoun met in the garden for the remainder of the month. Azoun kept her posted on history, family legends, court gossip, and local custom. "Right now all the petty nobles are in their country estates overseeing the plantings and first shearings. Come month's end, they'll all descend on Suzail. There will be a great ceremony that takes forever as each family lists its triumphs since the close of the last noble season. Naturally there will be intrigue and fistfights over who gets to be presented to my father first."

Amedahast told the young prince about elven poetry, news of the outside world, and ancient legends of heroes and wizards and great threats from beyond the borders of Cormyr. Azoun sat in rapt attention as she recited from memory the epic poems and love sonnets popular in Myth Drannor.

And each evening Baerauble would ask her what she had learned and correct the more obvious errors in Azoun's stories. Once or twice she had argued with the mage over a point of history, but the old wizard pointed out how it could only happen in one particular way, and if young Azoun's version was true, then all manner of other things should have occurred, which had not. Amedahast conceded the point, but grudgingly.

One afternoon, during their studies, Azoun turned to her and said, "You're going to be my wizard. Do you know that?"

Amedahast was taken aback. "Baerauble is the King's Wizard. I'm merely his apprentice."

"The old scarecrow is my father's wizard and High Mage to every Cormyrian king back to the beginning of time," said Azoun. "But he's never taken on an apprentice before. That means he's finally feeling his age. I think he's about to retire, or become a lich, or whatever old wizards do. And you're going to be my wizard."

The idea of becoming the master mage of Cormyr unsettled Amedahast slightly. Yes, she thought, she probably would like to attain high station and respect. But Baerauble had outlived all but the eldest of elves, enhanced by his magic and enchantments. Even in his frail state, he seemed invulnerable and eternal.

She crept around to the topic at the dinner table that evening. The old wizard nodded slightly and said, "Cormyr has always had a king, from the very first. It has always had a wizard as well, to advise, correct, and aid the king. Without its wizard, Cormyr would not be a true nation. Eventually you will assume that position, though not for some time. You still have much to learn."

The month ended and the noble season began in Suzail, a brief spate of celebrations in the capital before the nobility took to their summer retreats. Amedahast was presented to King Anglond and Queen Eleriel and swore fealty to the crown on Symylazarr, the sword also known as the Fount of Honor. She was presented before any of the nobles. Standing there after swearing the oath, she saw both Baerauble and Azoun smile at her, the former's tight and approving, the latter's open-mouthed and proud.

The feasts and revels were rougher than the elegant court of Myth Drannor, but held a vitality lacking among the elves. The dances were reels and progressions, and what they lacked in organization, they made up for in enthusiasm. The mysterious mage, Baerauble's pupil, stunning in her green gown with reddish hair wrapped with gold filigree, was a center of attention and danced with the noble sons and gossiped with the noble daughters. When those fine folk looked at her, their eyes held curiosity and just a touch of respect and fear.

She liked that very much—both the attention and the respect. Part of her told herself that it would fade in time, when she was no longer the Wonder of the North, when she truly took on responsibilities. But for the moment, her heart sailed on the winds of praise and adoration.

Then she noticed that Azoun was nowhere to be found.

Of course he would want to dance with her, she reasoned. And all the other crowned heads were present, as well as the High Mage, so it wasn't as if there were some affair of state to be tended to. She disengaged herself from a chatty young Turcassan who was extolling his virtues in bear-slaying and went looking for the handsome young prince.

She found him in the garden, in the gazebo. He was not alone.

They did not see her approach, but Amedahast got close enough to see the pair, she lying with her head in his lap, he dropping grapes into her overly reddened mouth. She was one of the lesser nobles, a debutante of the Bleth household perhaps. She wore a gown with a southern cut, low to the point of indecency and flaring at the hips. From his position above her, Azoun had a grand view of her charms.

Amedahast was close enough to hear them as well, the noble girl's giggles and the young prince's words. He was reciting poetry to her, dropping a grape into her open mouth at the end of each stanza.

It was elven poetry. Poetry that Amedahast had

taught him. She realized she was trembling, though the night was quite mild.

Amedahast wheeled and headed back to the castle, where the warm lights beckoned and cries of celebration filled the evening air. She stopped at the doorway to raise her hands briefly to her face. No tears. At least that was something.

Yet her face told the tale as she entered the hallway. She nearly collided with an older noblewoman, of House Merendil, if her studies with the treacherous young Azoun had been correct. Azoun had described the ruling matron as a vengeful, petty old woman, and Amedahast vaguely recalled a story that she had caught Azoun stealing apples as a lad.

Now she thought about that story again. Lady Merendil had three daughters. Azoun had probably been caught with more than apples in his hands.

Lady Merendil shot a sudden, questioning glance at Amedahast, then looked out into the garden and smiled. "Ah, the young prince strikes again."

Amedahast choked out her words, "Frankly, I don't care what the 'young prince' strikes. Or whom."

Lady Merendil laid a hand on Amedahast's shoulder. "You are not the first to have fallen to his charms, my dear. Did he let you think so? I am afraid he is like all the other Obarskyrs. Once their passions get involved, their common decency vanishes."

Amedahast said nothing, and her ladyship steered her into a side alcove. She spoke in a low whisper. "I can see that you are hurt. You must understand that you are not the first in that respect. Azoun and his kind will continue to act in such a fashion until they are taught otherwise, much as a hound struck across the nose will think twice before stealing food from the pantry again."

"He just makes me so—" Amedahast searched for the proper word "—so *angry*. I trusted him." She began to feel the tears pool at the corners of her eyes, but she fought back the feeling of despair.

"Poor dear," said her ladyship. "I know of a way to set the balance right. Are you interested?"

Amedahast thought for a moment, then nodded. He used poetry she'd taught him for his cheap conquests!

"I know of a group of foreign merchants. Let us call them the Steel Lords," she said, smiling. "They have been hurt by some of King Anglond's taxes and want to reopen negotiations. These Steel Lords think the king needs a message sent to him. I think young Azoun needs a lesson taught to him as well. Perhaps we can kill two birds with one stone."

Amedahast said, "Kill? No, I—"

"Forgive me . . . a poor choice of words," said Lady Merendil, her smile becoming beatific. "We are no longer savages here in Cormyr. The plan would be to capture the young prince and simply hold him for a few days, then let him go when the Steel Lords have their concessions. A simple transaction. And if it becomes clear that his wenching brought him to this pass, I'm sure His Majesty will keep Azoun on a shorter leash in the future."

Amedahast was silent. Perhaps it would be good to throw a scare into him before he brought ruin on the good name of Obarskyr.

Merendil brought her face close to Amedahast's. "Is there a time when he is alone? A place where he has few guards or watchers?"

Amedahast thought. There were no guards whenever they met in the garden. Which meant . . .

Which meant the young fool had planned this from the start. It was no random meeting a month ago. She was just a petty dalliance until the noble season began.

There is no coincidence. First Law of Baerauble, indeed!

"We get together in the garden," she blurted, "in back, at the gazebo. After his ride. Though I don't know if he will ever be back now."

Merendil smiled like the canary-consuming cat. "Excellent," she hissed.

"He won't be hurt at all?" Amedahast pleaded.

"Dear girl," said Lady Merendil, "where would the fun be in that?" And with that, she glided off to rejoin the party.

After a few minutes spent composing herself, Amedahast rejoined the throng as well. Most of the young nobles had paired off, and only a few were still spinning on the dance floor. Most were along the perimeter, gathered in tight little knots of deep conversation.

She found Baerauble ensconced in a chair, trapped in conversation with one of the rotund elder Crownsilvers. His face almost brightened upon seeing his pupil. To the Crownsilver, he said, "You must pardon me, for my student needs to walk her master home."

Crownsilver bowed and backed away. Amedahast helped the old wizard to his feet. He felt frail now, as if the life had gone out of him.

Once they were in the hallway outside their rooms, he said, "I thank you for rescuing me. If I had to hear Lord Crownsilver's epic treatise on rebuilding Marsember one more time, I would go quite mad." The old mage weaved a bit, and Amedahast smelled ale on his breath.

"My lord?" she ventured.

"Hmmmm?" was his reply.

"Have you ever served an evil king?" she asked. "I mean, a really bad and foul man?"

"Two separate questions," slurred Baerauble. "Cormyr has been blessed never to have a truly evil king. Mad, yes. Insufficient, yes. Greedy, bad, violent, petty, yes, yes, yes, yes. And lust-driven . . . oh, my, yes. But the Obarskyrs have been blessed with never having an evil king. The elves did well when they let the Obarskyrs stay."

"But if they were mad and violent and . . . lust-driven, why did you serve them?"

The old mage turned and regarded Amedahast. "I serve the crown, not the head it rests on. I have lived for over four hundred years, and in that time I have seen this nation grow from a single encampment to something worthwhile. And if continuing that achievement means doing my best in the face of adversity, so be it. We do not rule here, pupil. But we do protect, and that means protecting men whom we might otherwise judge weak or foolish, because there is always hope with the next generation. 'Do what you can,' I always have said, 'and it will be enough.' "

They reached Baerauble's quarters, and the old man bade her good night. Amedahast stood in the hallway for a long time. In another part of the keep, the dance continued, and high, spirited music wafted weakly, lacelike, down the halls. She listened to it for a moment and thought of foolish men and weak women.

Then she returned to her own quarters and pulled down the ancient texts and spell grimoires she had brought with her from Myth Drannor.

* * * * *

On the next afternoon, Azoun was late and looked more than a bit bedraggled, but he did show up, dressed as always for riding. He hurtled up the stairs two at a time.

Amedahast looked up from the tome she was reading and regarded him unemotionally. "You are later than usual."

"Kings set their own hourglasses," he said cheerily, adding, "That was a wondrous dance last night. I missed you at the end."

"Indeed," she said calmly, "Lord Baerauble needed my assistance, and some of us still have duties, even in the midst of the season. I want to talk to you about the possible resettlement of Marsember."

"Oh-ho! Crownsilver got to you," said the young prince, giving her a smile that she now thought of as annoying. "He'd get the bulk of the farmland if it were truly reestablished. And his cousins in the Truesilver clan would benefit if we ever finally got rid of the pirates and smugglers once and for all."

He went on about the ins and outs of the Marsember

question, but Amedahast was only half listening. She scanned the surrounding garden. The flower beds, now in full bloom, seemed to hold menace, and every statue was a perch for a possible assassin.

Suddenly she saw it, a mere rippling of light along the side of the garden maze. Just the slightest shimmer, as if the holly leaves were caught in a breeze that existed nowhere else. The movement would be unnoticed by anyone not looking for it specifically.

But Amedahast was looking for it and knew what it meant. Elven cloaks, smuggled out from Cormanthor. They would bend the light about them, such that the wearer would be well-nigh invisible against an immediate background. With those cloaks, the kidnappers could come right up to their prey.

No, not kidnappers. There was the tiniest flash of silver blades and steel-tipped crossbow bolts. They were intent on sending a message, but the message was to be a stronger one than she had been told.

Azoun was going on about the various factions lined up for and against the Marsember question. "So the Silver families are straight-ahead on this, but need the support of the Dracohorns, Bleths, and Turcassans, who don't want to see them get any stronger. And then the newer houses, like the Cormaerils, are in the— Hey!"

Amedahast leapt at the first sight of a weapon being raised, springing forward with frantic haste.

She was much lighter than Azoun, but the prince wasn't expecting an attack, and the pair of them went sprawling off the bench. A crossbow quarrel buried itself in the wood where Azoun's head had been a moment before. Another marked Amedahast's last position.

The young mage came up shouting, bellowing the incantation she had searched for the previous evening. Her fingers lit with eldritch fire at the tips, and then the dancing flames arched forward into ravening streams that roared through the quiet garden air as they transversed the grounds. Each found the face of a different target. They did not even have time to scream.

As they fell, the assassins' cloaks peeled away, drifting from the bodies, to reveal prostrate forms on the flower beds.

She had not felled them all; her first warning of that was when the last two assassins tore away their cloaks and charged the stairs of the gazebo. She readied another spell, but by this time, Azoun was on his feet, with his short blade drawn.

He ducked under the first assassin's vicious slash and planted his sword deep in the attacker's chest. The man gasped out blood and fell backward, taking the blade with him.

The other assassin tried to take advantage while the prince was engaged with his fellow attacker. His cutting blade was swung too fast, too short, and missed. He snarled—and caught an oversized riding boot in the face. The man's head jerked back, and he crumpled like a sack of potatoes.

Amedahast looked around for other targets. Nothing else moved. Then the far gates of the garden and the doors of the castle flew open, and two units of the king's guards poured into the tranquil space. The flames on her fingertips ebbed, flickered, and died.

Azoun was shouting orders to the men, gathering up the dead and healing the wounded to be questioned later. Baerauble appeared, moving slowly and leaning heavily on his staff.

"My lord," began Amedahast firmly, "Lady Merendil . . ."

". . . is probably halfway to the Chondathan colonies of Sembia by now to rejoin her daughters," the mage said smoothly, old and knowing eyes on hers, "but we'll send a message ahead on the off chance we can snare her. That was foolish, trusting that you could take them on by yourself, but I suppose you wanted to prove you could do it."

Amedahast started to explain, then shut her mouth. "Yes, sir," she said at last. "I will be more cautious in the future."

Azoun came up to the two wizards and threw an arm around Amedahast's shoulder. "They would have gotten

us both if not for your student, Lord Baerauble. She's
going to be a *great* High Mage!"

Amedahast delicately grasped Azoun's wrist with her
still-tingling fingertips and gently removed it from her
shoulder. She looked at the young prince stonily and
spat, "Remember this, *Sire. If* I become High Mage, I will
pledge to serve the crown. Not you, but the crown itself,
regardless of whether the head beneath it is hollow as a
gourd or *not!*"

Amedahast wheeled and stomped back to the royal
court. Azoun watched her slim form diminish in the distance for a time, then turned to the High Mage, his face
a question.

Baerauble merely shrugged.

15

The Common Room
Year of the Gauntlet
(1369 DR)

t's best not to ask what's in the sausage rolls, lad, but by the gods, they're good!"

"Oh?" Dauneth tried to sound unconcerned and cosmopolitan, as befitted a nobleman and a warrior. It didn't work.

"First time in Suzail, lad?" the merchant asked heartily. "Well, I'll grant you're as hungry as a war-horse after the ride from High Horn, but let me warn you away from the sweet-spiced fish rolls they seem to like in this town. Sickening things! And I suppose while I'm about it, I'd best give you a warning. If you bite straight into a sausage roll like those you're drooling at, while it's steaming like that, it's your own burnt mouth and tongue you'll be tasting—for the better part of a tenday!"

"My thanks to you, goodman . . . ?" Dauneth said, more to slow the flood of advice than to learn the man's name.

"Rhauligan. Glarasteer Rhauligan, sir, dealer in turret tops and spires, stone and wood both—you order 'em, and we'll build 'em—fast and cheap, and they won't fall down!" There was a cadence to his words, and they sounded like an oft-repeated slogan. Dauneth wondered just how much trade the man actually did. But the neatly bearded trader was raising a wintry brow and saying, "Say . . . does your castle need a bit of spire work, now?"

"Ah, no, actually," Dauneth said. "It's not my castle to expand or alter, at any rate."

"And you are . . . ?"

The tall, gawky man sighed inwardly as he heard himself saying, "Dauneth Marliir." If this garrulous merchant really did go around the realm fixing towers, Dauneth was probably earning himself a wagonload of questions.

"Of the Marliirs of Arabel?"

Sigh. Here it came. "Yes," Dauneth said firmly. "Ah—is this our hostess?"

Rhauligan cast a look over his shoulder. "Yes, that's Braundlae, right enough, but if *that's* what you want, lad, you've come to the wrong place! The red lantern est—"

"I came in here for some food," Dauneth said rather desperately. "Standing in line after line up at the court for hours is hungry work, and hard on the feet, too!"

The merchant whistled sympathetically. "Been up at court, have you? Gods, but the place must be buzzing like a ruptured wasps' nest right now!"

"There did seem to be a lot of whispering and people glancing around and then ducking behind doors, yes," Dauneth agreed, "and people rushing about, too—but isn't that what usually goes on?"

"Gods, no, lad. If you're up at court and want to show everyone how important you are, you don't rush anywhere, see? You saunter unconcernedly and wear a little half-smile, like you know all sorts of secrets that these poor fools around you don't, because they're not half so important and close to the crown as you are. See?"

"I'm beginning to, yes," Dauneth said, keeping weariness from his voice with the skill born of long schooling. The Marliirs had fought against Dhalmass at Marsember, had been part of the Redlance Rising, had made the mistake of backing the regent Salember, and had gotten into more sordid troubles with the Keepers of the Royal Rolls over taxes since. The family had to acquire certain skills merely to keep their necks away from executioners' swords and their behinds out of dungeon cells. Smooth talking, superb acting, and a heightened sensitivity to the attitudes of others were prominent among these. Dauneth had acted the part of a gentle, considerate young man of breeding for so long that he'd become one somehow. One of chief skills of young nobles—if they wanted to become old nobles, that is—was the ability to mask boredom behind feigned interest and attention.

"If the dust grows on your eyeballs, lad, you're doing it wrong," the merchant whispered loudly across the table as he bounced a friendly fist off Dauneth's forearm. Dauneth winced; the man had seen right through his politeness and had actually echoed a phrase one of his uncles had used once while teaching him how to sleep while appearing to be still awake. It had served him well with family-hired tutors ever since. "So the Marliirs are trying to get back in the royal good graces, eh? Well, they picked a fine time to send you here, what with the king dying and all!"

"*I* heard he died yesterday, and they're just keeping it a secret," the servingwoman said as she came up behind Dauneth with a platter loaded with two large, misted tankards, a round loaf of hardbread, and several covered pots and dishes. She set it down with a clatter.

"Gods, no, Braundlae," the merchant said. "If the Purple Dragon was dead, all the up-noses like the lad here—ho, beg pardon, lad, I didn't mean ill of you and your house, mind—wouldn't have anyone to line up to talk to and arrange all those last dirty deals with before His Highness croaks!"

"Hah!" Braundlae put her hands on her hips. "Do you think the High Wizard keeps the place crawling with war wizards for nothing? They keep poor old Azoun's eyes and mouth moving and a voice coming out and suchlike with *magic*, and all the high-and-mighties go away thinking they've made an agreement with the king, when all they've really done is— Oh, sir," she broke off, turning to Dauneth. "I took the liberty of bringing you our home brew and some sausage rolls, as I heard Master Rhauligan praising them to you earlier! Would you like something different?"

"Ah, no, no. This'll be fine, thank you, good lady," Dauneth said hastily. The woman gave him a merry smile and bent in a court curtsey, saying to Rhauligan, "You'll note the lad called me a 'good lady,' Rhauly. Good manners might not come amiss from you on occasion, mind!"

"Ah," the merchant said, bending forward over the table with a leer, "but then the lad doesn't know you as well as I do, does he? 'Good,' aye, I'll grant that, but—"

He ducked the playful snap of her apron with the ease of long practice, snatching up the lid of his bowl in mock fear to serve as a buckler. Dauneth glanced idly at the contents of the bowl and then stared down at them in horrified fascination. The merchant caught sight of the look on the young man's face and followed it down to his bowl.

"What's the matter, lad? Never seen eels in mint-and-lime hot sauce before? If your family was originally from Marsember, by the dragon, you *must* have eaten eels once or tw—"

"Oh, I have," Dauneth said faintly, "though they're no favorite of mine. But I've never seen anyone eat them alive and still *moving*—"

The merchant gaped at him. "But that's the best way, lad! Why, of *course* you disliked eels if they brought 'em to you all dead and cold and rubbery! Why—"

"I think," Dauneth said firmly, "that I'll take my sausage rolls upstairs. . . ."

"Why, yes, *do* that, lad—and when I'm done chasing these 'ere eels around the table, I'll bring you a second tankard. How's that?"

"Splendid," Dauneth said through clenched teeth. "Simply splendid." He'd grown quite pale, and at the temples his skin almost matched the color of his gray eyes. "I'll see you then. . . ."

He rose hastily and clumsily, the heavy broadsword at his hip banging into his chair. He turned to leave with a dignity that was somewhat spoiled by his having to turn back to the table to take up his forgotten tankard, then strode to the stairs.

"Sir!" Braundlae's voice was friendly but swift. "That's a full tankard of our best Black Bottom, and three piping-hot sausage rolls with Silver Dragon Sauce, too! How will you be paying for that?"

Dauneth turned. "Oh. Sorry. I thought that upstairs . . ."

"Is the Roving Dragon, sir. Caladarea's place—not mine. I'm sure she'll not mind you bringing in food that's better than she'll ever serve, but I'll certainly mind if you walk out with it!"

"That was not my intention, lady," the tall, gangly youth said stiffly, trying to fish in his belt purse with a hot covered dish in one hand and a tankard in the other. The purse looked heavy, both Braundlae and the merchant noted professionally. He plucked out three coins and laid them in her palm. Braundlae peered at them rather suspiciously and then gasped.

"Three golden lions! Sir, *one* will settle everything ten times over! I'll have to go hunting, this early, for coins enough to change—"

"Keep it," Dauneth told her quickly. "And cover Master Rhauligan's bill with it, if you would. Only don't let him bring any eels upstairs." And without looking back, he dashed up the stairs, bumping his elbow on the rail and his scabbarded sword on several steps along the way.

"Yes, sir! May the gods smile on you this month, and the next, too!" Braundlae said enthusiastically. When the young man was gone around the bend in the stair, she turned to Rhauligan and murmured, "Is he crazed?"

"No, just rich," Glarasteer Rhauligan said cheerfully. "Probably one of the richest young men in all Cormyr right now. Of noble Marsembian blood, here to ingratiate himself at court."

Braundlae lifted eyebrows that had seen much travel in their day and said, "Well, when there's a healthy king again—or a new one—it won't take long for the throne to smile upon him if he throws money about like that." She stared down at the coins in her hand as if she still couldn't quite believe it, which was the honest thing to do, because she couldn't.

"No, wench, it's loyalty the Obarskyrs value, not money. Loyalty."

Braundlae lifted her eyes from the gleaming gold to stare at him, and then up at the empty stairs where the young noble had gone. "Disloyal? Him? I'll not believe that."

Rhauligan shrugged. "He just gave you far too much money; of course you'll not think ill of him. What matters is how many young noblemen far shrewder than him buy friendships and allies daily."

"I'm sure," the hostess said cynically. "Besides, who's to say the king he'll be kneeling to will be an Obarskyr?"

"There's Tanalasta," said the merchant, "and Alusair."

"Both hide from the task," replied the hostess, "one in her account books, the other behind the sword. I repeat, will the next king be an Obarskyr at all?"

"How could it not be and this land still be Cormyr?"

Braundlae shrugged. "One family does not a realm make—or keep. There're no secret male heirs locked up in palace closets so far as I know, so if the king and the baron go down, as everyone's saying they will or in fact have already, there can't help but be another line of kings on the Dragon Throne! Now, once someone has taken the crown, I don't know how long they'll be able to hold on, once all the nobles see how one of their own is lording it over them, and they start thinking about how easy it'd be to supplant them in turn."

"Have you hired a mage to fireproof your shutters yet?" the merchant asked quietly.

Braundlae frowned at him. "What? Why d'you prattle on about . . ." She fell silent, looking troubled.

"As you said," Rhauligan said in a low voice, "once one

noble takes the crown, what's to stop another from trying for it? We'll have daggers in the alleys and then swords in the streets, until armies are riding into Suzail to make this noble or that one our sovereign! And the court is right across the flaming road from here, Brauna! Where do *you* think the wars'll be fought?"

"Oh, gods," the hostess whispered, her face gone pale, her apron bunched up to cover her lips.

"It could go on for years, with young hotheads riding around the realm declaring for this family or that, tearing the realm apart, with no crops to take in and no laws to shelter us. You'd better hope old Azoun *doesn't* die!"

" 'Young hotheads'? Oh, some noble sons are like that, to be sure, but this Dauneth, now, was perfectly nice!"

"Yes, and his family has been so disloyal to the Obarskyrs that the Royal Magician's probably measuring out dungeon manacles for him right this minute."

"Him?"

"Indeed. His family's rebelled against the crown a time or two, forgot to pay their fair handfuls of coins in tax to the throne . . . and rode with bloodied sword at the orders of Salember the Serpent!"

"And they kept their heads? How does he dare come here at all?"

"Why do you think young noblemen like him are coming here now, with the king dying? They say he was poisoned. Anyone like this Dauneth who's been here a month or so could have done it, or known it was going to happen and hovered like a vulture to seize whatever power came loose for the taking. Soon the city'll be full of all the other young noble sons, come to join the circling cloud around the king-to-be-corpse. You won't be able to ladle sauce fast enough to keep up, Brauna!"

The hostess looked at him grimly, and then said sourly, "You make the days ahead seem dark indeed! Finished your eels yet, Doomtongue?"

Rhauligan grinned at her in answer and opened his mouth wide. A last eel quivered and wriggled on his tongue, seeking freedom.

Braundlae shuddered despite herself and flung out a pointing hand. "Get you gone!" she ordered. "Up into the Dragon—with a fresh tankard for that nice young man!"

* * * * *

The Roving Dragon, as Rhauligan had informed Dauneth earlier, was currently the most popular bun-and-ale for working Suzailans to stop in at, once a day or so. For years, it had seemed there was no room left on the Promenade for a relaxed, reasonably priced establishment that could serve food quickly, where people could sit at tables and talk—gossip, business, court politics, or whatever.

Caladarea Ithbeck had changed all that. Newly arrived from Chessenta a season ago, she saw the lack of the sort of place she liked to eat at, its windows overlooking somewhere busy and important, and saw something much brighter: If one rented out the upper floor apartments of a row of shops, and then joined them into one long series of private little rooms by knocking doorways through the connecting walls, one suddenly had a large new dining hall right on the Promenade. Add a few *very* exclusive guest apartments for visiting nobles or rich merchants, make peace with a tavern or two by letting them take the lion's share of the low-bottle drinking trade and in return getting their stairs to serve as entrances, make sure that the food was simple and good—and the Roving Dragon was a sure success. It was seldom, even in the slow midmorning and waning noon hour periods, that the rooms with the best views had fewer than a dozen patrons lazily sipping at cider and making meat tarts or soup last as long as they could.

There were a dozen in the Snout Room—the sunny chamber at the east end of the Dragon, with its view of the royal gardens past the end of the sprawling court buildings—right now.

Two merchants were chuckling together at one table, a veritable forest of tankards rising from around their elbows. Another, leaner merchant sat with a smoothly amorous lady who was probably getting paid for her caresses. A table of six priests of Tymora were leaning noses together, speaking in low and excited tones—no doubt about how deliciously risky, and therefore favored by the Goddess of Luck, the present time was in Cormyr, with the king's life hanging by a magical (none doubted) thread. A mercenary captain sat silently at a small corner table, his booted feet occupying its only other chair, obviously waiting for someone. His breast badge was a wolf leaping into view between two trees.

And there was Dauneth Marliir. He'd been staring at the mercenary's badge from time to time, and at other times gazing at the head of the stair that led down to Braundlae's Best, and devoting the rest of his time to the huge tankard, which seemed all but empty now. The ale had a rough-edged, smoky taste, but it was good. He licked his lips in consideration. The best thing about this day so far, in fact. For all his patience, he had not yet had a chance to see the dying Azoun in the flesh, his progress in the long lines halted at the next-to-last chamber.

He could still remember the only time he'd seen the king, as bright and as clear as if it had happened only yesterday and not over a dozen summers ago when he took Arabel from Gondegal's forces. A bearded, laughing man, standing tall in his saddle in a leather forester's jerkin with his hands spread wide to acknowledge the cheers of his people. Power and grace and surging vitality, the sense that all the might of Cormyr was flowing into that man as he rode past, every inch the rightful and natural king of the Forest Kingdom.

And a young, excited Dauneth had roared out Azoun's name and waved his hands and wept along with all the rest, there in the streets of Arabel, and felt at one with men he'd never met in his life before. Old warriors who walked slowly and proudly toward the sunset of that day as if they wanted it never to come, while they told and retold, almost reverently, tales of when they'd knelt to Azoun or talked with him or fought under him, and they stood unashamed while tears ran down their wrinkled cheeks and dripped from their mustaches. He'd known from their voices and the way they all looked from time to time down the road where the king had gone, hours before, that they shared the same heart-light feeling that he had, touched with wonder.

"Warmed by the reflected fire of the crown," he'd heard a minstrel describe that feeling once. Whatever. To Dauneth, that laughing man spurring past on the magnificent horse would always be King Azoun, no matter what passing years and the poison or disease or whatever it was had done to the man now, and he would fight, even die if need be, in Azoun's name because of that bright memory. Let Cormyr always have such men riding across it, laughing and exultant, the Purple Dragon bright on their breasts, the sun smiling down, the—

"Drunk already, lad? Should I let you have this second one, or 'twould it be an act of kind charity to drink it all myself?"

Dauneth jerked back from that jovial voice to blink at Rhauligan, for a moment measuring one laughing man against another . . . and then surging Azoun on his horse was gone, and the loud, living, and very boisterous merchant was thunking two tankards as tall and as cold as the first pair down on the table and following them to a seat on the other side of the table, while calls came from across the room of, "Rhauly!" "You old snake!" "Where're the two tankards you owe *me?*" and "So who's your friend, Old Rolling-guts?"

Glarasteer Rhauligan grinned at the room in general and bellowed, "Ho, Tessara! Got a kiss for me yet?"

The amorous lady untwined herself from the merchant enough to lift a slim, black-scabbarded longsword into view and say, not unkindly, "In here, Old Shortcoin!"

"Ah," the merchant said, leaning forward, "but what if I showed you a man just swimming in golden lions, eh?"

"I'd show you the next man to become your victim," Tessara told him promptly, "but as you're not likely to do any such thing, why don't you introduce your friend—or is he just the dupe who paid for your tankard?"

"Well, yes," Rhauligan admitted, sinking down behind his ale with a rueful smile and a wave of surrender. Amid general snorts and exclamations of mirth, he added, "But I'll do as you bid . . . and do it proper, too. Know, Dauneth, that the lady with the sharp blade and sharper tongue is Tessara, now company-for-hire but once a pirate on the sea that roils past the very docks of Suzail."

Tessara essayed a small, swaying bow and smile, without leaving the arms of the lean merchant, whom Rhauligan loudly introduced as Ithkur Onszibar, an independent long-haul caravan merchant from Amn hoping to find a business partner in Suzail to anchor the eastern end of his trade route. The man winced at this shrewd intelligence, whereupon the others in the Snout Room—save for the staring, disapproving table of priests and the silent, watchful mercenary—all roared with laughter.

Rhauligan made a mock bow of his own and identified the other two merchants as Gormon Turlstars, a dealer in blades and fine-tempered tools from Impiltur—the grim one—and Athalon Darvae, a textiles dealer from Saerloon who'd been thinking of moving to Suzail but was now having second thoughts. That observation brought as big a wince, and laugh, as Rhauligan's daring sally about the caravan master. When the jovial merchant introduced Dauneth Marliir, however, there were a few whistles and the room—the *entire* room, Dauneth noted uncomfortably—grew silently attentive.

"In town to watch an old foe die?" Tessara asked boldly, but Rhauligan saw the sudden flush of crimson cross the face of his newfound companion, from ear to ear to fingertips, and made a swift interjection.

"Now, now. How can the lad be doing that when he's but newly arrived in Suzail and doesn't even know what's going on? I'd like to hear the latest myself, O most masterful of gossips and spies!"

The room erupted in chatter as all four of Rhauligan's

acquaintances spoke at once. Dauneth thankfully covered his face with his tankard and thought about how good the Black Bottom ale was beginning to taste. The cacophony went on for some time, as none of the four, once started, had any intention of yielding to silence, but in the end it was the grim, stolid sword dealer who by dint of ponderous patience went on speaking after the others ran out of breath.

". . . and the Royal Wizard continues to meet with every noble that he can pry out of the backwoods," Turlstars concluded, his eyes rising suddenly to transfix Dauneth as if on a sword blade. The young noble almost choked on his ale.

As soon as he could safely speak, Dauneth filled the lengthening, expectant silence with the words, "Ah—no summons came to us from court that I know of, but several of my elders had been telling me for a season or more that it was high time I presented myself to the king, and I was told rather firmly about a month back that now was the time."

"About a month back," Darvae, the cloth merchant, echoed meaningfully, gesturing at Dauneth with his tankard.

Tessara snorted. "You see conspiracies and cabals under your trencher every evening, Athalon, and under your bed every morning, too!"

"You can get *under* his bed?" Rhauligan murmured. "This I must see!" The look Tessara gave him in return, amid the rising chuckles, had edges to it.

The caravan master Onszibar cleared his throat and said, "Athalon's inference is, however, an interesting idea. Is this affliction of the Obarskyrs the result of a plan so wide-ranging that someone's thought to drag all the young nobles of the realm here to Suzail to provide possible suspects for the attack on the royals?"

"Or to gather together nobles who are in on the plot," Rhauligan put in eagerly, "without rivals, such as the other noble houses, noticing amid all the arrivals?"

"Or," Tessara said softly, "to bring the nobles together

so that rivals are within easy reach, so whoever's behind this can more easily cut down foes and folk of families not in their favor?"

Caught in the center of a web of thoughtful glances, Dauneth felt suddenly that he was all too alone in a city of watching, waiting eyes where many blades were seeking his innards, rather than the exciting, bustling heart of the realm where one young Marliir in dusty boots was unknown and ignored. An unsettling view. He sighed and took another quaff from his tankard, hoping no one would see that his hands had started, ever so slightly, to tremble.

"But who has the wits to plan so deftly and bring Azoun to the edge of death and hold him there for so long?" Turlstars asked, bringing on a tense moment of silence that was ended—reluctantly—by the cloth merchant.

"Vangerdahast," Darvae said, waving one of his soursweet fish tarts for emphasis, "and his war wizards."

Rhauligan snorted. "If they wanted the throne," he said flatly, "they could've had it years ago, without all this drama. A few quick spells and a mind link or a crowned puppet wearing the face of a tracelessly-disposed-of Obarskyr, and none of us the wiser. This feels like the work of someone who's had to be very clever to *avoid* the war wizards."

There were nods at this, but the caravan master said, "I can't think our High Wizard's behind this either, but he is the busiest man in the kingdom right now, flitting from one back room to another with scarce a stop for the chamberpot in between."

More nods. "With most of the important nobles of the realm," Tessara murmured.

Turlstars chuckled and waved at Dauneth with his tankard. "He'll be getting to *you* soon, lad, just see if he doesn't."

"I'll be pleased to assure him of my loyalty to the crown," Dauneth said rather stiffly.

"Ah," Tessara said, leaning forward in her chair to

waggle a warning finger at him, her elbow on one knee, "but what if he comes to ask you to join in a task or two that leads to a new order in Cormyr?"

"A kingdom ruled by wizards?" Rhauligan said in disbelief. "The Sembians'd never stand for it. They'd hire every ambitious mageling they could find to smash such a realm!"

"Only to find their hirelings wiping out Vangerdahast's lot and then taking their places! Wizards with power never wish to give up that power, be it magical or political." The cloth merchant Darvae set down his own drink with a solid *thunk* to underscore his point.

"I'd not want to be a mage that tried any such thing," Ithkur Onszibar said dryly, "in a world that holds the Red Wizards of Thay, the Zhentarim, and the mage kings of Halruaa. Once the mage realm is built, what's to stop anyone with greater spells from taking it over from within?"

Turlstars waved a dismissive hand. "All this is hard-flying fancy, people. All we know is that Duke Bhereu has died, the king and Baron Thomdor linger near death despite wagonloads of priests and winged carpetfuls of war wizards laboring night and day, and our Royal Magician is trotting around meeting privately with various nobles, while all the younger sons of those same noble families, and all their elders who like to play at politics, converge on Suzail as if free dukedoms are being handed out at street corners."

"As indeed they soon may be," Athalon Darvae murmured.

Turlstars ignored the comment and continued. "Some folk think the wizard is just binding loyalties to the crown with threats and promises and making all the up-noses feel personally important. Others think he's adding heads to his *own* little organization."

"Or handing out orders to a cabal that's long since established, and using the other little talks to hide that, or even to lay little tracing or thought-probing spells on the nobles who aren't in his camp," Tessara put in, with a meaningful nod of her head in Dauneth's direction.

"But why all of this?" Rhauligan protested, waving his hands. One of them held a tankard, but as far as Dauneth could tell, the merchant had emptied it already. "We've all heard about the suit of armor that can heal and purify the man who sleeps in it and the spells that can grow new kings from a few pieces of the flesh of old ones."

"New kings for old!" Tessara called softly, grinning. "New kings for old!"

"Stow it," Rhauligan told her, not unkindly, and continued. "There are said to be thick-piled webs of safeguard spells on all senior Obarskyrs and heirs, as well as on the palace and the court and the royal hunting lodges and houses . . . and outback privies, for all I know! Have they *all* failed at once?"

"If a traitor among the wizards worked carefully to avoid detection," Tessara said gently, "I'd be surprised if magic that is done could not also be undone." Turlstars nodded grimly.

"I've heard," put in Darvae, "that Lady Laspeera and some of the other war wizards started searching the vaults under the palace for a cure, but Princess Tanalasta had them turned out and ordered the undercellars sealed."

"Seems as though she wants dear daddy to die," Tessara muttered.

Darvae spread his hands in a what-do-I-know gesture. "She said what struck down the king may have come from there, and it was best that such perils stay shut away until 'the realm is out of danger.' She must know what the vaults hold better than any of us."

"The Doom of the Obarskyrs," the caravan master intoned somberly. "The armories of the war wizards, full of stolen spells and locked lich tomes and strange things that flash and whir about but haven't yet been probed for their secrets. Iron statues that walk. The Cursed Crowns. The meeting room of the Sword Heralds. The—"

"Lost Wyvern of Menacha. Yes, yes, and the stuffed remains of the Obarskyrs' adversaries," Turlstars said

Ed Greenwood and Jeff Grubb

dismissively. "We've all heard the legends, and they're just more flying fancy. I suspect that a lot of the talk I'm hearing around Suzail is the stuff of dreams, too . . . but we may as well wade through it. . . ."

"Especially as some of it is *really* rich," Darvae agreed with a grin. "Would you believe that Gondegal the Lost King has been seen in Marsember?"

"High Horn, I heard," Tessara said quickly. "And he's behind all this!"

"He and a hitherto unknown descendant of evil Prince Regent Salember!" Onszibar put in.

"What?" Turlstars asked sarcastically. "Not Salember himself?"

"Well," Tessara said, leaning forward to speak in low, urgent tones, "you may all laugh about wild rumors, but I was told by a friend I trust well that Lady Laspeera of the war wizards—second in rank of them all, after Vangerdahast himself—has disappeared. Some in the palace are saying she may have been entombed alive in the palace vaults when the Purple Dragons sealed them, at the command of the princess."

"That may just be true," Turlstars said thoughtfully, but Darvae made a rude sound of disagreement.

"I doubt soldiers as busy as they are right now could find the time to seal off all the ways a wizard might find to get out of a cellar," Darvae pronounced.

"Busy?" Rhauligan pounced.

The cloth merchant grinned wryly. "They're saying down the Promenade that there's a private war going on between Purple Dragons loyal to Tanalasta and those cleaving to the old wizard, Vangerdahast. Most of the court officials, like the sages Dimswart and Alaphondar, are supporting the wizard, but one wing of the palace is supposed to be awash in blood . . . entire hallways choked with armor-clad corpses."

"Some folk have vivid imaginations," Tessara murmured. "I heard that Alaphondar the sage was slain defending the queen from assassins, and the queen lies on her deathbed mere feet from her husband."

"But that's just it!" protested Onszibar. "What do we know to help us sort out the fancy from what's actually going on in the palace? What do we really know?"

Gormon Turlstars nodded, saying heavily, "On the way here I heard two nobles discussing where to hide. They think someone is stabbing all the nobles who dare to go to see Tanalasta and leaving them to die in the palace or to crawl out!"

Darvae nodded. "I heard that, too. It seems one made it as far as the royal gardens yesterday before collapsing."

"I can crown all," Rhauligan said grandly, holding up a hand for attention. "A guard in the palace who's been stationed close to the dying king says that the priests have been defeated by whatever ails him, and that they plan to keep our Azoun on the throne by using dark magic to make him undead!"

Turlstars snorted. "Even if you believed the priests could agree with each other to do that, do you think the people would stand for it?"

"Would they accept a regency where Vangerdahast rules, after marrying Queen Filfaeril?" Tessara asked. "I've heard that rumor several times."

"Yes, yes," Turlstars said disgustedly. "And the Purple Dragons, the war wizards, and the nobles are all planning to seize the throne. Red Wizards and Zhentarim have been seen openly walking the Promenade—"

"Well, they have!" Rhauligan said sharply. "I myself saw a man I know to be a Zhent mageling! I've heard that a man walking north of the court, near the royal gardens, was seen to change shape! If that isn't the work of a wizard . . ."

Tessara sighed. "So the realm is falling apart as we watch, and loyal Vangerdahast is to blame, either because he's causing it—"

"Or he's not stopping it," Turlstars agreed heavily.

Dauneth had been sitting silent behind his tankard, listening with growing horror . . . and then, slowly, a rising anger. How cynical these folk were—all of them! Did the king's life mean nothing? Did they believe no word spoken by anyone of the court? He saw again Azoun laughing in his saddle, arms spread wide, and heard a voice saying angrily, "From where I come from, the word 'loyal' is not an empty joke. The crown is worth upholding, worth fighting for. It is what makes us better than the money-grubbing Sembians or the savages of Tunland. Have a care for your words, for I will fight to see that King Azoun's name remains unsullied!"

The young noble blinked. They were all staring at him. He had half risen from his seat. It seemed that the angry voice had been his own.

"Ah," he said in some confusion, noting that even Glarasteer Rhauligan was gaping at him, and sat down again. "What I mean to say is that Lord Vangerdahast is older than the mountains. Why would he be a traitor? It sounds to me like he's just trying to keep the court running until the king is well again."

Tessara's dark eyes narrowed. "That's a peculiar way for a Marliir to talk—supporting the crown."

"What do you mean?" Dauneth asked softly, feeling a trembling rage surging up in him. Without thinking, his hand reached for his blade.

His fingers met the cold edge of a drawn sword, blocking his way to his own scabbard. Tessara's eyes were as wintry as the steel under his fingertips as she said, "Does your family not speak of such things as their war with King Dhalmass? Or the Prince Regent Salember? Or do they prefer not to deal with past defeats?"

"I—" Dauneth began hotly, and then fell silent because he realized he had nothing to say. His family didn't speak of such matters, and this woman looked as if she knew exactly what she was talking about . . . as well as how to handle a sword. He'd not even seen her draw the blade that she was now slowly pulling back, tip lifted a little to catch his gaze as a warning. He looked past it and into her eyes, and suddenly he thought how beautiful she looked, hard and confident, and . . .

He knew he was blushing again and managed to say,

"Lady, I meant no offense to anyone here. I was simply shocked by the way all of you—"

"Spoke lightly of the realm?" Rhauligan said roughly. "Lad, that doesn't mean we don't love it!"

The short silence that followed his words was broken by a drawl from Darvae. "Well, it seems the young high-boots is a panther, after all."

Someone started to laugh, but fell silent. The entire Snout Room joined in the sudden, tense stillness.

A man had come into the room, walking alone, a stout man in a plain brown robe, bound about the waist with a tasseled rope of the palest mauve. He looked about, his brown eyes almost stern, and Dauneth felt as if the man's brief glance had named, measured, and taken inventory of all the clothing and gear of a certain young Marliir.

Though many would not have called the paunchy, bareheaded man in robes impressive, everyone in the Roving Dragon had fallen silent—and stayed that way as Vangerdahast, the Royal Magician of Cormyr, went to the table where the mercenary captain was sitting. They exchanged wordless nods, and the wizard sat down, favoring the room with a wry little smile as he did so. Abruptly the sounds of chatter, creaking cartwheels, and shouting street vendors filled the room. The sounds of the Promenade outside, somehow brought in to swirl about . . .

Magic. Of course. To keep others from overhearing. Dauneth gaped at the stout wizard, who was leaning forward, elbows on the mercenary's table. They talked briefly and quietly, then nodded and rose together, striding out without looking around or acknowledging a tentative hail from Rhauligan. The sounds of the street went out with them, leaving the end room of the Roving Dragon silent again.

It was Tessara who broke the stillness, asking in a low voice, "Now, why does the Lord High Wizard of Cormyr need to hire mercenaries? To fight off rebellious nobles? Or Purple Dragons?"

"Yes . . . and Dragons loyal to whom?" Turlstars said grimly.

"We'll know soon enough, I fear," Rhauligan said almost wearily. He looked up at Dauneth. "You picked a bad time to come to Suzail, lad."

The young noble shrugged, affecting a confidence he did not feel. "If the realm needs me . . ."

Tessara smiled suddenly. "It saves riding here, you mean?" She shook her head and added, "You may be called on all too soon. The realm needs strong, orderly rule, or your fellow nobles, locked in feuds and rivalries that go back past all our memories, will tear it apart like hungry wolves."

"I've never seen darker days in Suzail," Turlstars said heavily. "What I want to know most of all is how can the realm survive?"

16

The King's Touch
Year of the Sea Princes
(432 DR)

t's never been this bad, thought Elvarin Crownsilver in the darkness. How can the realm possibly survive?

She looked around the night-shadowed forest. Here were the last of the great House of Obarskyr, huddling in the dark, waiting for a traitor to bring them their first victory.

Their first victory in three long years of being hunted through the king's own forest. Or their final defeat.

It all had begun with Baerauble's death, of course. Everything was always traced to the death of the original High Mage. Without his steadying hand, every wobble of fate seemed to bring the realm closer to its destruction. He seemed to be eternal, Cormyr's protector forever . . . and then he was gone. Amedahast, his student, was the best mage Crownsilver knew, but she was a mere shadow of her mentor.

And how could they have known that their proud, prosperous kingdom was a merest soap bubble, which must be constantly protected from the harsh realities of the outside world lest it collapse and swallow them all?

A plague came first, borne by merchants from

Marsember, decimating the folk of the countryside and turning bright Suzail into a charnel house where the dead lay in heaps on the streets. At first the priests fought it as best as they could, but when the sickness spread so fast and they had only so many healing spells and so many prayers left, the holy folk chose to keep their healings for themselves. A bad decision, since the city dwellers had more swords. When the dust cleared, there were no priests to be found save those of Talona, who spread the plague further.

Then dragons descended on Suzail and Arabel and every small encampment from the mountains to the sea. Great blues settled upon the fields and tore apart houses, and massive reds laid fiery waste to entire regions. Greens raided the few ships and caravans that sought to reach Cormyr. Even the mythical Purple Dragon was reported in an attack on the western settlements.

Arabel was gone in a night, this latest rebellion championed by a "Merchants' Revolutionary Committee." But now other holds and homesteads had risen and rebelled as well. It was hard to send men to aid the beleaguered crown when half the population was dying and the other half fighting dragons in the fields. Crown agents were killed, and government coffers looted.

Then the orcs arrived, driven south by some nasty battle in the Stonelands. Normally such a threat would bring Arabel back into the kingdom, but now there was little in the way of a Cormyrean army to send aid. The goblin-kin seized the heart of the King's Forest.

And when King Duar set out to defeat the orcish army, his own father-in-law, Melineth Turcassan, sold the city of Suzail to the pirates for five hundred sacks of gold.

His Majesty destroyed the largest of the orcish armies, but returned to find his throne stolen and the gates of his city barred against him. Worse, the pirate lord, Magrath the Minotaur, kept the crippled city as his prize and plundered the treasury for mercenaries to expand his reach into the rest of Cormyr.

That was three years ago, and in three years, those loyal to the crown had seen their numbers ebb—from battle losses, from treachery, and from raw despair. Many of the nobles, Crownsilver included, had shipped their families north to the Dales or west to Waterdeep. The loyal nobles broke into smaller groups, and still smaller bands. Duar's present band numbered only twenty.

Elvarin looked about the glade in the full moonlight. She and her cousin Glorin Truesilver. Jotor Turcassan, who had broken with the rest of his treacherous family; Omalra Dracohorn; and Dintheron Bleth. The men were the last of the Purple Dragons, their adventuring group from before everything collapsed. The rest of their ragged band were non-noble swordsmen and retainers. And King Duar, of course, and Amedahast.

Duar waited in the darkness, looking more like a funereal statue than a living soul. He was a giant even among Obarskyrs, but his great, muscular shoulders seemed weighed down by more than the crown he still wore. The betrayal of Melineth had almost broken him, and it would take a long time for him to truly recover. The death of the Turcassans later that year, at the hands of their treacherous allies, eased the pain only a little. He slept in his armor, and his tabard and robes were tattered and grimy. The only new item on his person was the sword Amedahast had crafted for him, Orbyn, the Edge of Justice, which slept for the moment in a battered sheath.

Duar had truly become King of the Forest Country, a refugee hiding in the broad expanse of the King's Forest. The orcs and goblins soon learned that this was not a land to settle in and retreated to the north. The dragons, too, had gone, returning to whatever slumber engulfed them after a rampage. And while Magrath the Minotaur put a price on Duar's head higher than what he'd paid for Suzail itself, he had few takers among the fearful common folk.

The common folk. Crownsilver shook her head at the thought. Entire hand counts of noble families switched sides at the drop of a crown. Cities like Arabel declared their independence with fickle regularity. But the common folk, the people in the farms and the villages and isolated homesteads, they always rallied around their king. Their group might be battered and beaten, looking little better than the brigands who now prowled the road from Suzail to Arabel. Yet one look at their grim king always brought out the best food and hidden weapons and the secret supplies. Despite threats and bribes, the common folk stood by their king.

And finally they heard some good news. Word came from her cousin, Agrast Huntsilver, that the High Horn had fallen into their hands, and the military units there were willing to throw in with the king. But only if Duar could produce a victory, and produce it fast. Crownsilver, His Majesty, and the mage frowned over the maps for all one long day before choosing the site of the attack. It was central to the kingdom, lightly guarded, and, most importantly, it was held by a noble family that had thrown in with Magrath's pirates: House Dheolur.

Elvarin frowned in the darkness. Duar's own grandfather had elevated the Dheolurs to nobility, and they'd spent the next three generations plotting and planning and scheming. They gained the right to put their stockaded settlement in the heart of the forest, and then did everything in their power to undermine the crown. When Suzail was seized, House Dheolur swore fealty to Magrath in an instant.

There was a noise in the distance, no more than the snapping of a twig. Everyone stiffened at the sound but Amedahast. The wizard stood up silently and looked in the direction of the noise. She had elven blood in her veins, but of late, Elvarin was sure it was ice water. Rumor had it that some Cormyrean noble had broken her heart at a young age. Elvarin just hoped for her sake that said noble was not a Crownsilver; Amedahast looked like a woman who held grudges.

Everyone held his breath for a moment as something moved at the opposite edge of the glade. A lone man appeared, moving cautiously. He was dressed in a cotton blouse and patched woolen pants, and his unkempt gray hair jutted in all directions from beneath a shapeless cap. He held an unlit lantern in his hand. He was clearly visible in the moonlight, as were they.

The old farmer waved the unlit lantern slowly.

Amedahast duplicated the motion in return, and the farmer limped forward, smiling.

Duar arose from where he'd been sitting. Upon seeing the king's face, the old farmer threw himself to his knees in respect. The king walked up to him and knelt as well, taking the old man by the shoulder and lifting him to his feet. Crownsilver had seen this many times now. Duar had become very good at it, and it sealed the loyalty of the peasants he embraced so. The touch of a king still held great power.

The two engaged in a conversation of hushed whispers. Amedahast and Crownsilver reached them at the same moment.

"Magrath is there," said Duar, smiling.

"So our information was correct," said Amedahast solemnly.

"Aye," said the farmer. "He's a hulking beast, Sire, with horns long as my arms. He's got his men up there, as well. They're in the main feast hall, and will be for the next several hours. There are a lot of them."

"So the victory will be that much sweeter," said Duar.

"You knew?" said Elvarin. "You knew Magrath would be here?"

"We suspected," said Amedahast. "It was one reason we chose Dheolur in the first place. We'll get High Horn's troops if we win a town, but we can throw all the pirates into disarray if we kill or capture their leader."

And what of the disarray if we lose you? thought Crownsilver. Instead, she said, "Is this wise, Your Majesty? We are but twenty, and it's a full-moon night. We'll be spotted as soon as we break cover."

"Spotted by drunken guards and watchmen more interested in what is going on within the settlement than without. Do you remember where the feast hall in Dheolur is?"

"Aye," said Crownsilver stonily. "I also remember the twenty-foot wall around the hold. What are we to do about that? Does Amedahast here have a spell that will allow us all to pass through walls?"

The wizard shot Crownsilver a look that froze her blood, but Elvarin did not care. If she was going to die following her king, it would not be because they had forgotten so simple a thing as the main gate.

"The plan is already well in hand," said Duar quietly. "Trust me and follow me, as you have followed me thus far."

With that, the farmer set off, followed by Amedahast, Duar, Crownsilver, and the others. They left their horses behind. Elvarin knew that if they needed mounts this night, it would be because their cause was already lost.

Dheolur was surrounded with a stout stockade, rising protectively around the warehouses and homes of House Dheolur. The traitor house. Elvarin remembered what she could not yet see in the darkness.

The place needed the protection of its wall, for even in the best of times, goblins and other monsters came wandering out of the King's Forest. Inside now would be Lord Dheolur, his loathsome and reptilian sister Pella, and Lady Threena, a Cormaeril who'd married into the household. Of the lot, Threena was the only one worth more than a bucket of warm suet. Elvarin hoped she would survive this night. But then, she hoped all of the folk with her, advancing cautiously through the forest, would survive this night.

The feast hall would also be the main warehouse, emptied for the revel. It stood to the right-hand side of the stockade, facing Dheolur Manor on the left, a large and ugly sprawl of pretentious turrets and wings built on the ruins of a temple that once stood there. And whose temple had that been? Elvarin thought for a moment. Moander, Threena Cormaeril had told her. Some minor and malicious deity of rot and decay.

Such a god would have a good home here. Dheolur was surrounded by low, peaty bogs and patches of marsh. This, more than any stockade wall, served it as protection. The farmer knew the way, and they kept to a series of forested rills, the ferns of the undergrowth slapping against their armored legs and thighs. All through their journey, Elvarin was concerned they'd be spotted, but if anyone noticed their passing, no alarm was raised.

They reached the clearing that surrounded Dheolur. The rebellious nobles had ordered the forest cut back a hundred yards in all directions but had not maintained their vigilance since that burst of good sense. Already ferns and spindly saplings were growing in the blasted land. Still, one had a clear view of the stockade, the gatehouse, and a crudely built watchtower. Despite the full moon, Elvarin could not determine if the dark wooden structure was occupied.

What now? Was Amedahast going to make herself invisible, fly over the walls, and open the gates for them? Elvarin could not believe the king would risk his last surviving mage.

Duar said something to the wizard, and the farmer drew close with his lantern. Amedahast muttered something short and sharp, and a flame appeared at her fingertip. The farmer held the lantern steady, its shutters closed. The mage lifted the glass globe and lit the wick.

The farmer faced the settlement and opened the shutters of the lantern, then closed them again immediately. Then a second time, this time a little longer, then closed again. Short-long, short-long.

There was a pause, during which all in the royal party held their breath. Then there was a response from the guard tower itself. Short-long, short-long.

Duar gave the signal to advance. The entire party, blades drawn, moved forward into the clearing.

The farmer remained, and Duar turned to him. Elvarin passed near as the two talked.

"You have the thanks of the rightful king. What is your name, good man?"

"Dhedluk, Sire," said the farmer, and he spelled it.

King Duar nodded and said, "When the victory is ours, you will be remembered." He laid a hand on the man's forearm, and the startled farmer clasped arms with his king, as equals. When Duar released his grip, the man dropped immediately to his knees. The king clapped him on the shoulder and hauled him up again. And with that, he and Elvarin joined the others.

Elvarin's breathing was tight and ragged as they crossed the blasted field by moonlight. Duar had a spy within, probably another farmer like Dhedluk. Or perhaps a guard who'd volunteered for watch duty while the others were occupied.

Or perhaps it was all a trap, and they'd arrive at the stockade with no open gate and no ladder or rope to gain entrance. Then archers would appear over the sharp rim of the palisade and cut them down like a farmer scything barley.

They were almost at the wall when a shadowy line appeared in it. The gate had been opened—not fully, just a crack. The opening would have been invisible if the moon had not been full.

They reached the gate, and Amedahast pulled it open enough to allow two men to pass through at a time. Elvarin was among the first into the encampment, alongside the king. They were alone on the other side of the gate. Of their benefactor, there was no sign.

Behind them, Amedahast stepped inside, closed the gate, and drove the bolt home. Then she spoke a few words, and the lock flared with a brief, yellow-green radiance. She had locked them inside. No one would be leaving this battle until it was over.

The manor stood on one hand, and the large improvised feast hall on the other. Crates and barrels had been removed for the celebration honoring Magrath and were piled untidily at the ends of the warehouse. There was no sign of any guards. The manor was shrouded in darkness, but the thin, high windows of the warehouse were lit from within. The shouts and laughter of drunken men, muffled only slightly by the walls, streamed from the interior.

Duar pointed at three of the common soldiers, and they crept forward with torches, again lit by the High Mage of the Wolf Woods. A pile of canvas sacks provided tinder, and the flames licked at a pile of crates bunched against the side of the warehouse. They caught fire almost immediately, and a deep roar began. Flames flickered hungrily upward, and the thatch roof flared with a crackle.

The reaction was almost immediate. There was a great chorus of shouting from within, orders were bellowed, women screamed, and the celebration became pandemonium.

The main doors of the warehouse, facing the manor house, burst wide open, and a press of humanity streamed out: serving girls and cooks, merchants and toadies, all sprinting and stumbling. And behind them, led by Dheolur himself, came the household guards. Behind those armored forms, framed in the growing radiance of the fire, was the shadowy hulk of Magrath himself.

The women and servants fled from the reaching flames to the manor, sobbing, and Duar's men let them go. The warriors saw their waiting foes and strode forward without pause. With a cry, the Purple Dragons engaged them.

Dheolur, resplendent in black plate armor brought all the way from Chondath, charged Duar. The chased and fluted armor was Dheolur's pride and joy, and he'd apparently wanted to impress his guests by wearing it. The renegade noble's helm was down, and he looked like an angry clockwork figure. His blade was long and slightly curved, and its edge glittered in the moonlight.

Duar stood to meet him, blade held out to one side, his tattered robes barely covering the chain mail beneath. The gold circlet gleamed on his head. As Dheolur rushed at him, Duar stepped aside with a grace that belied his large frame. The renegade lord's blade sliced through the night air, the force of his cut turning him halfway around.

Before Dheolur could recover, the king's blade arched upward. Orbyn's own soft glow rivaled that of the moon as it rose. There came the wet scream of cloven steel and flesh, and Dheolur's body and helm fell to the ground and bounced, in separate places.

Elvarin's enjoyment of the traitor's demise was hampered by her own difficulties, in the form of three of Magrath's crew, two men and an orc. All wielded short blades, and one had a hook for a hand as well. Her sword gave her a longer reach than any of them, but they surrounded her, one keeping at her back at all times. She was forced to wheel, beat back an attack, wheel again to strike aside another attack, and turn swiftly once more to avoid yet another blow. They'd tire her out quickly at this game and then close in for the kill, she realized, thrusting in unison. They knew her fate as well, for exultant laughter was rising from their drunken lips.

Hook-hand was at her back now. He lunged. Elvarin did not turn quite fast enough to avoid the blade, and she could feel the sharp burning sensation of the chain links of her vest being driven through her sweat-soaked fabric undershirt—and into her flesh beneath. The sword's cutting edge had been stopped, but she could feel the wetness of blood oozing out between the links.

Hook-hand's blade snagged for a moment, caught in the ravaged chain mail, and Elvarin took advantage of the distraction to sway back from the slashing blade of one of her other attackers and reach out with her free hand as she did so. She grabbed the hooked hand of her assailant and pulled. The startled man snarled and tried to wrench free, but Elvarin planted her feet firmly and jerked him off-balance.

Hook-hand let out a cry as he was dragged by his hook. Elvarin swung him in a wide arc toward the orc.

That twisted humanoid, the most drunken of the lot, only had time to look up and grunt a vague curse before his companion-at-arms slammed into him. Both crashed to the ground.

With two down, the third pirate was child's play. Two quick slashes, and he lay on the soft earth at her feet, moaning and clutching vainly at the deep wounds in his belly.

Twice Elvarin thrust down pitilessly. Hook-hand and the orc would not be getting up. Almost as an after-thought, she slashed the third pirate's fingers away from his dagger, flicking both flesh and steel away out of his reach, and stepped back. Firmly bidding the pain in her side to begone, she looked around.

The manor yard had become a proper battlefield around her, and carnage pooled and flowed in tight little knots. Truesilver was on the ground, his inert form being beaten with furniture by three goblins. Dheolur lay be-headed not far away. King Duar was engaged with Ma-grath now, the minotaur keeping glowing Orbyn at bay with a huge double-headed axe. Of Amedahast there was no sign. Fifteen or so other small battles between king's men and renegades swirled in the space between the burning warehouse and the manor.

Then Elvarin saw her. A figure in dark robes moving stealthily opposite the fire, a flitting shadow in the night, circling to attack the king from behind. Her hood was down. It was Pella, Dheolur's sister, her cruel lips set. No doubt she was as poisonous and foul-tempered as ever. For a moment, her hand showed in the full sleeve of her garment, and a dagger with a wavy, crooked blade glittered in the firelight.

The king did not see her approach, but Magrath did. He worked to keep Duar busy, not pressing his attack but hammering down so many quick, darting blows that the king was held in one place. Time and again Duar would lunge forward, only to have his blade turned aside by the battle-axe's thick ironwood haft. Pella circled around, placing herself behind the king.

Elvarin shouted and charged forward, leading with her unwounded side. She did not try to use her blade, but instead slammed into Pella with her shoulder, sending the woman sprawling. The wicked dagger spun away into the darkness.

The force of their meeting sent the staggering Elvarin to the ground as well, losing her grip on her blade. Pella recovered before she did, and in a moment, she pounced on the Crownsilver warrior with serpentlike grace. Throwing herself on top of Elvarin with thrusting knees, she clawed at the warrior's face.

Elvarin heaved and gasped, trying to shift the woman off her, but Pella seemed to have the strength of a huge beast, not the puny might her fairly small frame should have commanded.

Then one of those clawing hands drew back to strike— and Elvarin saw the horror of Pella's palms. Instead of unbroken, cupped skin below her fingers, Pella Dheolur's flesh was split with twisted mouths filled with sharp teeth and framed with oozing green lips. Elvarin struggled frantically and turned her head to one side, but Pella brought her open, toothy palm down on the Crownsilver's bare cheek. Elvarin screamed as needle-sharp teeth bit into her flesh. Pella's haglike laughter rose harsh and shrill around her.

And then the laughter broke and ended. A slender hand had taken Pella by the hair, pulling her backward. The Dheolur noblewoman was unprepared, and the jaws closing on Elvarin's face loosened for a moment.

Elvarin blinked back tears of pain and shook her head to shake away the blood and let her see.

Amedahast was hauling Pella over backward by a hand locked in her hair. The noblewoman was clawing the air vainly, trying to reach the wizard, as she was peeled bodily away from Elvarin.

Then the High Mage shouted a spell, and her free hand burst into a ball of cold blue flame. Pella clutched at Amedahast, but the fangs in her palms seemed unable to gain purchase on her.

Amedahast shoved the small fireball into Pella's face. The noblewoman screamed and writhed as roaring flames spread along her cloak and into her hair. The High Mage let go and stepped back. Pella tried to rise, her eyes glowing holes against an ashen skull beneath. She staggered forward, faltered, and with a banshee's wail collapsed in a tattered heap of burning rags.

Pella's final scream distracted Magrath the Minotaur, and that was all Duar needed. He drove his blade forward, glancing off the axe to catch the minotaur at the base of his breastbone, and shoved the steel upwards into the creature's rib cage.

The great beast was pinioned on the blade like a bug on a needle. The great axe fell, and a choking howl burst from the pirate leader as blood gushed from his mouth. Then slowly the minotaur sagged down on the blade, flung up one arm, and twisted around, convulsing. Finally he fell backward.

With the death of Magrath, the fight went out of the rest of the defenders of the hold. Some laid down their weapons immediately, while others, particularly the goblins, sought to flee from the stockade. They were stopped by Amedahast's sealed gates. The would-be escapees tried to make a stand, but the king's men grimly cut them down where they stood.

Elvarin stood up slowly and painfully, retrieving her blade. The wound in her side and the deep cut on her face rivaled each other for pain. The gouge on her cheek would likely scar, but at least she'd have a tale to tell for it. Amedahast could probably tell her what spell or curse had given Pella Dheolur biting mouths in her palms ... and if the wound itself was poisoned.

There was a flash of blonde hair and blue cloth from the manor house door. Elvarin raised her blade, but Amedahast put a restraining hand on the swordswoman's shoulder. Threena Cormaeril dashed down the steps and embraced the bloody Duar. The force of their laughing embrace spun the weary king around, and he almost fell over.

Ed Greenwood and Jeff Grubb

Elvarin chuckled, pain making the sound harsher than usual, and said, "So that was our inside agent. I should have guessed. There has always been more than one way to conquer a town."

Amedahast made no reply. Elvarin looked at her. The High Mage was stony in her silence, her brow furrowed deeply as if she'd been revisited by some old pain. Without a word, she turned and walked away, making for where the wounded were being gathered.

In the light from the blazing warehouse, Elvarin watched the king and the lady holding each other. Victory. They had captured Dheolur, and with Threena's aid, they'd be able to hold it. The forces from High Horn could then commit to a forest campaign . . . and with Magrath dead, the pirates might even abandon Suzail rather than face a siege. The days—the years—ahead would not be easy, but Cormyr might survive after all.

Never underestimate the power of the king's touch, thought Elvarin. Using her sword to support herself, the warrior limped to where Amedahast was already unpacking the healing potions and poultices.

17

Meetings
Year of the Gauntlet
(1369 DR)

he man in the gem-studded tunic and cloth-of-gold breeches knelt, drew his sword, and laid it at the feet of the silent man in robes.

Still on his knees, the gaudily dressed nobleman looked up and said firmly, "I, Embryn Crownsilver, being mindful of what I do, solemnly pledge my honor, my blade, and the arm that wields it to support you as Regent of Cormyr. I will fight to bring about the downfall of the decadent Obarskyrs, who have ruled *far* too long." His last words rang around the small, high-ceilinged antechamber.

"Take up your sword," the man he was kneeling before said quietly. "Your words will be remembered."

Rather uncertainly the Crownsilver noble rose from his knees, jeweled blade in hand. Sheathing it with a flourish, he turned, half-cloak swirling, and strode hastily away.

The man in robes watched him go. The nobles of this realm certainly talked to one another swiftly. That was the fifth pledge this morning, and nothing had been said in public yet about a regency. Not that such a silence was all that surprising; to many, in Suzail especially, the

Ed Greenwood and Jeff Grubb

word 'regent' was synonymous with 'tyrant.' Or one could just say, "Salember."

Vangerdahast the Royal Regent. The robed man smiled thinly and struck a dramatic pose, shading his eyes as he stared at the far wall of the chamber, an imaginary crown on his brow. Then he snorted in self-mockery and turned back to his spellbooks. Strange things happen to kingdoms when folk start getting ideas. . . .

* * * * *

Not all that far away from the palace, in the nearest wing of the court, one nobleman turned to another and said, "If my son ever gets back from traipsing around the wilderness with Princess Alusair, I'm going to send him away from the realm for a month or so. I don't want someone thinking he might make a good king, then sliding a sword through him to preclude that chance."

"A Skatterhawk on the throne?" Sardyn Wintersun mused. "You know, I can see that. Does your son still think the moon, sun, and stars ride in the heart of the wayward princess?"

Narbreth Skatterhawk looked a little smug. "He does, my lord, and I can say more. A Purple Dragon she sent back from Eveningstar with their last report says he saw her kiss him, right on the lips, and hungrily, like a tavern wench, in front of everyone!"

Sardyn chuckled and ran a hand through his white-streaked hair. "I mean no slight to our friendship, my lord, but it's not for nothing that the common folk say Alusair would kiss her horse if it trotted up to her!"

The head of House Skatterhawk laughed, a little stiffly, but whatever he might have said was swept aside by a cheerful greeting from behind them both. "Well met this fair day, pillars of the realm!"

Sardyn rolled his eyes once in silent eloquence before he turned, and Narbreth almost sputtered with laughter. Almost.

254

Ondrin Dracohorn was resplendent in flaming scarlet, his swept-sleeve tunic open clear down to the waist to reveal a heavy row of golden spanglestars and medallions that resembled, but did not exactly duplicate, some of the medals awarded by the crown to valorous soldiers.

The hue of his wardrobe was matched by the daringly slit gowns worn by the ladies on each of Ondrin's arms, ladies whose beauty both of the other nobles had admired at feasts and revels before. They were the finest that discreet money could buy in Suzail. Their graceful elegance made the little man strutting between them look like a puffed-up peacock.

Neither Sardyn nor Narbreth bothered to tell him that, of course. Their houses, the Skatterhawks and Wintersuns, were minor nobility and country nobles to boot, and it would be ungracious to offend one of the more established city families. Instead, they put on broad smiles and said, "Ondrin, old friend!" and "How goes the Dracohorn all men of sense listen to?"

"Things couldn't be better, my lords, couldn't be better," Ondrin said with an airy wave of his hand. "I've just heard that Embryn Crownsilver's been to see our court wizard about a certain matter."

The heads of House Skatterhawk and House Wintersun exchanged glances.

"We've heard about that affair, Ondrin. You can speak freely," Sardyn replied, and then winked at one of the hired ladies. Said lady, a safe pace behind Ondrin and a head taller, was mouthing a wide-eyed and silently dramatic 'No! Please, no!' plea against his invitation to Ondrin to talk.

Ondrin chuckled like the man of the world he was. "I have secrets that I dare not yet reveal, even to such old and trusted friends as you! I'll say only this." He leaned close, like a small boy furtively passing secrets, and whispered loudly, "You'd better go see the Royal Magician. I'm setting him up as regent, you know."

* * * * *

Ondrin's supposed regent was at that moment slipping behind a curtain in the garderobe attached to his chambers. The little corner of the room facing him held a marble bust of a bored-looking Baerauble on a pedestal to Vangerdahast's left, and a shelf full of neatly folded towels and dishes of scented soaps on his right. A row of carved gargoyle faces, which bore an uncanny resemblance to the four previous High Mages of the realm, ran along the wall, and the floor here was tiled in a chessboard pattern of alternating dark and light squares.

Ignoring Baerauble's unmoving gaze, the Royal Magician put one hand on his head, stretched forward uncomfortably to touch the fingers of his other hand to a certain gargoyle nose, and then touched the toe of his right boot to a particular tile square. Silent radiance rose and sparkled around him.

When it faded, he was somewhere else, somewhere piled with towels and soaps. It was the servants' closet off the retiring room in one of the royal apartments. The voices he'd hoped to hear came clearly to his ears as he made a certain gesture, then sat down comfortably on nothing to listen, his generous behind perched on empty air.

". . . I know things seem dark, Tana," Aunadar Bleth was saying soothingly, "but Cormyr has faced tougher times than this and survived. If the gods gather in your father, you'll just have to take the throne and rule as well as he would have wanted you to."

The young princess's only reply was a royal sob.

"Whatever you decide, I'll be here," Aunadar went on in a low voice. He was probably holding the crown princess with one hand and stroking her hair with the other, the wizard thought. He almost smiled, but instead, the young Bleth's next words made him stiffen.

"I, and a few others like me, will stand with you, whatever the old wizard tries to do. He's gathering the nobles to proclaim him royal regent, you know. I've even heard he's going to use spells to fabricate some document or other, signed by your father, authorizing him to rule . . . a document whose signature magically comes from some other writ, of course. He'll say he just plans to run the realm until you feel better able to do so—or until you produce an heir—but once he gets his hands on the Dragon Throne, no one of Obarskyr blood will ever sit on it again."

There was another sob, and then an agonized, whispering voice. "But what shall I *do?* He has all those spells! And he knows where all father's magic and wealth lies hidden, and—and just what old feuds and embarrassments and promises will make all the nobles dance to any tune he plays!"

"Not all, Lady Highness." Bleth's voice was firm. "Some few men stand ready to defend the cause of right. Some valiant few. I count myself fortunate to stand among them, when the realm needs me so—when *you* need me so, dove of my heart!"

"Oh, Aunadar," the crown princess said with a thankful, tearful sigh. "I don't know what I'd do without you! All of these grim men stride around demanding that I make decisions, and all the while, they're waiting for me to say one thing wrong . . . *one thing!* Then they can smile and nod and say, 'Aha! I *knew* she wasn't fit to rule! See what a mess she's made of our land? Best she be slain forthwith, or sent to one of our beds, to produce an heir *we* shall rear to be a proper king!' "

"I think you are fit to rule, my princess. I stand ready to fight with this sword to give you your chance, and I'll face all the wizards in Faerûn if that's what it takes!"

"Oh, Aunadar!" Tanalasta gasped again. In the gloom of the servants' closet, Vangerdahast made a mock vomiting mime of disgust. If he had to listen to much more of this . . .

The wet, murmuring sounds that were coming to his ears now meant that they were kissing. Long, hungry, tightly embraced kisses of the sort that made ladies-in-waiting swoon and old crones go all bright-eyed with nostalgia. Vangerdahast almost tore the closet door open and growled at them to get *on* with it.

Ed Greenwood and Jeff Grubb

Then Aunadar spoke again. "I must leave you now, my sweet. The wizard's plots and schemes are relentless and spread even as we speak. My friends and I must work against them tirelessly, or not a noble house in the land may be truly loyal to the new crowned Queen Tanalasta!"

"Aunadar, don't say that!" the princess protested. "Father's going to get well, and—"

"Of course," the young nobleman said quietly. "And when he does, you'll be able to show him a decisive, even-handed, masterful stewardship of the realm—your work of devotion during his infirmity. I know you will. Fare thee well, Tana, until next our lips meet!"

"Oh, Aunadar, do take care! The wizard's folk are everywhere! Keep safe, will you?"

"Princess, I will," the young Bleth's voice came distantly, and a door closed. Tanalasta erupted into sobs.

Vangerdahast listened to her for a time, pity on his frowning face, and then shrugged. So she wanted to be a true Obarskyr? Then 'twas time, and past time, that she showed her mettle. Rule over a realm was not something to be *played* at.

He opened the door soundlessly and walked to the low divan where she sat bent over, her face in her hands. It seemed to be her favorite place, and no doubt had seen much use over the last few months, what with the young Bleth sitting sideways on it holding her hands between every court meal!

Vangerdahast sighed loudly and sat down with a thump beside the princess. Tanalasta's head jerked up. Her face was as white as a statue except where two silvery trails of tears ran down her cheeks from red-rimmed eyes.

"You!" She said in horror. "How did you get in here?"

Vangerdahast gave her a merry smile. "Magic, Lady Highness. You know—waggle the fingers and . . . It's what keeps Cormyr strong!"

Tanalasta drew herself up, then rose to stand facing him, eyes glittering with hatred. "Are you threatening me, wizard?"

258

The Royal Magician met her daggerlike gaze calmly and said, "Child, I never threaten. I promise."

Tanalasta's lips drew together in a tight line. "I ought to have you thrown in irons, whipped, and then beheaded for bursting into a woman's chambers unbidden! You might be here to get a heir for yourself!"

Vangerdahast rolled his eyes. "Nothing so energetic, Lady Princess. No, I'm here for another reason." He reached into the breast of his robes and drew forth a folded parchment. Tanalasta's eyes widened when she saw the royal seals. Then they narrowed.

"No, this is not the forged writ that young Aunadar has been going around telling people I was making with magic," the wizard said testily. "If you care to examine it yourself, you'll see that the seals are unbroken and that none of them are Azoun's."

He held out the parchment, and after a swaying moment of indecision wherein she obviously feared some sort of magical trap, the princess snatched it from him and stared at the seals. The state seal, the old court seal—which was in the keeping of her mother, the queen—and Filfaeril's own seal, with the two small Obarskyr pendants she always added.

Impatiently Tanalasta broke them, froze for a moment for fear that she might have ignited some waiting magical trap, and then—when nothing happened—unfolded the parchment.

"As you can see," Vangerdahast said almost wearily, "it is a fresh writ of regency, signed by your mother, Queen Filfaeril. Since both you and your young Bleth seemed so contemptuous of King Azoun's own authority on an earlier document, and that of his father Rhigaerd, I took the precaution of procuring yet another authorization for my authority. As you can also see, it awaits your signature. My first concern, as always, is the safety of the realm, but I have no interest in ruling over the strident objections of the Obarskyr heir if I can possibly avoid doing so."

"You expect me to sign this?" the princess snapped, nostrils flaring.

"I expect you to consider the implications of everything you do, with the greater good of the realm, and not what you may personally want, always foremost in your mind. It's what your ancestors—and the wizards who have served them, from Baerauble the Wise to, well, myself—have always done. It's what sitting on the Dragon Throne has always been about."

"You just want to force me into giving *you* the crown," Tanalasta whispered, her voice trembling with rage.

"No, lass, I don't," the wizard said flatly. "If wearing the crown were all that mattered to me, I could take it in an instant. You know that. As Aunadar never tires of reminding you, I *do* have all those spells."

"Then why haven't you taken it? Or named yourself regent?" Tanalasta almost screamed. "What is your game, wizard?"

"Life is my only game, Tanalasta—the life of the realm, and of every last scheming noble, tame dog, and silly princess in it. I work to make Cormyr ever stronger—not larger, not more decadent, but always a better place to live. It's a long, long game, but then, I've never been a short-bet man, myself."

Tanalasta frowned, and with her eyes steady on the wizard's, slowly started to crumple the parchment. There was a flash, a soft numbing movement through her fingertips, and she was holding empty air.

Vangerdahast was holding the parchment himself. In fact, he was waving it at her. He raised his eyebrows and asked, "I take it you'll not sign this?"

"Never!" Tanalasta spat. "I don't know what vile magic you used on my mother to get her to sign it, but you'll never get me to give in to you and your schemes! What have you done with her?"

Vangerdahast blinked. "Done with her? Nothing, child. You read too many hot romances."

"Get out!" Tanalasta shrieked, pointing an imperious arm at the door. "Just get out!"

The wizard rose. "You can't run away from problems forever, you know. If you don't bother to rule the kingdom, someone else will step in and do it for you."

"Such as you, perhaps?" the crown princess said with a sneer.

The Royal Magician shrugged. "Or anyone . . . if you don't care who does it, literally anyone could take the throne. A grasping Sembian merchant, perhaps. Or a Zhentarim. A priestess of Loviatar, who might find it fitting that royalty feel pain every night. Who knows? Deciding to rule, or not to rule, and what to do if you do wear the crown is a decision you must make—and, Princess, it is best for the realm if you make it alone. Not with Aunadar. Not with your ladies-in-waiting. Not with Alaphondar or Dimswart or even me. Otherwise, it won't truly *be* your decision."

"The door still awaits you," Tanalasta said coldly.

Vangerdahast bowed his head, then sketched a bent-knee court bow. "Until next we meet, Princess."

"I hope that's *never!*" she cried, the fury building in her voice.

"Shall I say until you make a decision, then?" he asked mildly, his hand on the door. A moment later he was through it and striding away, listening to the shattering of expensive glass and china as the weeping princess hurled perfume bottle after cordial decanter at the closed door.

"It's always so tiring," the Lord High Wizard told no one in particular as he wearily walked the halls back to his own apartments, "when one has to deal with children. There is such a thing as sheltering little girls too much from the world." Then he thought of Alusair as he'd once farscryed her, hacking through a band of brigands, her hair flying around her, and her half-naked body drenched with blood, and said wryly, "And then, of course, there's the other way."

* * * * *

When the radiance faded this time, Vangerdahast was a safe few paces outside whatever wards the magess Cat might have set to protect Redstone Castle. The front gate stood ajar, of course. He stepped inside, glancing critically at the gardens, and noted approvingly that Lady Wyvernspur seemed to have taken things strongly in hand. Wearily—was a wizard's work *ever* done?—he strode up to the hall.

As he approached the steps that led up to the front doors, they opened, and Giogi Wyvernspur stepped out, resplendent in fawn-colored leather breeches, a purple shirt with cloth-of-gold sash and half-cloak, and a pair of old, battered, comfortable-looking brown boots. Vangerdahast sighed with relief; just whom he'd wanted to see. Now there wouldn't be a hour wasted on challenges and servants' questions and little lads goggling in awe at the mightiest wizard in the land. . . .

Giogi sniffed the air, smiled happily, and glanced about, nearly falling off the doorstep in surprise when he saw the old bearded man in plain robes looking up at him from a few steps away.

"Gods! What— I mean, heigh-ho, Vangy—ah, Lord High Wizard," he said with a grin. "How's the ruling-Cormyr-from-behind-the-throne business these days?"

"That's what I've come to talk to you about," Vangerdahast said gravely, taking the noble by the arm. "Do you still have some of those silly stone benches about?"

Giogi sighed. "This sounds serious. You're going to talk a bit, aren't you?" He pointed and sighed again. "Over here."

They sat, and the Royal Magician said quickly, "You may or may not have heard that Duke Bhereu is dead, Baron Thomdor hangs on the edge of his grave, and the king is gravely ill and expected to die, too. Rest assured that this much, at least, is the truth."

Giogi grew somber at once. "We had heard rumors, even out in the countryside, but no details. How?"

"A hunting accident, involving possible treason," Vangerdahast said grimly, "which we haven't yet gotten to the bottom of. I'll tell you more later, but first I must tell you why I'm here."

Giogi was still gasping like a fish on the Immersea docks. "Ah—uh—"

"For the good of the realm," Vangerdahast said gravely, "I think I must assume the title of regent at this time. Filfaeril's out of her head with grief, Alusair's nowhere to be found, and Crown Princess Tanalasta is head over heels in love with a grasping young noble who'd love to tell her what decisions to make for the realm. Unfortunately, she wants to do more crying than ruling, so I feel I must rule from the foot of the throne for a time."

Giogi's eyes narrowed. "And so—?"

"And so I need to know who will support me as regent—in particular, if Princess Tanalasta or a large group of nobles says I should not be or presents rival temporary rulers for our land. If Vangerdahast declares himself regent, will I have the support of the Wyvernspurs?"

Silence fell. Giogi cleared his throat finally and said, "Uh, well, this is all so sudden—"

"That's more or less what Tanalasta's been saying, as the days pass," Vangerdahast said dryly. "I need to know, Giogioni, and I need to know soon. Where do the Wyvernspurs stand?"

"Uh—hah! Well," Giogi said, floundering, and stood up to pace. His hand drifted to his sword, and he suddenly looked down at the old wizard, his hand on his hilt, and asked sharply, "So Thomdor's still alive? The king lives too?"

"Yes and yes," the Royal Magician replied, nodding.

"And Princess Alusair—she's on a foray up in the Stonelands, isn't she? Have you sent her a message?"

"I have," Vangerdahast confirmed. "Why do you ask?"

"I can't speak for my kin until I have enough answers to give so I don't appear a complete fool," Giogi replied. "So what did Alusair say?"

"There has been no reply," Vangerdahast said gravely.

The Wyvernspur frowned. "There's something you're not telling me about this. . . . What is it?"

Ed Greenwood and Jeff Grubb

Vangerdahast's brows drew together in a frown. "Many nobles of Cormyr—folk of good families, with reputations for honor that go back generations—have gladly given their support for my regency without demanding answers to a lot of pressing questions."

He stood up slowly, a glint in his eye. "If you don't feel you can support me, say so—but if you want Cormyr to be a friendly home for you and yours in the future, perhaps you'd best get on the boat, or it just might sail away without you."

Giogi's slim, jewel-pommeled rapier slid out of its scabbard. "The Wyvernspurs—so far as I can recall, right now—have always been loyal to the crown," he said coldly, "and that's not going to change while I stand ready to defend the realm. I challenge you, wizard, in the name of Azoun, rightful King of Cormyr! I shall fight you here and now unless you promise you'll do everything in your power to keep the king alive—and if you fail, you'll then support an Obarskyr to assume the throne and obey *her* as loyally and as diligently as you did her father!"

The old man in robes looked up at him with disgust on his face. "Do all you young idiots keep your brains in those slim scabbards? What good will challenging me do? I'm not in the habit of making promises under threat, and if you believe anyone will keep such promises, you *are* the fool you've so often been labeled." He matched the angry nobleman's swordsman's stance, empty-handed, and added, "Besides—I fight with spells, not swords."

Sudden radiance flickered around one of the Royal Magician's arms, flowing up and down it like racing flames.

Giogi gulped, threw his sword behind him, and suddenly became a rising, shifting thing of red scales. His sleepy eyes became large and golden, and his arms began to meld into wings. The gift of the Wyvernspurs, sometimes called their curse as well, was the ability to transform into the winged dragonlike beast they took

264

their name from. For all his apparent foolishness, young Lord Wyvernspur knew what he could do in wyvern form.

"Oh, no, you don't," Vangerdahast said levelly. "Let's not play at battling old mages this afternoon, thank you!"

The flowing radiance on his arm raced down into his sleeve and touched a wand that hung half-concealed there. The wand flashed, shuddered, and spat forth a stream of eerie golden-green light that swirled around the rapidly growing form of the wyvern, and suddenly there was another blurring and a strange singing sound, and Giogioni Wyvernspur stood in his own form once more, blinking at the Royal Magician.

"Before this continues and one of us does something extremely foolish or gets hurt," Vangerdahast said, "I'd best—"

The Lord High Wizard of Cormyr was not young and had seen his share of spell battles. Moreover, he was very quick and expecting trouble. It never seemed to take him too long to find it. Wherefore when he heard the first whispered syllable from up the steps and off to his right, he willed his ready spell shield to coalesce.

The spell that should have hurled him clear out through the front gates of Redstone Castle instead struck the mystic shield and simply washed over the wizard in flickering, impotent streamers of radiance, then faded into the air.

"Well met, Cat," he said calmly, turning from the dazed Giogi to face the furious copper-haired woman at the castle door. "I've just been talking to your Giogioni, here."

"Talk?" Cat snapped, her green eyes blazing. Gods, but she was beautiful, the old wizard thought. Was he himself the only homely male who wove spells in this kingdom? "Is that how the Royal Magician talks to people?"

Vangerdahast made a gesture, and Giogi's rapier flew smoothly up to its owner's hand. Still looking dazed and shocked, Giogi slid it back into its scabbard. The old wizard nodded. "Good. I hate trying to talk to folk who are trying to kill me."

"What is this all about, lord wizard?" Cat demanded, hands on hips now. "You come here and attack my Giogi right on his own front steps . . ."

Vangerdahast held up a hand to halt her angry torrent. "Please desist. Accept my apologies. You have every right to be furious. The Lord High Wizard of the realm humbles himself before you."

"But not too much," Giogi added, managing a smile. The old wizard's face split in an answering grin—his first real one that day, as it happened—as he clapped the noble on his shoulder and urged him up the steps to the waiting, still-angry Cat.

"If you'll protect me against your good wife," Vangerdahast said gravely, "I'll have the chance I need to talk to you both—for the good of the realm."

"Trying to convince us you'll make a good regent?" Giogi asked grimly, but he did not slow their climb up the steps together.

Vangerdahast shook his head. "You have made your choice, while most of your fellow nobles of Cormyr are still sizing up the contenders. You have queried, while others have gladly grasped. We must talk, young Wyvernspur."

"You're not going to try to keep me out of this?" Cat asked in a dangerously soft voice.

"Lady," the Royal Magician replied in solemn tones as the three retired to the halls of Redstone Castle, "I'd not dare to."

* * * * *

Elsewhere, a man fidgeted nervously in a hidden room, waiting for his assignation, rubbing his hands nervously as he paced. He couldn't spend all afternoon in some broom closet! Where was she?

The broom closet in question was a small secret chamber, unused for years. The dust lay heavy on the low stone bench and polished duskwood table that were its only ornament. A pair of narrow passages, so narrow that only a child could move easily through them, led off to either side.

The man's candle flickered, and he was aware she was coming. The air over the table thickened and curdled, turning into a ball of serpentine smoke. At the center of the ball lay a pair of eyes, the color of flaming jets—black with red pips dancing at their centers.

"Hail, Cormyrean," said the eyes in a soft, purring voice.

"Brantarra," snapped the man in response. He was sure that name was no more her true appellation than the writhing mass was her true form.

"I trust that everything has gone smoothly."

"Not smoothly enough," said the man, "The king still lives, and one of his damnable cousins as well. Your clockwork toy did not work as well as hoped."

"Not my toy," said the swirling mist calmly. "Only my venom, carrying its deadly disease. The golden creature is known to Cormyr, if not to its current rulers. I think that an extremely amusing jest. How fares the king?"

"Badly," said the man. "There is little hope for him, though for now there is no way to get near him. He is surrounded by guards and priests and other nobles at all times."

"If you are to kill a king, you must strike surely with the first blow," said the soft feminine voice.

"Your venom was supposed do the job at once," hissed the man.

"A poor workman blames his tools," said the voice, and the man was sure there was a smile on the lips that spoke those words.

"Regardless," said the man, "Azoun lingering on his deathbed does not help our cause. The king's wizard is already meddling and dabbling. Can you not do something?"

Now the voice laughed. "Do something? Like magically teleport myself into that sickroom, flinging fireballs and loosing lightning bolts? If I had the power to destroy Vangerdahast and his war wizards, do you not think I would use it? Nay. Patience is the better course here."

"Brantarra—" began the man, but the voice made an urgent, shushing noise.

"Patience," it said. "We will both get what we wish. In the meantime, I have another toy for you." A tendril of mist extruded from the smokey mass and touched the table. When it withdrew, there was a large ruby glittering on the duskwood surface.

"When you first activated the abraxus, you sacrificed one of your own servants to bring it life," said the voice. "This ruby will allow you sacrifice another at a distance."

"But the abraxus has been dismantled," said the man. "The remaining pieces have been locked away."

"Hush," said the voice. "Give the stone to another. Not a royal, and not a wizard. Someone who will be near you when the final confrontation comes with that overweight slug of a Royal Magician. When the time is at hand, you will know how to use it."

The man picked up the stone, turning it over in his black-gloved fingers gingerly, as if it would explode at any moment.

"I do not trust you fully," he said at last.

"Nor I you. Fully," said the mist. "Yet we trust each other enough to join together for a common goal. Maintain your act, your lordship, and all will come to you!"

With that, the fiery lights within the smoke dimmed, indicating the audience was over. The man looked again at the blood-colored gem, then placed it in his pocket. Then carefully, using his candle to guide his path, he slid back along the narrow passage, heading for more populated parts of the castle. After he left, the smokey lights flared briefly, and the flame-jet eyes opened once more.

"That one has spine," said the glowing eyes softly to the darkness, "and magical protection of his own now. Perhaps it is time to pull the strings of other puppets, if the throne of Cormyr is truly to be mine."

18

Cats and Wizards
Year of the Empty Hearth
(629 DR)

handerahast, newest member of the Brotherhood of the Wizards of War, eased himself carefully along the ledge. He could have used a simple spell to allow him to climb the side of the building, but he trusted Luthax to have wards against spells and those who used them. So it was back to the old ways of his childhood.

The chill autumn wind whipped around and through him, and he wished he were wearing something heavier than his dark shirt and leather leggings. A cloak would flap with an incessant thunder in this thin, stiff breeze, and a full set of wizard's robes would catch in the wind and send him spiraling head over heels over the slate roofs of Suzail like an errant kite.

Luthax would be amused by that, but then Luthax would be amused by anything that involved maiming his junior officer.

"Listen, orc spawn," Luthax had said on Thanderahast's very first day, "the only reason you're here is that your Auntie Amedahast is the High Magess. But that doesn't cut clean with me, and I'm going to be on your back like a tick on a bullock until you decide to take up another line of work."

His relationship to Amedahast was distant but distinct, though there were few wizards in the line. Indeed, Thanderahast would rather be picking through the ruins of ancient Asram and Hlondath or studying in the elven libraries of Myth Drannor than playing spy on the lonely roofs of Suzail.

At first Thanderahast thought Luthax believed that his junior mage was competition. Baerauble the Venerable had chosen one of his bloodline as his successor, and possibly Luthax worried that Thanderahast would be a similar replacement to the aging High Magess. But it went deeper than that. Luthax was mean clear through to the bone, and he obviously enjoyed assigning the younger mage the most unpleasant and difficult of tasks and telling others, including Amedahast, of his failures. Most of the court already thought Thanderahast was a fool, thanks to Luthax's slander.

There were footsteps on the cobbles below, and Thanderahast froze, holding his breath. A pair of Purple Dragons, the king's own elite, were on patrol through the district. Their deep violet capes were bunched tightly around them, and they looked neither right nor left as they passed along the row of stone townhouses.

Looking up the hill at the castle, Thanderahast waited until the armsmen had rounded the corner. Rebuilt, along with most of the rest of Suzail after the Pirate Years, Castle Obarskyr sprawled over the low hillocks, surrounded by broad lawns and concealed redoubts. No one would sneak up on the Obarskyrs again.

Thanderahast considered returning to the castle and waiting for Amedahast's return. She was away on court business, as she was so often these days. Thanks to Luthax's malicious gossip, Thanderahast's stock at court was none too high, so he had to play spy on his own.

Luthax was up to something, of that Thanderahast had no doubt. The burly wizard, senior mage in the kingdom behind Amedahast, was the Castellan of Magic and the effective leader of the brotherhood. Yet he was a nasty customer, unctuous and fawning to his betters, boisterous and bragging to his equals, and Gehenna-on-a-plate to those he thought his inferiors. Like junior officers. Like Thanderahast.

But for the past month, his actions had been even more intriguing. Mysterious comings and goings, particularly with the other noble houses. Sudden "retirements" of high members of the order, and the promotions of Luthax's friends to brotherhood offices. The junior officers and lesser mages were being treated more as pawns than as students.

Thanderahast had mentioned all this to Amedahast, and her only response had been, "Then you had better keep an eye on him, hadn't you?" Which brought him to this wide stone ledge on the outside of a noble's house in the city on a cold autumn night.

He edged forward and almost pitched off the side of the building as one of the shadows moved before he set his foot down. A night-black cat jumped up from its hiding place, stretched, and meowed irritatedly at the young mage.

What was a cat doing on a third-floor ledge? wondered Thanderahast, at least after his heart had regained its normal rhythm. Cats were everywhere, it seemed. The High Magess had imported them after the last plague from Marsember, and their presence seemed to have acted as a talisman, protecting the city from other such diseases.

Amedahast favored cats, and during visits to his notable ancestor, Thanderahast, had noted that there were always about a dozen running free in her chambers at any one time. If they weren't hissing at each other over stacks of spellbooks, they were regarding the young guest scornfully from high, secure shelves, or dancing their way through forests of glass alembics and other delicate instruments.

King Draxius Obarskyr, on the other hand, did not like cats. It was no ill experience or sneezing sickness that motivated him, folk said, just a disdain for their familiarity and their lack of devotion. If cats would act like dogs, the king would have no problem with them. Amedahast remembered that the king had once banned cats from the castle, until the vermin grew so numerous that the cooks complained.

The black cat, thin and Untherian in origin, shivered and laced itself around Thanderahast's ankles. It had a typical cat's ability, the young mage noted, to put itself just where you wanted to step next. The small creature looked up, revealing a white dollop of fur beneath its chin. It regarded his with emerald-green eyes and mewled imploringly at him.

"Sorry, kitty, I have no food," Thanderahast whispered, but the cat would not be denied, circling around his ankles, its meows becoming louder and more urgent. Finally the young wizard picked up the cat and cradled it against his breast. The lean black cat was a ball of furry warmth and immediately cuddled against him, purring loudly.

Thanderahast gave a mighty sigh and then inched onward. Why couldn't Luthax have chosen to have his clandestine meetings in a basement somewhere?

His goal was a set of thin windows along the front of the building. The house belonged to the Emmarask household. One of the noble Emmarasks, Elmariel, was a trusted crony of Luthax's, and so, of course, he had now risen to be almost as powerful as Luthax himself in the brotherhood. If this house matched a dozen seemingly identical others scattered throughout the city, the street side of the third floor would house the reception parlor.

Thanderahast was not disappointed. The closest of the thin windows, mostly lead and iron enwrapping bits of colored glass, had been cracked open. The warmth of a fire and the smell of wizards' pipes spilled out. The cat Thanderahast held yawned deeply at the smell, gave a cat-sized sneeze, and resumed its slumber against the young wizard's chest.

"Weakness," Luthax was saying. Thanderahast could identify that booming voice across a crowded hall, and the senior wizard was in full form. "That is what we are worried about. The court wizard grows older and more enfeebled with each passing year. And we remember what happened when Baerauble passed on. Without a strong mage behind the throne, the kingdom quickly falls to ruin. The vaunted Obarskyr blood provides the realm no protection without the power of magic behind it."

Thanderahast leaned forward to survey the room. There were about thirty people inside. The top six officers of the brotherhood were there, in their black and red robes festooned with eldritch symbols and self-awarded medallions. The rest were lesser nobles and some of the most prominent merchants in Suzail, but Thanderahast's eyes widened as he recognized members of the Bleth, Dauntinghorn, Illance, and Goldfeather houses, plus one or two minor Crownsilvers. A powerful group to be gathered in such a small room. Luthax stood by the fire, Elmariel Emmarask at his side.

All eyes were on Luthax . . . powerful, broad-shouldered Luthax. The robes hid most of his paunch, and the hearth accentuated the deep crags in his face and overlarge nose, making him look all the more serious and wise. His beard was long and reddish-brown, and it was said he shaved his head daily to make himself look more sage and puissant.

"When magic was not strong," said Luthax, "the kingdom was not strong. Kings and princes are irrelevant to stable governance of the realm if good spellcrafting does not exist. This is one reason we formed the Brotherhood of the Wizards of War."

Thanderahast stifled a snort. Amedahast formed the brotherhood, not Luthax. She did so to supplement her own abilities with a school of mages loyal to the crown, but also to keep track of the wizards who were appearing in greater and greater numbers in the Forest Kingdom. "Popping up like mushrooms after a good rain," as she said to Thanderahast once.

Luthax paced as he spoke, punctuating his points with an upraised finger. "Now the High Magess grows feeble and spends her time with her spells and her travels. She is more often than not away in some distant plane, as she is this evening. She has lost interest in Cormyr and its petty kings. Yet she still refuses to step down."

There was a murmur of assent in the room, and a sudden steaming of hard-drawn pipes. Thanderahast did not like where this was going.

Luthax continued. "At the same time, Draxius himself has passed harsh laws against further logging in the King's Forest, and denied the rights of the noble houses there. And while he conquered Arabel, he did not give those lands to the nobles who fought beside him, but rather left the noble families there in place, as if their defiant rebellions had never occurred. And *this* at the recommendation of the senile High Magess."

More murmurs, and a 'hear, hear,' probably from one of the Illances.

"So the blood of the Obarskyrs has run thin, and the High Magess of the realm has become an old crone, leaning on her staff and weaving insane plots."

More shouts of assent. Luthax was twisting the hearts and minds of this audience, using his own personal charm and argument to make his points. Thanderahast bridled at the description of his seven-times great aunt. Amedahast was no crone, nor did she need any support. "The day I need a staff is the day I die," she had told him once.

"Now is the time for action. Now is the time for heroes. Now is the time for a new way of doing things in this nation, if Cormyr is to survive."

Luthax coughed and then raised his voice again until it rang from the rafters. "You, gathered here, are the vanguard. You are the best and the brightest of the merchants, the nobles, and the mages of fair Cormyr, who have labored all too long in the shadows of foolish kings and vain high wizards. We have it in our power to take command of this land and lead it to greatness. All we need is the proper weapon."

Luthax was pacing now, back and forth, his favorite mannerism when speaking. "My companion Elmariel has returned from exploring the ruins of Netheril with an elder prize," the senior mage said triumphantly, "a bit of magic from the lost days when mages ruled the world. With this weapon, we can rid ourselves of those who would impede us."

Luthax's voice caught for a moment. Thanderahast ducked away, then froze. Had he been spotted at the window? No, the senior mage resumed his discourse, and when Thanderahast looked again, had taken up pacing again, too.

"We are truly the wise heads of Cormyr," Luthax proclaimed, and waited for the assenting murmurs of the crowd before continuing. "We can rule more wisely that any blood-tainted king or everlasting magess. We judge ourselves on merit and on real, tangible power. And we must be ready to move—and move quickly!—when the time comes to take the reins of power from old, enfeebled hands."

Thanderahast would have wanted to hear more of Luthax's schemes, but the cat against his chest began to squirm and howl, not the mewling cry of an imprisoned feline, but rather a deep-throated grumble that spoke of immediate threats. The cat's tiny claws pierced his cotton shirt and drove shallowly into the young mage's flesh.

Thanderahast stepped back from the window and pulled the cat away from his breast. Its fur was all on end, and its eyes were wide. It did not try to struggle against Thanderahast's grip, but instead spit and hissed at the autumn air.

No, not the autumn air, the young mage realized. Rather, the cat hissed at something hanging *in* the air. It appeared as little more than a ripple in the starlight, a slight flickering of the few windows still lit. It was wholly invisible save for its edges, which shone like a soap bubble to reveal its troll-like form and its teeth, which gleamed like clear icicles.

275

Thanderahast retreated two more steps along the ledge, cat at his bosom, mind racing through his memorized lore to identify the creature. This must be Elmariel's creature from Netheril. He'd been spotted after all, and this beast had been dispatched to take care of him.

The junior mage began an incantation of protection, but it was already too late. The beast swooped down upon him and gathered him up in invisible arms that coiled around him like serpents. Thanderahast choked back an involuntary shout, for those in the parlor would not come to his aid.

The invisible beast pulled Thanderahast off the ledge and suspended him over the street below. Thanderahast hung there as the night lights of Suzail swam all around him.

Then it threw him to the pavement from three floors up. The young mage clutched the cat and screamed.

He landed too soon to have fallen that far. It appeared to be a dimly lit hallway. He had not fallen more than three feet, and he had struck not rude cobbles but solid flagstones. The chill was gone, and the wind as well. He was inside a building, and a sharp pain was blossoming in one shoulder, where he had struck the flags. The cat had leapt out of his arms when he struck and was now calmly cleaning itself a few feet away.

He knew this place. He was not just in a building. He was inside the castle itself. Could the Netheril creature have thrown him that far? Or magically transported him there?

"You must get to the king," said the cat.

Thanderahast shook his head, certain that a speaking cat was the result of wits dazed in his fall, and looked at the cat. Its eyes were glowing a radiant green, and it spoke with Amedahast's voice.

"You must get to the king," it repeated, "before Luthax's beast does. He is in his quarters. I will take care of the conspirators." The glow faded from the small creature's eyes. It resumed grooming itself, oblivious to the spell that had surrounded it.

Thanderahast nodded and scooped the cat up, starting down the hallway. This part of the castle was strange to him, since he had never been in the royal wing. But all knew where the king's quarters were; the light from that room's fire would burn long into the night.

The hallways were empty, and Thanderahast's soft-soled shoes slapped hard against the flagstones. Right, then left, then an immediate right, and there would be . . .

. . . a hulking guard in the violet and ivory of the Purple Dragons, standing before the door that led to the king's chambers. He held up one hand. A war axe gleamed in the other. "Hold, young wizard," he said, eyes stern. "Why are you here at this late hour?"

Thanderahast drew a deep breath. What could he say? He'd been spying on the leader of the war wizards, and a cat had told him the king's life was in danger?

Instead, the mage thrust the cat up into view. As the guard stared at it, Thanderahast barked a series of short syllables that were old when Netheril was young and thrust out his free hand to touch the guard on the forehead. The guard managed to let out a mild curse as he slumped against the wall and then sagged there, snoring softly, as magical slumber claimed him.

Thanderahast burst through the doorway into an empty antechamber, then through its low arch into the king's own private quarters.

There was an immediate squeal, and a flash of pink flesh and blonde hair as the woman in the king's bed burrowed deeply beneath the covers. His Majesty himself was standing before the fire in a long nightshirt, a poker in hand, turning with a frown from tending the fire. Beyond him, the window was open to better vent its smoke.

Draxius's expression began with bewilderment and clouded toward anger. "What is the meaning . . . ?" he began.

Through the open window, stars rippled, and Thanderahast caught sight of a flash of icicle-clear teeth in the darkness outside.

He threw the cat at the shimmering stars.

The small creature screamed a high-pitched howl as it flew across the room. That challenge was matched by another, throatier roar as the cat's claws dug deeply into invisible flesh. The cat seemed to spin in the air, raking the unseen assailant.

Long tears of blood appeared in midair. Apparently the creature's interior was not as proof against vision as its skin. The beast bellowed again, and the cat let go. The feline skittered across the room to the far side of the fire.

The blood remained, marking the creature's presence. Draxius charged and laid into it with the poker, battering it as if the cold-wrought iron was a battle mace. To Thanderahast, he shouted, "My blade . . . by the bed!"

The wizard snatched up the blade, oversized and unwieldy for his slight frame. When he turned back, the monster was more visible than before; blood painted a battered, teardrop-shaped head with a fanged mouth. From the bed came a muffled sob of hasty, fervent prayers.

Thanderahast shouted a warning and the king stood back. The wizard threw him the blade, sheath and all. Draxius caught the sword and spun it once to shake it loose from its sheath. Then he dropped the poker and returned to the fray.

Now the king of Cormyr cut long, deep slashes into the creature's blubbery hide. He roared in exultation as his blade bit deep. Advancing across the bed chamber, Thanderahast was shouting as well. Old spells, taught by the High Magess and spoken in forgotten tongues. Thanderahast's hands gleamed with pearly blue light, and out of its glow spewed a battery of darts made of solid magecraft, which leapt from his fingertips to lance into the beast's flesh.

The creature stumbled, tried to rise, and stumbled again. Its teeth were sharp and visible now, coated in its own blood. King Draxius stepped forward, and with one last, mighty blow cleaved the monster down the middle.

Sudden stillness fell in the room. The Netherese beast was dead, the last of its lifeblood a spreading pool before the fire. King Draxius looked down at its corpse with his blade ready in his hands, panting slightly, until he was sure that the ichor-stained beast would never move again.

"Well, that was a bit of excitement," the king said at last, exhaling deeply. Then he looked up at Thanderahast. "You're Amedahast's young whelp, aren't you? How did you know to come here?"

Thanderahast stammered for a moment. "The cat . . ." he began.

"Your Majesty," interrupted Amedahast, and the young mage nearly jumped. Even the king gasped and took a startled pace back.

No, his teacher was not in the room, but her magical image was. She hovered, ghostlike, in the bed-chamber air. Her hair was a silver rain, wild and free down her back. She had a staff at her side, but did not need it for support.

The illusion of the High Magess spoke again. "I have sent my successor, the young mage, Thanderahast, to you to prevent a magical assassination attempt. If you are hearing this, he has been successful. I would have come myself, but I will be dealing with the conspirators who sent this evil creature to you. They are powerful mages, and if I do not return, know that the young mage has my complete confidence."

Then the image faded. Thanderahast swallowed; he'd never seen her so grim, her face drawn so tight. She could defeat Luthax, of course, but rank upon rank of treacherous war wizards?

Then he remembered the staff, and her words: "The day I need a staff . . ."

Outside the window there was a bright flash: the magical detonation of a lifetime of spells ignited in a single moment. Its brilliance overpowered the fire in the room, and for a long moment, Draxius and the mage were etched in sharp, white relief. Then the sound came, a huge, rolling boom that shook the very stones of the castle.

By the time Draxius reached the window, a column of flames was rising from the lower city. He turned to Thanderahast. "Wait outside. I'll get dressed and join you. Two minutes."

The young mage nodded and headed for the door. He knew what had happened there, and what they would find. The top of the townhouse would be blown out by a single blast, created by a powerful magess breaking a powerful staff over her knee to release the energies within. The bodies of all the others would be sprawled around the room, the torn tatters of their shattered magic drifting around them. The message would be clear to any conspirators fortunate enough not to be in the room at the time: The price of treason was death, and no sacrifice would be judged too difficult to bring about that payment.

The sleeping guard had slid entirely down the wall. Thanderahast let him lie in peace, and in the promised two minutes, Draxius emerged, dressed in a fine shirt and simple leggings. He had his crown on now and his scabbard belted to his side. "Come on, lad," he said. "We may have to call out the war wizards on this one."

"No," Thanderahast replied and met the king's eyes squarely, feeling the weight of his new responsibility settling onto his shoulders. If he were as loyal and true as the High Magess had been, only his death would lift that burden. "The war wizards," he said firmly, "or at least the brotherhood's leaders, *were* the conspirators. I heard that myself."

Draxius looked long and hard at the wizard, then nodded. "Then we'll manage on our own as we always have. And, lad," he added, placing a friendly hand on the young man's shoulder, "I know you'll think long and hard about what happened here and tell your stories about it accordingly."

Then the king kicked the guard awake and bellowed that an armed, full-strength party should be readied to investigate the explosion immediately. The groggy Purple Dragon hurried off, and the king strode along in his wake, bellowing orders to the bleary-eyed staff as he passed.

"Think long and hard?" repeated Thanderahast. Did the king not want it known he could handle a sword, or that there existed invisible creatures of ancient magic . . . or that the war wizards themselves had betrayed the throne?

Then he thought of the flash of blonde hair and pink flesh in the king's bed and realized what Draxius meant. The queen had red hair and was as tan as a polished duskwood tabletop.

Thanderahast smiled slightly and went off after his liege, following the sound of shouted orders.

19

Chess
Year of the Gauntlet
(1369 DR)

wo men sat in an antechamber of the palace. Ostensibly they were off duty, enjoying a quiet game of chess in the quiet of the royal wing. In reality, they were war wizards, and they were very much on duty. They were here to ensure that none of the nobles gathered to see the dying king wandered where they weren't supposed to . . . such as into the presence of the crown princess. With both the royal cousins dead or nearly so, no one but a war wizard could comfortably order about a noble of the realm without unpleasantness. War wizards could, however, because they were experts at unpleasantness.

The drifting silvery spheres in the water clock patiently marked the passing minutes as Kurthryn Shandarn frowned over the forest of tall, spindly white pieces sculpted of moonstone. They were emblazoned with the Purple Dragon of Cormyr, and the carved features of the king were said to be a good likeness of the long-dead King Galaghard. That wasn't going to help his position much, though. He sighed, moved the turret carved with the arms of Arabel along a file of the board, and looked up.

Huldyl Rauthur met his gaze and made his move without hesitation. He was a short, stout man whose temples were almost always beaded with sweat, but he was a better crafter of new spells than Kurthryn, and they both knew it. For all that, Kurthryn outranked him. The war wizards were funny that way; a lot of enforced teaching and learning of humility went on, and there were still a lot of covert tests of loyalty. Those who failed such things usually simply vanished.

Kurthryn frowned down at the board again. Then, reluctantly, he moved his other turret, the one that bore the arms of Marsember, and sat back to survey the board. Huldyl's bat riders—mounted wizards on oversized bats that were the counterparts of Kurthryn's noble knights—were slashing through his line of soldiers. Huldyl moved a bat-mounted wizard and took one of those pawns now.

"One little dragon down," he announced calmly. Kurthryn nodded absently and frowned down at the board again. The palace was as silent as a tomb around them, with the king still dying and all, and they'd both had ample opportunities to lose games of chess to each other yestereve and today. The other shift of war wizards, Imblaskos and Durndurve, were dice-and-cards men who played Wheel-of-Spells and Chase the Dragon and left the chess pieces undisturbed. Which had led to this long multishift match and Kurthryn's present grim position.

Damn these dark days for Cormyr, anyway! Kurthryn tried to concentrate on his increasingly muddled defenses, noting that one of Huldyl's death priests was threatening to slash in and take any one of three of his little dragons if he wasn't careful.

A shadow flickered at the edge of the mage's vision. Kurthryn looked up to see Aunadar Bleth stride past, on into the royal wing. The young nobleman was frowning and seemed to have acquired new lines on his face over the last few days. Kurthryn looked over to Huldyl, who had obviously been watching Bleth's approach for some time, and the junior war wizard met Kurthryn's eyes and shrugged. Technically the young noble was one of the very people they were here to stop, since he was a young noble. But then this particular young noble was the favorite of the crown princess, perhaps the next king of Cormyr—no, he'd be called a prince consort, wouldn't he? Neither of the mages felt like denying Tanalasta what little comfort she could find just now . . . or offending the possible future queen.

Moreover, Tanalasta *was* Azoun's eldest daughter, and word was going around the palace that the Lord High Wizard Vangerdahast himself, head of their brotherhood, was a traitor to the crown in her eyes, trying to make himself regent while Azoun lay dying downstairs. Fear made few folk love war wizards at the best of times; if the people came looking for scapegoats, Suzail—nay, all of Cormyr—might suddenly become a very unsafe place for those in the purple robes of the war wizards.

So where did the Royal Magician stand now? Several nobles had said loudly that any man who'd try to climb on the Dragon Throne while the king lay stricken in a bed not far off was a scoundrel, even *if* pieces of paper protected him from the charge of open treason. Such a man was morally unfit to be lord of anything, let alone the most powerfully ranked mage in all the land, whatever his true magical might.

One war wizard, an earnest young man from the Wyvernwater shores called Galados, had even confronted old Thunderspells about it last night—and had not been seen since. Whispers were spreading among the Brotherhood even now—wild rumors about a lot of things. Unable to concentrate on his game, Kurthryn Shandarn rubbed his eyes and voiced one of the rumors now.

"Anyone heard from Galados yet?" he murmured across the board. Huldyl did not look up.

"Nothing," he said in a low voice. "Yet remember, none of us has been able to find Princess Alusair, either. She *must* be shielded. I wonder why."

Kurthryn shrugged. "Who knows what precautions

she usually takes in the Stonelands? They say Zhentarim lurk thereabouts all too often. *I'd* carry a magical device to hide my presence from other mages if Lord High Thunderspells'd spare me one."

Huldyl grunted. "When you rise to such importance, let me know."

Kurthryn chuckled and made a mildly rude gesture.

Huldyl returned it idly and asked, "Are you going to move another piece tonight, or shall we just talk?"

"I'm thinking, I'm thinking."

"As the sage said to the serving girl," Huldyl responded wryly. "Old Thunderspells is probably fretting behind a shield of his own right now."

"Fret? Him? Why?" Kurthryn moved a noble knight, and then, seeing the weakness he'd left, winced.

Huldyl shrugged and moved his death priest to topple one of the little dragons, ignoring the move Kurthryn had feared he'd make. "Our elder wizards, Vangerdahast among them, can't even get any straight answers out of Princess High-and-Mighty about the governance of the realm."

Kurthryn's eyebrows rose, and he looked involuntarily over his shoulder to make sure that the outermost door of the chain of rooms that led to Crown Princess Tanalasta's apartments was closed. It was. "Couldn't Laspeera Inthré penetrate the royal thoughts?"

Huldyl smiled thinly. "She could if Tanalasta and her fiancé Bleth weren't both wearing spell shields taken from Azoun's personal cache of seized and pillaged magic."

It was Kurthryn's turn to shrug. "Ah, well, if you've got it, use it. Handy, being king. Down through the years, you can seize a lot of magical gewgaws from the disloyal." He looked down at the board in front of him and moved one of his bishops out of harm's way.

"Mother Laspeera," Huldyl said admiringly. "Now *there's* a woman I could wish was younger, and I older. What a worker for the realm—and mother to us all."

"And naught has been seen of her for days. She has

gone missing in all this," said Kurthryn. "Like Alaphondar the sage."

"And like Galados," added Huldyl, snaking a hand over the board. His death priest moved again, and another of the little Purple Dragons died.

Kurthryn sighed at the discarded chess piece as his colleague set it down beside the board, the latest member of a slowly growing group. He laid his hand on his queen to move it in front of old Galaghard, but the piece felt somehow warm and wet and uncomfortable under his fingers, and he drew his hand away again. Studying the board, he suddenly saw the sly attack Huldyl had prepared, and he hastily moved his king instead. The bishops and the noble knight were just going to have to take their chances.

Huldyl smiled. "I'm glad we don't use that foolish rule the Calishites prefer . . . touch it and you must move it."

"Oh—yes," Kurthryn responded. "Small-minded etiquette for small-minded folk, eh?" Then he sighed again as Huldyl's smile widened, and the junior war wizard brought that damnable death priest back across the board again to menace both Kurthryn's turret of Arabel and his other knight.

"Who taught you to play this game? Old Thunderspells himself?" Kurthryn protested, looking down at the shambles of his position. Huldyl was going to be able to strike down his choice of at least two pieces while Kurthryn tried to move the rest of the Glory of Cormyr out of the way. He peered across the board at the enemy witch-king—Gondegal, some called it—secure behind the pair of black turrets, and sighed. There was just one chance . . . time for a little distraction. He leaned forward to deliver his most juicy secret.

His colleague was chuckling smugly. Kurthryn stilled that sound and left him gaping with his softspoken words. "I've been told that certain senior priests in this city, with the aid of a powerful archmage whose identity they are keeping secret, have discovered the cause. The poison that killed Bhereu and bids fair to kill both Thomdor and the king is a liquid-borne toxin that works through the bloodstream inside a man. The reason spells have failed to neutralize this poison is that it generates its own dead-magic zone." He moved his knight.

Huldyl whistled low. The dead-magic zones, proof from any spellcasting, were a legacy of the Time of Troubles, when the gods walked Faerun. "So can they foil it now?" Huldyl asked, wild-eyed, leaning forward over the board in his excitement.

Kurthryn shrugged. "They're working on it."

The junior wizard sat back, rubbing his chin. "Who could have crafted it? A Red Wizard of Thay, perhaps, or another powerful lich or archmage? But who did it? Almost absently he moved one of his pieces.

"Who's trying to become ruler of Cormyr?" Kurthryn responded grimly.

Huldyl threw up his hands, barking out a short, mirthless laugh. "Every third noble between here and Arabel, that's who! There's no shortage of those who might want to." He rubbed his chin again and added thoughtfully, "And when subterfuge, plotting, and poison are the means, those who might not have spells nor swords strong enough to take the throne might have their chances."

"You mean this man who's wooing Tanalasta might really be after the crown?" Kurthryn shook his head in disbelief. "If it's him in truth, why does Bleth not marry her first and make his claim clear before starting all the bloodshed?"

"It could be someone else," Huldyl said, with another shrug. "I mean only that soft words and velvet handshakes have won as many thrones as the rising and falling of blood-drenched blades."

Kurthryn waggled his eyebrows. "Been reading too much Tethyrian poetry, have we?" He moved his knight again.

Huldyl snarled in mock rage. "Aye, the same place you were reading books on how to play chess!" His death priest slid delicately across the board to slay Kurthryn's advancing knight. "So much for sneak attacks, 'good my lord,' " the junior wizard added.

With a weary sigh, Kurthryn moved one of his bishops. If this game bore any relation to reality, Cormyr had not long to last. "So what do you think of this young Bleth?"

Huldyl shrugged again. "It's the princess who has to kiss him, not I. You know how I feel about sneering, lazy, idiot nobles. Granted he's been crisply and ably delivering what few orders Tanalasta has deigned to decree thus far, but who's to say how much of those orders are his intentions or embellishments? She never steps out of her chamber of sorrows to check!"

"Sounds like the Obarskyrs need a bit of steel in the old bloodline," Kurthryn murmured.

"Hah! The line forms down the hall to marry the crown princess and father a long line of strapping sons," Huldyl said sarcastically. "Shall I save you a place?"

"Nay. I fear, 'good my lord,' that I lack what is most needed," Kurthryn replied, mimicking the tones of a cultured court official.

"Stamina?"

"Deafness," Kurthryn replied flatly. "Have you heard Tanalasta when she's in one of her moods? Such as when she is going over the account books, and finds a three-silver-piece error? Or hounding down some delinquent creditor or slipshod contractor? Nothing's worth years and years of that! Not Cormyr, not fabled Myth Drannor at its proverbial height, not gold-buried Waterdeep right now!"

Huldyl chuckled and moved his much-traveled death priest back to a safer spot. "So what's the latest out in the city?"

Kurthryn's senior rank brought more reports to his ears than Huldyl ever heard, and he shared the relevant bits of the most recent one now. "Well, our esteemed Vangerdahast does have some significant and slowly growing support for his regency—the old heart-of-the-realm noble houses, mainly—but this Bleth, pet hound of the crown princess, is lining up nobles as fast as he can hand out bribes and twist arms on behalf of Tanalasta ruling as queen."

"So who will win?" Huldyl asked quietly, and before Kurthryn could even lift his shoulders to shrug, added, "Nay, forget I asked that; instead, tell me: Who do you think offers the better road ahead for the realm?"

"I've thought about that a lot," Kurthryn admitted. He grinned weakly when his colleague made a silently sarcastic so-who-hasn't? gesture. "Both sides have their merits. I think Vangerdahast has the wisdom and experience to be much the better ruler, and without courtiers and senior nobles and royal cousins and what-all between him and us, he can use us of the war wizards far more swiftly than Azoun could move us to his will. Cormyr will be less corrupt and faster to respond to crises."

"Yes, but will the people believe that?"

Kurthryn frowned and shook his head slowly. "No, they won't. They never do. They'll never trust magic, because they think of it as something their nasty neighbor would use against them if he could, and they're always afraid the lot of us are as bad as their nasty neighbor. And with respected bards reminding them from time to time of how High Magess Amedahast died all those years ago battling the first war wizards, who can blame them?" Moodily he moved his king again.

Huldyl was nodding in somber agreement. "There's another thing, too," he added. "With a clear, unbroken Obarskyr line, everyone knows who has the right to sit on the throne. The moment a regency muddies the waters and someone marries one of the princesses, a rival noble will think he's better suited to rule than the one who snared the princess—and once that starts, we won't have a Cormyr unless the land can somehow endure every last noble family in it killing off all their rivals, until there's no great house left. Then one of us will have to choose a commoner to wear the crown."

"Ah, yes," Kurthryn agreed grimly, "choosing the right

commoner. The fun never ends, does it?"

"We probably won't have to worry about having to make any such choice," Huldyl said. "Remember, this whole thing has been forced upon us by a treasonous murderer, or perhaps a band of murderers. You really think they don't have something of their own in mind for Cormyr? We'll be lucky if we even find out who they are before they have our heads bouncing and rolling down the banks of Lake Azoun!"

"I think it's Sembians—perhaps with help from Westgate, or even Amn. Merchants, anyway, who look upon Cormyr as a rich little breadbasket that they can empty faster if they don't have a king in the way of their grasping hands," Kurthryn said. "They may have bought or duped a few Cormyreans, and they'll probably put a puppet noble house on and around the throne, but it's outlanders doing this to Cormyr. I'm sure of it."

"I'm not," Huldyl replied in a voice of doom. "This has all the feel of a home-brewed plot."

"How so?" Kurthryn asked dubiously. "You think some old noble with a grudge or ambitious young one can get his hands on a dead-magic toxin? Someone who's very powerful in magic must be involved, someone better than even our Lord High Wizard, or he'd have cured the king by now."

"Unless he's behind it all," Huldyl returned. "Who better placed to lead priests astray? And those of us who tried to help, too? All your point about the means of slaying really tells us is that the traitor or traitors have money enough to *buy* powerful magic. The deadly means might have come from anywhere in Faerûn . . . perhaps the far Tuigan Wastes, or the lands of the far south, or across the seas to the west. What better place to find something that'll baffle our best healers?"

Kurthryn nodded. "That feels right, that argument—but nothing in your words really proves it's traitors here at home. Cormyr has no shortage of foes who'd like to see it gone . . . rich Sembians who'd like to expand their holdings, in particular."

"Ah," Huldyl said, leaning forward, "but which of those outsiders wants their prize of Cormyr damaged or ruined by strife? None of them. Who can't see any way to what they want *but* strife? Someone who dwells here and has a place in society he knows he can't be budged from. And who would benefit most from Azoun's death and chaos in Cormyr?"

"Well," Kurthryn responded, "who? You tell me! Alusair doesn't really want the crown. She's happiest playing lady adventurer across half Faerûn, at her own whim. Apparently Tanalasta doesn't want it either. This Bleth would probably be happy as prince consort, but he dare not move quickly to take real power or half the nobles in the realm'll set him straight—and have him murdered if he ignores their rebukes. All of the nobles would probably like to strengthen their influence, wealth, and holdings, but no one noble house will be allowed to rise above the rest once the Obarskyrs are gone. They all regularly backstab each other, and they have no central leader. Their distrust of each other is so strong that they could never have one!"

"Go on, O master plotter," Huldyl said eagerly, waving at his friend to continue.

Kurthryn took a deep breath and added, "The military is loyal, by and large, to whoever sits on the Dragon Throne. The people always suspect us war wizards of treachery against the crown, but surely if there was some plot within our ranks, we'd have heard of it or smelled something. Besides, Vangerdahast keeps us on a short leash."

"It all comes back to Vangerdahast, doesn't it?" Huldyl said grimly.

They nodded to each other, both facing the same unpleasant possibility. The Lord High Wizard was powerful enough, perhaps, to create the deadly poison. One war wizard who'd confronted the old mage about his planned regency had disappeared. Vangerdahast was spending a lot of time trotting around, whispering with nobles, but he had said nothing, beyond a few curt orders, to his own war wizards. Moreover, he was usually a master at spreading rumors and swaying the people—yet this time he'd done nothing in that line, even with the folk of Suzail blaming the royal plight on any wizard who was handy. What was the old vulture's game?

"Well," Kurthryn said heavily, "at least we know at last what has laid the royals low. If I know old Thunder-spells—and he is as loyal as I believe him to be—we'll probably have a cure for it in days."

"Too late for Bhereu."

"Too late for him, but we could even lose Baron Thomdor and survive. So long as the king does not die, Cormyr will see itself through this crisis as it has through so many others. Even a king lying abed for years will save us from civil war . . . I hope."

"You have more hope in you than I do," Huldyl said gloomily. "And—"

Whatever else he may have said was lost forever as a lone figure in blue and silver, stumbling a little, came forlornly up the hall toward them. It was the priestess of Tymora, Gwennath, coming from the direction of the royal quarters. She was as white as Kurthryn's chess pieces.

The war wizards exchanged a look, and Kurthryn put out a gentle hand. "Lady? Is there aught we can do for you?"

"Pray," the priestess said in a trembling voice. "Pray for me . . . and for him . . . and for the realm. I have failed. Baron Thomdor is dead."

She shook off his comforting hand, burst into tears, and strode away, sobbing out a prayer to Tymora.

The two wizards looked at each other again. "Check," Huldyl said bitterly, moving his bat-mounted mage to threaten Kurthryn's king.

Slowly Kurthryn reached out and tipped Galaghard over to signify his surrender. "We'd better go see," he said wearily, and they got up in a swirl of robes and strode down the hall. Although they hurried, there was really no need to hurry now.

When they were gone, the moonstone queen that had felt odd to Kurthryn's fingers earlier pulsed, shifted its position slightly, and then slowly flowed, like syrup, down over the edge of the board to the floor, where it rose, growing with terrifying speed, to become . . . a woman in a plain, dark, revealingly cut gown. She wore a locket on a black ribbon at her throat, with hair the color of honey and eyes like warm flames.

Emthrara the Harper, who with Laspeera had unlocked the secrets of the abraxus, unclenched her right fist. In her hand was a white chess piece: the queen she'd been. She set it on the proper square of the board, murmured, "Check indeed, good sirs," and glided to one wall of the antechamber, where her deft fingers probed, pushed, and finally opened a hitherto hidden door in the paneling. Without a backward look, she slipped into the darkness beyond and was gone. The door shut behind her with the faintest of clicks, leaving the room dark and empty. Once more this part of the palace felt like a tomb.

20

Battle of the Witch Lords
Year of the Thirsty Sword
(900 DR)

t was not a meeting they had time for, thought Aosinin Truesilver, but then it was not a meeting they could afford to miss, either. By rights, King Galaghard, his noble court, and High Wizard Thanderahast should be seeing to the last details of the planned assault in the morning. But these were elves, and these elves demanded immediate attention.

Their appearance was both ominous and telling. For the past three months, the Glory of Cormyr, the army of the king, had met and routed the Witch Lords' armies time and time again. At the fords of Wheloon, at the forgotten temple, at Juniril and again at the Manticore's Crossing, each time overrunning the Witch Lords' position and trampling their undead troops beneath the hooves of good Cormyrean steeds. Yet their foe had risen from the dead again and again—literally.

From each battle, the most powerful Witch Lord necromancers slipped away, to regroup with forces of moldering fighting men freshly disinterred. Now the Glory of Cormyr had ridden to the limits of their supplies and trapped the remaining human mercenaries and levies of the Witch Lords flat against the western verges of the Vast Swamp. A victory here would break their power in Cormyr forever and free the eastern half of the realm from their threat.

Yet on the eve of the assault, a rider arrived, with the news that a great pavilion had suddenly appeared behind the king's forces. Its green and yellow spires rose like new mountains in the darkness, lit from within by their own radiance.

These were not simply elves of the woods, who had always passed through the kingdom, moreso since the fall of their greatest city. They were noble elves, the first to arrive in Cormyr since the fall of Myth Drannor. Noble elves who demanded a reception.

"They couldn't have picked a worse time," muttered Thanderahast as they drew near the entrance. Save for the wizard, everyone in the small party of Cormyreans approaching the pavilion was in full battle armor, including the king, the High Priest of Helm, and several nobles, among them Aosinin Truesilver, the king's cousin.

"You would snub them, then, and risk seeing their forces arrayed alongside those of the Witch Lords?" asked the king in a low voice.

"We may see them there yet, Sire," said one of the Dauntinghorns. "The elves have always been treacherous. Not fifteen winters ago, they repelled the Sembians and their Chondathan mercenaries in the Battle of the Singing Arrows despite the fall of Myth Drannor."

"Don't speak nonsense," snapped the wizard. "The Sembians were logging elven lands heavily, thinking that with their cities gone, the elves would be weak. The power of the elves has never been in cities but in the forest itself. Now, hold your tongue, for the ears of the elves are as sharp as their skin is thin."

One of the Illances made a joke about the sharp, pointed nature of elven ears, but he was shushed by his fellows. The party entered the pavilion.

Its interior had a ghostly, ethereal quality. There were elves on all sides, lounging on broad pillows. They sipped fluted glasses of glowing fluids, regarding the passing humans as if they were mongrel dogs who had wandered into a dinner party. Then the elves turned their attention back to their own dealings. Somewhere in the distance, a sad lute was being played, joined by a wispy thin, haunting voice that just caught the edges of their hearing.

The greatest chamber of the pavilion was nearly empty. A pair of guards stood at the entrance, clad in finely-made but archaic chain mail. Across the chamber stood the twisted stump of an ancient tree, a living throne into which three seats had been carved. Two of the seats were empty. The third, the farthest to the right, was occupied by a single cadaverous figure.

Aosinin reached for his sword, thinking this was one of the Witch Lords and that they were standing in the heart of an enormous trap. He relaxed only when he realized that the figure was an elf . . . though a very ancient elf, it seemed.

The figure on the throne was clad from head to toe in chain, its ornately shaped links as fine as any that could be crafted in Suzail, even by dwarven hands. Its design, like the mail worn by the guards, was archaic, and many of the links were thin enough from wear to appear nearly translucent. The elf's face was elongated, his cheeks and eyes deeply sunken, his remaining hair silver-white and flowing from a receding forehead.

Aosinin had never seen an elf this old before. And yet something about the figure seemed familiar . . . like the mage Thanderahast. There was something similar in the elf's fluid, well-practiced movements, the grace of . . . well, a near immortal, Aosinin supposed.

The elf lord waited for the royal party to reach the foot of the throne before speaking. His voice sounded like an old book opening for the first time in a century. "So these are the children of Ondeth and Faerlthann? Somehow I expected more."

The king took a pace ahead of the others. "I am King Galaghard the Third, royal head of Cormyr, called the Forest Kingdom, the Wolf Woods, and the Land of the

Purple Dragon. This is my Royal Wizard, Thanderahast, of the blood of Baerauble himself. And the mightiest men of my noble court."

The elf regarded the humans for a long moment, and Aosinin wondered if these elf lords could cast death magic without moving an eyelid. At length, he said, "I am Othorion Keove, last of the house of Iliphar Nelnueve, the Lord of Scepters. Do you remember me?"

Thanderahast stepped forward. "We know of the tales of great Iliphar and of that first coronation of Faerlthann nearly nine centuries back. I fear we have lost much of the records of his court, but we welcome you back to Cormyr."

The elf regarded the wizard stonily. "You are the blood of old Baerauble Elf-friend? The blood must be thin indeed by now, though I believe something magical pulses through your veins, allowing you a long life as old Baerauble had."

Instead of replying, the wizard chose to ignore the venom in the remark. "The same magic that probably pulses through your noble brow as well, lord elf. I am surprised to see one so ancient outside the elven homeland of Evermeet."

The elf nodded. "I have resisted the call of Evermeet the Fair for many years in order to fight against the human incursions, to fight against the fiends of the pit who claimed Myth Drannor, and lately to fight against the southerners who sought to claim our forests unasked."

King Galaghard stepped forward. "May we ask why you are here, lord elf?"

"I thought to do a little hunting," said the elf. "Tell me, do you still have forest buffalo here?"

Thanderahast broke in. "I fear not, O Venerable Othorion. They vanished long ago."

"Giant owlbears, then?" suggested the elf lord. "Or envenomed pumas, or great ruqs?"

"They are no more as well, lord elf," the wizard replied.

Ed Greenwood and Jeff Grubb

Othorion Keove regarded the humans coldly. "You haven't really taken care of our lands very well, have you?"

Now the king stepped forward once more. "We tend to the land as best as we are able. There are still great forests in Cormyr, which cannot be said of neighboring Sembia, and trees here that stood when your Lord of Scepters was here last. The forested domains are smaller, but they have served us well and have been well tended and mastered."

Thanderahast tried to speak, but the king gave him no chance, continuing, "We have defended this land from dragons and from orcs, from pirates and from evil sorcerers. On the morrow, we set out in one last battle against the evil forces of the necromantic Witch Lords. We have protected this land and its people because long ago we made a promise to your liege to do so. We have nothing to apologize for to any elf, lord or no."

Aosinin thought he saw a small smile break across the elf lord's face. "I see the blood of Faerlthann runs thick and true in his descendants. Your first king had such fire, and his words were sharp, while those of Baerauble were cloying and tricky. It is pleasant to see that threats and bold speech, at least, have not changed. Am I not welcome to hunt within your woods?"

"You are welcome, Othorion Keove," said the king quickly. "Welcome as an old friend of the land. I apologize in advance for not keeping sufficiently dangerous creatures at hand for your return. I ask only that you trouble none of the citizens of this land, nor harm them in any way. For they, like the land, are in my trust, and I am obligated to protect them."

The elf nodded silently and the king continued. "If you will excuse me and my brethren, then, we must prepare for our own hunt on the morrow. There are few hours between now and then, and we must make the best use of them."

The elf lord nodded and raised a hand slowly in dismissal.

Thanderahast said quickly, "The battle tomorrow, O elf lord . . . we could use any aid you could muster."

A wintry smile twisted Othorion's lips. "The Witch Lords' representative has been here and gone already with a similar invitation, hedged with hidden threats and blatant promises. I will tell you what I told him: I am here for the hunting. But that one did give me a message for you, child of Baerauble. He said that Luthax sends his regards."

The mage's face went pale, and he stiffened visibly. Then he bowed low and joined the others in leaving the tent. None of the elves paid the grim, armored humans any attention.

The ride back was a time of low whispers. They did not talk of elves, but rather of the upcoming battle. Marsember had sent some desperately needed infantry, fresh but untried. They would stand on the left flank. The veteran Purple Dragons would hold the right, backed up by Thanderahast's apprentices. Arabel had sent troops, but even their marching was a shaky, undisciplined affair; they might well prove unreliable. Their ranks would be seasoned with veteran militia from Suzail and placed in the center, near the king and the main vanguard. Those nobles not leading specific units would be mounted and go into battle flanking the royal forces, behind the central troops.

They returned to the camp to find nothing amiss, though there had been activity and many fires in the Witch Lord encampments. The goblins and orcs in the necromancers' host preferred to fight in the dark, but the presence of human troops meant that they would have to wait until daylight.

The nobles congregated to confirm the battle plan one last time, then broke for the evening. The nobles who had brought their own units returned to their camps, and the wizards retired to their meditations. Soon only a handful were left.

Throughout, King Galaghard was mostly silent, marshaling his words as if they were strength, even after the others had dispersed. At length, he rose. "I want to check the perimeter one last time. Truesilver, walk with me."

Aosinin strode alongside the king, and the two paced in silence along the hard-packed earth. Finally Truesilver could contain himself no longer and asked, "Cousin, who is Luthax?"

The king looked out over the wide valley that come the dawn would be their battlefield. High fires blazed in the Witch Lords' camp, and he could imagine the orcs and ogres and trolls dancing about the flames. He said, "Luthax is an old rival of Thanderahast's, I believe, from before he became the High Wizard."

"I cannot imagine anything still being around from before Thanderahast was High Wizard," said Aosinin.

Galaghard smiled in the moonlit darkness. "Wizards live forever, and their rivalries longer than that. I worry that the wizard will forget his loyalty to the crown in the heat of battle, particularly if an old foe has aligned himself with the Witch Lords. Yet many beings in Faerûn are older than Thanderahast. That old elf lord, for one. He was hunting here before our ancestors arrived."

"I didn't think elves lived that long," said Aosinin.

"They don't," responded the king. "I think he has some of the same magic that keeps Thanderahast and the other wizards going for centuries. Yet he, the elf lord, expected to return here and find all as it was—forests instead of fields, monsters instead of cattle, trees instead of homesteads. It makes me worry."

"Worry, Sire?" asked Aosinin.

The two passed a guard. Salutes were exchanged, and Galaghard continued only once they were well past. "All that we have achieved, all that we have built, has happened in his one lifetime. Were we to fail tomorrow, to fall to the necromancers, would any record of us be here in another nine hundred years? Would the forests reclaim our fields and the monsters lair in our ruins and no one remember our names?"

"We will not fail tomorrow," said Aosinin quickly, unsure of what else to say.

"We have been on campaign for three months," said the king, "three months of living in our saddles and sleeping in our armor. If we fail tomorrow, would I rather have spent those three months with my family, with my wife, with little Rhiigard and Tanalar and Kathla? And will it matter in the long run who truly rules Cormyr?"

Aosinin was silent. Thanderahast was obviously not the only one shaken by the elf lord's appearance. "We will not fail, my lord," he repeated at last. "You know you have the loyalty of every Cormyrean on that battle plain tomorrow. They look to you for support, for leadership. If you are sure of yourself, they'll follow you into the Pits of the Abyss itself!"

"And if I am myself unsure?" asked the king. "If I feel tired and unwilling to go another step? What then, Cousin?"

"Then I will stand by your side, Cousin," Aosinin replied, "and remind you of our duty to protect the land of Cormyr. If we fail, no amount of time will eradicate the curse of the Witch Lords. And I will remind you that *I* am sure you know what you are doing."

They passed the last of the sentries. The sentry was little more than a boy, but he snapped to attention at the king's approach and saluted crisply. Aosinin saw the lad's eyes in his small watch fire. They glowed with pride and respect.

Aosinin looked at his king. Galaghard's features were lit by the flames. His jaw was firm, and his eyes sparkled. He managed a small fatherly smile.

The men would follow him, and that was important, Aosinin thought. After the battle, the king could retire to his home and hearth and family, and his worries would be laid to rest. And if they failed in the morning, they'd all be beyond such worries in any event.

* * * * *

That morning came all too soon for Aosinin and the others. With the first touch of redness in the eastern sky, the squires were up and about and soon roused their masters as the troops, most of them sleeping little themselves, donned their shirts of mail and leather and saw to their weapons one last time. For some of them, it would in truth be the last time.

The squires brought Aosinin and the rest of the nobles their great suits of plate mail and slowly ratcheted the bolts home, encasing the valor of Cormyr in steel. Metal covered their outer legs, their waists, and torsos, and a combination of plate and chain wreathed their upper limbs. Aosinin chose his open-faced helm, as would Galaghard. Despite the risk of arrows, the king needed to be seen, and Aosinin and the rest of the royal nobles would not let their cousin take a risk they were unwilling to engage themselves.

Across the vale, there was the sound of drums and horns. The enemy was preparing, too.

The sun's disk was just breaking the horizon when the troops of Cormyr formed their battle lines. Patriarchs of Helm the Watchful strutted along the line, each with an attendant acolyte and a bucket of holy water. The patriarch would dip a hollow mace, its head pierced with a hundred tiny holes, into the barrel, then fling the water over the waiting troops, blessing them en masse with the Tears of Helm.

Aosinin was on his brown gelding by this time, a huge, heavy beast barded with interleaved plates heavier than his own. His squire secured the last of the bolts and latches, then retreated to ready himself. The squire, one of the young Dauntinghorns, would march with the infantry, providing some backbone to the Arabellan troops.

The men of Arabel looked nervous but resolute, Aosinin thought, eager to prove their worth and banish the last vestiges of the term "rebel Arabel." Yet a mantle of fear hung on them that even the blessing of watchful Helm did nothing to dissipate.

The troops from Marsember were descendants of the original smugglers and pirates who had founded and refounded that swampy, independent city. They looked fully capable of taking on the Witch Lords by themselves. Indeed, if the king hesitated any longer, they would do exactly that.

The mages signaled that their preparatory spells were complete, and Thanderahast rode to join the king. The wizard's mount was a light pony, a dappled veteran of many battles. It had been trained to retreat if Thanderahast left the saddle, and it had survived a number of nasty frays as a result.

The king was mounted on his black charger, a magnificent mount clad in ivory-shaded barding. The charger's armored headpiece had been fitted with a unicorn's horn, no doubt further enchanted by the Royal Wizard to protect the rider. Galaghard's own armor was polished to a luster that caught the sun's rays and threw them back like a mirror. On his chest was the painted symbol of Cormyr, the Purple Dragon, adopted officially since the years of pirate exile.

Across the shallow vale, the horns grew louder and the drums began to roll, a long, ominous sound that would end in a charge. The Witch Lords' troops would not wait for the sun to fill the vale; their inhuman troops preferred to fight in the shadows. They would move soon.

There was one last, lingering blare of horns, and the drums fell silent. The armies of the Witch Lords roared in unison and surged forward down the gentle slope. Goblins and orcs trotted on the flanks, their ranks sprinkled with the hulking forms of ogre captains. In the center ran the human troops, bolstered by a few knots of loping trolls. There was no visible sign of the Witch Lords themselves, but then there hadn't been at any of the previous battles, either.

The Marsembians started to advance in response, only to be hauled back by the shouted curses of their noble leaders. Marliir was the name, Aosinin thought.

The king held up one hand, his eyes locked on the advancing line of nonhumans and traitors. If he had any doubt in his heart, it did not show on his face. The opposing forces had reached the bottom of a shallow delve and were now slowly working their way up the other side.

King Galaghard lowered his hand, and the silver horns of the Cormyrean army roared out in response. Like one vast, amorphous creature spread out over the hilltop, the Glory of Cormyr spilled into the valley. Aosinin rode in the main vanguard, alongside the High Wizard on his pony. An eager-looking young Skatter-hawk rode on Thanderahast's other side, paired with an older, grimmer Thundersword. As they rode, both nobles waggled the blades of their swords to flash reflected sun into the eyes of their foes.

They had closed about half the distance to the enemy line when the bats appeared. The ungainly creatures lofted up from the back of the enemy lines, great fur-covered giants with twisted faces and dead-white skin, shadowing the morning light with their numbers. Humans rode the backs of the daunting beasts—humans wearing dark helms bedecked with stag antlers. The lieutenants of the Witch Lords.

They swooped over the Marsembian troops, and lightning bolts laced down. The bolts were erratic, gouging the soft, peaty earth more than the troops, but for every two Marsembians who fell, only one rose again.

On his left, Aosinin heard Thanderahast let out a shout of anger, then call out Luthax's name. His personal enemy was among the bat riders, though how the mage knew, Aosinin could not guess. Thanderahast began to bark the ancient phrases of a spell. Aosinin realized what the mage was doing and reached out to stop him, but his armor did not allow him such swift, stretching overbalancing, and the mage finished the spell and lofted himself out of his saddle, flying upward to meet the bat riders. The pony, as trained, immediately halted and started to trot back up the hill.

Aosinin bellowed at his cousin, and the king nodded grimly. From other wings, Thanderahast's pupils were rising as well, abandoning their troops in order to join in the airborne carnage.

Ahead, the Witch Lords' troops halted on the near slope of the valley. Ogres were bellowing orders, and orcs and goblins were desperately trying to form a line, spear-points out, to break the Cormyrean charge. Most would not complete the maneuver before they were struck down.

Above their heads, the bat riders and flying mages wheeled and dodged. Lightning cracked across the clear sky, and the Royal Wizard's pupils replied with gouts of fire. Here a human form would plummet to the earth, and there a flaming bat wing would flutter downward, trailing ink-black smoke down to its death. Thandera-hast had removed the danger of any unopposed, con-certed attack from above, but at the cost of any protection of the line troops on the ground if the Witch Lords had any other tricks up their sleeves.

The next horror of the necromancers was apparent when the two armies fully closed. At first Aosinin thought he faced humans—traitors, rebels, and merce-naries. They might have been once, for he recognized some badges on the armor they wore. But now they were marching dead things, the remains of their eyes hanging bloody in their sockets, and their flesh drained of all blood. To a man, they had deep slashes across their ex-posed throats.

The walking dead! Zombies, Aosinin realized with a groan, magical creations under the control of a powerful necromancer. And unlike the animated skeletons they had fought in previous battles, these were recently made and still had some of the power they held in life. The noble thought of the fires and the drums of the previous evening and realized that it had not been a rallying cele-bration, but a grisly enchantment. The Witch Lords had consumed their own living troops to provide fodder of the utmost loyalty for this crucial battle.

The Arabellans in the front line quailed when they saw what they faced, and several began to retreat. Galaghard rode among them to the front of the line, rais-ing his arm and sounding the attack. The Arabellans stiffened at the sight of the king and, with a shout, pressed forward into the undead.

Aosinin spurred his horse forward to follow his king, and all around him, the battle lines disintegrated into the usual chaos of hacking and thrusting and dying as the ranks of soldiers broke into a swirl of smaller conflicts—man against goblin, against ogre, and against undead abomination. The Truesilver wasted no breath on battle cries but set his teeth and hacked at the butchered humans, seeking to carve a path to the king, who wheeled and slashed again and again against the undead horde.

At the king's flanks rode two priests of Helm the Watchful. Golden lights danced from their palms as they drove the animating essences from the fighting corpses. As Aosinin watched, one of the priests was overwhelmed by a wave of clutching undead and dragged from his mount. Aosinin did not see him again. Instead, the Truesilver found himself beset on all sides by swarming goblins, who were spilling into the heart of the Cormyrean host in the wake of the undead, slashing at zombie and Cormyrean with equal abandon.

The world became a small, blood-red, frantic place of wheeling and cutting and slashing, Aosinin's horse bucking under him like a mad thing. He trampled foes who sought to gut his mount and drag him down. He made little charges to nowhere, wheeling as his mount lashed out in all directions with steel-shod hooves, then surging back along the line of destruction he'd already cut, to reap more goblin lives. Twice he was nearly torn from the saddle, and once his gauntlet was ripped clear from his hand. A goblin tried to climb up on his mount, its clawlike fingers scrabbling against the horse's barding, clawing at Aosinin's face. The Truesilver cursed and ran the small creature through. As the goblin fell away, Aosinin saw young Skatterhawk, transfixed by three black goblin blades, topple from his horse, knocking over three zombies. There were yet more of the undead to swarm over the fallen noble's body, and more orcs and more goblins. Aosinin's world was reduced to the length of his sword.

When Truesilver did have time and breath to look up again, he was wet with blood clear up to his gorget, and half the nobles of the Glory of Cormyr were down. Cormaerils, Dauntinghorns, and Crownsilvers had vanished from their saddles and now lay dead and trampled beneath feet and hooves in the battle. The king was farther away now, driven apart from his cousin by the weight of the advancing undead.

As Aosinin cursed and fought to bring his mount around, he saw a huge shape rise up from among the heaped dead. A monstrous troll, larger than any Aosinin had seen, cunningly hidden among the undead troops and goblins, surged into battle with the king. Galaghard's mount reared, whinnying in fear, and the king fought to keep it under control.

Another horseman spurred into the space between the king and the troll. One of the Bleth boys, by his markings. To the troll, one human was as good a victim as another. One swipe of its huge claws unhorsed the impulsive Bleth, and another ripped his armor open from neck to waist. Blood fountained, and the young noble threw back his head in a cry of agony that Aosinin could not hear. He fell out of view, lost in the press of staggering zombies and desperately thrusting Arabellan billmen.

Bleth's sacrifice bought the time the king needed. Aosinin realized that, besides himself, Galaghard was now nearly the only mounted knight left. The king wheeled his charger and brought his sweeping blade around nearly level with the troll's neck. As the horse plunged forward, the monster's head was cut from its shoulders and bounced into the throng of advancing goblins.

That would not kill the creature, thought Aosinin, but the loss would keep it busy for a while. Indeed, the troll had already abandoned its attack on the king and was now throwing goblins about like handfuls of straw, searching in the confusion for its lost head.

The king wheeled again, this time facing Aosinin. Seeing his cousin, he raised his sword in salute, and the Truesilver returned it, seeing Galaghard give him a bloody smile. There were no doubts in his liege's mind this day. No hollowness in the king of Cormyr.

The king used his uplifted blade to point to the left flank, where the Marsembians were slowly being driven back by a wedge of orcs and goblins. Were that wing to fail, the Witch Lords could drive around behind the Cormyrean lines, surrounding them, and force the Glory of Cormyr into a knot of men too tightly packed to fight. Then the outermost could be slain at leisure, while those on the inside were crushed or trampled to death.

Aosinin rallied a small band of Arabellans with hoarse shouts and windmilling waves of his sword—by the gods, was his arm going to fall off?—and led them in a charge across the field of heaped and broken bodies, seeking to reinforce the Marsembian foot soldiers.

The Arabellans took heart for the first time that day and began to shout as they came down on the orcs from one side.

Their cries were drowned out by the sound of horns, shrieking like great hunting hawks. Aosinin had heard only one horn sound like that—a trophy horn carved all of one piece of crystal, as smooth as glass, that resided on a cushion in a room deep in the palace. An elven horn!

Heart rising in sudden hope, he stood in his stirrups as his faithful steed raced along, and he looked beyond units of snarling, hurrying ogres in time to see the elves arrive on the battlefield. Some were flying, and these joined the wizards in their airborne struggle with the bat riders. The remainder rode great stags, giant elk whose heads were heavy with iron-tipped antlers.

This was the true Glory of Cormyr, Aosinin realized. The armor of the elves glowed, as their tent had the night before, in a scintillating pattern of green and gold. They were few in number, but to an elf, they were heavily armed and armored.

The Witch Lord line disintegrated as they struck it full force, the ogres falling like crops at harvesttime under the wicked, slender blades of the elves. In mere moments they were slain, and the elves were through to the heart of the wedge of orcs.

Without their leaders, the goblins and orcs dropped their weapons and tried to flee, only to be cut down as they ran. Aosinin heard exultant singing and realized that it came from the elves. More of the goblin troops fled at the sound.

The glowing wave of death caught up with Aosinin's band and passed on by, and the Truesilver urged his Arabellans to join the flank of the stag riders. One entire wing of the Witch Lords' army was in flight before them, and individual elves were breaking away to chase down stragglers.

Now the charging elves struck the zombies at the heart of the Witch Lords' host, troops too mindless to run. Bright blades flashed, and graceful bodies leaned and slashed and rose to slash again in a deadly dance that separated limbs from bodies and forced the dead to fall. In less time than Aosinin would have believed possible, the undead had also fallen beneath the hooves of the rushing stags. The Cormyrean infantry could clearly see what was happening now and raised a great cheer as they hacked at orcs and goblins with renewed heart.

The elven riders swept up to the king of Cormyr, whose mount was picking its way gingerly over a mound of undead and goblin bodies that the royal sword had slain. Galaghard raised his bloody blade in greeting and bellowed, "We appreciate your aid!"

"Aid?" Othorion Keove grinned down from his high saddle. "I said I came here to do some hunting, and when I awoke this morning, I decided I had a taste for orc, goblin, ogre, and undead. Care to ride with me?"

The king spurred his own mount alongside the elf lord's stag, and together they swept down on the surviving wing of the Witch Lords' army. It was mired in combat with the Suzail militia, but it shattered like ice as the elves and men bore down on it. Weary Cormyreans from all over the field trotted over to be in at the kill. Few foes of Cormyr would be slipping away from this last stand.

Overhead, the surviving bat riders wheeled and fled into the Vast Swamp. Two were immolated as they flew, but another half-dozen outran the mages and elves and disappeared into the misty bogs beyond, flapping frantically.

Their mounts exhausted from the charge, Aosinin, Galaghard, and the elf lord rode slowly to a low hillock overlooking the battle. Below, the priests of Helm were tending to the human wounded and dispatching dying orcs. Several smoldering piles marked where trolls had fallen; they would have to be immolated later to make their deaths final. Thanderahast landed nearby, his robes bloodied and scorched. He nodded to the king, and Galaghard saluted him formally. Words would be exchanged later, Aosinin knew, about the High Wizard abandoning the knights of the court to pursue his own personal vendetta.

The elf lord turned to the king and said, "A good day's hunt."

Galaghard shrugged his heavily mailed shoulders. "It is good to see that Cormyr still offers something suitable to your tastes."

"It does, in many ways," said the elf, and then, after a visible hesitation, he rode nearer and laid a slender hand on the king's arm. "Hear me, human, for I have altogether too much wisdom bought over long and bloody years. It is easy to rule from a distance, but difficult to lead from the front of a battle. It is easy to order, but hard to inspire. It is simple to conquer, but hard to rule. That is why you triumphed this day over the unseen necromancers. I had my doubts as to your fate, and your worth, until I saw one of your brother humans sacrifice himself in the fray to purchase you time. Such loyalty is more precious than all the gold in your vaults."

"Aye," said the king huskily, smiling. "And here—" he

thumped his chest with one bloody gauntlet—"it is valued more than all the gold in all the cities of humans all over Faerûn. I can believe in my power—my just authority—only as long as others believe in me." He looked at Aosinin.

"You probably don't know how important this is," the old elf added, "but I have to say you've done a fair job with this tract of land. Iliphar would approve, and probably Baerauble as well."

"Will you be staying, then?" asked the king. "You will be most welcome, for I shall ensure that all Cormyr knows that the realm survives because of your aid here today."

The elf waved a dismissive hand. "For a year, perhaps two, we shall abide here," Othorion replied, "but no true elf can resist the call of Evermeet forever. Yet in these fair forests, I think there will be good hunting for a small while."

As the three men and the elf went slowly down from the hill, their trembling mounts moving no faster than the walking wizard, men of Cormyr walked about on the bloody field under the bright sun of morning.

The foot soldiers gathered mementos and told their companions about how they'd almost died *here*, and had hewn that one down over *there*, and as the tales went on, the tellers were already expanding their heroisms. By nightfall, all of them would have personally rescued the king and led the elves onto the battlefield in the charge that won the day and preserved the realm.

21

Spells and Politics
Year of the Gauntlet
(1369 DR)

he Royal Magician's eyebrows rose. "Impressive shielding spells," he said, watching the three hired mages at work. Two were Calishites, whose sash symbols showed that they were both Exalted Masters in at least two schools of sorcery, and the third was a Nimbran. By the looks of the rippling prismatic domes and spell-stop fields they were weaving around the room, any two of them could probably defeat him in a battle of spells. The house of Cormaeril spared no expense in seeing to the safety of its own . . . or in attempts to impress their Lord High Wizard.

The man he was here to meet inclined his head and smiled slightly—a smile that did not reach to his eyes, which were hard, black, and cold. "One can never be too careful," he murmured and went on waiting, leaning casually against the wall.

One after another, each of the wizards signaled that his spells were complete. Vangerdahast's host gave them each the same hand sign in return, and each sat down on a bench facing Vangerdahast, drawing out a pair of wands to hold ready. Their purpose was clear. If the Lord High Wizard didn't keep to his best behavior during the

312

interview ahead, he would not be Lord High anything for very long.

Vangerdahast smiled slightly, to let his host see that he'd understood the rather unsubtle point, and sat down on a solid bit of nothingness he'd conjured. That opened some eyes over on the bench; none of them had seen him do the necessary casting. Perhaps this old fool was mightier than they'd thought, their eyes seemed to say.

The old fool crossed his legs, leaned back with his behind resting on empty air, and said, "I'm sure you already know why I'm here."

The cold-eyed young noble lazily pushed himself away from the wall with one boot and set down his slender tallglass of dragondew wine on the ornate table that bore the arms of his family.

"You'd like to proclaim yourself regent of Cormyr sometime during the next two days," Gaspar Cormaeril replied coolly. "Or has the information reaching me been incorrect?"

"You've stated my aim," Vangerdahast agreed. "I can, and shall probably have to, wait as long as six days or more." He met Gaspar's gaze and added, "To achieve this at all, however, I'll need support. The support of prominent nobles . . . such as the house of Cormaeril."

Cold eyes met his steadily. "I'm sure you're used to a lot of coy and flowery speech, sir mage," the young noble said, "but I've grown enamored of rather more direct talk these days—in particular, when every fleeting breath we take costs me coins." He inclined his head toward the three watchful mages on the bench. Vangerdahast nodded and spread a hand, indicating that he should continue. The gesture caused at least three wands to lift warily.

Gaspar smiled thinly. "Know then that it is my intention to support you as regent of Cormyr, on a permanent basis if you desire, so long as you meet my conditions. I'm not one of those who hates or fears the idea of a mage-king; in fact, I consider that your lot have demonstrated wise and deft statecraft through the years and

313

may save us all from a lot of the nonsense attendant on the vanity and, er, lustier side of the Obarskyr monarchs."

Vangerdahast nodded. "I am pleased to hear this. May I know your conditions?"

Gaspar smiled again. "It is a pleasure to work with someone so . . . practical. My conditions are this: As regent, you must agree to work with a small council of nobles—a dozen or so, no more, whose initial membership I must approve. Have no fear of facing an outrageous roster. I realize, as I'm sure you will, the necessity of recognizing the noble families of Bleth, Cormaeril, Crownsilver, Dauntinghorn, Emmarask, Hawklin, Huntcrown, Huntsilver, Illance, Rowanmantle, and Truesilver." He paused in his leisurely litany and turned to fix Vangerdahast with a direct gaze. The old wizard noticed that his position ensured that none of the mages on the bench would have any trouble firing both of their wands at Cormyr's Lord High Wizard. "Before we proceed, tell me, my lord—do you have any essential dispute with this notion?"

"None," Vangerdahast replied. "This—as outlined thus far, at least—corresponds with my own prior intention. No regent should attempt to rule without the direct aid and support of the people of the realm."

The young Cormaeril nodded. "It is good to hear that. It is my intention that the families I've named—and I believe I could agree to one or two more, perhaps the Houses of Wintersun, Marliir, or Wyvernspur—be free to send any designate of their choice to sit on the council. Initially, of course, the heads of the houses will want to attend. Later on, I suspect that most will delegate this duty to more junior family members, or those who particularly enjoy intrigue." Gaspar allowed another small smile that did not reach his eyes to cross his face and continued. "This council of nobles will advise you on all affairs and meet at least once a tenday—every third afternoon would seem to be more appropriate. You must agree to place all major matters of state before it, including any measure involving taxation, the war wizards, the Purple Dragons, envoys of the realm to external powers, and measures that alter the powers of the crown in any way. No royal business—or rather, the business that was formerly royal—is to bypass the council or be concealed from it."

The Royal Magician of Cormyr nodded. "I agree. This is to be a voting council, I take it?"

Gaspar smiled thinly again. "It is, and by any majority vote, it will hold veto power over all decisions and decrees of the regent. *All* decisions, my lord." His eyes flicked to the three wizards and back again, in another not-so-subtle warning.

Vangerdahast smiled politely. "So far this seems not unreasonable. I trust matters of scrutiny and reportage can be worked out in the council once we begin?"

Gaspar inclined his head. "Indeed. An integral part of council powers, in my view, will be the right of every sitting member to employ as personal bodyguard one mage of his own choosing, whose name and sigil will be known to you but whose other particulars will remain secret from the regent, the war wizards, other council members, and all other arms of state."

Vangerdahast's eyebrows rose. "On the surface, an understandable guarantee of autonomy, yet in the long run, I can see this as a grave source of trouble for the realm. You deem this wise?"

"I deem it necessary." Gaspar's calm was glacial. "Rest assured, sir mage, that none of my thinking in this has been hasty. Yet, prepare: I have not yet enunciated my two more unusual conditions."

Vangerdahast almost smiled. The lad was uncanny in his maturity and cold-blooded poise but a young and excited boy underneath, nonetheless. "And these are?"

"You will intend all council meetings and have a vote. However—and this you will keep secret, revealing it to no one upon pain of death—your vote will always be cast as I, or another Cormaeril family representative acting in my stead, directs."

"In other words, House Cormaeril will have two votes," Vangerdahast said softly. "A public one and a private one."

"Indeed," the young noble replied. "The other condition must also remain secret, for obvious reasons, and also depends upon your ability to act convincingly. Although you must never betray this by your manner or words, you must place no credence in the counsel given by House Illance."

"Chief among the current enemies of House Cormaeril," Vangerdahast murmured. "Are there other conditions or details?"

Gaspar took up his glass again. "None. I take it you find these conditions somewhat more restrictive than you'd intended to place upon yourself?"

"A trifle," Vangerdahast admitted, "and yet they are not unreasoned, nor are they unworkable if the council acts with alacrity. May I in turn demand that no council member—including, I suppose, myself—have the power to delay votes by absence or protest, and that any efforts to delay decisions require at least a two-thirds majority?"

Gaspar frowned slightly, then said, "I think that provision is reasonable enough. You need a council that cannot bring the business of the realm to a halt out of spite or internal bickering."

Vangerdahast nodded. "I do."

"I agree to that, then," Gaspar replied. He sipped at his wine and added, "Of course, no mention of this meeting or our agreements must ever pass your lips, or—" He inclined his head meaningfully towards the wizards on the bench.

"I have been the essence of tact for some years, sir," Vangerdahast replied gravely, "and fully understand such things."

Gaspar smiled, looking very like a satisfied snake, and said, "You're now wondering just how you can evade these conditions, or whether you need the support of the Cormaerils at all, given this rather steep price for your title. Know, sir mage, that I have been very busy over the last few days—and, in other ways, for some time before that—in discreet inquiries among certain of my fellow nobles. Be advised that I have seen to it that the major houses I have mentioned—beyond, perhaps, the three royal houses, which will tend to prefer the crown princess on the throne to any sort of regency—will never support you unless you agree to my conditions. You can abandon all thought of formal rule. I predict that the crown princess will shortly banish you from the realm, for she has been soliciting support for such a decree from my house and others. Or you can be regent, but only under my terms."

"It certainly sounds as if you've fully prepared for this, ah, discussion," Vangerdahast said mildly. "I hope you won't be overly offended if I express my surprise that so young and hitherto nonprominent member of the Cormaerils should hold such power within his house. Can you really speak for your entire large and far-flung family?"

Gaspar gave the Royal Magician his serpent smile again and replied with a question of his own. "I presume you are acquainted with both Ohlmer Cormaeril and Sorgar Illance?"

Vangerdahast nodded. Ohlmer was an outwardly respectable patriarch of House Cormaeril, given to kidnappings within the realm for the purposes of slavery, illicit smuggling dealings with pirates, and the mistreatment of young female slaves who came within his reach. Sorgar Illance was a cruel ex-adventurer, now balding and bitter as well as cynical and cultured, who'd risen to become head of House Illance, a position that had not slowed his compulsive thefts and love of slaying men in brawls. "I know rather more about both men than I care to," he remarked carefully.

Gaspar smiled once more. "Then you will probably not be overly distressed to learn that both will die mysteriously tonight. I shall take no part in it; you may observe my revels, if you wish, at the newly opened Cormaeril Club dining hall. Await the news . . . and come morning, you'll see how effectively Gaspar Cormaeril can rule the House of Cormaeril."

Vangerdahast raised an eyebrow. "I'd not be upset to hear of such . . . unfortunate demises, yet I'd be concerned for any noble in Cormyr who might begin to fall too much in love with boldness, and so start off on the trail that leads, sooner or later, to overstepping oneself. Too many nobles dying would be suspicious, my friend."

Gaspar shrugged. "Whereas overmuch caution, as practiced by the incumbent heads of all our noble houses, leads to bitter, building resentment and unrest and the slow decline of the realm into the chaos we face today."

The man was as cool as the depths of an icy cave. The Royal Magician raised one last warning. "Whenever kin die violently, there arises the dreadful prospect that one could awaken to find his family torn apart in clan strife, as has indeed happened before to those who have forced their fellows to choose between blood and country."

Gaspar set down his empty glass gently and came to stand over the Lord High Wizard for the first time. He looked down.

"Far worse fates can befall a kingdom," the young Cormaeril said softly and menacingly, "when its senior families have long reaches, deep pockets, and surprising allies."

And with those grand words, Gaspar turned on his heel and strode away, gesturing to his hired wizards. The two Calishites rose and faced Vangerdahast with leveled wands, while the Nimbran hastily sheathed the two he held and brought down the shielding spells.

The Calishites looked at Vangerdahast with open contempt. "This realm of Cormyr must be barbaric indeed if one fat old man with such paltry magic can be its titled high mage," one remarked loudly. The other chuckled.

Their chuckles died abruptly, an instant later, when Vangerdahast stood up and made a rather rude gesture and the two mages suddenly found themselves surrounded by a ring of over thirty identical Vangerdahasts, all of whom licked their fingers, made another leisurely impolite movement, and then waved a cheerful farewell before fading away.

* * * * *

Vangerdahast faded back into solidity elsewhere—the Tower of the Balconies at the front of the royal court, to be precise—just in time to look out of its windows and down into the courtyard to see Gaspar Cormaeril saunter out of the Dragon Door and stop to talk with Aunadar Bleth.

The two greeted each other as old friends and chatted casually. The young Bleth reached into his pocket and pressed something into Cormaeril's hand. From a distance, it appeared to be a large crystal, the color of sunset, or perhaps a small decanter or large piece of jewelry. Long reaches, deep pockets, and surprising allies, thought the wizard.

"Long reaches, deep pockets, and surprising allies," Vangerdahast said quietly to the unhearing figure below, "and far worse fates indeed."

22

The Last Dragon
The Year of the Dracorage
(1018 DR)

hate this," pouted Crown Prince Azoun, the second of the royal line to bear that name. "We're sitting here like coneys waiting for the hunter."

"Your objection is noted," the young mage Jorunhast said icily, "and duly ignored."

"You don't want to be here either," said the crown prince.

"You are correct," the wizard replied, his voice verging on a snarl. "But I have to be here to protect you."

The wizard had no love for this crown prince, and deep in his heart, he hoped that Thanderahast would hang onto life long enough that Jorunhast could be the court wizard of the *next* King of Cormyr *after* Azoun. But not this one. Any king but this one. To swear fealty to such an egotistical, pampered, self-centered child! To call him "Sire" and "liege" and "master"! Jorunhast shook his head.

Even the young prince's voice was shrill, tinny, and irritating to the mage's ears. Only three years separated the two in age, but the young prince still sounded like a petulant child.

The bickering pair waited on a low, windswept hill outside Suzail. They made an odd pair as they sat astride their light message ponies. The crown prince was whipsaw thin and gangly, the apprentice wizard broad-shouldered and well muscled. An impartial observer would probably have judged that the lean, hungry one was the mage and his larger companion had Obarskyr blood in him.

Behind them, low on the horizon, the smoke from the wreckage of Cormyr's capital city spiraled up into the warm summer air.

The great rage of dragons had descended on Cormyr without warning and without mercy. Arabel, Dhedluk, Eveningstar, and a score of other settlements had gone up in flames. Small hamlets were reduced to kindling, and the roads would likely once more become haunted, dangerous paths through lawless wilderness.

But it was Suzail that had suffered the worst. Three great dragons, red wyrms of huge dimensions, had descended on the city like eagles among sheep. The docks and the lower wards, built mostly of wood, roared up in flames. Most of the stone buildings weathered the initial blasts, though glass melted and scorched wooden doors caught fire from the heat. Those buildings that still stood, the dragons ripped apart with their claws, seeking the humans cowering within.

Castle Obarskyr sat above the conflagration, separated from the flames by wide gardens now wilted from the heat. Protected by generations of spells, wards, and glamors, it became the rallying point for the city. Here the nobility fled, and here, in the scented chambers of King Arangor, the response was launched.

Three wings of Purple Dragon guardsmen had erupted from the secure doors of the castle. King Arangor, barely fitting into his own armor, led one wing south to the docks, accompanied by Thanderahast. The future King Azoun II led a similar wing of troops to the west, where the smallest of the three dragons was ravaging the warehouses and taverns. The third wing struck north and east, where the noble manors were clustered along the base of the hill. This was the smallest of the

groups but contained many of the nobility of the realm—
the Crownsilvers and Truesilvers, the Dracohorns and
Dauntinghorns, the Bleths and Ilances. This group was
led by Lord Gerrin Wyvernspur and aided by Thanderahast's pupil, Jorunhast.

Each of the groups met their dragons and triumphed.
The crown prince's soldiers drove out the dragon to the
west. The dragon on the docks was trapped against its
own burning work and slain, but at a heavy cost—the
king was sent flying from his saddle in the fray and severely injured.

Lord Gerrin's party found the third red dragon prowling the cobblestoned streets of the noble district like a
huge hunting panther, sniffing at cellar stairs to discern
which houses had plump aristocracy hiding in the basement. The noble knights struck hard and fast, and
Jorunhast barely had time to unleash a few spells before
they had run the dragon through.

Jorunhast was standing over the still-cooling body of
the red dragon in the wreckage of House Illance when a
great shadow passed over his face. He looked up to see
only darkness as a great shadow blotted out the sun
itself.

A fourth dragon, larger than any they had seen before,
descended on Castle Obarskyr.

It had come out of the north, and Lord Gerrin's party
saw it first. The nobles and their retainers could do
naught but gawk at the immense size of the creature, as
if one of the moons had been pulled down and now hovered over their city. Jorunhast was caught in the spell as
well. It was the largest creature the Cormyrean born
mage had ever seen.

All they could do was watch as the monstrous creature
banked its mighty wings and settled over Suzail.

The new arrival was three times the size of the great
elder wyrms they had previously fought. Its once ebony
scales were purple and gray with age. As it beat its
wings, the rushing winds extinguished some flames in
the lower city, fanned others, and caused many damaged

buildings to collapse. It landed on the castle, and the west wing collapsed beneath its prodigious weight.

The purple dragon, the *true* Purple Dragon of Cormyr, had returned.

Lord Gerrin, strongest and most noble of the knights, was the first to recover, shouting out a curse as he began to run up the hillside. Jorunhast and the others, wounded and tired, followed more slowly. Elsewhere, the sorely wounded king and the crown prince were also rallying their troops and climbing the low hill to the place where the dragon that was too large to be true was destroying the Obarskyr family home.

Jorunhast stumbled after Lord Gerrin, trying to shake the image of the beast in flight, blotting out the sun itself, from his mind. The dragon was immense to the point of being overwhelming. The mage wracked his brain for a proper spell to use against a beast so huge, but all he could come up with was a name. Thauglor. Thauglor, the Black Doom.

The Purple Dragon continued its slow, leisurely destruction of the castle's western wing. Ancient stonework crumbled under its weight, and the slate roof shrieked and crashed inward. Jorunhast was relieved. Most of the noble refugees were in the east wing. The west wing contained the guest quarters, the scriptorium, and the library . . .

And Thanderahast's spell-chambers, filled with all manner of dangerous devices and explosive magic. Jorunhast forced himself into a panting run, catching up with powerful Lord Wyvernspur halfway up the hill. Behind them trailed the armored knights, struggling in their heavy armor. The young mage opened his mouth to warn the Wyvernspur lord.

They were too late. The dragon crushed something better left uncrushed, probably in the wizard's chamber of alchemy itself. There was a fierce white flash and a roar, and the ground beneath them rolled and surged.

Their boots had already left the ground behind. The two men tumbled end over end, blown halfway down the hill by the force of the explosion. The brightness of the flash was later reported to have been seen in Arabel, a brief, flickering star on the horizon.

By the time Jorunhast had recovered his wits, the dragon was gone and the rest of the castle was in flames. The great purple dragon, the Black Doom of myths and legends, was a large blot flying north and west, still huge even at a distance. The refugees who had sought the safety of the Obarskyr fortress now spilled out the doors and windows, seeking to escape the flames that raged unchecked within.

Jorunhast and Lord Gerrin reached the front of the castle, and the Wyvernspur noble started shouting orders, telling the screaming courtiers to clear the area and make for the noble houses. Jorunhast remembered feeling at the time that Gerrin Wyvernspur embodied all that was noble in Cormyr. He was strong, brave, and utterly fearless, not an overweight relic of the past like the king or a wastrel like Arangor's only son.

Jorunhast heard screams from above. In an upper chamber window, one of the younger ladies-in-waiting was sobbing for help. The wooden frame of the window had already been touched by flames, and smoke poured out from behind her.

Jorunhast worked a minor magic then, one of the few spells he still had. He cleared his mind of the smoke and the noise swirling around him and muttered a few ancient words. Then slowly, carefully, he began to walk up the wall.

He reached the open window less than a minute later. The lady-in-waiting was red-eyed from the smoke and in a trembling panic, ready to jump. She wrapped her arms tightly around the mage's neck and held on with all her strength, practically throttling him in the process. Jorunhast gasped calming words and slowly brought her down to the earth.

By the time the pair of them had reached firm ground, the other knights and nobles had reached the summit as well, and they were beating back the flames with tapestries, cloaks, and whatever came to hand. Gerrin had organized a bucket brigade down to the lake named after the first Azoun, and Thanderahast was working a spell of weather summoning, calling thick, rain-bearing clouds to Suzail to help battle the blazes that raged at the castle and across the city.

Upon reaching the ground, the young maiden refused to release her tight grip and pledged eternal love and loyalty to her brave rescuer. Jorunhast accepted the praise—and kisses—warmly, then lifted his head to see the crown prince staring at him icily.

It was then that the broad-shouldered wizard suddenly remembered the young lady was one Azoun himself had been courting.

Carefully the wizard disengaged himself from the young woman, but the damage had already been done. The crown prince was not as handsome, as tall, or as well mannered as the apprentice mage. Jorunhast could feel the burning royal jealousy. Indeed, had not young Azoun driven off a dragon, only to find the wizard had been declared a hero thanks to some bit of parlor magic?

That was three days ago. Since then, the citizens of Suzail had buried their dead, put out their fires, and picked through the remains of the city for survivors and salvage. A full half of the buildings in the city had been destroyed, and a third of the population killed. A quarter of the castle was shapeless ruins, and most of the rest was smoke-gutted and scorched. Yet some god or other had been smiling on the Obarskyrs, it seemed. The throne room had survived, as had the Shrine of the Four Swords and the great treasures of the kingdom. The heart of Cormyr had survived the flames, but just barely.

Arangor, whom Jorunhast thought had grown fat and lazy in his long, peaceful rule, lost no time in regaining order. Outriders and heralds were posted to all the major towns and villages for reports to determine the extent of the dragons' depredations. Most of the noble knights, led by Lord Huntsilver, rode north to Arabel, where a pair of green dragons had emptied the city.

Then the word had come from the marshalling grounds near Jester's Green, once known as Soldier's Green. The Purple Dragon, Thauglor, had been spotted in the King's Forest, apparently licking its wounds from the explosion at the castle. It had not flown off into the mountains for a long slumber as it had apparently done many times before. It had remained within striking distance and might, when it recovered, strike at Suzail again.

A council of war was held in the king's quarters. Despite the efforts of the best surviving priests of the city, Arangor was unable to walk more than a few paces without great pain. Pillows were tucked in on all sides of his throne, and a heavy blanket was spread across his legs. He accentuated every statement with a low moan.

A weak king, thought Jorunhast. His mentor's words of loyalty to the crown rebuked him for such thoughts. Thanderahast had to have served forty kings in his time. Were they all as mewling and sad as this one?

"That Purple Dragon is behind all of this," said the king, planted firmly among his pillows. "Thauglor is leading this attack."

Lord Gerrin Wyvernspur shook his lean head, "No. Dragons don't think in terms of leaders and attacks. They are much more independent."

"How do *you* know what dragons think?" asked the king sharply.

Gerrin looked at the Royal Wizard for support. Thanderahast put in, "Lord Gerrin means that what our sages know of dragons states that they swear fealty in matters of recognizing territory, but they do not band together in organized attacks. I think whatever roused these dragons to attack Cormyr also brought Thauglor back as well. He is not leading the attacks, but he is benefiting from them."

The wounded king put his head in his hands. "Why now? Why did he suddenly appear *now?*" The unspoken words in his anguished query were "during my rule."

Thanderahast shrugged. "No one knows why there are

Flights of Dragons, and this one is as bad as any previously recorded. As far as Thauglor the Black is concerned, he has been sighted before."

"Before," repeated Arangor bitterly. "Out in the wilderness, far from any city and any king. And each time his appearance has marked a weakness in the crown and the nation. What are the people saying now that the Purple Dragon has attacked the castle itself?"

"What matters now," said Thanderahast calmly, "is what we are going to do."

The decision that followed had brought them both to this wind-whipped hilltop: Jorunhast, armed with one of his mentor's wands, and the young crown prince, lightly armored. They sat in the saddles of their spindly-legged ponies, waiting for the dragon to arrive. The elder wizard had set out with Lord Gerrin to flush the dragon out.

"I don't like it," said Azoun.

"You've said that before," said the wizard-in-training. "Why didn't you say such things when it was proposed?"

"And have everyone think me a coward?" protested the crown prince.

"Best to speak up and be thought a coward than to fail in action and be proved one," said Jorunhast calmly.

The slender young prince looked hard at the mage. Loudly he said, "And I don't particularly like *you* either."

"I don't believe they make you a court wizard based on popularity," said the mage, turning in his saddle to face the younger man. "It's sort of like kings that way."

"Ah, but I *am* popular," the prince replied, smiling tightly.

"With the ladies, I'm sure," snapped the wizard. "Ah—some of them, at any rate." He allowed himself a small smile and ignored the fuming prince.

"If *I'd* been there *I* would have rescued—" Azoun began, but the rumbling cut him short. The sound seemed to rise out of the ground itself, and both young men could feel it through their saddles as well as hear it. It was a roar that seemed to envelop their world, coming from the east. Both men looked to that direction, where a

327

small dot blossomed on the horizon.

It was on top of them in an instant. In fact, there were two airborne figures, one pursuing the other. In the lead was Thanderahast, mounted on a wyvern's back. The wyvern was a smaller kin of dragons, lacking forelegs, and this one was marked with orange and red striations. Of Lord Gerrin, who had accompanied the mage into the woods that morning, there was no sign.

Behind the wyvern and mage came the dragon. Jorunhast clearly saw it approach, and it still looked huge. Its ancient scales reflected in the morning sun in shades of lavender and lilac, belying the powerful muscles that lay beneath them. It beat the air heavily and steadily, as opposed to the wyvern's quick, panicked wing thrashings. The Purple Dragon was gaining. Magical energy danced from the old wizard's fingertips, and the bolts of power he hurled ricocheted off the dragon's ancient scales.

Prey and predator were over their heads in a heartbeat, the windy wake of their passing carving furrows in the tall grass. The wyvern banked sharply after it passed over them, and the great flying behemoth banked in pursuit. Its large size took it into a larger turn, and its massive wings nearly scraped the ground as it swung about to follow its smaller prey.

It was even bigger than Jorunhast remembered. Now, without the city around him, without the protection of walls and redoubts and buildings, it dominated the young wizard's vision. He suddenly felt very small and exposed and alone on that bare hilltop.

Something cold and clammy settled in Jorunhast's stomach and clung there tightly.

The dragon passed over them again, and the wizard was aware that the young prince was shouting something at him.

"The wand!" he bellowed, his smooth, beardless face almost apoplectic. "Use the damnable *wand!*"

The wyvern-mounted mage banked again, and the Purple Dragon followed, this time pulling out of its turn almost directly behind its quarry. The two young men on the hill saw the monstrous creature's throat bunch and swell. Azoun was shouting again, and Jorunhast was fumbling frantically with the wand.

The dragon breathed a huge gout of acid—and the wyvern and mage evaporated. Jorunhast thought he saw his mentor move his arms in sudden spellcasting before the heavy, scintillating spittle struck, then both wyvern and wizard were lost to view, swallowed in the flow of the dragon's breath. After the acid gout had passed, the great purple dragon was the only thing in the sky.

Jorunhast screamed a magical word of old Netheril and felt the wand glow and pulse in his hand. A bolt of flame burst from its tip and lanced upward. Jorunhast did not aim it, but the dragon was so huge he could not help but strike it. The lance of flame raked along the orchid-hued belly plates of the beast.

The great monster screamed.

The Purple Dragon convulsed and pulled itself into another tight, air-shattering turn. Fighting for calm, Jorunhast readied his next spell.

Beside him, Azoun shouted after the great beast's retreating form, "Hail, old lizard! Think you can defeat the *true* rulers of Cormyr?"

The lad's voice cracked, and Jorunhast would have sworn that the wind blew the remains of his words away, but the dragon apparently heard them well enough. It responded with a great roar.

Jorunhast muttered the last phrase of a new spell and slapped the withers of both ponies. The pair sprang forward as if released from a starting gate, their powerful legs enhanced by the magic. The ponies ran as they had never run before, sped by Jorunhast's hastening spell.

The dragon surged through the air behind them, but the pair slowly began to increase the distance between them and their pursuer. Jorunhast looked back.

All he could see was the dragon's open jaws—a huge, fang-toothed mouth surrounded by ancient wattles of flesh. He turned around again and bent low to spur on his mount, urging it to even greater speed.

Ed Greenwood and Jeff Grubb

Then he heard laughter and looked to his right to see the crown prince smiling in the racing wind. Had the dolt lost his mind?

Jorunhast turned in his saddle again. They had gained more distance, and now the dragon was gaining altitude behind them. Jorunhast pointed the wand and shouted the eldritch words again. The wand pulsed, and a lance of flame streamed over the great creature's head. The dragon dodged it easily but came down lower now, only slightly higher off the ground than the two riders ahead.

Jorunhast and Azoun plowed forward up a shallow wash. On either side rose grass-swept slopes topped with brush. At the far end of the wash, the ground climbed to a small hillock.

Both young men dug spurs into their mounts, and the message ponies once more increased their speed, topping the end of the wash with a few dozen strides. They reined and wheeled in place, and the young Azoun raised his arm, sword in hand.

The dragon was coming in low and fast, nearly touching the grass beneath it, gliding with its wings outstretched, grazing the soft hills on both sides. Azoun dropped his arm in a short, chopping motion.

The brush lining the ridges on either side dropped away, and two lines of Cormyrean archers unleashed steel-tipped volleys against the great beast.

Had they aimed at the creature's scaled body, their shots could have done little more than annoy the beast. Instead, they shot for the wings, riddling the tough membrane with a myriad of holes. A few shafts caught at lucky angles and tore great gouges in the wing surfaces.

The dragon was coming in too low to recover as the air beneath its wings suddenly streamed through the holes. It tried to land on its massive haunches, but it was moving too fast and sprawled forward as it landed, its head and long serpentine neck plowing a furrow along the base of the sod-covered wash. There was a sound like a ship's mast being rent in twain, and Jorunhast knew it

330

had to be one of the dragon's massive wings doubling under it.

They had knocked the creature out of the sky. The soldiers on either side of the wash threw down their bows and snatched out their swords. They lowered their helms over their faces and, with a single shout, spilled down from both rises to where the wounded dragon thrashed.

Azoun dismounted and pulled out his own blade. The mage nearly fell from his mount trying to stop him.

"Those are my men," said the crown prince angrily. "I should fight with them!"

"And further risk the loss of the heir to the throne?" Jorunhast dismounted and put a firm hand on the young man's shoulders. "I think not. Let them wear the beast down. By then Thanderahast and a *real* warrior, Lord Gerrin, will be— Oof!"

The crown prince moved more swiftly than the wizard had thought possible, elbowing him sharply in the gut. Jorunhast felt the air rush from his body as he fell to his knees, gasping helplessly. By the time the world stopped spinning around him, the young royal warrior was halfway to the battle.

The soldiers swarmed over the great dragon like ants, and with about the same effectiveness. They hacked at the great beast's scales, and occasionally an armsman would loosen one sufficiently to strike at the meat beneath. For Thauglor, it was akin to being stung to death by gnats.

The great beast had its own bag of tricks. The one good wing swept a half-dozen attackers into dazed and bruised ruin. Its tail smashed another two. Its claws gutted a pair of warriors where they stood. And its huge jaws ran bloody as its head snaked out again and again to snuff out the life of another Cormyrean soldier.

And the only heir to the throne of Cormyr was charging into that maelstrom of death.

Jorunhast looked around. If Lord Gerrin was coming, he was taking his damned time about it. Thanderahast was wounded or dead. The mage raised the wand but saw that the crown prince was in the way. The insufferable, irritating, impulsive crown prince. A lance of flame would burn through him and into the dragon itself. Perhaps Cormyr would be a better place without him.

Jorunhast paused for a long moment, then cursed and ran down the hill after the prince. Even with all these warriors rushing about, you'd think less work would be needed to get a clear shot at something as large as the dragon. And as he ran, the mage swore to himself that, even under torture, he would never admit he was running to Azoun's rescue.

The young prince reached the dragon and struck. His blade bit deep. The sword, supposedly crafted long ago by Amedahast herself, parted a scale as if it were jelly and slid into the creature's haunch, striking to the bone.

It was as if the dragon had been struck by lightning. It heaved itself from the ground, shuddering, and tried to roll away from the attack, crushing a half-dozen soldiers and almost snatching the blade from Azoun's hands.

But the scion of the Obarskyrs would not let up. He tore the blade free and cut another long, shallow wound along the dragon's belly. It gave out a great scream and spat a huge gout of acid. Men screamed where the acid struck, but the dragon had little time to enjoy their deaths. Its serpentine neck snapped around, and its jaws closed on the small form of the crown prince.

Jorunhast shouted, but then he saw that Azoun had avoided the fanglike maw of the beast and was hanging by the loose wattles at the corner of the creature's mouth. The dragon shook its head like a dog trying to dislodge a tick, but the young monarch held fast. The wizard saw a white flash of clenched teeth as he stared at Azoun's blurred form.

Wildly, Jorunhast tore his gaze away and looked about. Half of the soldiers were dead, and there was still no sign of the elders. Where had they gone? The mage was close enough to use the wand of flame, but it might bounce back off the dragon's scales to consume him as well. And if he missed and cooked a certain crown prince . . .

The wizard ran to the gaping wound along the dragon's belly, now seeping thick, deep purplish blood. He glanced up to see the young prince still clinging to the hide beside the dragon's mouth. As he watched, Azoun drove his blade deep into the wyrm's eye. Dark, gold-flecked fluid sprayed out.

Jorunhast hastily bent his head away from the bloody rain he knew would come and shoved the thin wand into the open wound and shouted the command word. The wand pulsed, and a jet of flame shot deep into the creature's body.

The dragon spasmed, its body arching and flexing from the agony of the ravaging fire inside and the blade in its eye. A huge clawed paw swept Jorunhast off his feet. He lost his grip on the wand, and his last sight was of Azoun driving his blade deep into Thauglor's reptilian brain with both hands.

Blackness overwhelmed the young mage when he struck the ground. It seemed to last for only a moment, but when he picked himself up, the dragon was sprawled dead on the floor of the wash. Priests moved among the fallen soldiers. A priestess of Lathander put her hand on Jorunhast's shoulder, but he shrugged it off and stumbled back toward the dragon's flank, where Gerrin and Thanderahast stood talking to Azoun.

Lord Wyvernspur was badly burned, the left side of his face and entire body raw and bleeding beneath the slimy ointments of the priests. Thanderahast was similarly burned and anointed, and in addition sported purplish ridges rising along the side of his head, bruises from some sudden impact.

Azoun seemed unharmed by his adventure. Jorunhast wondered at the luck of children, fools, and royalty.

"You are back with us, lad," said the elder mage. "We could not return as soon as we'd hoped, but I see the pair of you were capable of handling things."

"It was a good plan," said the young mage, still light-headed. He blinked hard in the sunlight, then added, "I lost your wand, I'm afraid."

Ed Greenwood and Jeff Grubb

Thanderahast chuckled. "A small loss, easily forgiven. Azoun told me of your bravery in charging the dragon and in waiting for the right moment to strike with the wand. We were worried you had panicked."

Jorunhast stared at the younger man. Hadn't he told them the mage had frozen up when the dragon first attacked? That he had tried to stop Azoun from entering the battle?

Azoun cocked his head and said, "It's good to see you back standing up. Want some help looking for that wand?"

Jorunhast gaped at the young prince for a moment, and then, slowly, nodded.

Gerrin and Thanderahast flagged down the priestess of Lathander for information about the wounded, leaving Azoun and Jorunhast alone. The two young men paced off to the trampled area near the dragon's body. They made vague sweeps in the splayed grass with the sides of their feet, looking for little and finding less.

At length, Jorunhast said, "I only charged in after you because you were going to get yourself killed."

"I know," said the slender man. "And they probably think something like that, but they never have to *know*. Despite it all, you did pretty well today."

Words burned in Jorunhast's throat like the black dragon's bile. Finally he spat them out. "So did you." And then he added, "Sire."

Azoun flashed a wide smile. "Mind you, I don't trust you, and I still don't like you. But with the beating old Thanderahast has taken, it's likely you'll be my wizard when my time comes. So I might as well get used to you."

The young wizard sighed. "And I to you. But do me one favor, my lord: No more charging into combat."

"Only when you're behind me with your magic," said the future king. "Only when you're behind me."

The young prince strode away, leaving Jorunhast to think that Azoun's voice was not so tinny after all.

23

Encounters and Expeditions
Year of the Gauntlet
(1369 DR)

I do believe, dear, that we can finally say that Arabel has become truly civilized," Darlutheene Ambershields declared, opening her violet eyes very wide and waving a ring-encrusted hand. Gems flashed and sparkled in the light of near highsun for a dazzling instant before her hand dipped, rising again with a fresh glass of cordial.

"Why, Darlutheene—that outpost of uncultured bumpkins?" Blaerla Roaringhorn asked in disbelief, opening her own brown eyes very wide as well. "Whatever do you mean?"

"Well," Darlutheene purred, "with the news this morning—of nobles found knifed in their beds, and the knives still buried in them, bearing the arms of rival noble houses—I do believe the intrigues of Arabel are finally approaching those of Suzail!"

"No!" Blaerla gasped, color flooding into her cheeks and eyes sparkling with fresh excitement. "Nobles? Knifed in their beds? Why?"

Darlutheene waved a languid, cordial-bearing hand and fluttered her long lashes. They were dusted with gold this morning. "They say that Princess Alusair led her band of noble young rapscallions into the city over the rooftops, to—" she lowered her voice dramatically— "work their deadly slaughter."

"But why would she do that?" Blaerla asked, brown eyebrows furrowed in genuine puzzlement. Then she added cattily, "I thought she *liked* nobles in their beds— male nobles, and lots of them."

Darlutheene gave a little crow of laughter that made her several chins shake heartily, then slapped at her confidante's arm with perfumed fingertips. "Ah, shrewdly said, Blaerla! Shrewdly said!"

Blaerla flushed with genuine pleasure and held out her own glass for a refill. Darlutheene awarded her with a delicate pouring of her best ruby-hued Elixir du Vole and continued. "Why, dear, don't you see? She's removing nobles who've declared their loyalty to our dear court wizard—because *certain* noble houses, I've heard, are hiring mages in Sembia, Westgate, and farther afield to organize a raid on the palace! She needs to be sure that the families working for the wizard won't foil them!"

Blaerla squealed with excitement, almost—but not quite—spilling her cordial in her bouncing breathlessness. Her low-cut gown briefly displayed movement akin to a ship breaking up in heavy, rolling waves. Darlutheene could only watch in fascination as the perfume wafted forth from her friend's heavily gem-and-fine-chain-adorned front. Blaerla asked, "Raid the *palace*? *Why*? Oh, Darlutheene Ambershields, before all the gods, tell me why!"

"I have heard they're coming for the king, of course," Darlutheene said smugly. "To wrest him away—sickbed and all—from Vangerdahast's clutches. Of course, with all the evil spells that have been laid on him by now, they're probably too late. For all we know, Azoun could be a zombie under our dear Royal Magician's control, *even as we speak!*"

"Oh!" Blaerla squealed, clutching her glass to her ample bosom, "this is all so *exciting!*" She felt the cold glass against her flesh, remembered what she was holding, and drained it in a single gulp.

Holding it out for more, she said triumphantly, "We are truly favored of the gods to dwell here in Suzail, with the eyes of all the world upon us, while all these . . . dramatic, *important* things are happening!"

Darlutheene patted her friend's cheek fondly, seeming not to see the empty glass held out to her. "Yes, yes, dear," she said fondly. "Of *course* we are."

* * * * *

Had Blaerla not been quite so excited, the two fine-gowned ladies might have heard a brief commotion in the street below. The Purple Dragon sword captain Lareth Gulur, a veteran of the Tuigan War, had just nodded a wordless greeting to a war wizard he knew slightly—Ensibal Threen, a mild-mannered sort—when out of the crowd strode a noble in deep-blue velvet and white shimmersheen, his fingers bristling with rings. One of the Silverswords, Lareth thought, wrinkling his brow as he delved in his memories for the man's name. He was rather chubby, with long blond hair and a wispy mustache of the same hue—gods, don't these young fools know what they look like, with a few brave hairs sprouting from otherwise bare upper lips?

"Know, Vangerdahast-loving wizard, that it is I, Ammanadas Silversword, who brings down upon you forthwith your richly deserved doom!" the young fop snarled.

Ammanadas, that was it! Lareth almost smiled at the haughty little puppy for his helpfulness—until he saw the long, glittering skinning knife flash out of the noble's sleeve.

The wizard Ensibal had turned at the sudden, ringing declaration, and in doing so presented his throat to the blade. The Silversword obligingly plunged the blade into the proffered throat. Blood fountained, and the war wizard collapsed like a toppled oak as screams went up on all sides and folk scurried about, either to get clear or to find a better view.

337

Ed Greenwood and Jeff Grubb

The Silversword noble made a disgusted sound and leapt back, almost into the Purple Dragon's arms. Lareth had his own dagger drawn by then. The Purple Dragon used the dagger's pommel with a heartiness driven by fury, clouting the young noble across the back of the head. Ammanadas Silversword fell limply to the cobbles, and Lareth stepped around him to see to the wizard.

Lareth Gulur did not need his battlefield memories to know that Ensibal Threen's life was hanging by the most slender of threads. He sheathed his dagger and waved at people to keep clear, in case violent magic was triggered by the wizard's death.

"Gulur? Gulur! For the throne's sake, man, what happened here?" The shocked and angry voice behind him belonged to Hathlan, a senior officer of the Purple Dragons.

"Get a priest. A noble knifed this wizard because he supported our Lord High Wizard, or at least the young fool thought he did. I knocked out the noble, and he might have his wits scrambled a trifle, but he'll live," Lareth replied without turning. His eyes were on the gathering crowd, looking for nobles—or anyone else—trying to slip away.

"All of them have their wits scrambled a trifle," Hathlan snorted. "There've been attacks like this all across the realm these last few days. The nobles are seizing their opportunities and settling scores, real and imagined." Then he was off, bellowing for a healer.

Lareth looked at his superior, then at the fallen war wizard. "Cormyr is balanced on a sword edge," he murmured, "with years of red war waiting on either hand should we fall."

* * * * *

"Have you heard the news? Some noble just slaughtered a war wizard right out on the street!" The speaker, a new arrival to the Snout Room, was breathless with excitement, but not so breathless that he couldn't gasp out news *this* good.

338

"It's beginning, then," Rhauligan muttered. He looked as if one of the high-quality turrets he sold had crashed to the ground.

Dauneth Marliir, the young Arabellan noble, was gaping at the new arrival as the man bustled on down the Snout Room, bawling his news. The man's words had distracted the young nobleman from the warm knee and rather revealing charms of the tavern dancer who sat drinking with them. She was an old friend of Rhauligan's, the merchant had said heartily, but was lavishing her affections on Dauneth.

The dancer, Emthrara, kissed Dauneth on the cheek, seeking to restore his attentions. Dauneth blushed and hoped the hunger he felt for the young woman wasn't showing too much. He swallowed. What was he doing, thinking about women when Cormyr was crumbling into war outside?

"They're saying up at the palace that Princess Alusair fled deeper into the Stonelands," Emthrara said in a low, husky voice. Dauneth felt smooth skin shift against his arm and swallowed hard a second time.

The turret merchant made a small chuckle. Rhauligan knew exactly what was going through Dauneth's mind about the dancer and did not hide his amusement. Dauneth tried not to look at the merchant's knowing smile across the table as Emthara said quietly, "I've heard more talk of Vangerdahast's possible treachery, too."

But surprise had seized hold of Dauneth. He turned his head to look at Emthrara and discovered that his lips were mere inches away from hers. He could feel the soft touch of her breath on his face. He swallowed again, grimacing. Stop it, Dauneth. This is too important!

"You were inside the palace?" he asked, his voice louder than he'd intended. Emthrara gave him a smile and a nod. Dauneth tried not to feel the soft brush of her honey-blonde hair on his cheek.

"I'm often up at the palace, Dauneth," she said, her voice deep and musical with soft mystery. "I—have work there."

Ed Greenwood and Jeff Grubb

"Oh," Dauneth said, and then realized what she meant. "*Oh!*" He hoped he wasn't blushing too furiously and thanked all the gods that neither Rhauligan nor the dancer laughed at him then. He struggled to think about what seemed more and more important and found himself asking, almost calmly, "Can you get me into the palace—unseen?"

"Why?" Rhauligan leaned forward across the table to ask that very direct question almost in a whisper. Dauneth was startled by the sudden proximity of those bristling eyebrows and lined forehead and shrank back.

"Ah . . . um . . ." he began auspiciously, and then, irritated at his own discomfort, he brought a fist gently down on the table and said grimly, "Something dark and treacherous is going on in this realm, and I'm going to do something about it."

The other two looked at him, and Dauneth felt a sudden swelling of pride. Again neither of them laughed at him, nor did they look anything other than serious as their eyes rested on him thoughtfully.

"I know of a way to get into the palace," Emthrara said then, "where few folk should see our arrival. A way I know of for . . . professional reasons."

"I've never been one for waiting overlong," Dauneth told her firmly.

"Aye," Rhauligan said dryly. "I've noticed."

He did blush then, but Emthrara laid a hand on his arm and murmured, "Come on, then."

Dauneth followed hard on the Harper's heels. Nothing else seemed to matter anymore. Finally he was doing something that mattered, and his skin fairly crawled with eagerness. Finally, after all these years, he felt truly alive.

* * * * *

"Lie down here, beside me," the tavern dancer said in his ear, and suddenly she went to her hands and knees and crawled in under the bushes. Dauneth cast a quick look around the royal gardens, noting the helms of some Purple Dragons not far away, and followed her. Patches of bare, hard-packed ground amid the moss told him that this was a way that had been traveled a time or two before. Emthrara was lying on her belly, stretched out along the wall. "Beside me," she murmured again, and Dauneth hastily lay down as she bade him. Emthrara added, "Watch, and then follow me quickly," and stretched out the toe of her boot to touch a certain small stone on the wall. It gave slightly. Holding it in, she reached out her arm until her fingertips touched another stone. It moved, just a trifle—and all the stones between them quietly folded down and inward, revealing a long, low slotlike opening. Without any hesitation, the dancer rolled sideways into it with a pale flash of exposed leg.

Dauneth propelled himself after her and promptly encountered soft flesh in the darkness as he rolled into her. Behind him, there was a faint grating sound and then suddenly complete darkness again as the stones rose back into place.

He lay there, smelling cold, damp stone and earth, and—just for an instant—wondered why he was doing this.

"Take this," Emthrara said into his ear, seeming to know exactly where it was in the darkness, "and put it into your inside pouch—the one where you keep the gems and the letters of reference your father gave you."

Dauneth froze. How had she known about that? He'd . . . then he relaxed. Probably just about every man she meets visiting at court carries pretty much the same things. He felt something smooth brush his fingers: a tube of parchment . . . a scroll, tied with a ribbon.

"Don't crush it," the tavern dancer murmured. "If anyone challenges your presence, show it to them and say you've been hired by a master you dare not reveal—Alusair, if they force an answer out of you—to give this message to the Lord High Wizard Vangerdahast personally. If you crawl straight ahead in the darkness, you'll find steps leading up. Stand up then, but not before, and walk up the steps. There's a door two paces beyond that; it opens inward by a pull-ring and leads to a space behind the hangings in the Blue Banners Room. Try not to be seen emerging; after you're out, walk along unhurriedly but purposefully, as if you know where you're going and belong there. Don't run if a guard challenges you—oh, and try not to burn the place down or kill *too* many people. Good luck, young hope of the realm."

And then a pair of soft, warm lips found his mouth in the darkness, kissed him fondly but thoroughly, and she was gone. Dauneth heard a soft swish of a shoe edge on stone, another small sound, and then nothing. He was alone in the darkness, under the very wall of the palace. His place and manner of entrance was probably not what anyone in House Marliir had intended. Dauneth grinned at that, made sure the scroll was secured, and crawled ahead into the darkness. The realm needed him, adventure awaited, and all that. Who *was* Emthrara, anyway?

* * * * *

"Oh, just to see him smiling again," the Crown Princess of Cormyr sobbed, "smiling for me!"

"The king your father lives yet," Aunadar said smoothly, putting a comforting hand on her shoulder. "Is that not proof enough of his strength?"

Tanalasta burst into tears—the deep, wracking weeping of a woman who makes no effort to cover her face or hold anything back—and went to her knees on the footstool in front of her. Aunadar circled around to embrace her from in front, and she buried her face in his chest and sobbed with such force that his whole body shook. Her fingers were like claws, and Aunadar bent swiftly to murmur in her ear as his encircling arm went around her shoulders. "Lady mine, all is not lost. Whatever befalls this fair realm and your ever valiant father, my hand and heart are yours. I shall serve you with all I have, never failing nor leaving you in need—especially now, when your need is greatest. Now, as the wolves circle Cormyr, waiting and watching for your weakness. Be strong, Tanalasta, queen of my heart! Be strong, queen of the realm!"

His voice rose in passion, and Tanalasta raised bright, desperate eyes to him, tears racing down her cheeks, and reached up to him, murmuring his name through ragged sobs.

* * * * *

Had the king died? A woman sounded in real grief, just ahead. Dauneth almost thrust the hanging aside and strode out to offer what comfort he could, but the word "Queen" once and then again stopped him. The hanging suddenly seemed a friendly but all too flimsy shield. He'd wandered through more rooms than he could keep track of and hidden behind a *lot* of hangings to reach this place. Surely he must now be in the royal wing.

He looked down to be sure that he didn't stumble and make noise. The floor was bare and clear. They even dust behind the hangings here! he thought with amazement. Then a sudden, chilly addendum struck him: When was the last time they had dusted? And would they dust again soon?

But the voices came again, and he heard the name "Tanalasta." The crown princess! Turning to . . . a suitor, it seemed, for comfort. A gap in the hangings was just ahead; with aching care, Dauneth crept forward, keeping well back against the wall, and peered out. . . .

A woman in a severe gown of the finest make knelt on a footstool with her head against the breast of a man whose arms were around her, his head bent over hers as he murmured comforting words. Dauneth knew him slightly; it was Aunadar, of the Bleth clan. All the talk he'd heard, then, was true. Above her head, Aunadar seemed almost to smile for a moment, and Dauneth looked hard at him.

No trace of the smile—if it had indeed been a smile

and not a mere twitch of tired lips—came again, but the eyes of the man whose arms were around the princess were cold and somehow triumphant.

If I were deeply in love and feeling grief for my lover, would I look like that? Dauneth drew back, troubled, but not knowing what to say or do. His discovery, if anyone found him here, could very well mean his death. So he held still, hardly daring to breathe, and listened.

"If you weren't here, Aunadar, I don't know *what* I'd do. . . ."

"Yet I am here, most royal lady, here . . . and your servant; forever, if you'll grant it so! Let me be the strong shield at your back, the faithful hound who walks at your side in the shadows . . . and together we shall win through to bright mornings ahead!"

Dauneth winced. Where did the man find such words? The best-perfumed chapbooks of Sembian love poems?

"Oh, Aunadar, I must go to him! He may be stronger, and if he should wake again, I must be there!"

"Come then, Lady Highness!" Aunadar said grandly, throwing wide a door.

"Oh, Aunadar!" The crown princess said in loving adoration.

"Tana!" he replied, in a voice deep with passion. "My Tana!"

"Yes," she breathed fervently, and they swept out shoulder to shoulder, fingers laced together.

Dauneth watched them go in thoughtful silence. There was definitely something amiss in this royal house, but he was too ignorant of the everyday feel of things here to put his finger on it. He had to talk to someone. Of course! Rhauligan! The merchant would know what to do now. Dauneth drew in a deep breath, squared his shoulders, and stepped boldly out into the open, as if he had every right to be there and was hurrying on his way, in the conduct of business crucial to the realm.

After all, wasn't he?

* * * * *

344

"Glarasteer Rhauligan, sir, dealer in turret tops and spires, stone and wood both—you order 'em, and we'll build 'em, fast and cheap an' they won't fall down!" the merchant introduced himself grandly as the newcomer tried to sit down next to him and Dauneth.

The newcomer peered at him suspiciously, snorted, and turned away from the table. "I was seeking someone else," he said curtly over his shoulder, leaving the young man and the merchant in peace. Rhauligan gave him a cheery wave of farewell that somehow became an impolite gesture and then—as chuckles from other tables made the man whirl around again—a signal for more service.

A waitress with the longest, smoothest legs Dauneth had ever seen on a human drifted over. "My lord?"

"A flask of firedrake," the merchant told her, "and two tall- glasses—one for my friend here."

The waitress started to turn, and Dauneth gave her a smile that bought him a frank and admiring one to match before she bustled away to see to warm firedrake wine and cold, salt-rimmed glasses.

"Well, lad?" Rhauligan asked in a low voice as the scion of House Marliir shifted to a more comfortable position in his chair.

Dauneth shot a dark look across the table. "No bodies falling out of doors or knife-wielding clusters of masked nobility," he muttered, "but I did hear Aunadar Bleth comforting the crown princess."

"And?"

"Something didn't seem quite right," Dauneth murmured. "He seemed just a little too happy about the king dying."

Rhauligan shrugged. "And why not? If he's Tanalasta's favorite and she becomes queen, he can run Cormyr without any of the perils of ruling it. He wouldn't be the first noble to be more in love with a woman's position than with the lass herself, now, would he?"

"That's true," Dauneth agreed reluctantly and sat back with a sigh—in time to look up with a hasty smile as the waitress bent over him and set their drinks on the table, gave his shoulder a friendly squeeze, and was gone again. Despite himself, he turned his head to watch her go.

Rhauligan grinned, shook his head, and poured them both firedrake wine, watching the glasses steam and fog as the warmed liquid met chilled glass. Ah, to be young again . . .

"On me, lad," he said as the young noble turned his head back to the table. Dauneth hadn't even managed to open his mouth to protest that it was his turn, even past his turn, to pay for things, when the merchant asked, "Did anyone see you? Should I expect Purple Dragons to come in here hunting young Marliirs?"

Dauneth shook his head.

"Did you have to show your scroll to anyone?"

Dauneth shook his head again, then frowned, set down his glass, and reached into the open front of his shirt, and fumbled with the wooden toggle that held his safe pouch closed. When he drew it forth, the scroll was only a little crumpled at one end. He stared at it curiously, turning it a little in his fingers. "I wonder what it says," he said slowly under his breath.

"So open it," the merchant urged, sipping warm wine.

"Oh, but Emthrara—" he started to protest.

"Gave it to you to let every hairy-nosed guard who might ask your business have a read," the merchant put in. "So . . . ?"

Dauneth looked at him doubtfully for a moment, and then, as if of their own accord, his fingers went to the ribbon that bound it, slid it along without untying Emthrara's knot, and let the parchment loosen of itself. Then, in sudden impatience at himself, the young noble spread the scroll out on a dry area of tabletop and read it.

There were only a few lines, in a fine, flowing hand: "The bearer of this note is Dauneth Marliir, of noble blood and on a mission of the greatest importance to the crown. If he would see Cormyr's future as bright as winter stars above the Stonelands, he will meet the azure-masked one in the Snout Room of the Roving Dragon at the lighting of the evening candles. Let him pass, in the name of Alusair." Underneath that was a little mark, or personal rune, that looked like a three-petaled red flower, or perhaps a stylized crown.

Dauneth looked up at Rhauligan. "Here! Read!" He thrust the parchment across the table. The merchant read it, let his brows rise for a moment and then fall again, rolled it up carefully, replaced its ribbon, then handed it back. "Well, now, that's handy, lad . . . 'twon't be all that long now till they light 'em."

The young noble sputtered. "Yes, but—but Emthrara gave me this! How did she know I'd be here? And now?" His eyes narrowed. "You told her!"

"By the gods, lad," the merchant protested, "you're beginning to see conspiracies behind every pillar in Suzail! Drink up and think awhile; things always go better when your thoughts go *ahead* of your tongue . . . if you take my meaning."

Dauneth frowned. "But who does she work for? Is this truly from Princess Alusair?"

The merchant poured himself more wine. "Lad, living high is the art of finding out answers to questions like that without ever asking anyone else . . . d'you see?"

Dauneth sighed. "That's right," he said, picking up his own glass, "go all wise and graybearded on me."

The merchant shrugged. "You had to have a woman show you how to get into the palace. I know of more than a dozen secret ways into that place, and I'm no war wizard nor courtier, O young wet-nosed conspiracy sniffer!"

Dauneth glared at Rhauligan for a moment, then slowly grinned. "All right, sir merchant. Your sword finds the gap." He sipped firedrake wine and then frowned again. "More than a dozen?"

Whatever answer the merchant might have made was lost forever in the sudden appearance of the waitress, who leaned over their table—making Dauneth swallow, and try not to stare—to light the candles that were descending on fine chain from the ceiling. She shook her taper to extinguish it and turned to smile at the young nobleman.

Just for an instant, an azure mask seemed to cover her apple-cheeked features, and she said, in a voice not her own, "The corner back booth at Urgan's Best Boots, as soon as you can get there." Then her face seemed to waver and was bare again, and she gave Dauneth a wink and glided away.

Dauneth blinked. "Did you hear?"

"Spellcraft for sure," the merchant said, draining his glass and pointing at Dauneth's own. "You'll be needing a guide there. Come on!"

* * * * *

Evening was when most shops in Suzail rolled down their shutters, set their door bars, and blew out their lamps, but down this short and apparently nameless side street, Urgan's Best Boots still showed a light over its door. Rhauligan clapped Dauneth on the shoulder and said, "I'm off, lad. Try not to get into too much trouble."

Dauneth nodded, replied, "You, too!" and, taking a deep breath, put one hand on his sword hilt and the other on the door handle.

He cast a last look around before entering. Rhauligan had already vanished, as if swallowed up by magic. The street was deserted. The young noble frowned, shrugged, and went in.

Urgan seemed to have vanished, too. The shop was lit but deserted. Dauneth looked around suspiciously, spotted the curtained changing booths, and headed for them, almost trembling with excitement.

He parted the curtain of the corner booth cautiously, using the hilt of his scabbarded sword. Inside stood a woman in a blue gown, her back to him. One of her legs was planted on a stool, and she seemed to be in the process of disrobing.

"Ah, I'm sorry," Dauneth muttered. The woman turned

her head as swiftly as a striking snake. Emerald eyes gleamed out at him, her other features obscured by an azure mask.

"What for? Your swiftness is commendable," was the calm reply as the woman turned to face him and let fall her gown, to reveal breeches and a tunic of the same sea-blue hue. "If you are Dauneth Marliir, I am very interested in working with you."

"I—have the good fortune to be Dauneth Marliir, good lady," Dauneth said, bowing low. He cast a look behind him as he rose, but the shop was still bare of Purple Dragons or anyone else. "And you are—?"

"A friend of the crown," the masked woman replied smoothly. Her voice was not Emthrara's, but it had a similar husky tone. The masked woman plucked up her gown from the floor and hung it on a wall hook. "I know you went to the palace earlier today. Will you accompany me there again?"

"Lady, I will," Dauneth said without hesitation. This didn't *look* like Princess Alusair, either, but then he had never seen her all that closely.

The woman seemed to know his thoughts. "I am not of royal blood," she said, "but I am loyal to the crown. Are you?"

Dauneth met those green eyes steadily and replied, "Lady, I am. I am prepared to swear by whatever you choose, if you will it so."

"I want nothing so dramatic. A man's word is enough . . . if it is the right man."

Her words made the scion of House Marliir feel good indeed. He grasped the hilt of his sword hard, smiling in pride that lasted only for an instant. The masked woman moved a table aside as if it were made of paper, rolled back the edge of a rug with her foot, and put two fingers into a hole in the floor. She pulled, and a square of wooden flooring rose. A trapdoor common to such shops, usually used for storage.

"Follow me," she directed simply and slid into the dark opening. Dauneth did so, finding stone steps leading down into a small room that smelled of old leather. He had a brief glimpse of shelves and shelves of boots in the radiance that suddenly bloomed into life in the palm of the woman's hand. She was a mage!

Emerald eyes met his, and then, without a word, the woman strode away into the darkness. Dauneth followed hastily along a narrow, stone-floored tunnel. Such a tunnel was not usually common for such shops, and this one smelled of earth and nearby cesspits. The tunnel went on for a long, long time before it met with a second passage. Dauneth and the masked woman turned left, took a few paces, and then turned right again and went on. The walk was even longer this time, ending in a few worn steps that led up before they emerged in a room full of dusty cobwebs and boxes.

The masked mage turned to Dauneth, her radiance dimmed by the simple method of pressing her palm against the base of her neck. "Keep close to me and be very quiet," she murmured. "We're in the under-court cellars, beneath the Noble Court."

The noble nodded, keeping a hand on his blade to prevent it from swinging and scraping against or knocking anything over. They passed through a succession of dark and dusty rooms, seeing glimmering lanterns in the distance twice, and then the woman in blue held up a hand to halt him and peered around a corner. Satisfied, she waved him on, and together they stepped past the sprawled forms of two guards, dice and cards strewn around them. "They won't sleep all that long," she murmured. "We must move briskly." Beyond the guards were steps, leading to an iron-banded door, barred on their side. Dauneth and the woman lifted the bar down together, and the masked woman touched the lock with one finger. The door clicked once and shifted open a little.

Beyond was another tunnel. "I could come to master these tunnels were there not so many of them," Dauneth muttered. The emerald eyes of the masked woman seemed to smile in answer as her head turned briefly. They went on along a dusty passage that seemed to hold a statue or something ahead.

As they drew nearer, Dauneth saw that it was a stone block, almost as large as a man, that had fallen from the roof above. He glanced up. The cavity it had come from fitted it perfectly, and a dust-covered chain descended from the darkness of the cavity to the block itself. This had been no crumbling misfortune, but a deathtrap. He looked down and saw yellow-brown bones protruding from under the stone and a skeletal arm, reaching vainly for somewhere safer. Somewhere forever beyond its reach.

He looked up to find the masked face watching his. "Don't walk this way without me," she said in a low voice. "There are two more of these ahead."

Dauneth nodded soberly, and they went on. At a certain spot that to the noble looked no different than the rest of the passage, the masked mage stopped and turned to the wall beside her. She touched something and then simply stepped into the wall, her body passing into the solid stone as if it did not exist.

The young noble stared, fascinated, at the hand that reappeared out of the solid wall and beckoned to him impatiently. He went to it, clasped it with his own, and was drawn through—nothing. They were in a side passage. He blinked at the masked face and the glowing hand that went with it, and then turned to look back. A sort of veil or misty curtain seemed to hang across the mouth of the tunnel they now stood in. He extended his hand through it and waved his fingers. There was no resistance. The veil must be some sort of magical illusion, an image of a stone wall that concealed this opening.

A firm hand came down on his shoulder. He turned and followed the masked mage again until she led the way up a steep, narrow stair and into a room, where she stopped and turned to face him.

"We're in the palace now," she explained, "or rather under it, in the vaults that the crown princess ordered sealed. We took this last, hidden way to avoid a guardpost. I can't risk this light any longer; stand still."

The radiance faded, and Dauneth had a last impression of her fingers weaving intricate gestures before two cool fingertips touched his eyelids. Startled, he stepped back, blinking, only to find that he could see clearly in what must be utter darkness.

Those emerald eyes seemed to be smiling at him again. Emboldened, he asked, "But if these are the royal vaults, how are we to get around? The bards always say only the Lord Vangerdahast and the royal family have keys! We'll—"

His words died in his throat as slim hands drew a chain up out of her bodice to reveal a trio of long-barreled, dark, ornate keys. "It seems the bards are wrong for once," the masked mage said softly. "Draw your sword now and keep watch. Danger awaits us."

Three archways led out of the room; the masked mage chose the one to the left, and they entered a room full of small casks branded with the device of a flying bird encircled by stars. The next room held stacks of crates, and its loftier ceiling was held up by three pillars. A ladder on wheels leaned against the central pillar, and as they approached, something seemed to boil down out of the tangle of railing and platforms at the top of the contraption. It appeared as tendrils of smoke, yet the misty tentacles moved of their own volition.

"Dauneth—strike at it!" the masked mage snapped, stepping back. Without hesitation, the nobleman thrust his blade into the heart of the smokelike mass. His companion snarled out some words, and something like lightning leapt from her hands to touch his blade.

The weapon seemed to leap and then hum numbingly in his hands, and Dauneth almost dropped it, but around him the smokelike thing seemed to be shuddering and fading all at once.

In another moment, it was gone, leaving the vault silent except for his loud breathing. Dauneth stared around to find that the masked mage was already continuing on down the room to the door at its far end. He hastened after her.

"What was that?" he panted.

"A guardian," said the mage, "one that my spells would have had little effect against. Hush now."

The woman in the azure mask muttered a few words, and the door swung wide. Something moved in the darkness beyond: a warhelm, hanging in the air as if it rested on a man's shoulders. It turned a little, and then flew into the room like a gliding bird, right over the mage's shoulder.

Fire blossomed from the helm's eye slits, twin beams of flame that stabbed out at Dauneth. The nobleman dodged behind the nearest pillar, hissing something that was half prayer and half curse. Fire scorched the stone, and sparks sprayed and tumbled around his head. Rolling, Dauneth tried to get away, keep hold of his blade, and find his feet all at once—and then purple fire exploded overhead, and the room shook soundlessly.

He scrambled up, still fleeing from the pillar, to see the masked mage gesturing him to halt. He did, staring around wildly. A pulsing, spitting sphere of purple radiance hung in the air not far from them. Dauneth stared at it. There was a round, dark shadow at the center of the sphere.

"The flying helm?" he asked, his mouth suddenly dry.

The mage nodded. "Now it will serve as our guide. We stay behind it for the next few rooms, and the guardians waiting there will leave us be, so long as you don't touch any of them."

They went on through chambers and down another flight of stairs into a long, narrow hall whose walls were broken by many niches, each home to a silent, unmoving suit of dark plate armor. The purple sphere floated ahead of them, and twice along the passage unseen magical barriers suddenly flared into violet radiance, flashed white, and then parted.

The masked mage ignored such displays, striding steadily ahead until she reached a closed stone door. Dauneth peered at it curiously; save for a pull-ring and a keyhole, it bore no mark. Was this what they'd come for?

The masked mage selected one of the keys, murmured something over it, put it to her lips, and then slid it into the lock.

Dauneth didn't know what he'd expected to see beyond the door—Vangerdahast and a dozen senior war wizards bound and gagged, perhaps—but he'd thought the royal treasure vault would have gates and an inscription and guards.

The masked mage in blue strode in without hesitation, glanced around quickly, and then stepped aside, the pulsing purple sphere moving with her. Dauneth followed, his sword raised and ready. Dust rose around their boots and hung heavy everywhere else, though someone—no, several someones—had come in and crossed the room recently. Armed men stood ready for them—no, just old and ornate suits of chased and gemstudded armor. Dauneth eyed them warily, then looked around.

Along the walls sat massive chests, except to the left, where there was a row of dragon skulls. Small purple gems gleamed along the brow of each of the great bone heads.

A stuffed, well-worn minotaur stood guard over a low table where a line of crowns sat, all of them grander than the simple circlet King Azoun favored. Dauneth blinked at the size of the gems in some of them—there was one ruby as large as his own fist—and then glanced quickly around the room again, still expecting some sort of attack. Another wall displayed a row of swords, halberds, and maces. Among them was a small glass case that held the scorched head of a sledgehammer.

The footprints in the dust led to an armoire of tarnished electrum that pulsed with a faint blue glow of guardian magic. Its double doors stood open, revealing a fire-ravaged interior where ruined things had melted and dripped down to puddle on the floor long ago.

The masked mage was peering carefully at a yellowed map. As Dauneth turned to look at it, she rolled it up, thrust it back into her bodice, and announced, "Right—

now we start back. My trap sphere won't last forever, and the helm will go free once the sphere evaporates."

Dauneth frowned. "We're leaving? Didn't we come here to find something . . . something to save the life of the king?"

The masked head nodded. "We did and we have," she said, turning to go. "We came to find if something was missing from this room, and it is. Now we know much more than we did before."

Dauneth's eyebrows rose in disbelief. "We do? *I* don't."

The masked head turned back to him. "Come," she said simply and went out the door, the purple sphere moving before her. He shrugged and followed.

The woman in blue reached past him to point and whisper. Her spell made dust swirl up from the floor of the room for a brief instant before it settled again, hiding the marks of their boots.

"The golden bull that struck the king down," she said crisply as they swung the door closed again, "was an automaton called an abraxus, a constructed creature animated by magic. One such beast appeared in Cormyr in the past and ended up—disabled—in this room. Now it's missing, and that means—"

"That someone who can get down here is responsible for the king's condition," Dauneth said slowly. "Either someone able to work the sort of magic you did to bring us past the guards and barriers, or someone in the palace." His eyes locked with hers. "Someone in the palace is a traitor."

"Quite so," the lips behind the mask said softly. "Which brings us to your more difficult task. . . ."

24

Sembians
Year of the Soft Fogs
(1188 DR)

ing Pryntaler stormed around the campfire, his arms pinwheeling so violently that Jorunhast thought he'd take flight right then and there. "If war is what they want, then war is what they'll get," he snarled for the fifth time during this current rant.

"War is *not* what they want," the wizard replied calmly. "What they want is Marsember. If they can get it without war, then so much the better."

The pair stood in the midst of a small encamped band of nobles, clerics, scribes and guards at the narrowest part of Thunder Gap, the traditional boundary between the Land of the Purple Dragon and the Chondathan colonies of Sembia. But now the Sembian cities were colonies no longer, but a nation of merchant cities ruled by expediency and gold rather than kings and wizards. The uplands around the storm-haunted peaks, which had been so much wilderness for so many centuries, were now regularly transversed by merchant caravans.

The Cormyrean group was camped on the near side of the pass, the Sembians in their oversized wagons on the far side. Their mutual meeting ground was at the saddle

of the pass, a great field where tents of purple and black
had been erected. The intention had been to hearken
back to the splendor and power of the elves, but instead
of radiant elven pavilions, these meeting tents looked
like smoky mountains made of storm clouds.

The activity within the largest tent was as stormy as
the color of its canvas. For three days, the king had met
with the representatives of the Sembian houses, and for
three days, he and Jorunhast had returned to their own
fires without a settlement. Each day Pryntaler's war
mutterings grew louder and sharper.

The sticking point was Marsember, of course. A nomi-
nally independent city-state on the Cormyrean side of
the Thunder Peaks, it had extensive ties, both legal and
less so, with Sembia. The more prestigious Marsemban
merchant families, craving respectability, favored merging with the Sembian state, while the nobles and the
shadier merchants wanted it to remain an open city. The
senior nobility, the Marliir family, sought the support, if
not the armies and taxes, of the Cormyrean crown.

Jorunhast was supportive of an independent Marsember, at least for the time being. There were many times
when the business of the crown needed to be dealt with
in the shadows of Marsember rather than braving the
bright scrutiny of many noble eyes in the halls of Suzail.
A measure of independence was needed for that.

Sembian rule would be worse. An established presence
of Sembians on the western side of the Thunder Peaks
would be an ever present encouragement for the more
adventurous among the merchant families. Once the
Sembians had one of their cities on this side of the Thun-
ders, what would keep other cities and towns—such as
Arabel, cradle of rebels—from swearing fealty to gold as
opposed to the Dragon Throne?

After a number of long talks with the young king,
Jorunhast had made the point that Marsember must be
protected, and called a parley with the Sembians. Officially they were here to settle the exact border between
Cormyr and Sembia, but the question of Marsember's

status overshadowed wilderness boundary decisions. Pryntaler's argument was simple and straightforward: An independent Marsember would be good for all sides, and its fate was essentially a decision for the crown of Cormyr, since Marsember stood squarely within Cormyr's sphere of influence.

And every evening, after a day of talk, they returned to their camp and Pryntaler exploded with ever-growing rage. Now he stalked around the glow of the fire like a caged lion, spitting out his words like venom.

"Gold-fisted, book-smart, thieving, lawyer-loving, scheming merchants!" he bellowed. "How did my ancestors stand to have such worms as their neighbors all these years?"

"They were far neighbors for most of that time," the wizard explained patiently, "and spent most of the time in frays with the elves and the Dalesmen to the north, and with their own Chondathan masters. Now that they are free of Chondath's tethers, they seek their own future."

"A future that includes Cormyrean territory, it seems," Pryntaler shot back. "Perhaps we should take the battle to them, instead of wasting time on words!"

The other nobles at the fireside raised a cheer, and Jorunhast saw a few of the servants and his own scribes nodding in agreement. He shook his head in amazement.

Pryntaler, son of King Palaghard and the warrior queen Enchara of Esparin, had grown strong and true, the very image of his father. He had his father's broad shoulders and piercing blue eyes. He had inherited his mother's fiery temper, however, and her ability to bring the troops to a blood boil. Which was, of course, exactly what this situation did not need.

Jorunhast sighed deeply. He had grown as well, though most of that had involved an ever-increasing waistline. His shoulders were still broad, and he had slowed the work of time sufficiently to keep his good looks. But next to Pryntaler, the wizard tended to resemble a baker or a contented Lathanderite friar. If

Pryntaler got his troops incensed, nothing would stop them short of war. And Jorunhast realized what none of his countrymen seemed to see: In any dispute that went beyond a single battle, Cormyrean steel could not hope to prevail against Sembian gold.

Jorunhast did not entirely blame his liege's inherited temper for these outbursts. In each of their meetings thus far, the five Sembians had behaved like moneylenders approving a loan, as opposed to diplomats meeting a king. Kodlos was their nominal leader, but he had to check with the others before deciding even on breakfast. The vulpine Homfast and vulturelike Lady Threnka were united in their lust to make Marsember Sembian. Old Bennesey was the scholar of the group and seemed to have every treaty, purchase, and chance meeting of the two nations committed to memory. And Jollitha Par sat there and said nothing but watched everything, a spider waiting at the center of his web.

At no time in the past three days had they received Pryntaler as a royal personage, or even a head of state. They would not call him "Majesty" or "Sire." They interrupted him often, with the air of merchants breaking into the ramblings of a junior clerk. They asked improper questions that time and again sent Jorunhast to check with his scribes, and then challenged their records while the king sat smoldering. Jorunhast felt they did not want war, but their treatment of the king sent them well down the dark road to the battlefield.

For his part, as the talks wore on, Pryntaler had become more belligerent and stubborn. Now he was refusing to even discuss minor matters of tariffs and exports, merely presenting the Cormyrean viewpoint and refusing to compromise. Jorunhast understood his mood in the face of the constant insults and spurious challenges of plainly established facts and historical records, but the Sembians were not rebellious minor nobles or haughty representatives of someplace so comfortably distant as Thay. These men had gold to spend, and they would send it to work in Cormyr, or they would send it elsewhere. And if they sent it elsewhere, they might use it to buy soldiers.

None of these observations would calm the angry king nor sway the other nobles and guards, so Jorunhast cleared his throat and said, "Perhaps we should merely decamp tonight and return to Suzail. Methinks the Sembians would get a very clear message should we not be here next morning."

Pryntaler halted by the fire, as if looking for an answer in its coals. Jorunhast knew that despite his bombast, the king would lose Marsember if discussions broke down now. Finally the king raised his head and snapped, "One more day. I will deal with those accountants and gold misers for one more day. Then they'll see what it is like to anger a Purple Dragon!"

He wheeled and stormed into the moonlit darkness. Instantly two of the nobles, Juarkin and Thessilion Crownsilver, fell into place behind him. Pryntaler thought of them as watchdogs. Jorunhast thought of the two nobles as the king's minders and, more importantly, as the wizard's informants.

They would walk down to the nearby lakeside, and the king would lecture them about how things weren't like this in his father's day. And the Crownsilvers would nod and listen and make stern grunts of agreement, until eventually the king ran out of steam and bluster. In the meantime, the other nobles, squires, scribes, and healers of the royal party would trade tales and speculate as to what the wizard Jorunhast would do to save the day in this particular case.

Jorunhast, in this particular case, did not have a clue. On one side, he sympathized with the king. The Sembians were a bureaucracy without a strong leader, and as treacherous to deal with as a community of drow. On the other hand, now was a time for speakers, not warriors. If the king could not deal with the Sembians, war loomed on the horizon, if not with Sembia, then somewhere else.

The Royal Magician smiled to himself, thinking of how things truly were in Palaghard's day. Pryntaler's father almost launched the nation into a war with distant Procampur soon after his coronation, when a new crown crafted for the coronation was stolen. The king thought the jewelers of Procampur were responsible, and he mustered the armies accordingly. The true thief, the pirate lord Immurk, was eventually revealed and the crown recovered. It was an ugly, top-heavy monster of sculpted gold, and after a few months, it was relegated to the family treasury in favor of the original three-spired crown. Yet that golden monstrosity had nearly started a war. And now, perhaps, the hardheadedness of the Sembians was going to create another one.

Jorunhast rose, dusted off his robes, and slowly and leisurely headed after the king, one of his own scribes following in his wake. Around the fire, a few heads were nodding to each other that the king and the Royal Magician would butt heads for a while away from prying eyes, and the wizard would eventually bring the Purple Dragon back to the negotiating table. And from the look in the eyes of some, that would not be the best thing for Cormyr, in their opinion.

Jorunhast walked slowly down to the lake, both to enjoy the scenery and to give the king more time to calm himself. The meadows were as close to high summer as they would get, and it was pleasantly cool around him. A light woods of small, stunted fruit trees ran down to the lake. Once it must have been an orchard or a grove planted for late harvesting, but its original planters were gone, leaving only the trees as a living memorial. A waning moon low on the horizon illuminated the path sufficiently that the wizard did not need magical light to see his way. Somewhere, night-blooming plants had opened for the bats, and their soft, fragrant scent hugged the ground.

Jorunhast was among the trees when he heard the sounds of battle ahead, at the edge of the lake itself. Human shouts were punctuated by the clang of metal clashing against metal. Jorunhast broke into a trot, his young scribe scrambling to keep up.

Ed Greenwood and Jeff Grubb

The two burst from the trees to see that the two
Crownsilvers were already down, and the king himself
was locked in combat with a great metallic gorgon. The
creature's scaled flanks caught the moonlight and reflected it back in shattered shards. Its massive head was
wreathed in clouds of greenish smoke.

Jorunhast turned to the scribe and shouted, "Get back
to camp and bring every priest and every man who has a
sword to swing!"

The young woman hesitated for a moment, her eyes
locked on the great metallic creature. Then the wizard's
shouted curse at her mazed wits broke her transfixed
state, and she went scrambling back up the path.

The king was fighting oddly, rushing forward to slash
at the creature and then dancing back again, then dodging aside when the great bull charged. Time and again
his blows skittered along the sides of the beast, and in
the darkness, Jorunhast saw sparks fly as the steel
struck against the scales.

The wizard knelt by one of the fallen Crownsilvers.
The youth was unmarked, but his face was drawn and he
was gasping for breath. Poison, then. Jorunhast laid the
young noble's head down—there was little to be done
until the healers arrived—and turned back to the battle.

The king was tiring, and the monster seemed unscathed by his attacks. Again His Majesty danced forward, slashed without effect, and dodged back, clear of
the creature's horns and breath. Not a gorgon, but some
relative, perhaps, thought the wizard. The monster
looked as if it could continue the battle until dawn. The
king, sweat already pouring down his face, obviously
could not. Pryntaler favored the wizard with a short, desperate look, then dodged out of the way of the beast's poisonous maw.

Jorunhast caught the pattern of the king's attack. It
would be tight, and he did not know if the magic he had
would affect the beast. However, he could not wait, and
the nobles and knights would arrive too late if he hesitated.

362

The Royal Magician raised his hand and started to craft the spell as Pyrntaler dodged in once more to strike the beast. His blow had no more effect than the others. When the king jumped back, out of range of the poisons that engulfed the beast's head, he hoped fervently, Jorunhast let loose his spell.

A bolt of lightning sprang from his fingertips and thundered into the beast. The blast of energy struck the side of the creature and spread along its scales, as if it were trying to slit the creature apart. The golden gorgon, or whatever it was, staggered forward for a moment, then halted in its tracks, as if turned to stone by the force of the blow.

Pryntaler's shoulders sagged in exhaustion, and he nodded his thanks at the wizard, panting, "The monster was waiting for us here when—"

Jorunhast held up a hand, and the king fell silent, puzzled. The gorgon was clicking, as if it had swallowed a giant ratchet.

The magician of the realm approached the stone-still creature. Yes, it was making the low clicking noise. Now he could see in the moonlight the beast was not a living thing, but rather an automaton or golem in the shape of a great bull. Somewhere within it, something was attempting to repair the damage of the lightning bolt.

Wizard and king looked at each other, and Jorunhast raised his hand again, signaling Pyrntaler to stay back. He approached the clockwork beast carefully, expecting it at any moment to spring back to life. Holding his breath, he ran his fingers along the thing's head and shoulders. He found a small tray tucked beneath its chin. He pulled it forth, and a smoking, greenish pile of herbs tumbled out. The poison, obviously herbal in nature, that had felled the two Crownsilvers.

Jorunhast stepped back two swift paces and let the toxic fumes waft away in the night air. Then he returned to the creature's side and resumed his inspection. The clicking became louder and more rapid. He ran his fingers along the ridge of the machine's back. There was a small stud at the top of the spine, directly behind the nape of the creature's massive neck.

Sweat gathered on the magician's forehead. The latch might silence the clicking or reactivate the beast fully ... or might cause it to explode. Should he wait for the other nobles, the knights, and healers?

The creature began to slowly move its jaws, opening and closing them in a jerky rhythm. Within the metallic shell, Jorunhast heard bellows flex, and the mouth hissed to exhale the now removed poison.

Jorunhast cursed, offered a silent prayer to Mystra, and moved the control.

The wheeze of the bellows died with the clicking. The beast became inert once more. There were shouts from up the hill as the first of the rescuers reached the abandoned orchard.

King Pryntaler examined the creature. "A magical device?"

Jorunhast nodded. "One not normally found in the wilderness of Cormyr. Someone put this here to ambush you."

The king snarled, "The Sembians! I swear this means *war*!"

"Yes and no," said Jorunhast. "Yes, it probably was the Sembians, or at least one of the merchants. But, no, I don't think it means war. They saw this creature as a tool to be used to solve the border dispute. Let us use it to the same purpose."

The king looked hard and long at the wizard, then nodded. Now the would-be rescuers were spilling down along the shore. The king turned and barked orders for the healers to attend the fallen Crownsilvers and left Jorunhast to examine his prize.

The mage hummed to himself as he peered at the creature, exclaiming as he found small additional latches and hidden panels. He called for the four strongest of the knights to remove their armor and be ready for some heavy lifting.

* * * * *

In the morning, the Sembians were already gathered at the purple and black pavilion, waiting and asking in thirty-second intervals what the time was. The Cormyreans arrived late, to five scowling faces.

His Majesty King Pryntaler, by contrast, was all smiles. If he had spent the previous evening battling for his life, he did not show it.

"You are late," said Kodlos gloomily, as if the king were a clerk sneaking past the noon bell. "Yesterday you spoke of our lack of respect to your claims, and now—"

"Not late . . . merely delayed," said the king, beaming as he interrupted the leader of the Sembian merchants. Kodlos blinked twice, and Pryntaler waved back at the entrance.

Two of the noble knights of Cormyr were wrestling a low, wheeled cart into the pavilion. On the cart stood a large object shrouded in a great swath of fabric. At one side of the cart walked Jorunhast, a contented grin plastered on his face. The merchants exchanged curious glances.

Pryntaler continued, not giving the Sembians the opportunity to respond. "Last night I went for a walk, to consider your offers and viewpoints. While I was doing so, I came across this in an abandoned orchard not far from here."

The king nodded. Jorunhast took hold of a corner of the fabric shroud and hauled it aside with a flourish, revealing the golden gorgon he'd first seen the night before.

Four Sembians leaned forward curiously at the sight of the golden bull. One, the ever quiet Jollitha Par leaned backward, his face turning an ashen gray.

Jorunhast called, "This is a wondrous creation, some sort of clockwork guard, apparently unaffected by the ages. But we do not know what it is. It—"

Old Bennesey, the scholar, interrupted just as rudely as he had for the last three days. "It is an abraxus, mage.

These were automatons, created by Chondathan mages, but they could be used by anyone. They were usually activated by an unwilling human sacrifice and served as both guards and assassins. . . ." Finally his brain caught up with his tongue and tripped up his flow of words. He stammered, looked at Jollitha Par, then stammered again.

Pryntaler broke in. "Chondathan, you say? Well, that would explain your knowing about it. I think this must have been an old guard for Sembia's Chondathan borders. Jorunhast, have you found out how to operate the creature?"

The mage bowed low. "I believe that there is a latch along the spine here."

Jollitha Par started as if he had been set on fire. "That will not be necessary!" he protested, his voice rising along the scale with every word spoken.

His Sembian fellows—or at least, Kodlos, Homfast and Lady Threnka—turned their heads slowly to stare at the spiderlike Jollitha. This was the first time the quiet merchant had spoken aloud, and it was as if the golden abraxus had suddenly broken into song.

Pryntaler went on. "I note that learned Bennesey, here, referred to this as a guard. If this is left over from the era of the Chondathians, it could be said that the original settlers of your country recognized the Thunder Peaks as the border between our lands."

Lady Threnka gave the king a small smile and adjusted her pinch-nosed glasses to regard Pryntaler with cold condescension. "You would have us believe that this creature has been sitting unaffected for hundred of years, just so that you might state that the borders of our lands—"

"What other explanation do you have, my lady?" said Jorunhast. "If it had not been left here by some previous Sembians, the alternative is that some present-day Sembians put it there. Then the question becomes who and why. Is this what you are saying?"

As he spoke, the spidery Sembian grabbed Lady

Threnka's arm and spoke softly and sharply in her ear. Her demeanor tightened as he spoke, transforming from haughty and superior to tense and worried.

She ignored the wizard's words and spoke to Pryntaler. "I see your point, Your Majesty. Perhaps we should adjourn for a short caucus, Kodlos, to discuss the merits of setting the official borders between our nations."

Kodlos made a puzzled noise. "My lady, we had just gotten started rather tardily—"

"And we will start again once we consider this." She rose to her feet. "Come. You will forgive us this leave, Your Majesty."

Pryntaler smiled and managed a small half-bow. "Always, your ladyship."

The five representatives and their aides made a quick retreat. Pryntaler turned to his wizard. "How long do you think it will take?"

"It depends," said Jorunhast, "On whether they come back to accept the Thunder Gap as our mutual border, or just head back for Ordulin right here and now."

"She called me 'Your Majesty,'" Pryntaler said.

"Twice," replied Jorunhast, nodding. "Though it looked as if she were gargling slugs as she said it."

"And you noticed Jollitha Par?" said the king.

"Aye," said the wizard, "and if you choose not to behead him right here and now, I guarantee he'll get a special magical visit later, and none will mistake the message or the messenger."

"Behead him?" thundered Pryntaler, smiling broadly. "The old spider has accomplished in one fell swoop what we've been trying to do for the past three days. I may give him a medal!"

25

Lies, Spies, and Assassins
Year of the Gauntlet
(1369 DR)

e're almost ready, you know . . . almost. Just a few more little details, and then we'll have to move very swiftly indeed." Ondrin Dracohorn glanced around the chamber once more and added apologetically, "One can't be too careful, you know. The war wizards have spies everywhere, and who knows just whom they're working for?"

The other noble, one of the middle-aged Daunting-horns, curled his lips. "Vangerdahast, of course."

Ondrin's watery blue eyes blinked up at him. "Well, some of them, of course, but I've reason to believe that a lot of them are working for other masters . . . noble masters. Trust me in this; my spies are everywhere, too."

His nose almost twitched with excitement. "As to why I counsel haste, have you heard what happened to Ohlmer Cormaeril and Sorgar Illance? Both old family patriarchs were found dead in their beds, and on the very same morning!"

The other noble nodded knowingly. "Just a little housecleaning for *those* two families. I'm always surprised those serpents didn't father thrice as many daughters as they did, to sell them into slavery—'guaranteed gently born noble bluebloods,' and all that."

Ondrin's eyes lit up. "Now, *there's* a chance for a handsome profit! Why didn't I think of that? I'll have to hire myself some lasses to breed with."

The older, taller noble shook his head. "No. No, you've got to free Cormyr first! And by the time you're finished accomplishing that high and splendid calling—and how many rich merchants can say they did *that*, toppling kings and setting new ones on thrones, eh?—other nobles'll have their broods well on the way. In a dozen years or so, after all the expense of rearing them and training them, you'll be ready to sell and find the market glutted."

"I suppose." Ondrin sighed, visibly crestfallen, and then said with a rush, "But I almost forgot to tell you! I've heard that the same men slew both old Ohlmer and the head of House Illance! Men working for the same patron, somewhere in House Cormaeril!"

The other noble's eyebrows went up; encouraged, Ondrin rushed on. "They're saying the war wizards were furious. They thought a few spells would find out who was behind it all, once they got hold of one of the assassins, but when they started fishing them out of the harbor, they were headless and positively aglow with deadmagic fields!"

The eyebrows went up again. "Dead magic? That sounds like the work of someone a little more powerful than your average war wizard!"

Ondrin seemed to purr with satisfaction. "And you know there's only one man in Cormyr who fits *this* little scenario! As it happens, I was talking with our esteemed Royal Magician just the other day—a few private matters, you know . . ."

* * * * *

The gong by the bath's door sounded faintly, as if a discreet fingernail had tapped it.

Gaspar Cormaeril lifted his mouth from the stunningly beautiful woman and smiled coldly. "Approach!"

he called, rolling her aside in the warm, languid waters with a firm hand and reaching for a glass of smoking blue wine, a rare and expensive import from a very distant place indeed, with the other.

Sensibly the lass settled deeper into the waters and nestled into the crook of the noble's arm. The scented waters were still roiling from her movements when the man in dark leathers padded to the edge of the pool, knelt, and murmured, "News you should hear, lord. Ondrin Dracohorn's been heard talking of the deaths and tracing them to House Cormaeril!"

Gaspar sipped at his wine. "Has he, now? Well done, Tuthtar! Send Elios to watch over our talkative little noble for the rest of the day, and then get yourself something to eat. I'll have something important for you later." He gave the man his serpent smile, nodded in dismissal, and turned back to the willing lass, sliding down into the deeper waters of the pool again.

She began to murmur softly; Gaspar let her do so for a very short time before he rolled over again and pressed a button that flanked the marble lip of the pool. A message gong sounded in the distance, and it had barely fallen silent before another man entered the room and knelt in smooth, practiced haste. "Lord, command me," he said.

Gaspar smiled coldly. "It has become necessary to remove Ondrin Dracohorn. Someone is bound to take him seriously, eventually. And see to poor Tuthtar as well. Ensure to his everlasting silence forthwith, before he has a chance to gossip in the kitchens."

"At once, lord," said the man and turned with a grin.

"A pity," Gaspar murmured, taking the willing lass into his arms again, "but I can't have folk around who know too much about two fates. Every mouth that can talk of such things is a peril House Cormaeril cannot afford."

He looked down at the woman; as her emerald eyes met his, they widened in sudden fear.

"Another pity," Gaspar said with a smile, as he pressed another button to summon a second assassin.

* * * * *

The man in robes strode past, looking grim. The two guards nodded in salute. When the man was safely gone and a stout door closed behind him, one of the Purple Dragons muttered, "That's the first time I've seen Lord Alaphondar in days now. Where's he been, I wonder?"

The other guard shrugged. "Best not to wonder, I've found. He's in there with Dimswart now, though, and by the looks of things, he's bringing along grim news with him." He frowned. "I wonder what. . . ."

Not far away, a dark figure peeled itself away from a pillar and stroked her chin. What indeed? And just where had the sage been? It was high time to get some answers. A black-gloved hand fell to the hilt of a ready dagger.

* * * * *

The Crown Princess of Cormyr buried her face in the pillow and sobbed as she had never sobbed before, until she strained for breath and her ribs ached. The handkerchief held beneath her cheeks was sodden, and her hair was everywhere, and she felt sick, yet still she could not stop weeping.

"Oh, *gods!*" she wailed in frustration.

"My lady!" Aunadar's voice came to her, and a moment later his soothing hands touched her shoulders. Tanalasta shuddered under him, wracked by fresh sobs of grief.

"Princess," Aunadar said gently, "I have just now come from where the king lay abed and found him gone from the chamber, but the priests there said he yet lived! High Lady, there is still hope!"

"My father is *dying*," Tanalasta sobbed. "Dying! He lies so near death that they've moved him to somewhere secret, and they've forbidden me—*me*, his only family present!—from seeing him. Only our Lord High and Mighty Wizard and his two cronies, the bloody-minded sages, can see my father! They'll not let me in to see him until all that's left is a cold *corpse!*"

She rose bolt upright on her bed and hurled the sodden pillow across the room. The heavy, waterlogged cushion struck an oval mirror as tall as the princess herself and shattered it into a spiderweb of cracks.

"Princess—" Aunadar said helplessly, and she answered him with a snarl of rage that rose into a scream, then thrust her fingers into the next pillow like claws, ripping and tearing.

Aunadar put firm arms around her and endured a few frantic moments of struggling and clawing before his lips found hers, and he began to stroke and soothe and rock her gently.

It seemed a long time before she broke free of his kiss, trembling, and said quietly, "I'm all right now, Aunadar. Let me go. Thank you."

Aunadar Bleth released her and sat back, concern darkening his eyes, and she managed a wan smile. "I'm not handling this very well, am I?"

"Lady," he said gravely, "I don't think anyone faces the loss of her father very well. We do what we can, as the gods made us, and that is all we can expect and hope for." He smiled faintly. "Right now, what I hope for is your smile. I haven't see you smile in days!"

Tanalasta burst into fresh tears, a short shower that ended in a lopsided, sputtering smile. She put a hand on his cheek. "You are the sweetest of men, my Aunadar."

"Oh? Deceived you, too, have I?" he teased, stroking her upraised hand. She chuckled weakly, and his lips found hers once more.

They rolled over on the bed, and Tanalasta came up alone. "No!" she said. "No, Aunadar . . . much as I'd like that right now, I can't—I—I just can't. There's too much to worry about! Nobles muttering everywhere, rumors of rebels gathering in the King's Forest and even somewhere right here in Suzail, that old wizard gliding around, smiling at me and waving his writ of regency whenever he passes! I can't spend what may be my last few days of life rolling around on beds with you! What if the nobles came in and stabbed us both? What then?"

"Then we'd be together forever," Aunadar said lightly, adding hastily, when he saw her brows darken in fury, "But you're right, Lady Highness, and I am wrong to distract you now. Your birthright is this fair kingdom of ours, and I must tell you that I have been very busy these last few days trying to ensure that what is rightfully yours does indeed pass to you!"

"What do you mean?" Tanalasta asked softly, her eyes dangerous.

"I've been talking to all the nobility I can find here in Suzail, putting to them the blunt question of their loyalty to you, should Crown Princess Tanalasta claim the Dragon Throne in the face of Vangerdahast as a declared regent—or anyone else who thinks the throne might be his for the taking, 'for the good of the realm.' "

"What did they say?" Tanalasta's voice was calm, but the last pillow she'd caught hold of was now a tortured rag in her hands.

"Most of them offered guarded support," Aunadar said carefully, "but many of them also complained about this and that which displeases them about the governance of the realm. I sense that if Cormyr is to stay strong under a ruling Queen Tanalasta—without its war wizards, perhaps—certain, ah, concessions to the nobility may be necessary to guarantee the security of the kingdom."

"Were they any more specific?" Tanalasta asked dully.

"Some of them want a small say in the policies of the realm," Aunadar said gently. "A council of nobles that you'd consult with, or something of the kind."

Tanalasta frowned. "I see. So say the nobles; what of the others who dance ever closer to my father's throne?"

Aunadar spread his hands, "Rumors, more than hard truth."

Tanalasta waved a despairing hand. "Rumors, then—speak!"

The young pride of the Bleths leaned forward in excitement. "Hear, then: Your sister, Princess Alusair, has been seen to flee with her war band deeper into the Stonelands, apparently afraid to return to court. She and her nobles rode away from a patrol sent out from High Horn specifically to speak with them."

"That sounds like my sister," Tanalasta said with a sigh. "What else?"

"I almost hesitate to say, High Lady, because it is but rumor and could well fly false," Aunadar said gently.

"Out with it!" Tanalasta ordered, exasperated.

The young nobleman bowed his head to signify obedience to her wishes and said gravely, "It concerns your mother, Tana. I was trying to find out if it was true before I told you. Queen Filfaeril has been stabbed by a would-be assassin's blade in Eveningstar and lies wounded and delirious there, in priestly care. Lathanderites, I would guess. I've heard no word of poison, but—"

"No," Tanalasta gasped, going very pale. "No—not Mother, too!"

Aunadar put an arm around her shoulders hastily, but she did not swoon or collapse into tears. He saw her bite a trembling lower lip and feel for a pillow that was no longer there. It was lying, now shredded, at her feet.

Gently he put another pillow into her hand, and her slim, soft white fingers—oh, he knew how soft—dug into the fabric like a falcon's claw.

Dug in, and then let go. The princess tossed the pillow aside, swallowed, and said firmly but very quietly, "I'm all right. Go on, my Aunadar. There's more, isn't there?"

Her comforter nodded. "It's Vangerdahast, of course."

A spasm of fury crossed the face of the princess at the wizard's name, and then was gone again. Her next words seemed to come with fresh energy she'd not shown before. "Yes? Speak!"

"He's been seen flitting about the kingdom," Aunadar said grimly, "and walking the halls of the court and the back alleys of Suzail even more energetically these last few days. Talking to nobles and giving them promises, spells cast to their order, or just plain gold. Gold from the royal treasury, of course."

"He's gathering his own following," Tanalasta said faintly. She seemed unsurprised and calm. Her mind was engaged now, calculating what it would cost to buy a kingdom. And, Aunadar thought, how much it would cost to prevent that sale.

"Exactly," Aunadar said, "and I've heard that both the court sages are off around the Realms gathering support—mercenary troops, even—for whatever he's planning."

"His royal regency," Tanalasta said flatly. "A wizard ruling the realm." She lifted her shoulders in a shrug. "Not a bad idea, actually," she added, "so long as the rule is just and the mage mighty enough to hold off the inevitable attacks from rival mages. As the Simbul holds off the Red Wizards, to keep her realm of Aglarond safe."

"Wizards can never be trusted, Tana," the young nobleman said, kneading her shoulders gently. "You know that."

His touch was bliss for her tight, tired neck and shoulders. The crown princess leaned back into his fingers with a sigh of pleasure. "Oh, Aunadar . . ."

"I'll always be here to do this if you ask me to," Aunadar murmured, close by her ear.

"Go on," she said. "Keep those wonderful fingers at work and tell me more about the old wizard."

She felt Aunadar shrug. "There's not much more any of us know, Tana. He's just here, and then there, and then gone. We don't have the spells to chase him around the kingdom or fight him if he notices us following. But one doesn't have to be a sage—even a court sage—to see that he's up to no good. Remember the old tales . . . Cormyr's wizards are loyal only to the crown, not to the one who wears it."

In a place of darkness not far away, Dauneth Marliir took his eye away from his tiny spy hole and nodded. The scion of House Bleth was right. He'd already felt the same thing, in his own now cramped bones. Vangerdahast was certainly up to something.

The princess sighed. "You're right, Aunadar." She

reached back and gently but firmly pushed away his massaging hands. "My thanks for that, but I must get dressed and get out of here. Even if I can't stop wizards from snatching Cormyr from me, I need fresh air and a place to walk and to be up *doing* something! I'm not going to lie in my bed until they come to turn me into a toad or charm me into marrying the noble of their choice or even—gods!—our Lord High Royal Magician himself!"

She stormed out of the room, hauling on the cord that summoned her ladies-of-the-chamber as she did so. "Step out into the receiving room, Aunadar," her voice came back faintly. "We're not officially betrothed yet, and I don't want people talking . . ."

From Dauneth's hiding place, the faint sound of Aunadar's assent drowned out her last words. They'd moved too far away for him to hear any more. Dauneth sighed, raked slivers of shattered mirror from his hair, took a last look through his spyhole, and crept away.

Someone else heard the faint sounds behind the wall and smiled. That would be young Marliir departing. She might as well follow suit.

The lady with eyes like flames spat out the rose she'd been absently toying with during her long, uncomfortable time curled up behind the wing tapestries of Tanalasta's bed. Its stem was almost chewed through. Emthrara, the Harper, sighed and dropped the rose, then rubbed at her aching back and slipped away.

When a maidservant came into the room a moment later with Tanalasta's discarded nightgown in her arms, she almost slipped on a rose lying on the floor. The servant picked it up and peered at it curiously. Someone had been chewing on the stem. She frowned, shrugged, and then carried it away for disposal, leaving the floor bare and unblemished once more.

26

Death of Dhalmass
Year of the Wall
(1227 DR)

hodes Marliir, youngest cousin of a minor relative of a fallen noble house, stalked the streets of Marsember hunting for the King of Cormyr. In its sheath, his serrated dagger wept sweet poison.

The fall of Marsember had come within a generation of the establishment of Sembia's western border. Once the Purple Dragon established a permanent border with Sembia, the slow, continual tightening of his royal gauntlet around the port city began. Finally, just to stay free, the ruling Marliir family had been forced to publicly endorse the pirate trade in the city and to declare hostilities against the Forest Kingdom.

And that's when Dhalmass, mighty Dhalmass, the Warrior King of Cormyr, crossed the marshes and took the City of Islands.

Rhodes Marliir was nobility in name only. His immediate family was not within spitting distance of the Marsembian throne, but his was the only branch that had not perished battling the invading horde. And now, blade in hand, the young rogue was intent on exacting his revenge.

The remainder of the town was in celebration, which angered Rhodes even further. These were the merchants and smugglers and thieves and petty nobles, like the Eldroons and the Scorils, who had loudly encouraged the ruling Marliirs to stand firm against the Purple Dragon. Then these supposedly loyal followers deserted the cause when the king's forces first entered the marshes, and some—Rhodes suspected the treacherous Eldroon household—even guided the Cormyrean army through the tortuous byways of the marsh to the city's open gates. Now those traitors tooted silver horns and threw gaudy bits of paper to celebrate their new masters and Marsember's incorporation into the nation of Cormyr. . . .

His uncles and great-uncles lay in Marsember Bog unavenged, along with the last of the Janthrins and the Aurubaens. Mighty Marsemban nobles all, who in life would not have allowed one such as Rhodes, born on the wrong side of the blanket to a poor relation, to pass through the door of any of their palatial homes. That did not matter to Rhodes. All he had gotten from his relatives was a noble name, and now, thanks to their bullheaded stubbornness, the power of that name was gone as well.

Still, Rhodes had his contacts in the city. Everyone knew Dhalmass had taken over the old Marliir manor as his base of operations a fortnight ago. But it was Halfhand Elos who reported that the newly arrived queen, Jhalass Huntsilver, had suddenly taken ill and the king was abroad in the city. The pawnmaster Jacka Andros told him the king was at the Cloven Shield, drinking with his victorious troops. By the time Marliir had reached the Shield, another source said that the king had adjourned to the Drowning Fish Festhall. And the proprietress of the Fish, the old crone Magigan, had noted gravely that his lustful majesty had just left, three empty kegs to the better, with a pair of young ladies, one supporting each arm. For a fee, Magigan would recall where they were going, and for a slightly larger fee, she would forget that fact—and her telling of it—forever, after she told Rhodes.

The last of the Marliirs paid the crone's fee and sought out the apartment Magigan had mentioned. It was on one of the city's outer islands, which served Rhodes well. Half of the city was located on a treble-handful of unnamed islands hunched along the marshy shore. These small islets were linked by innumerable bridges of crumbling stone and sea-weathered wood, which added further to the mazelike nature of Marsember.

The narrow streets and bridges of the inner islands were packed with revelers and soldiers. More warriors had fallen in the last two tendays to inebriation and exhaustion than had died in the brief siege of the city's low walls. The two-tenday anniversary of the takeover, prompted by the arrival of Queen Jhalass and rumor of the king being abroad in the city, had served as reason enough to spark a new wave of revels hard on the heels of the previous ones.

The outward island was practically deserted. The last bands of partygoers clustered along its bridges, tossing empty bottles and insults at the barges beneath them. Here the buildings leaned against each other like drunks, and shadows seemed darker and more forbidding in the dying rays of the sun. The address the old crone had given proved to be a two-story, slightly leaning house of stucco and weathered lumber, its roof a rambling ruin of shellacked wooden shingles.

The girl was running out as he stalked in. Half-dressed in a light shift of Theskan silk, she was clutching a blanket over her bare shoulders. She was small and blonde, and her blue eyes were wide and full of tears. She halted upon seeing Rhodes, then sobbed and fled, her bare feet slapping the cobbles, the blanket trailing after her like a cape.

He found the other girl sitting on the second-floor landing. She was dusky-skinned and almond-eyed, with long, dark hair worn loose in ringlets. She also wore only a light shift as she sat with her knees up, clutching an overly brocaded pillow. She stared at the open doorway wordlessly, seeming dazed.

Was the king he'd come to slay some sort of devouring lusty lion who drove his partners to madness? Rhodes edged around the doorway to see a room in the disarray of passion. Discarded clothing of both sexes littered the room, cast over chairs, tall chests, and nightstands. The room was dominated by a single huge bed with an over-stuffed straw tick. Its covering quilts lay thrown to one side. In the center of the bed, tangled in the cotton sheets, sprawled Warrior King Dhalmass, naked—and dead.

Rhodes Marliir carefully approached the bed, his hand on his dagger. The huge, muscular body of the king was already turning blue in its swath of sheets. The royal mouth gaped open in one last, endless battle cry, and the royal eyes stared unfocused at the ceiling. Rhodes touched the body with the back of his hand. It was cold and clammy. The last of the body's heat had departed with the king's fleeing life.

The young noble cursed. How *dare* Dhalmass die, here and now, before Rhodes had a chance for revenge!

There was a subtle change in the stifling air of the room, as if a window had been opened for a moment and then shut again. Rhodes realized he was no longer alone in the room with the dead king.

He turned. The new arrival was a broad-shouldered man whose large gut spilled over the top of his belt. He wore red and black robes of vivid hues and expensive make. A mage's sigil in gold thread was embroidered over his heart. Rhodes did not know the symbol, but he knew who the man must be from Halfhand's descriptions of the royal court. This was Jorunhast, Royal Magician of Cormyr.

Rhodes began to stammer that he'd found the king this way, but the wizard swept him aside with one arm and went to the bed. He touched the king at the neck, the breast, and the inside of the thigh. Then he cursed mildly and pulled a small book from his vest. He raised the book and muttered something in an alien tongue. Sparks of light danced around the pages and grew swiftly in brightness and number, to orbit the volume like the streaming stars in the skies over Faerûn. The wizard laid the book on the king's forehead.

The sparks danced, flared once, and then died. Dhalmass continued to lie there, blue and stiff. The wizard leaned on the bed with both fists, his shoulders slumped in defeat. He cursed again, longer and louder this time.

"That's it, then," said the wizard. "He's well and truly dead. His mighty heart failed him, obviously in a moment of passion. Even the Book of Life could not bring him back this time."

He turned his head to look at the young noble. "Were you here when it happened?"

"Me?" asked Rhodes, then shook his head. "I've only just arrived. He was, uh, entertaining." The young Marliir pointed his chin at the open doorway. Beyond, the dusky-hued girl was watching everything with staring eyes.

"The only witness?" asked the wizard.

"There was another young lady," said Rhodes. "She left suddenly."

Jorunhast cursed again and looked hard at the noble. "And you were here with the girls?"

Rhodes straightened his shoulders and looked the wizard in the eye. "I am no panderer, mage. I am of the blood of House Marliir—one of the last, thanks to this man."

"So you came here, poisoned blade in your sheath, seeking revenge," said the wizard.

"I came seeking justice," said Rhodes. "I regret that I was too late to mete it out."

"*Justice!*" the old mage spat the word like a curse. "Is that what they call unthinking bloodlust these days?"

Rhodes Marliir's eyes narrowed. "And how did *you* know where to find him?"

Jorunhast held up a hand. "I came bearing sad news. Her Highness Queen Jhalass has perished, apparently in an allergic reaction to some fish served at dinner. Like Dhalmass, no amount of herbcraft or priests' magic could save her. Both of the rulers of Cormyr have perished within hours of each other. I fear for your city, Marliir."

The news amazed Rhodes. It was as if the gods themselves were saying, in their unsubtle way, that conquering Marsember was not the wisest of moves for the Cormyrean crown. He forgot that Jorunhast had not exactly answered his question.

Then the mage's last comment registered, and Rhodes asked sharply, "You *fear* for my city, mage?"

"Aye," said the Royal Magician, his face a mask of concern. "Once word gets out that both king and queen died in Marsember, regardless of how, there will be a gnashing of teeth and a seeking of revenge. Or, as you would call it, 'justice.' Seven companies of Purple Dragons walk—and drink deeply—in this city right now. Tell them their king, their warrior king, is dead, and his queen alongside him. Can you imagine the carnage and rioting that will ensue?"

For the first time, Rhodes really thought about it. "They'll destroy the city," he said quietly, seeing in his mind islands that were only ashes, houses put to the torch, the bridges broken, the vultures swooping down . . .

"Marsember would be abandoned once more," the Royal Magician intoned, "and its abandonment would not be peaceful. It is well that you had no hand in his death, for revenge would be swift and hard, and no mage or warrior or pirate could shield you."

He looked down at the spread-eagled corpse on the bed again and sighed. "Even now, I fear Marsember will be devastated by these deaths. And some of the same conspiring merchants who opened the gates to us have crept away during this last tenday. They might well return after the fury has abated and the city has been torn apart and try to establish their own kingdom. Then Cormyr would return. Death upon death, year after year. Feuds that die not, and children who do. Sometimes the gods play savage jests on us all."

Rhodes Marliir stared at the wizard, realizing the man was truly sad at the thought of Marsember's fate.

He felt tears rising in his throat, and at the same time a curious thankfulness. He'd never stood thinking beyond his own pride before—thinking down the generations and ages, of the fates of realms and cities and peoples. No wonder folk thought wizards strange.

Rhodes thought of the many islands of the city that was his home, the rat warrens of twisted streets and ancient, decaying buildings. The sagging wharves and inns and taverns and festhalls. All gone in a passion as hot and burning as his own hatred of the king. Marsember, swept away . . .

"What if he did not die here?" Marliir asked suddenly. "What if you teleported him back by magic, to lie beside the queen, and men thought they died together in their sleep?"

The Royal Magician shook his head. "They would still both have died in Marsember, and enough people heard Queen Jhalass complain of the food that the assumption would be that they were poisoned by rebel Marsembians. The fire and rampage would follow, inescapably."

Rhodes sighed in sudden despair. "Then my city is doomed. I wish I'd slain him myself! Then I'd be the only one held responsible, and not all the people of Marsember."

"A noble thought. Yet dark times will come indeed," said the mage, "unless . . ."

"Unless?" echoed Rhodes.

The Royal Magician of Cormyr drew himself up and asked formally, "Rhodes Marliir, will you pledge your loyalty to the crown of Cormyr, which will now pass to Palaghard, son of Dhalmass?"

The young noble looked at the mage, dumbfounded. Had the man not heard him confess his desire to kill the king?

"Knowing," the wizard continued, "that in doing so, you'd save Marsember from much rioting and ruin and gain a full noble title and rewards for you and your surviving house?"

"I suppose . . ." Rhodes shrugged, and then their eyes

met. He sighed again, drew himself up, and picked up Jorunhast's book from the cold forehead of the corpse.

The wizard made a sudden movement and then froze. The Marsemban nobleman handed him his book, looked into the eyes of the mage, and said firmly, "To save Marsember from seven companies of drunken, enraged Purple Dragons, I will so swear. I do so swear—if you will protect this city."

Jorunhast nodded. "Done . . . I hope."

Rhodes raised an eyebrow, and the wizard started to pace the room. "Dhalmass was a great war leader, but only a fair-to-middling ruler. He was too much the slave to a lust for battle, as well as for . . . other, more earthy lusts. By rights, he should have died in battle. We can ensure that if you're willing to assist me."

"Willing in what way?" Rhodes asked, eyes narrowing.

"His Majesty must be seen leaving this place and returning to his quarters, where he will sleep undisturbed through the night," said the wizard. "I will teleport back to Marliir House with the body and store it, say within the royal carriage that brought the queen here. We load Queen Jhalass similarly. In the morning, the king will be called back to Suzail. He will go by carriage to be with his queen, and will not take escorts on this safe trip through known country. Regrettably they are ambushed on the coast trail by known rogues and brigands. How do you feel about the Fire Knives?"

"Marsember has no love of the Fire Knives thieves' guild," Rhodes replied stiffly.

"Then the Fire Knives it is," the wizard said with a grim smile. "The king dies protecting his queen and passes into history as warrior king rather than libertine. And it all happens far from the walls of Marsember, which allows this fair city to drift easily into the arms of Cormyr without further bloodshed."

Rhodes was silent in response. The plan had more bizarre angles—and perilous steps—than the trader's market in Marsember. Nevertheless, if all went well, it would work.

He asked, "You want me to impersonate the king? Aren't there laws against such a thing?"

"If caught," the wizard said with a shrug. "And, Rhodes Marliir, I pledge to you my aid in getting you out if you are. Unless someone has the unusual presence of mind to check once and again to see that their drunken monarch truly *is* their drunken monarch, no one will know. Indeed, if there is any doubt, they'll likely summon me to determine your identity."

Rhodes smiled grimly. "And in return I get my noble house in Marsember?"

"You get your noble rank," said Jorunhast, "but too many questions will be asked if it is in Marsember."

"I don't want to be a petty lord of some sheep path," Rhodes said grimly, folding his arms.

"What about Arabel, then?" suggested the wizard. "A large city with a number of local nobility, far from the easy reach of the throne."

"Arabel would be suitable," agreed Rhodes.

"And it revolts against the crown every hundred years or so. You'll fit right in." The wizard smiled again. "Moreover, I can see my way clear to losing enough gold from the royal treasury that—when you're as old and as fat as I and have sons of your own, mind—you can buy any islands you want in Marsember again. But you must give me your most solemn oath that you'll *never* speak of this to anyone. Not a wife, not an heir, not a crony!"

Rhodes Marliir nodded. "I so swear on my noble name and my loyalty to House Obarskyr and Cormyr. And so let me hear you swear that you will protect Marsember."

"More than that," the wizard replied. "Dhalmass would have looked upon Marsember as an irritant removed, but in the end no more than another trinket of conquest, to be forgotten after it is acquired. Palaghard, or rather King Palaghard the Second, is a more thoughtful man. I think it will be easy to convince him to improve upon his late father's acquisition, to bring in stone and new construction. I swear I will move him in that direction. Agreed?"

385

"Royal Magician," Rhodes said softly, "you have yourself a deal. I will be true to this, before all the gods you care to summon."

Jorunhast clucked disapprovingly. "God summonings? I leave *that* sort of truly dangerous nonsense to young nobles. Folk think them strange, you know."

Rhodes chuckled helplessly.

Jorunhast scowled at him. "Stand still," he said, "or I'll have to shock you senseless and put you in bed with Dhalmass, there, to try to get you into his likeness!"

The young noble stood very still. The wizard peered at him and set to work, slowly cloaking Marliir with the seeming of the king. When the last spell was done, Rhodes examined himself in a cracked mirror and then looked down at what lay on the bed. The match was perfect, rendered by an expert who'd known the original subject from birth.

"Don't talk while you're on the road, for that I cannot fix now," said the Royal Magician. "Limit it to grunts. That was about the level of the king's speech when he was drunk, in any event."

"One last thing," said the "king" with Marliir's voice. "Are you going to do this same magic for the queen?"

Jorunhast paused. "I suppose so. I'll recruit some serving girl for the impersonation. Someone of strong will, like yourself. Many of the court know of the queen's illness, but almost none of her death."

"One of the queen's servants would be missed," said Rhodes.

"You have a suggestion?" asked the wizard.

Rhodes looked out the door. Following his gaze, Jorunhast saw the dusky-skinned woman. She was still sitting there, eyes and ears open, and had been watching them, not daring to make any sound by moving. Her eyes were very large and dark.

"Lass," Jorunhast said, "know that I am the Royal Magician of Cormyr, and hold the power in my hands to cook dragons to ashes." He raised one of his hands meaningfully and added with a smile, "On the other hand, I also have the power to transform young wenches into queens. . . ."

It took only a little coaxing to convince the young woman to throw in with the plan, given the choice between horrible death—now or at any time in the future, if she spoke out—and nobility, a manor house full of fine gowns, with good food in plenty, servants, a swan pond, and the ear of the Royal Magician to pursue any interests that might come to her. To say nothing of a husband, if she could see eye to eye with the darkly handsome young man she'd seen change into the king before her eyes. She looked at him now and frowned.

"Strip," she told Rhodes calmly, "and put on all the things he tossed around the room. You're the king now, and none of what you're wearing fits."

Looking down, the young noble saw that she was right. His clothes and dagger went onto a sheet, and the body of Dhalmass was rolled onto it and then wrapped up in a tight bundle. The wizard glanced around the room, nodded, and made a quick, intricate gesture.

He, the shrouded corpse, and the girl began to glow with a soft radiance.

"One last thing," he said as the glow spread and gained strength. "Dhalmass was well loved in Arabel. You might consider putting up a statue for him."

"When I hear of improvements in Marsember, I shall," the young noble replied tartly, then grinned in real pleasure for the first time he could remember.

The radiance rose to blinding intensity, and then abruptly faded, leaving him alone in the upstairs apartment.

Marliir checked the room over for any fallen royal jewelry or other evidence they might have overlooked that would tell a nosy Cormyrean that his king had been here—and died here. He found nothing.

The temporary king closed the door on the squalor of the room where Dhalmass had died and headed down the stairs. The king had been—well, *was*—a taller man than he, and it was more difficult than he'd thought it would be to maneuver his new body down to street level. Fortunately, Rhodes thought, the original King had been drunk; a few staggers would be forgiven.

He met the other girl, the blonde, at the doorway. She was creeping timidly back in to see if the drunken monarch had truly died in her arms, and she nearly leapt out of her skin when confronted with His Majesty, hale and hearty, seeming none the worse for wear.

Marliir kissed her gently on the forehead, then winked and weaved off into the city, on his way back to the official royal residence at Marliir House. There'd be other lasses to kiss on his journey. If he did this properly, many eyes would see and remember King Dhalmass this evening, and in the morning he and his queen would board the coach to take them back to Suzail. And in a week's time, there would be mourning across an entire realm for the fallen crowned heads of Cormyr—and a new noble lord and lady sitting at ease by a swan pond in Arabel.

27

Deals
Year of the Gauntlet
(1369 DR)

The old nobleman finished speaking and fixed the wizard with a level eye, trying to determine if the wizard had truly been listening.

"Legitimate concerns," Vangerdahast repeated the old noble's words gravely, nodding—and meant it.

Albaerin Dauntinghorn had a remarkable skill for seeing clearly through dishonesty, deliberately obtuse courtly phrases, and misleading impressions.

Unfortunately, that's precisely what the Royal Magician of Cormyr did not need right now. He was going to have a lot of hasty and hardy work ahead of him as it was to keep the court from becoming a graveyard of nobles wearing daggers in their ribs over the next tenday or so. The nascent factions seeking to remake Cormyr had their respective bits between their teeth and were starting to pull on the realm trapped between them. The image of Cormyr as the helpless victim being torn apart between four horses was all too painfully accurate just now.

Vangerdahast gave old Albaerin his best confident smile and told him, "You have my word that, if I am named regent, I will bring the matters you raise before the open court and see that they're dealt with directly, rather than festering unattended through the months ahead."

They exchanged the curt nods of old, wise equals who dealt with each other in mutual respect, then parted. The court wizard turned along the Hall of Honor, where the names of common soldiers who had died valiantly in the service of the realm were graven on the stones of the wall, and headed for Gemstars Hall, where there were bound to be some nobles muttering together about the dark future of Cormyr. It was time to fill a few more gullible heads with promises of what could be theirs if a certain wizard were made regent.

He was halfway there when a page in the tabard of palace service hurried up to him, bowed, and said in a voice sharp with excitement, "Revered lord, Lord Aunadar Bleth would speak with you in the Flamedance Hall at your earliest convenience. He says the matter is of utmost urgency to the security of the realm."

"Of course it is," Vangerdahast said, almost soothingly, and added, inclining his head in dismissal, "My thanks. I shall attend Lord Bleth directly. If you have been charged to bring him a reply, you may inform him so. If not, spare yourself the run; I shall not keep him waiting long."

The page bowed and ran off toward the palace. Of course, thought Vangerdahast, and looked up and down the Hall of Honor to see if he was being observed. The page dwindled into the distance and turned down the east stair; there was no one else in sight. The wizard nodded in satisfaction, laid his hand on a particular inscription on the wall, and spoke a certain word. The block seemed unchanged, but his fingers sank into it as if it no longer existed. He reached in, plucked a certain ring, a pendant, and an armlet from the small cloth bag that he knew would be there, and drew them forth, speaking another word that made the stone solid again.

Donning the three items, he resumed his walk, heading not for Gemstars Hall any longer but for the palace and the soaring hearths of Flamedance Hall. The flames would be illusory during weather this warm, but their endless leapings were fascinating to watch nonetheless. It would be best to get this over with, now that he was protected against poisons, normal missiles, steel weapons of all sorts, and the effects of hostile gases. It would be most indecently hasty to try to strike down the Royal Magician of all Cormyr, leaving the land mageless once more, but then, these ambitious young nobles seemed to care not a whit for the safety of the realm nor for rules, courtesies, and conventions. Truly a wonderful future lay ahead for the kingdom.

Two belarjacks nodded to him respectfully at the threshold of Flamedance Hall and drew the doors wide. The old wizard strode in calmly to find only one figure waiting for him, with a decanter and two glasses. Vangerdahast smiled slightly as he heard the doors close softly behind him, and walked steadily forward.

"So this day finds you desirous of converse with the wise old mage of Cormyr, does it?" he asked cheerfully. "Well, then, speak! I bring both time and interest to hear you out."

Those piercing brown eyes locked with his, and the thin lips beneath the thinner mustache twisted slightly. "That is convenient, lord wizard, for I find I have matters of crucial import to the future of the realm to discuss with you."

Vangerdahast stopped a few paces away from the young noble and raised both of his bushy brows. "How so? A man who's spent so much of his time in recent years hunting boar and deer carries matters of crucial import about with him—and undiscussed?"

Aunadar poured himself a glass from the decanter, amber and sparkling—old, fine flamekiss, by the looks of it—and said almost wearily, "Whatever you may think of me, Lord Vangerdahast, I am no longer a boy but a man—moreover, one affianced to the future Queen of Cormyr. I have the ear of the crown princess and eyes

391

quite able to see the future ahead of us all. Pray do me the courtesy of dispensing with the old-wise-one-patronizing-the-self-important-puppy act. It demeans you more than it does me."

"Speak, then," Vangerdahast said calmly, shaping something in the air behind him with one hand.

Aunadar laid a hand on the hilt of the court rapier he wore. "Casting spells when discussing affairs of state is a dangerously bold breach of courtesy," he said, gliding a step forward.

Vangerdahast finished his gesturing and sat down calmly on the empty air, as if reclining in a comfortable chair. He made a flippant gesture of dismissal with his fingertips and said, "Lad, casting spells is what wizards *do*. If you don't like being around castings, don't summon wizards into your presence as if they were your servants. And of the two of us here, I shall be the judge of what court courtesy is or may be. All these veiled threats and posturings demean *you* more than they do *me*, to borrow a much-overused phrase."

Aunadar's mouth tightened, but he let go of his sword. Facing the wizard, he struck a pose—probably unconsciously, the wizard judged; these well-muscled noble sons with their sleek good looks started doing such things the moment they noticed that the world held women—and said, "I'd like to dispense with all the fencing between us for an hour or so."

Vangerdahast raised an eyebrow and gestured at him to continue at his pleasure; the wizard would attend to his words. Aunadar raised a matching brow of his own, drew a deep breath, and said, "We are prepared to accept you as regent of the realm if—and only if—you agree to certain conditions."

" 'We'? Are you speaking for the princess? Surely not, without her writ or herald! Or are you speaking for your father and your older brothers, Faern and Dlothtar? Or the entire House of Bleth?"

Aunadar's mouth tightened again. "I speak for myself and for the nobles, both within my family and without, who stand with me on this point. Rest assured that I can muster to support me more nobles of Cormyr than any other person in the realm, including, my lord, yourself. Do you want to hear my conditions, or shall I inform them that you are a mad old tyrant best removed from Faerûn forever?"

Vangerdahast smiled. The youth spoke of "my" conditions, not "our" conditions, and failed to notice the slip. The wizard nodded. "I do indeed wish to hear them. Perhaps we *can* deal together for the continued good governance of the realm."

* * * * *

"Brantarra? We're here!"

The small disturbance of whirling lights and roilings of the air in front of the young noble promptly grew two burning eyes, then sighed. They were within the palace itself, in one of the innumerable hiding holes and hidden passages. This one had seen only a few booted feet disturb the dust.

The spectral appearance sighed again, a soft, feminine sigh. It seemed to say, Were *all* the nobles of Cormyr as excited as young boys, creeping around and whispering? Was this all she had to work with?

"That is good," the burning eyes said instead. At the sound of her voice, the five men in their gaudy court dress tensed, drawn swords glittering in their hands. All gulped and drew in breaths.

The woman who was using the name Brantarra went on. "Are you ready to forge a glorious future for Cormyr and for yourselves?"

The boldest of the nobles—Ensrin Emmarask, the one she'd first contacted—took a nervous step nearer her mystic portal and stammered, "Y-Yes, lady, we are."

"Then hold out your cloak under my eyes—well below them!"

Tentatively Ensrin did as he was bade, and the whirling lights so close above him spat out something.

393

Ed Greenwood and Jeff Grubb

He flinched but managed to catch it in his cloak. It rolled over once, twice, and stopped: a ruby as large as his thumb. The radiance pulsed again, and another stone joined the first. Three more joined it before the voice said, "One for each of you, to start with. Earn them now."

"How, Lady Brantarra?"

"Go to the shrines just established in the palace, where Crown Princess Tanalasta worships. She will be on her way there shortly to kneel in prayer. Slay her."

Someone gasped, and someone else swallowed noisily. The room was suddenly full of nervous shiftings and the flashings of moving blades.

Ensrin then did the bravest thing he'd every essayed in his young life. "Kill the crown princess?" he asked.

"Yes—and bring away her head with you, to hide in the place where first we met. Strike now; the princess must die this morn. It's best if your attack comes at the altar of Tymora, when the princess is kneeling, far from guards or alarm gongs. Only one priestess should be in attendance. If you tarry, be warned that the chamber consecrated to Tyr is staffed by several heavily armed Warpriests of Justice."

Ensrin swallowed, raised his blade in salute, and quivered in excitement. "Lady, it shall be done!"

"Aye," the others echoed in a ragged chorus. The eyes of fire looked around at them all, and the voice of Brantarra said, "Good. Do this, and the wealth I promised is yours. You'll never have to lift swords—or anything else—again. Go!"

Ensrin nodded sharply and drew a black silken mask from a belt pouch. As he drew it on, the others followed suit, and the little sphere of whirling lights sighed again and faded away.

Five masked men boiled out of the room and hurried along darkened back passageways of the palace. It was too bad for the lone Purple Dragon who happened to round a corner in front of them. Swords plunged into his face and throat without hesitation, and he fell against the wall and then slid to the floor without making more noise than a gurgle. Dealing death, it seemed, was very easy.

Back in the hidden room, the last motes of Brantarra's light finally faded away, and something promptly moved atop an armoire in the corner. A moment later, a woman in dark mottled leathers, who wore a locket on a ribbon around her throat, dropped lightly to the ground and hurried to the door. The nightmare—young nobles rushing around the palace with blades ready in their hands and the will to use them—was beginning at last.

Emthrara raced down the corridor, drawing her own blade as she ran. If the gods smiled for once, perhaps she'd not be too late.

At the first corner, the fallen form of a Purple Dragon lay sprawled. A hulking form, his back to Emthrara, rose up from the body, the spilled blood spreading around the man's feet in gleaming ribbons. The Harper rushed toward the man, raising her blade for a thrust that would slay him before he had time to react.

She was delivering that deadly thrust when the man looked straight up at her. Emthrara shouted as she saw his face, her sword in midswing.

He ducked, but it was too late. She half checked her swing, and instead of biting into flesh managed to strike the hallway corner. Her sword left a pale chalky streak where it clanged against the metal.

"Rhauligan!" she shouted. "You didn't—"

"Of course I didn't," said the turret merchant, looking down at the fallen Purple Dragon. "Whoever did passed this way recently. The body is still warm, and no one else has found it yet."

"Then who did this?" asked the Harper.

"And more importantly, where are they now?" said the merchant, pulling from his belt a long, wickedly curved knife. "What say we find out?"

* * * * *

Aunadar smiled silkily. "Hear me, then, wizard: I, the nobles who stand with me, *and* my lady, the princess,

will accept you as royal regent of the realm for a brief
period of clearly proclaimed duration, during which you
will involve the princess constantly in all of your decisions so that she can learn how you govern the kingdom.
We will not accept any regency of more than five winters
in length. Have we any dispute on this?"

The Royal Magician shook his head in agreement.
"Your words thus far simply define what a regency is, a
definition I have no quarrel with." He smiled thinly. "So
I'm sure there are more conditions."

"Just one," Aunadar said coolly. "One that a mage who
likes authority so little and counsel so much should have
no difficulty at all in accepting: a regent's council of a
dozen or so nobles who have the right to overturn or stay
your decisions by a two-thirds majority vote."

"And who will choose these nobles? And how will they
be unchosen?" the wizard asked.

Aunadar frowned. "Unchosen?"

"If council members do not serve for finite periods and
then leave office, you do not have a council," Vangerdahast said pointedly, "but a dozen or so petty kings. A
realm under such chaos would be ungovernable and is
something I'll never agree to."

"Your alternative?"

"A two-year term for each councillor, followed by two
years in which the same woman or man could not serve.
Every two years each councillor can nominate one candidate for the council, each local lord of the realm can nominate one candidate, I nominate one, the Lord Sages
Alaphondar and Dimswart each nominate one, and each
living member of the immediate Obarskyr family who is
able, or of age, to speak for herself can nominate one candidate each. A simple majority—not a two-thirds count—
will serve to appoint a candidate to the council."

Aunadar's eyes narrowed. "What if we vote in more
than a dozen councillors?"

"Then the council grows, at least temporarily."

"And if less than a dozen can be agreed upon?"

"Then I shall name one person to the council, the Marshal of the Realm or senior officer of the Purple Dragons will name one, the two sages will each name one, the Obarskyrs will each name one, and so on, until we have our dozen—or more. These namings would be binding appointments, not one-man, one-vote proposals, and the only beings in all Faerûn who could refuse them would be the named candidates themselves."

"While the council sits powerless? That's hardly fair."

"Ah, but knowing that such a fate awaits the realm, the council will have to agree on some candidates rather than simply refusing everyone proposed as their successors."

"And if they refuse?"

Vangerdahast shrugged. "Then I ignore them, and their vetoes fail—as they will in any case whenever I resign my regency and an Obarskyr takes the throne."

"Need our ruler be an Obarskyr?"

The wizard shrugged. "If you want to remain in the Forest Country, technically the answer must be yes. The original elves who kept this land and entrusted it to the Obarskyrs might take a dim view of other hands being found at the helm."

Aunadar sneered. "Spare me the fairy tales, mage! Keep to the serious! Are you telling me that after all these years, the elves would return and press a claim against a land we've ruled for thirteen centuries?"

Vangerdahast did not answer, but instead let the question hang in the air for a long moment. The point had been made. Aunadar did not know if the old wizard was telling the truth. Indeed, there was much the young Bleth did not know.

The noble looked deeply into the hearth, then turned with the agile grace already displayed on many a dance floor. "Let us agree—for the moment, as an abstract point of debate—that we accept your view of council servitude and powers and your contention that one of Obarskyr blood must lead us." He smiled softly and turned to fix the mage with a steady, searching gaze. "Tell me, then, is one born directly from the seed of an

397

Obarskyr king not of Obarskyr blood?"

"You speak in this case of the many King Azoun has fathered, or is rumored to have fathered," Vangerdahast said calmly. "Yes, they are of Obarskyr blood and stand in precedence ranked by senior birthdate, *behind* all of the pure House of Obarskyr. If I, the sages, the wizardess Laspeera, and the major priests of the realm agreed to by us and the High Heralds we shall call in—if such a determination ever becomes necessary, and not before then—can all agree on the lineage of each bastard candidate. We alone shall investigate such claims, not a whispering cabal of nobles, and I warn you, young Lord Bleth, that if we are ever forced to mount such an indelicate investigation, we shall thoroughly delve into, bring to light, and proclaim throughout the realm every illicit birth connected to every noble house in the land." The Royal Magician smiled faintly. "Nary an escutcheon shall remain unblotted, to quote the old saying."

Aunadar made a gesture of uncaring dismissal. "Fair enough. Who, in your view, is to name our first council?"

Vangerdahast replied promptly. "I could ask nobles to nominate themselves and put them to a test. Those who pass are councillors; those who fail will be dead."

"A test," Aunadar said darkly. "A dangerous quest, no doubt? Or face-to-face personal spell duels with you?"

"Both of those seem excellent proposals," the wizard agreed brightly. "Which do you prefer?"

"Stop playing with me, mage!" Aunadar snapped. "So, say we agree to your vote of heralds, and the council forms, and they vote you down on something—what then?"

"I accede to their wishes," Vangerdahast replied, "but continue to formulate policy for the realm. They are to act as reins on me and the princess under my tutelage, not as commanders over us. Moreover, voting us down does not make her an un-princess or oust me from my office as Royal Magician of the Realm."

Aunadar nodded slowly, stroking his chin. "I can see us coming to an agreement on this," he said slowly. "Tell me, what do you really think of such a council?"

"A good notion," the wizard said. "It's high time some of our nobles saw the decisions a ruler faces clearly, rather than through the bellyaching, self-serving blinkers most of them habitually wear."

"*What?*"

The wizard held up a hand. "Don't roar at me, young Bleth. You wanted plain speech, remember?" He waggled a finger. "Besides, I need to know *your* answer to a question."

"And that question is?" Aunadar Bleth snapped, still visibly angry.

"Our council and regency are installed, and both run more or less smoothly—let us say." The wizard leaned forward to fix Bleth with a searching gaze. "What happens if, after five years, Tanalasta is no more capable of taking up the reigns of power than she is now?"

"And who would judge such a thing?" Aunadar replied softly. "We both know that she'd never measure up—in *your* eyes—to what a monarch of Cormyr has to be."

"It's nice to know that you already know what we'll both think five winters hence," Vangerdahast said dryly. "No wonder every last noble in the realm thinks he knows exactly how to govern Cormyr."

Aunadar Bleth sighed and set down his glass. "You can never stop teaching the fools that the gods set all around you, can you?"

The wizard almost smiled. "It's one way to spend a life," he said mildly.

The young noble shook his head, sighed, and then said briskly, "In answer to your question, the council would see to it that the crown princess ascended the throne in any event, proclaiming the situation throughout the realm. I doubt even a Lord High Wizard could last long if every last hand in the kingdom was raised against him. No matter where you slept, there'd always be a forester or farmer or goodwife, skillet or something in hand, to smite you down."

Vangerdahast raised his brows but said nothing.

The young noble smiled triumphantly and added, "One more thing. I know that one of the Obarskyr family treasures is an item that protects the mind of its wearer from sorcerous influences. I want Tanalasta to wear that item, and I want it examined by a neutral wizard—one not from this realm—to be sure that it hasn't been tampered with. I want him to ascertain and tell all of the council the precise limitations of its powers, and I want enchantments that duplicate those powers placed upon items worn by all members of the council, including myself. I'm afraid that, as one of those arrogant young nobles you speak of, I can't find myself ever linking the word 'trust' and the word 'wizard.'" He gave Vangerdahast a saccharine smile and picked up the empty glass. "Something to drink?"

The wizard shook his head. "Everyone seems to be buying his poisons from Westgate these days, and they always make things too salty so they can water down the stuff, because folk are driven to drink more of it."

Aunadar's lips tightened. "I don't like your inference, mage."

"Whether you like or dislike what I do or say is immaterial, noble," Vangerdahast replied easily. "I am trying to govern a realm, not win fawning popularity contests among young noble boys."

"Yes," Aunadar said softly, "that's precisely what you're trying to do—govern a realm. And for the good of our realm, I am going to stop you. Wizards have twisted the lives of all in Cormyr long enough."

"Ah, that grandest of phrases: 'For the good of the realm.' It can cover everything from outright murder to poisonings, smashing down buildings, setting the country to war, or starting plagues—and has." The wizard's tone was biting. "When someone says he's acting for the good of the realm, it labels him either a self-righteous fool or a self-righteous villain. Which are you?"

Aunadar's nostrils tightened, and he strode forward. "I trust the lore you were taught was specific on the subject of the last regency, wherein the faithful regent refused to give up power after his time had passed."

"Oh, yes," the mage replied softly. "My tutelage on that was thorough. I remember the tales of the last regency very well."

Aunadar stepped back a pace, face paling—and in his hiding place behind the hearth-surround peepholes, Dauneth Marliir shuddered for the same reason: the ice in the old mage's voice.

28

Dragons, Red and Purple
Year of the Rock
(1286 DR)

ing Salember stalked the halls of Castle
Obarskyr, bellowing for the courtiers, for his
guards, for the servants. None answered his
summons, and no one knelt, awaiting orders, at
any corner he turned. His footfalls rang heavily through
the stone halls and echoed in the distance.

The guards were gone from his doors, the servants
from their hiding holes, the fawning courtiers from their
appointed places. Where were the scribes, the healers,
the pages? Where was his court?

They could not all have left him, he thought. Defections had been rife, true, but he'd kept the rest of the
rabble in line. And they could still win. He had led the
country for nine years and led it well. "Cormyr stands
strong!" he bellowed, just as he had done in so many
speeches before. The echo came back to him mockingly.
Couldn't the people *see* that things were better now
under his regency? Had been better, at least, until the
upstart prince started making trouble.

Everything had been knocked askew by this upstart
prince. Work was undone, crops unharvested, deals unmade. Even the castle itself was filled with projects half

accomplished before the servants fled. Tapestries were half hung, shields of treacherous houses pulled from the wall but left lying when they fell. Salember passed the Blue Maiden, a favorite statue, resting beside its plinth, waiting for the workers to lift her up to the pedestal. Salember cursed at the sloppiness of the staff, along with their weak loyalties.

Salember paused by one of the great gallery windows overlooking the city. The sun was westering, and most of Suzail lay at his feet, already cloaked in the deep shadows of early evening. There were fires in the city tonight, fires unnecessary for so close to Midsummer Eve. They marked the sites of battles between his faction and that of Rhigaerd, between the Reds and the Purples, between those who served the rightful ruler and those who followed a pretender to the throne. The flames of burning buildings made him think of red dragons against the shadowed city, but the spiraling smoke reminded him of purple dragons in the dying sun.

Out there in the city and in the countryside beyond the walls, the factions were sparring and battling. In the streets of Arabel and swampy Marsember, in forested Dhedluk and mountainous High Horn, the country was riven. The Purple Dragons were torn apart, with units and mages taking opposite sides. The Battle Brotherhood had been shattered into a hundred individual mages, all of whom had headed for their towers and lairs. Even the churches—the Helmites, the Lathanderites, the Mystrans—were riven by the choice.

And all because some folk would fling aside a capable sitting regent for the unproven whelp of the previous king.

Nine years ago Salember's brother, Azoun III of the Forest Country, had died, leaving behind a son too young to rule a nursery chamber, let alone a kingdom. Jorunhast came to Salember then with the offer of a regency—a temporary rule until Crown Prince Rhigaerd was of age. Salember stepped up to the Dragon Throne, a position he'd never sought.

And he'd served for nine years, and served well. People were living better, imports were up, and the depredations of orcs, goblins, brigands, and dragons sharply on the downswing. So after nine years, it made perfect sense to keep the same steady hand at the helm.

But, no; the traditionalists, the monarchists, the mired-in-rules old thinkers resisted. Rhigaerd demanded the crown, then fled into the wilderness to marshal his own forces. He took the banner of the Purple Dragons with him. Salember flew the Red Dragon, a color of battle and blood, over the castle.

Salember removed his heavy crown and set it on the sill of the gallery window. He'd taken Palaghard's crown from a century ago as his own, and the ornate, gem-encrusted helm weighed heavily.

He sighed. When the Purples were crushed, then perhaps the old crown would be fetched from the vaults. Yes, when the rebel Purples were crushed and Rhigaerd routed from whatever burrow he'd squirreled himself away in. When Rhigaerd's Purples were finally destroyed, everything would fall back into place. And at last affairs in Cormyr would get back to normal, and he could forge ahead to make the land ever mightier. "Cormyr stands strong," he muttered, bringing his fist down on the sill slowly and gently. Like a storm giant, he must be careful, he thought, lest his great strength break things around him that he held dear.

A distant sound came down the hall, a single, short slam or thump, booming along the bare walls.

The Red Dragon King turned and shouted, "Jorunhast? Is that you?"

The Blue Maiden looked up at him, calm and unchanging, from the floor beside the plinth he'd ordered her placed upon—how long ago had it been? A tenday, now? A life-sized, sculpted maiden of smooth blue glass, sitting gazing up at the dragon coming to devour her, the sages said. Her hands were too large, and her feet, too, some folk said, but Salember liked her strength, her courage to sit naked but for a cloak held against her, awaiting doom. That was the sort of spirit more folk in Cormyr should show. Besides, the sages said the maiden was linked to the good fortune of House Obarskyr and should never be smashed, disgraced, or lost. He'd have to give that order again and get her up on the plinth where she belonged without further delay. If he could only get the damned servants to answer his call. . . .

"Jorunhast?"

The wizard would still be there. He was tethered to the crown like a mongrel dog, as all the Royal Magicians, Crown Wizards, and Lords of Magic of the past had been.

Yes! He, Salember, had found that in Baerauble's original books: The wizards were magically bound to protect the crown. Others had forgotten that, but not wise old Salember. Whatever else happened, the Royal Magician would be loyal.

But Salember's voice echoed down the halls to no response.

Cowards, thought Salember. No fire in the belly, no passion in the heart for a good fight. All the Daunting-horns and Marliirs and Wyvernspurs, retiring to their country holdings to wait out the storm. Truesilvers, Crownsilvers, and Huntsilvers! They were cousins to both him and Rhigaerd, yet they mumbled their loyal oaths and equivocated and minced when pressed for troops and aid!

Salember held the high ground, the crown and the throne and the castle, and so the nobles remained loyal at first. Then slowly they started to drift away. Not to Rhigaerd, of course . . . never to Rhigaerd. They valued their own hides too much. A few traitors had died horribly, as examples. Salember had used his gold well, and the Fire Knives were very effective at creating examples.

And yet the cowardly nobles went on drifting away. They swore their fealty and tugged their forelocks, and then hied for the countryside, taking their students, scribes, and servants with them. What kind of kingdom could shine with such weasels, such men of straw, as its backbone?

Salember shouted again, an incoherent bellow. There came the clear sound of a door closing and latching somewhere in the distance.

A servant seeking to hide from his sire's wrath? Or had Jorunhast finally returned? You'd think with all the magic at his fingertips, the old mage could find the errant prince with the simplest of divinations. But instead, the old wizard was continually abroad, overseeing this outpost or tracking down that lead or reporting on such-and-such a battle.

Salember padded down the hall and slowly made his way down the stone spiral staircase to the main floor. His tired footsteps echoed ahead of him. To the right was the throne room, the Hall of the Dragon Throne. Probably some loyal courtiers and captains were already gathered there, waiting to be reassured by their liege that all was proceeding smoothly, that the rebels were on the run. To the left were the four chambers of the Great Swords.

Salember turned left. The captains and courtiers could wait.

The king was sure that Jorunhast or one of his predecessors had ensorcelled this part of the castle, making the air heavy and muffling all sound. Even when the castle was bustling and vibrant, it had a tranquil, hushed nature to it, like the nave of a great temple to Helm or Tempus. Visitors once streamed here to see the Great Swords, but there were no visitors today . . . nor had there been on any day for weeks past. There were no visible guards, either.

Here, on velvet plinths, rested the four great blades of Cormyr. Ansrivarr, the Blade of Memory, was the first, a large, crude sword that hearkened back to the days of wilderness and elves. Symylazarr, the Font of Honor, upon which the treacherous nobles had sworn fealty, was as broad as the Blade of Memory and etched along its blade with archaic runes. Orblyn, King Duar's mage-forged sword, with which he rallied the kingdom during the Pirate Exile, was a thinner, more modern blade. And Rissar, the Wedding Blade, small and delicate and finely shaped, was used for marriage vows and blood promises. So much like Cormyr today—ornate, gaudy, and ineffective in a real fight.

Salember lifted the crystal dome and removed Orblyn from its cradle. Somewhere in the far distance a single gong rang, but there came no scurrying of booted and mailed feet, no hue and cry of guards, no panic among the Battle Brotherhood's wizards, and no manifestation of guardian creatures.

Orblyn was covered with fine runes lightly etched into the blade. Salember had to hold the blade up to the light to see them clearly. The magical inscriptions seemed to twist and writhe as he watched. After all these years, Orblyn had held its edge and its sharpness.

Salember slid the unsheathed blade into his belt. Yes, now was the time for true battle. King Salember had the crown, the throne, the castle, and the blades. He had the loyalty of the remaining troops and the support of the people bought by nine years of peace and prosperity. He cared little for the false friendship of the nobles. Once the Purples were crushed utterly, those nobles who survived would come crawling back for his approval and forgiveness. Some he would spare. Others he would make examples of.

Now to the Hall of the Dragon Throne. Now to rally the troops and impress the remaining nobles. Now to ride to destiny and strike at his foes in their lairs. Even before the rebellion, Salember had remained too long in the castle, overseeing accounts and treaties and forecasts. And for too long after Rhigaerd declared his revolt had he stayed within, protected by stout walls and powerful magic. Now was the time for the Red Dragon to be unleashed on the countryside itself, he thought, and he smiled at the prospect.

No guards flanked the doors of the throne room, just as no guards had protected the chambers of the Great Swords. Had they all finally fled, or were they in the city, battling fires and treacherous Purples? The doors stood open.

The throne room was one of the oldest parts of the castle, the heart of the Obarskyr family's lair for over a millennium. To one side stood the great sealed stone tomb of Baerauble himself, its surface worn smooth by the touch of a million hands over the ageless years. To the other side was the low rise of steps that led to the throne itself. Sometimes there were two chairs on its highest step, for king and queen. At the moment there was but one.

There were three figures standing just shy of the top level, a woman and two men. As he stepped into the room, Salember wondered if they were real or merely some magical vision.

Jorunhast was there, of course. Where else would the Royal Magician be save here, protecting the crown? Yet Rhigaerd, the treacherous pup, was also here, dressed in the white and purple of his rebellious band. And Damia Truesilver, most cowardly of the cowardly nobles, Rhigaerd's confidante. The woman's belly was swollen with child, and Salember remembered Lord Truesilver himself begetting her with another whelp ere he died in battle.

Had Jorunhast brought the conspirators here for sentencing and punishment? He should have teleported them directly to the deepest dungeon instead.

The wizard looked haggard and worn, as if he had spent the last three nights sleeping in roadside hedges. His shoulders were slumped with age and care. The battles had taken their toll on him as well. "You are here at last," he said. "We must end this, and end it now."

The old wizard stepped down from the dais and positioned himself to one side, between the king and the rebellious prince. The wizard wanted a parley, then. For all the good that would do.

"Greetings, Uncle," said Rhigaerd, his young face struggling to look somber and serious.

"And to you, Nephew," said the king. "You have come to your father's house to surrender yourselves and end this bloody folly?"

"I have come to my father's house, yes," said the Prince, "and I seek to end this folly. But I am not here to surrender, but to talk."

Jorunhast put in, "I convinced Rhigaerd to seek peace with you. We have come from a bloody battle near Wheloon, where the Red and Purple factions beat each other to corpses thick upon the ground . . . to no resolution."

"If we continue this bloodshed, there will soon be no Cormyr to rule," Rhigaerd added. "Already the Sembians are making restless noises about protecting trade. And agents of the Black Network and the Thayvian wizards cross our borders freely. This must end."

"Agreed," Salember replied coolly. "I am willing to accept your surrender. Your men will be spared. You, of course, will have to accept exile in Waterdeep or the Dalelands."

The young prince's face reddened, and he sputtered a curse. Behind him, Damia placed a gentle hand on his shoulder, and he collected himself. "Surrender my throne?" he said at last.

"*Your* throne?" mocked Salember. "Nay, may I remind you who has guided this country through nine years of peace? Who has sacrificed his own life for the good of the nation? Who has spent all his waking hours of time and energy living up to the Obarskyr name? The same hours of your youth that were spent hunting, adventuring, and gallivanting about, while I have done the real work. Do you think I'd entrust this great realm to an untried child?"

Salember's face had turned beet-red by now, and the king felt the fire of renewed energy rising up within him. No pup of an upstart was going to waltz in and steal the crown from him without a fight!

Rhigaerd said, "The Obarskyr line has always passed to the oldest suitable direct male candidate. There have been exceptions, and Obarskyr queens have ruled when no male has been available. For nine years, there has been no child of Azoun the Third suitable. Now there is."

"And now you expect to gain a full kingdom as if it

were a present for your seventeenth birthday?" snarled Salember.

Rhigaerd's face reddened again, but he held his voice calm. "While you were secure here in the castle with your account books and courtiers and your petty intrigues, I was out in the land itself. You call it gallivanting, but I see it as learning about my country. I have hunted in the King's Forest and drunk deep with the soldiers of High Horn. I have dug the good ground with farmers, spoken with smugglers, fought brigands and goblins, learned language from wandering elves, and my accounts from visiting Sembians."

"A well-spent youth," snapped the king.

"I know my people and my land. I am ready to take on my father's burden," finished the young prince. "I do not want to fight you for it, but fight I have, and will. Do not, I entreat you, divide our people more than they already have been."

"A pretty speech," Salember spat. "Did Lady Damia help you? No, young nephew, you have insufficient knowledge of court politics. The courtiers would eat you alive."

"From the looks of things, it is the courtiers who were eaten alive in this castle," Rhigaerd drawled. "Or fled to our camps, or hid themselves until we two could come to agreement."

Lady Damia put in, "We thought, Lord Salember, of recognizing your wisdom with a continued advisory role for you, perhaps a barony or dukedom of the kingdom."

"I should surrender the crown to a child for a handful of crumbs and a smattering of titles?" Salember snarled, the fire coiling like a serpent in his belly.

"I admit your experience would be invaluable in—" Rhigaerd began.

Salember cut him off. "In cleaning up after your mistakes, Nephew? In supporting you as king? In doing all the work and gaining none of the credit?"

"It does not have to be immediate, Uncle," said Rhigaerd calmly. "Three more years of regency, then a smooth changeover."

"No!" Salember shouted. "You will get the crown only when I have no earthly need for it! Surrender to me here and now, young prince. If you truly love this country as you profess, *prove it!*"

Rhigaerd's eyes blazed with anger. "I do love the Forest Kingdom," he said, voice rising, "and honor my ancestors. Yet, Uncle, you *must* step down. Can't you hear the sounds of men dying? The sounds of the realm ripping itself apart? We cannot survive with two kings, one rightful and one temporary."

"Agreed!" shouted Salember and turned to Jorunhast. "Kill them, wizard!"

Silence wrapped the four of them like a cloak, the echoes of Salember's orders rebounding from the walls like ripples of water.

Jorunhast looked at the king stonily. "Excuse me?"

"Kill them!" bellowed the king. "Kill them now! This is our best chance to end all of this destructive nonsense—now!"

"Prince Rhigaerd came here on my assurance of personal safety, Sire," the mage said calmly. Rhigaerd moved to stand in front of Lady Damia, and his hand drifted to the hilt of his peace-bonded blade.

Salember's eyes burned with fury, and his own hand now rested on Orblyn. "I am your king, and I demand your obedience! Kill the pair of them! A snake without its head cannot long survive!"

Jorunhast looked at the young noble and pregnant noblewoman on the dais, then back at the king. Salember's face was a mask of rage now, spittle flying as he shouted.

Jorunhast looked at his king and said simply, "No."

Salember's face was as crimson as a red dragon's now, the fire surging through him. "I found Baerauble's records, mage! The elves have forced your kind to serve the crown. You *must* follow my orders! You must deal with the threat to the crown! Kill them!"

Jorunhast blinked at the raging king and said quietly, "Sainted Baerauble was forced to serve the crown, yes.

Amedahast, Thanderahast, and I—we served through choice and through loyalty. Loyalty to the crown, but also to the king and the people and the country itself. Let it end here, Sire. Even Iltharl the Insufficient knew when to step aside. . . ."

Salember was no longer listening, for the fire pounded in his temples and his ears, and in his heart something snapped loose from its moorings and catapulted him to action.

With an incoherent scream the Red Dragon King pulled the blade of King Duar from his belt and charged the pair on the dais.

Jorunhast stepped forward as the king charged and whipped out a massive hand, grabbing Salember's face with widely splayed fingers. The mage barked a few ancient words, and a tomblike carrion smell swirled through the chamber. He let go of his king.

Salember stumbled forward a half-step and fell to the floor, Orblyn skittering away on the flagstones in one direction, Palaghard's gaudy crown in the other. The carrion stench returned again, and this time Salember's tattered scream was borne on the whispering wind.

Rhigaerd bolted down the dais stairs and knelt by the king's body. "He's dead."

"Aye," said Jorunhast softly. "I had to deal with the threat to the crown." The mage held his arms before him, hands interlocked in the opposing sleeves, as if hesitant to show the deadly weapons again.

"The king is dead," said Damia Truesilver.

Jorunhast nodded and pulled from his robes the crown, the original elven crown of Cormyr, slender with its three amethyst-studded spires. He handed it to Lady Damia. The young prince knelt, and the noblewoman placed the circlet on his brow.

"Long live the king," said Damia, "Arise, King Rhigaerd the Second of Cormyr. Would that your coronation had been a celebration, but your kingdom has need of you."

Rhigaerd stood again, and Jorunhast saw that his eyes were wet.

The young king's voice was firm, however. "You have my thanks, wizard."

"I had to deal with the threat to the crown," repeated Jorunhast sadly. "I am sorry there was no other way. He was my friend as well as yours."

"Let him be remembered in his strength, not in his madness," said Damia, as if finishing a litany.

"Yet you have killed a king," said Rhigaerd solemnly, "and for that, the sentence is death. I hereby commute that sentence to eternal exile. You will leave Suzail, wizard, and never return to it again."

Jorunhast opened his mouth, then shut it again and nodded.

"None will trust a kingslayer, regardless of his motives," said Rhigaerd, "and none will believe me to be truly a ruler if I keep Salember's chief plotter as my own."

Jorunhast nodded again and said, in tones almost of relief, "As you wish, Sire. I follow your orders out of my loyalty to the crown. I will gather some things and then be gone." The mage retreated to the door of the great throne room.

"Hold one moment, wizard," said Rhigaerd, and the mage paused by the doorway.

"Sire?"

"Cormyr has always had a wizard, but now will not," said Rhigaerd carefully. "In your exile, find and train the best young mage you can find. When I marry and produce an heir, I will send word far and wide, to where you cannot help but hear—and I bid you then send your pupil to become my son's tutor. Cormyr can survive without its wizard, but not for long. In this, I command you."

Jorunhast bowed deeply. "As you wish, my liege."

"And thank you," Rhigaerd added softly. "Thank you for the crimes you committed in the name of the crown."

Jorunhast's eyes were as wet as those of the new king.

"I do my duty out of loyalty and love," he said roughly, "and I will teach my pupil to do the same."

And though no one saw him leave, Jorunhast was never seen in Suzail again.

29

Treachery
Year of the Gauntlet
(1369 DR)

Lady of Fortunes and Mysteries," the priestess said reverently, "hear us." Striking the silver gong just inside the door, she threw off her sea-blue cope to reveal vestments of shining silver, took three slow, measured paces forward, and knelt. She touched the silver disk at her throat, the symbol of her goddess. "Tymora, hear us."

Behind her came the soft rustle of the crown princess removing her own overrobe and slippers. Gwennath remained on her knees until Tanalasta joined her, murmuring her own "Tymora, hear us."

Gwennath reached out as she did every morning to clasp the hand of the heir to the throne. Tanalasta's grasp was firm this time, yet thankful—not the trembling clinging it had been on earlier days. Such a contact was not actually part of established ritual, but the crown princess need not know that. Gwennath had thought she needed it that first day when a pale and visibly grieving princess had come to the clergy of the goddess and almost pleaded for the consecration of a temporary shrine, so that she might have swift access to divine guidance whenever she felt need of it. High Priest Manarech had agreed without hesitation, with an eye to the future favor of the Dragon Throne, but Gwennath knew, and had a shrewd suspicion that Tanalasta did, too, that the old patriarch had no intention of any shrine to the goddess being temporary.

No matter. The silver disks, symbols of the goddess Tymora, were hung along the walls and the site consecrated. The crown princess of the realm got on her knees to Tymora every morning and evening, and the clergy of fair fortune were well content, even with the establishment of a companion shrine of Tyr, the Lord of Justice, barely a room away. However devout Tanalasta really was, she did seem to find comfort in the prayers, she was obviously seeking guidance, and her visits to the little room with the altar did give her some peaceful time alone every day—time without Vangerdahast glowering at her or young Bleth murmuring in her ear.

Tanalasta cast a sidelong glance at Gwennath, and the priestess gave her a quick smile before she broke their handclasp and rose to begin the supplication. If the goddess granted it, she might come to know this one as a true friend in times to come.

"Lady of Favor," she began, seeking that wholehearted nearness to Tymora that devotion required, "hear now the—"

There was a sound in the passage behind them, the quick and frantic sound of booted feet running—lots of them. Whatever could it be? Were these soldiers coming? Gwennath's heart sank. Had the king died?

Her duty was clear. The supplication must be seen through. She raised her arms to the altar and—

Tanalasta screamed.

Gwennath spun around in time to see the crown princess fleeing, wild-eyed, past her, trying to get around behind the altar. Trying to escape from the five masked men with glittering blades who were flooding into the chamber. Their eyes were on Tanalasta, and they held murder in them.

Nobles, to judge by their rich clothing, and coming

fast. They'd cut down a young priest at the doorway without even slowing, and Gwennath was unarmed.

"*Lammanath Tymora!*" Gwennath snarled, flinging up her arms. The foremost noble slashed viciously at her, and she ducked low, swayed away from his flashing blade, and then launched herself into him shoulder first. As the breath whooshed out of him and his feet left the floor, she got in one good punch, discovering with satisfaction that his codpiece was only soft gilded cloth. The man made a strangling sound as he and the priestess crashed to the floor together.

By then her spell had filled the room with whirling disks. Her desperate shout had snatched all of the platter-sized holy symbols of Tymora from their hooks on the walls and animated them to her will. She sent them slashing, edge on, against the rushing men. She was rewarded with shouts and startled curses.

"Princess!" she called, rolling away from the man she'd felled. "My mace lies beneath the altar! Defend yourself!"

One of the nobles barked out a contemptuous laugh and leapt past one of the discs, heading toward the priestess. Gwennath glared at him and brought a disk swooping down sharply from the air overhead. She'd only a few moments more before this magic ended. . . .

It was enough for this foe, at least. The disk sliced into his hair and the head beneath, and the man gasped, spat blood, and went to the floor, still wearing a goggle-eyed look of surprise and pain.

Another noble was rushing past toward the altar, and all of the disks were falling now, the power of the spell expired. Gwennath ran to intercept the man. The princess cowered low behind the holy table.

A dagger flashed end over end across the room and thunked into the back of the attacking noble's head. He staggered, wobbled—and the priestess was upon him, snatching the man's own dagger from his belt as she moved quickly inside his sword arm. Gwennath drove the hilt of the stolen dagger hard into its owner's temple and then shoved him against the wall. Turning to see

417

what new peril she might face, Gwennath found herself staring at the bloody point of a blade as it burst through the front of an elegant silk shirt.

Behind the dying noble, as he sagged, was a face she'd seen before: a woman with eyes like two merry flames and hair the hue of honey, who gave Gwennath a merry smile and said, "Catch!" as she tossed the noble's cosh into the air.

Gwennath gave Emthrara the Harper a smile in return, plucked the falling weapon out of the air, and spun around to see to the safety of the princess.

Tanalasta was dodging around the altar, dragging behind her a mace she obviously found too heavy to use, with a snarling noble in hot pursuit. Even as Gwennath cried out in alarm and raised her hand to hurl the dagger she still held, someone else—a merchant in battered boots, who was waving the longest knife she'd ever seen—vaulted the altar and crashed solidly into the noble. The knife flashed once as they went down together, and there was a short, wet gurgling sound from behind the holy table. She wasn't surprised to see that only one man rose again—and that it wasn't the one who wore the mask and fine clothes.

The last of the nobles—the one Gwennath had struck in a sensitive place—had risen behind the priestess, sword up and red rage for the Tymoran in his eyes. Gwennath did not see him, but Emthrara did. The lady Harper shouted a warning, but nothing was going to be able to stop that blade in time. . . .

And then Emthrara saw another figure rise up behind the noble, the altar stool raised in one trembling hand. White to the lips, Crown Princess Tanalasta of Cormyr brought her improvised weapon down with all her strength.

The noble's sword went one way and his head snapped to the other, blood spraying from the force of the blow. The impact left the noble's head no longer round, but it managed to make a rattling noise before plunging heavily to the floor with the noble's dead body.

The princess stared down at what she'd done, gasped, and promptly emptied her stomach in revulsion.

Her shoulders were still shaking as more armed men, priests of Tyr and Purple Dragons, all waving ready weapons and glaring around at the carnage, burst into the room.

"What happened?" one of the guards demanded and strode forward with one hand out to roughly grasp and spin about the sobbing woman in front of him.

He stopped abruptly when she turned of her own accord and he recognized her face. White it might be, and blue about the lips, but he could not mistake the face of the heir to the throne. The eyes in that famous face were wet with unshed tears.

"We—I was attacked by these . . . traitors," the princess, said, her breathing suddenly fast, "and all of these other folk slew them for me."

"Other folk, High Lady?"

Tanalasta glanced around. The merchant and the woman with the sword had vanished as suddenly as they had appeared; only the priestess of Tymora stood with her. The grim-looking priestess now stepped forward and said firmly, "Her Highness prevailed against these men, blade to blade and eye to eye. Let word of this travel throughout the realm, that justice and right have made the crown princess victorious in battle against five experienced fighting men . . . who also happened to be foolish nobles. They found the fate that awaits all traitors."

The eyes of the guards and priests looked at Gwennath and then turned back to the princess.

"What *really* befell here?" a grizzled Purple Dragon asked bluntly, rising from the blood-smeared flagstones where he'd been examining the man Emthrara had run through.

Tanalasta gave him a wintry glare. "It was *just* as the holy lady has said," she snapped, and she turned away to kneel before the altar. "Now, if you gentle sirs will clear away that carrion, my prayers are unfinished. . . ."

"Well said, Your Highness," Gwennath whispered as

she knelt beside the royal supplicant.

Tanalasta surveyed her with a sidelong glance and whispered back fiercely, "When I rise from here, I'm going to expect some answers! Go nowhere until I give you leave."

Gwennath smiled and bowed her head. "Of course," she murmured, and she lifted her voice to sing the first call to the Lady of Fortune.

* * * * *

The eyes behind the azure mask almost seemed to glow with interest. "And what else did Bleth propose?"

Dauneth Marliir shrugged. It had been a long, cramped day for him, skulking in this hiding place or that in the palace, and the mage seemed serenely unconcerned with the palpable villainy of the Royal Magician. "I've told you all," he said, a trifle sharply. "He made it clear he'd not accept an endless regency and warned Vangerdahast that he'd raise the whole country against the wizard if he tried any such thing." He frowned. "But you seem to be missing my point: The Lord High Wizard was agreeing to all this, it seemed, and fighting only over the details of how this council would operate! Both he and Bleth seem to think of the princess simply as a—a pawn, to sit on the throne and do as either a wizard regent or a council of nobles tells her to do! Vangerdahast *is* as cold-hearted as all these scheming nobles! He doesn't care about the Obarskyrs at all, any of them! He claims he serves the crown, but that seems to mean that he just wants the realm to stay stable while he goes on wielding the power he has now, no matter who is—in name—ruler of Cormyr!"

The woman in azure robes nodded almost absently. "Many have said such things, through the reigns of a host of Obarskyr monarchs and the service of more than one of the faithful mages this realm has been blessed with—and yet time and time again, the wizards have served Cormyr with staunch and shrewd deeds when it

420

was required. Vangerdahast seems quite capable of looking after himself *and* Cormyr for the time being. I'm more interested in what Aunadar Bleth said to Tanalasta—and his tone of voice and facial expressions as he uttered those words. Let's go over it again—slowly, and in as much detail as you can recall. Don't invent or embellish just to please me. I know that I'm asking for more than you can remember. Just give me all you can."

Dauneth did, and it took a long time. More than time enough for the young noble to begin to wonder just who this woman who hid herself behind an azure mask was, and what she was really hoping would happen in the days ahead. It was easy to claim that one loved Cormyr and was working in loyal service to, or in the best interests of, the realm, but who judged such things? And why wear a mask to do them?

That last question stayed with him, and he grew quiet enough that the mysterious lady in the blue mask told him to go to wherever his lodgings were and get some sleep for as long as his body needed. If he were reeling with weariness when something important did happen in the hours or days ahead, he'd hardly be able to do anything useful about it.

Dauneth nodded curtly, agreed, with every appearance of weariness, and took his leave. He was careful to stumble along the street in case she was watching. When he turned the corner, the scion of House Marliir promptly sprang onto a rain barrel, used it to reach a balcony, and from there took a perilous leap onto a roof by way of a carved gargoyle rainspout. She might leave by a spell or another of those mysterious tunnels that these northerly reaches of Suzail seemed to be positively riddled with, but . . . He shrugged. She might also simply walk out of the place. If he could only get to its roof so that he could watch both its front entry and the back way. . . .

Dauneth hurried and, just in time, fetched up at his destination in panting haste. She went out the back way, of course. He watched which way she was heading, keeping low and immobile until she was out of sight, and then moved. He was going to have to be very careful if he hoped to keep her in view and escape being spotted. Whoever this blue-masked mage was, she was certainly no fool.

He'd suspected all along that she was noble-born or connected with nobility or the court itself and that she'd get to the Promenade before long, and he was right. Crouched in the lee of a potted pricklethorn bush that was decorating the steps of some grand townhouse or other, Dauneth saw the lady in blue turn out of the side street he was watching and walk briskly along the Promenade toward Eastgate.

She wasn't going out of town. No, she'd turn off westward before the gate and head back into the Nobles' Quarter on the pleasant hedge-lined street that crossed Lake Azoun by that beautiful arched bridge . . . yes! There she was! Dauneth raced along the top of the ornamental wall that separated the holy ground of Deneir from the meadows of the rich merchants next door, down to the edge of the lake. He just had time to crouch down behind the last sculpted stone book, spread open forever on its wall-top pedestal, when she stopped on the bridge and looked back and down the lake, scanning the gardens . . . for him?

She looked down at the gentle waters for what seemed like an eternity to Dauneth but was probably only a short time, enjoying the evening stars swimming in Lake Azoun. Then she turned and went on down the far slope of the bridge, heading for—Dauneth squinted, and finally climbed right up onto the stone book to see properly—Wyvernspur House!

Yes, she was glancing up and down the street, up at the sky, and then . . . she went inside. Dauneth clambered hastily down from his perch and almost fell as a calm voice from just below him said, "Yes, a lot of folk seem to find that inscription particularly interesting."

He stared down into the kindly eyes of an old bald priest, who nodded a grave greeting, and said, "Personally, I think the next one over is more profound, but then, the variance of opinions is born of the strife between the gods that gives us all life and striving. What do you think?"

Dauneth Marliir looked desperately from book to book, seeing that both of them sported—amid spots of bird droppings—long and carefully carved inscriptions, half seen in the moonlight. He didn't have time for this. . . .

"I think," he said carefully, looking at the grass of the lawn outside the temple wall and glancing up that long sward, "that the future of the realm depends upon my acting now and thinking later!" And with that grand declaration, he hurled himself backward off the wall, hopefully out of reach of any spell that the priest might use against uninvited night intruders.

He landed running. He heard only a single faint, dry chuckle behind him as he hurried along from dock to garden seat to fence to the next dock, and so on, until he finally reached the rising stone wall, topped with large stone spheres, that joined the bridge parapet. He was gasping by then, but for Dauneth Marliir, there could be no rest until he uncovered one more secret allegiance. Just one more . . . His feet took him to the crest of the bridge in a rush, and then he slowed, noting that Wyvernspur House seemed to have no guards and to be darkest on the lake side. The imposing edifice of the Cormaerils across the street, however, seemed to bristle with watchful guards, several of whom were already staring his way. He gave them a casual wave of greeting, as if they were old friends he'd expected to see, and turned along the shore beside Wyvernspur House, as if he were strolling along a way he knew well.

As he'd hoped, a footpath wound along the water's edge. He slipped past a prowling cat, ignoring the brief snarl of greeting it made, and vaulted the low wall that marked the Wyvernspur boundaries, hoping he'd triggered no alarm spells or deadlier guardian magics.

He crouched tensely on a cobbled garden path amid gardens where water chuckled endlessly over stones somewhere nearby, moving only a few quick steps to be away from the place where he'd first intruded . . . but nothing happened. No guards or seeking spells came his way. After a long time, he relaxed. He was being overly fearful again. It seemed even nobles couldn't afford to cover every inch of their holdings with defensive magic.

Right, then. Dauneth Marliir took hold of his scabbarded sword to keep it from knocking against anything and glided forward. A window sat invitingly open, framed by garden flowers and occupied by an orange tabby on the sill. He eyed the dark room inside narrowly, looking for guardians. Surely it wasn't going to be *this* easy.

But it was. The cat on the sill stretched, yawned, thought for a moment, and then bounded away into the night gloom of the garden, leaving the sill unoccupied. Dauneth was up and over it in an instant, crouching on bare flagstones in the dimness beyond. This was some sort of plant room, leading into . . . a servants' stair. Dark, narrow, and offering a high window with a ledge!

There seemed to be no cat in residence up there just now. Dauneth found the servant's footholds on the wall, spaced so that someone shorter, older, and grumpier than he could reach the window occasionally to wash it, and used them. He hadn't even settled down to think of his next move before he heard the voices.

A man and a woman, in the next room, talking with easy familiarity. He knew the female voice: Lady Bluemask. Dauneth became an intently listening statue.

"Cat, the nobles can't *all* be base, blackhearted villains. *I'm* a noble! You're a noble, too!"

Lady Bluemask—What had he called her? Cat?—sighed. "Giogi, my own, it doesn't take all of the nobles to hack our country down into war. Almost all of them with any influence, or more money than fear, are up to something right now. Who knows how many quiet little deals are being hatched over wine around this city right this minute?"

"None that I know of," came the reply. Giogi—Giogi Wyvernspur, of course, the adventurer! One of the country-squire nobles. His voice continued. "And there may be none at all!"

"Say you're right," Cat replied, "and there are none at all. That still leaves the two factions we *do* know of . . . without any chance of mistaking what they're up to. Agreed?"

Giogi sighed, and Dauneth heard liquid splashing into a glass. "Agreed," he said. "Anything new with those?"

"Well," Cat said as glasses clinked together, "the only news out of the palace today is that five nobles grew so impatient that they tried to murder the crown princess this morning, cutting her down at prayer." Dauneth stiffened and almost cried out in astonishment before Cat's next words dumbfounded him. "She slaughtered them all."

"*Tanalasta?*" Giogi's voice was a cry of disbelief. Dauneth echoed it silently.

"A Harper and a friend of hers, plus the priestess at the altar, did the killing, I believe. Gwennath spoke to me after all the Purple Dragons had finished huffing and snorting and looking grim all over the place."

"So, which nobles?"

"Young blades, all of them—Ensrin Emmarask, a Dauntinghorn, a Creth, an Illance, and Red Belorgan."

"Him—huh! Any chance to kill anything, *he'd* be in on it," Giogi said disgustedly.

"They were all carrying huge rubies," Cat added.

"No! Not the Secret Society of Men Who Carry Huge Rubies!" her mate protested with mock incredulity. "Say it isn't so!"

"Dolt," said Cat affectionately. "Rubies or no, they're dead. That leaves us with all the usual villains."

"Aunadar Bleth and Gaspar Cormaeril and their nobles' council. An idea silently supported by at least some members in all the oldest, largest houses and feared by the minor nobles, who know they'll be left out of all decisions . . . and profits."

"Exactly. Everyone from the Huntcrowns to the Yellanders wants the council. Even the Illances have set aside their old feud with the Cormaerils to be in on this . . . and upstart houses such as the Flintfeathers are pushing the council as their way of gaining respect among the 'heavy houses.' They all—even the three so-called royal houses—see it as a way out from under the tyranny of the Obarskyrs."

"Into the tyranny of their rivals and neighbors," said Giogi, "a tyranny that will undoubtedly soon spill over into open violence when various stiff-necked families seek to get even with each other over 'you voted against me' grudges."

"Five months?" Cat asked, considering.

"Nearer three." Giogi nursed a thumb under his chin. "And that's assuming that the big houses, who stand to lose everything they've gained if the country is plunged into war, try to keep tight reins on things. If just two of the large old houses get annoyed at the same time and don't work hard at keeping the peace, we could have massacres and then raids and then full-scale battles in a month."

"That's right, lift my spirits! Even the young lion I recruited to help me get to the vaults seems to be going sour," Cat said bitterly. In the darkness, Dauneth's lips twisted wryly. "Tell me who stands on the side of the wise old regent."

"Well, there're the Wyvernspurs!" said Giogi brightly.
"And?"

"Well, there're the Wyvernspurs," Giogi added, in mimicry of his own breathless tones.

"Go on," Cat said, a clear warning to become more serious in her tone.

"Uh . . . most of nobility with country estates and holdings: the Dauntinghorns, the Skatterhawks, the Immerdusks, the Wintersuns, the Indimbers, the Rowanmantles, House Indesm, and the Rallyhorns—but not the Roaringhorns, who want king or council and no ruling queen."

"Could that have anything to do with the fact that the Roaringhorns detest both the Bleth family and the wizard Vangerdahast?" Cat asked with a smile.

"Never," Giogi said, with mocking shock in his voice. "No noble house of *this* realm would ever sink to such a shortsighted, personally vindictive level. Not when they can proclaim such actions as part of a grander, higher-minded policy of supporting only what is best for fair Cormyr."

"Speaking of what is best for fair Cormyr," Cat asked, "how is our guest in the basement?"

Giogi shuddered. "The guest in the basement," he declaimed grandly, "is fine. I, however, am frazzled—distinctly frazzled. See?"

He shuddered dramatically, then sighed and said in tired, serious tones, "Restless and ill-behaved children are less problem. Our guest does only three things, and all of them all too well: demand, argue, and worry." He sighed again. "I'm going to be very glad when all this is over."

Cat wrinkled her nose. "I've hated all this deception and spying on perfidious nobles from the very beginning," she said firmly.

Giogi sighed. "I feel the same way, but you must remember that we're proceeding exactly as Vangerdahast planned, and he's been at all of this a lot longer than we have."

"And quite successfully, too," Cat said. "Dealing smoothly with the mundane work of statecraft as the Royal Magician for years, while crafting spells and making alliances behind the scenes. All in the name of service to the crown."

"He's smooth," Giogi admitted, filling his glass again. "I'll give him that. Smooth as a greased basilisk. Or something similarly smooth."

In his dark window, Dauneth nodded grimly. Good old Vangerdahast was the true villain, then—the shadow behind all of the troubles now besetting Cormyr. Of course, if his magic had laid the three royal hunters low, that same magic could keep the puzzled priests and baffled sages from curing his victims.

There was a sudden flash of light from outside. Dauneth looked out the little window to see what had caused it and smiled, slowly and grimly.

The gods did have senses of humor and justice, after all. Here was the fat old spell-hurler himself, come calling on his conspirators with a big smile all over his face! This would save much chasing about and creeping through wizardly defenses, the young Marliir noble thought, reaching for his blade.

Vangerdahast had appeared out of the now fading glow by magic, transporting himself from the palace, and was humming pleasantly as he swung wide the door of Wyvernspur House and strode in.

Moving hastily, Dauneth's shadowy form dropped down from a balcony and silently slipped in through the slowly closing door, blade glittering in hand. It had been a frantic few minutes of running and clambering and lurking to get here while the stout wizard strolled leisurely among the garden plantings, seeming highly satisfied with Cormyr in general and himself in particular.

Yet he'd made it, and the fat fool hadn't even noticed the noise or the shadow . . . the shadow that had skulked long enough!

Dauneth raised his glittering blade and took two catlike, velvety soft steps forward. He did not hold with putting steel into men from behind, but with wizards, all principles were laid aside. The death of Vangerdahast would end a threat to Cormyr as grave as anything the legendary Baerauble had ever dealt with! If a mage had to die by a surprise thrust from behind, then so be it!

Die, wizard! he murmured inwardly, not quite daring to say it aloud, and his blade flashed down. . . .

Let it be swift, let it be now, and let it be for Cormyr!

30

Adventurers
Year of the Grimoire
(1324 DR)

he Royal Magician thundered on the inn door
with his fists, the thick frame nearly rattling
loose from its hinges. "Balin!" he bellowed. "We
have to get on the road!"

On the other side of the door, there were sounds of gig-
gling and hushed, urgent whispers.

Vangerdahast shouted, "Get out of there *now*, or I
swear I'll teleport you to your father, along with any
'guests' you may be currently entertaining."

The whispers were replaced by the sounds of hasty
movements. Vangerdahast counted to ten. Then he
counted to ten a second time.

He was up to eight on his third counting when the
door cracked open and Crown Prince Azoun, son of Rhigaerd and the fourth Obarskyr to bear that name,
squeezed out. He opened the door only sufficiently to
allow his growing frame to pass and held the door shut
behind him with one hand, tucking his shirt into his
breeches with the other.

"Do you have to shout, wizard?" asked the prince in
groggy exasperation.

"It's the only proven way to get words through your

ever-thickening skull," the mage replied. "Unless, of course, you'd rather I took to suddenly manifesting in your sleeping quarters with attendant flashes of fire and smoke."

Prince Azoun, traveling through his own country as Balin the Cavalier, muttered something definitely un-royal and then said, "Give me ten minutes to gather my gear."

"Make it five minutes. That way you won't get distracted again by the young lady."

Azoun grumbled an assent, and six minutes later he was out in front of the inn, yawning loudly. His pack was on his back, his short sword sheathed on his belt, and a shapeless, wide-brimmed hat covered his head and most of his features. At nineteen winters old, the young noble was already broad-shouldered and handsome. Soon he'd have to make use of magical disguises to avoid being recognized at once.

The larger and more portly Vangerdahast was similarly attired and equipped, save that he had a short walking staff instead of a sword. Azoun had no doubt that the leather-shod walking stick held more magic than any gnarled staff wielded by a more powerful mage.

"Where to today, O learned elder?" asked the prince.

"Eveningstar," said the mage. "It's about two days' jaunt from here. I thought we'd walk half today and rough it overnight, and make the town by dusk tomorrow."

"We could make in a single day if we rode," the prince observed, not for the first time.

"Aye," said the wizard. "And we could travel in comfort if we took a carriage, and we could make it in an instant with a spell. But with a spell, we'd miss the countryside, and with a coach, we'd not meet anyone else in our travels. And with horses, we'd not have time to talk," he added meaningfully, "and for me to help you review your lessons."

The young prince grimaced. "One day, you know, I'll have my own band of heroes and adventurers, mighty warriors all! And *we* will ride horses!"

"So you will," said Vangerdahast with a smile, "and you'll be able to tell your brave companions about every bend in the road and every inn in Cormyr, because you saw them all on foot as a boy."

"Boy!" spat Azoun. "My father was king at my age!"

"And with Tymora's grace, you'll be spared the pain that he had to go through, wizardless and alone!" retorted the wizard. "So tell me, O learned young one, what other kings of Cormyr took the throne at such a young age?"

Azoun grumbled and rummaged through his memory as the two set out, leaving the Old Owlbear Inn behind them. The wizard chose a path along the banks of the Starwater, as opposed to doubling back to the main road itself. It was little more than a footpath that followed the course of the river, meandering along beside it beneath the shade of early summer leaves.

Azoun recited the names of the nineteen young kings and seven warrior queens, starting with Gantharla, and of the four recognized illegitimate kings. He listed the current noble houses with ease, though he needed prompting to recall all the names of the dead houses that had ended through lack of heirs or loyalty. He recalled perfectly the lyrics of the song "The Cormyte's Boast," including the lewd ones, which he had learned the night before from a bard at the Old Owlbear. Of course, eventually the conversation would come back to sore feet, tender calf muscles, and the pain of traveling overland on foot and incognito.

"I still don't see why we can't tell anybody who we are," Azoun complained, shaking his left boot while on a rest break. A single small pebble that had pained his footsteps for the past quarter of a mile dropped out.

"Two reasons. The first is safety. I shouldn't have to remind you that we're far from war wizards and Purple Dragon guards and the relative safety of home. I can aid and protect, but I cannot be all-wise or all-vigilant, so our best protection is secrecy. Enemies of the crown think the Obarskyrs cling to their castles and high society. We should do nothing to dissuade them from that view."

The young prince waved away the explanation. That one he understood. The elder mage was certainly being a mother hen about the dangers abroad in the kingdom, but at least Vangerdahast now let him journey forth from the castle for these little forays.

"Secondly, when you wear a crown, the rest of the world is transformed. People tend to tell you what they wish you to hear, as opposed to what you need to know. Truths are shaded, identities are hidden, and facts are concealed. Would any troubadour dare teach his king the racy lyrics of 'The Cormyte's Boast'?"

This was the argument Azoun was prepared for. "So what you're saying," he said sharply, "is that the king has to seem something other than he is in order to get to the truth? That he has to deceive his own people?"

"I am saying that no one is what he seems," said the portly mage, "and the king should recognize that fact and plan accordingly. That young waitress at the inn, for example."

Azoun blinked. "What of her?"

"I noticed she was rather cold and aloof to you last night. Obviously the situation had changed by this morning. I trust you did not, by any chance, happen to let slip that you were more than Balin the Cavalier last night after I retired?"

Azoun reddened slightly and shrugged his shoulders. "Perhaps I did. I can't remember." He straightened his shoulders and added, "We were drinking parsnip wine," as if that explained everything.

"Ah, but that's exactly the point. We are travelling Cormyr on foot, not for my health nor for yours, but to understand both the land and the people. And even the most good-hearted may not be what they seem, and even the coldest may warm to the glow of the royal crown."

They traveled for another two hours in the bright forest of morning, breaking once for another boots-off rest and once for an early, dry lunch. Vangerdahast lectured

on the history of Eveningstar and the monster-haunted
halls that reached through the gorge north of the village.
This region had been his own playground back when he
was a boy. It was here, he would point out, that he'd first
decided to become a wizard, and there, he would note,
that he was later taken on by Jorunhast, the last Royal
Magician of the Court.

"I haven't heard much about Jorunhast," said Azoun,
"save that he backed the wrong side during the reign of
Salember, the Rebel Prince."

"That and more," said Vangerdahast. "Actually, he
killed Salember when the Rebel Prince threatened to kill
your father and your grandmother Truesilver. Then your
father thanked the mage and banished Jorunhast from
the court. Cormyr was without an official mage until
your elder sister was born, and I was sent for to act as
her tutor, and yours as well. However, King Rhigaerd has
withheld the official title of Royal Magician from me, as
is his right."

"Yet if your teacher saved my father . . ." began the
prince.

"Jorunhast killed a *king*," said Vangerdahast. "A bad
king, but a king nonetheless. I think your father was
worried it might become a habit. And there are lessons
here."

"Such as?"

Vangerdahast sighed. "Returning to Suzail twenty
years after Jorunhast left, I saw that the kingdom had
survived being officially wizardless quite nicely. Thirteen
centuries of careful and not-so-careful building had left a
good foundation that two passing decades could not de-
molish. But small things had cropped up—the weakness
of the battle wizards, the growth in power of the thieves'
guilds, the erratic politics of Arabel, and the shady dealings of Marsember. All small things in themselves, but
with great future consequences if they were ignored.
Your father chose not to ignore them and sent for Jorunhast's pupil. In this your father showed great wisdom; a
lesser king might see Cormyr's prosperity and decide it

did not need an official wizard after all."

"Whatever happened to Jorunhast?" asked Azoun.

"I think Jorunhast was right, you know," said Vanger-dahast, ignoring the question Azoun had asked. "He had to make a choice between a mad current king and a young, untried would-be ruler. He made the choice, and in so doing, he knew he would be banished for his actions. Yet he spared your father any need to slay Salember, even with the excuse that he was defending himself. Jorunhast was willing to make an unthinkable choice if it was what was good for the realm. That's an important lesson for both of us."

Azoun was about to press the question of Jorunhast's eventual fate again when he heard shouts from up ahead. Two people were running toward them, shouting and waving their hands. A older man and woman, just past their middle years, wearing dressing gowns and sandals. Not the sort of garb one chooses for a hike in the woods, thought Azoun.

"Ghosts!" cried the man. "Our house has been possessed!"

"They've taken over," the woman gasped, "and driven us from our home!"

"You appear to be adventurers licensed by the crown. You must help us!" said the man.

"Let us be calm," replied the wizard soothingly. "I am Borl the Proficient, and this is my young companion, Balin the Cavalier. You say you have ghosts?"

"We are but humble farmers," said the man. "We've been living on an abandoned estate a mile up the trail, rebuilding the house and clearing the old fields."

"That's when the old nobles came back," the woman added, tears forming in her eyes, "screaming and moaning, and drove us from the house!"

"Which nobles?" asked the disguised prince.

The old man blinked. "I don't know. There was no indication, and there are so many noble houses in Cormyr. But it was a right fine building; it must have belonged to aristocrats."

"And the fact the ghosts have returned proved that," the woman added, almost triumphantly. "Only nobles care so much for their property they come back from the dead to protect it!"

"What do these noble ghosts look like?" Vangerdahast asked quietly.

The couple stammered as one, and then the old man's voice trailed alone out of the confusion, admitting, "We've not exactly *seen* them."

"No?"

"Oh, but they put up a *horrible* racket," the woman exclaimed, leaping in. "Down in the basement, and up in the attic, making dreadful moans and cries for vengeance. For three days and three nights, we've huddled in our beds, but we could find nothing amiss in the light of day. We found one of the chickens dead this morning—brutally slain! We had to flee for our lives!"

"Sounds like something worth investigating," said Azoun.

Vangerdahast shrugged. "There are hauntings aplenty in this Forest Country. All too much history assures us of that."

"But still, our duty to the crown, that document we signed when the king allowed us to pass through his lands . . ." Azoun began, smiling.

The wizard waved him to silence. "Well, if it's on the way . . ."

"And they're not going to move Eveningstar in the meantime," the young Prince added helpfully. Vangerdahast gave him a look, and Azoun fell silent. But he did not stop grinning.

* * * * *

The manor house was only about a quarter of a mile off the Starwater trail. The man gave them directions, but the couple would not leave the main path, declaring they'd go nowhere near the house until the two adventurers had cleared it of all risen spirits.

The house itself was fashioned in a style some called "Cormyr Sprawl." The main house was a foursquare, sturdy block of fieldstones on the ground floor and brick for the floor above, thickly covered with ivy along its southern face. On three sides, additional wings had been built of stone or lumber or unfinished wood. The result looked like three houses had collided in the depths of some dark night, and no one had bothered to disentangle them since. Over the door was a faded and battered heraldic device.

"Goldweathers?" said Azoun.

"Gold*feathers*," corrected the mage. "A minor house from a few hundred years back. They fomented an unsuccessful rebellion in Arabel years ago and were stripped of their rank and lands. Those commoners have clear title to this land just by occupying and clearing it."

The immediate surroundings had been cleared, but the fields beyond were still overrun with brambles and young trees. There was a coop, but no chickens or other animals on the property. Azoun thought that strange and mentioned it to Vangerdahast.

"Aye," said the wizard. "Perhaps our ghosts have an interest in live chickens and goats."

"I wondered the same thing myself," said a voice from above them.

The speaker swung down from the branch that had been her perch. She was almost as tall as Azoun, but slender and as lithe as a panther. She wore leather trousers that hugged her muscular thighs and calves, and a loose cotton blouse with a heavy leather vest that did nothing to conceal her charms. Her auburn hair was braided in a whiplike tail down her back. Her eyes were bright and green, and she carried a thin, double-bladed sword.

Vangerdahast started to move forward, putting himself between the newcomer and the young prince, but Azoun stopped him with a hand. The wizard looked at his liege and saw *that* look on his face, eyes determined and serious, mouth in a wide smile. It was an Obarskyr look, and Azoun got it when faced with a new challenge or a new woman.

The woman held her weapon at her side and said, "I am Kamara Brightsteel, errant adventurer and solver of mysteries. And you?" Her voice was husky, and she rolled her *r*'s slightly. The accent made her all the more attractive.

"Balin, a wandering cavalier," Azoun replied, "and his manservant and instructor, Borl." The young prince ignored the fat mage's harrumphed protest and went on. "We met the inhabitants of this homestead on the road, and they said there were ghosts here."

"I think I also saw their 'ghosts,'" the young woman said. "I saw them leaving in haste."

Vangerdahast raised an eyebrow, and she continued, "There were a couple of men, or at least manlike forms, moving around the sides of the house. I think they were gathering up the chickens and goats, but I didn't get all that good a view from my hiding place. Three or four, I'd say. They didn't look like anything special."

"So you think . . . ?" prompted the wizard.

"I think a pack of brigands came upon the house and chased the couple out with spooky noises and rattled chains. They can't have much spine, or they'd simply have killed the two. I think they're nothing more than chicken thieves with perhaps a little more imagination than usual."

"Then let's clean out that nest of chicken thieves," said the wizard.

"Let us do it," Azoun said, still wearing *that* look. "I mean Kamara and I. It'll be good practice for me. Why don't you go back to the trail and fetch the old couple? By the time you return, we should have taken care of this little problem."

Azoun expected Vangerdahast to argue, but instead, the wizard stared off into the forest for a time, his mouth a firm, straight line. At length, he said, "Very well. I bow to your adventurous spirit. Be careful now." And with that, the wizard padded back down the path, leaving the pair alone before the house.

Kamara watched Vangerdahast's retreating back dwindle into the distance. "Funny old man," she said. "Mage?"

"Scholar," replied Azoun, sticking to the story they'd crafted at the outset of their trip. There was no need to brag of Vangerdahast's abilities, in any event. "I am the warrior of the pair."

"And a brave young warrior at that," Kamara said gently. Her eyes sparkled as she spoke.

A silence fell between them for a moment. The man and the woman stood facing each other. Azoun stared into the young woman's eyes; they seemed like jade coins from some distant and forgotten empire. Somewhere in the distance, a hawk cried out.

Azoun broke the locked gazes first. "We should take care of our 'ghosts.'"

The woman managed a small smile. "Indeed. It would not do for your scholar to return here to find us mooning about with brigands in the house."

Side by side, the pair ascended the porch steps of the old manor house. The front door was unlocked, and Azoun went in first.

The interior was fairly typical of a country house. A slender hall ran from front to back, dividing the ground floor in two. All the doors along the hallway were closed.

On the right would be the dining room, and behind that, a kitchen overlooking cooking pits behind the house. On the left would be a sitting room, parlor, or library. The bedchambers would be upstairs, reached by a narrow wooden flight of stairs. Azoun tried to imagine brigands getting the goat up the stairs. He shook his head. They must be hiding the livestock somewhere else.

The building was too quiet. Even if the livestock had been shoved in the basement, they would make some noise. There would be the soft sounds of their calls, or at least the slight shifting of floorboards as they moved about.

Kamara hung close behind him as he entered, and he could feel her soft, warm breath on the back of his neck.

Had the brigands taken the chickens and left? Mentally he figured the time it would take Vangerdahast to return to the main trail and bring the old couple back. More than enough time to get comfortable with a fellow seeker of adventure. And perhaps enough time to "let slip" one's true identity and reap the benefits of that admission.

Kamara shut the front door behind her as Azoun opened the door on the right. As he thought, it was the dining room, with another door beyond leading to the kitchen. The furnishings were sparse but of high quality, probably the salvageable remains of the original Goldfeather stock. A great table dominated the room, and the walls were covered with cabinets, all open, their contents spilled on the floor. In the center of the table, a box of silver flatware, another legacy of the Goldfeathers, was rudely overturned, the knives and forks carving fresh scratches in the deep polish.

The thieves came after chickens but did not stop for the more valuable silver, thought Azoun. Perhaps they were still in the building. He held his breath and looked at Kamara. She hung back from the dining room and was scanning along the hallway. Her muscles were tense, as if she expected an attack at any moment.

Azoun brushed past her and tried the door opposite, which should lead to a parlor or sitting room. The door was stuck, and the young prince had to shoulder it open. Something heavy and wet slid along the floor, pushed out of the way of the door, leaving a crimson streak on the floor behind it.

It was a goat. A dead goat in the sitting room, propped against the door. Azoun had found the missing livestock.

The sitting room had been turned into an abattoir, its old furnishings covered with blood, fur, and feathers. There were a trio of old goats, including the billy goat that partially blocked the door. Their throats had been torn out by crude daggers or teeth. The chickens, great black hens with crimson bellies, had their necks snapped and were strewn about the room. Some had been half eaten, but most had been slain and discarded in an orgy of slaughter. Feathers blotted the sticky pools of blood.

Azoun began to say something to Kamara, something about these invaders being more than mere brigands or even ghosts, when he heard her growl behind him.

He turned and realized what the supposed ghost had truly been. Brigands had never been inside the house. Someone else—some*thing* else—had created the bloody carnage in the sitting room.

Kamara growled as her shoulders slumped and narrowed, her jaw elongating into a fang-toothed muzzle. Her eyes went from jade coins to cat's eyes, as bright and sharp as the claws erupting from her fur-covered hands. Her flesh grew orange fur, striped with black.

Kamara was a weretiger. She dropped her sword and leapt, snarling, at the young prince, paws outstretched, slavering maw open.

Azoun shouted and ducked beneath the leap, desperately bringing his blade up as he did so. The steel raked deeply down her chest and belly, jarring his arm. Then she was over him, carried into the bloodstained room by the force of her leap.

Azoun wheeled and saw the tiger-woman kneeling among the slain goats and chickens. She held her split belly together with one paw, and the young prince could see the slashed sides of the wound he'd made crawling, meeting, and flowing together—healed. Lycanthropes could be only affected by silver or magic. And Azoun had sent his magical support away.

Kamara crouched again, and Azoun's free hand lashed out, grabbing the doorknob and pulling the door shut in the weretiger's face. A moment later, the boards above its central crossbrace splintered under the force of her charge, and with a horrible tearing sound, the boards gave way. Cruel black claws batted the air inches in front of his face. Azoun staggered back.

His sword was useless, and he could never hope to outrun the transformed lycanthrope. By the time Vangerdahast returned, the heir to the Dragon Throne would be in the same state as the chickens in the sitting room. Kamara was ripping apart the door and would be through in a matter of seconds.

Then Azoun remembered what he had seen earlier, and he fled from the hall.

When Kamara tore apart the last of the door and sent its remnants spinning from their hinges, she found the young royal's sword lying abandoned in the hallway. The front door remained shut. Her prey was still somewhere in the house.

There was a noise, the shifting of weight on floorboards, directly ahead. The dining room! Kamara sprang across the narrow hall and into the doorway directly across from her . . .

. . . and caught a thrown steak knife in the ribs. The cut was shallow, but it burned like acid!

Silver! The quivering blade was silver, a legacy of the Goldfeathers.

She hissed, spat, and jarred the blade loose. Two more daggers, crudely thrown but accurate, caught her in the arm. Kamara the weretiger howled in pain and threw herself at her assailant.

Azoun stood at the far end of the table, the spilled silverware arrayed before him. He managed to dig one more thrown knife into her thigh as she vaulted the table. She came within striking distance, and he lashed out with his hand, catching her full in the side of the face with a silver teapot.

Kamara sprawled to one side, wide of her mark. Already a hideous swelling had erupted from where the pot had struck. The knife wounds were not knitting. Blood seeped through her shredded blouse and leggings. Azoun readied the teapot for another attack. It would not be a battle he'd brag about, but it would be one he would win.

The weretiger seemed to recognize that as well. She leapt up, and Azoun raised the pot in one hand and a knife in the other. Kamara snarled, but instead of pouncing on the waiting prince, she leapt for the window, smashing through it to land heavily on the porch beyond.

441

Azoun charged forward, but by the time he reached the empty frame, she was gone. The young prince saw a flash of something orange disappearing into the trees.

He sighed, retrieved his sword, and checked the rest of the house. There were no robbers, ghosts, or weretigers left in the building. By the time Vangerdahast returned with the old couple, the young prince was sitting on the front porch, head between his hands.

The old couple shouted in alarm when they saw the smashed window, demanding to know what had happened. Azoun sighed and explained. "Your 'ghost' was a weretiger who wanted your livestock. So she drove you off, then killed your chickens and goats. There were no real ghosts here, only a hungry predator. I drove it off. It won't likely be back, but you should get some silver weapons just to be sure. Be careful going into the front room—it's a bit of mess."

So warned, the couple hurried into the house. The woman shrieked and then sobbed, and the man made comforting noises.

"I can't leave you alone for a moment, can I?" Vangerdahast asked softly.

"How was I to know?" the young prince protested.

"You weren't to know," the wizard said severely, "but you should always be cautious."

The pair remained at the old Goldfeather Manor for the remainder of the day. Azoun removed the rest of the shattered parlor door and used the boards from it and some additional lumber to patch up the front window. When they reached Eveningstar, he'd send a carpenter for the door and a glass glazer for the window, compliments of the crown, to make full repairs. Vangerdahast helped the old woman clean away the carnage in the parlor room and dress the chickens and goats. One of the goats made an excellent dinner at the close of the day, and the old woman proved to be an excellent cook.

The weretiger did not return.

They talked late into the evening, the old man telling tales of when he was a lad, when the kingdom was torn apart in the War of Red and Purple. When he started to nod off, the old woman told her guests where beds had been made ready for them, shook her husband awake, and the couple retreated to their own room.

Vangerdahast and Azoun sat by the last dying flames of the hearth fire. Neither moved to put more wood on the waning blaze.

"You're right, you know," said Azoun at last.

"Right about what?" said the wizard, his eyes red and tired beneath half-closed lids.

"No one is who he seems," said the young prince, stretching, "and while I should not be paranoid about it, I should be aware—and therefore wary."

"A lesson learned," said the wizard. "The day is not a total loss."

Azoun rose from the hearthside and went to the door, waving his arm to loosen a bruised and tired shoulder. "You know," he said thoughtfully, "It's amazing that our morning discussion had such an immediate reinforcement. If I didn't know better, I'd swear you planned all this, just to drive home a lesson."

The young king-to-be shook his head, half smiled, and was gone, leaving the stout wizard sitting beside the last cooling coals in the hearth, alone with his thoughts.

"Then there's hope for you yet, boy," Vangerdahast said softly to the embers as he rose stiffly to seek his own bed. "There's hope for you yet."

31

Loyalties
Year of the Gauntlet
(1369 DR)

ur shy crown princess certainly showed some fire," Rhauligan remarked, raising his glass to his companion in the Snout Room. "I guess we'll just have to get a stool into her hand more often."

"As she governs Cormyr, you mean?" Emthrara responded with a smile, clinking her glass gently against his.

Rhauligan nodded. "I'm getting just a trifle too old for such frantic scramblings as this morning's little fray."

"You're getting just a trifle too fat, you mean," Emthrara replied, shaking her head to tell an approaching patron that she wasn't interested in dancing just now. The man held up three golden lions hopefully, but she continued to shake her head. He raised his eyebrows and pressed on through the crowded Roving Dragon in search of a lady who'd say yes. Rhauligan watched; the patron's trip was not a long one.

"At least the threat to the throne is ended," he said, licking his lips and gazing into his glass appreciatively.

"*This* threat to the throne is ended," the Harper corrected him. "There'll be others, knowing our valiant nobles."

* * * * *

In a place much darker and quieter than the Roving Dragon, where two hallways met in a little-used back corner of the sprawling royal court, a young, cleft-chinned nobleman stood talking to nothing, keeping his voice low.

"I'll ask you the same thing I asked Vangerdahast and Gaspar Cormaeril," Immaril Emmarask, cousin to the now-deceased Ensrin, said calmly. "What's in it for me?"

"Loyalty to Cormyr?" the woman's voice came back to him. "A bright future for the realm?"

Immaril shrugged. "Grand goals, bandied about all too much by folk seeking justification for small and dirty things they want done right now. Offer me something I can have and hold for my loyalty."

"A typical noble son of Cormyr," said the voice that came out of the small, whirling cluster of winking lights.

Immaril shrugged again. "I prefer to see myself as slightly more honest than most. I don't bother to hide the same feelings that drive most of my fellows. We see others enjoying wealth and power in return for things done, or silences kept, for the crown. Why should we not have the same things?"

"Why indeed? If I fill your hand with rubies right now, will you serve me?"

Immaril hesitated. "I need to know just a bit more about you first. Am I hitching myself to a lich righting age-old wrongs? Or a dragon seeking an even more ancient revenge on the realm? Or a Red Wizard seeking to gather an entire kingdom of slaves? Or some other archmage, out to smash a realm for mere entertainment?"

"This is something it would be better if you did not know," the voice told him, "but let us share a few secrets. Tell me who stands with Vangerdahast, and I'll tell you what—not who—I am."

"Fair enough," Immaril said, glancing around. "The Dauntinghorns—most of them—the Rowanmantles, the Rallyhorns, the Skatterhawks, the Immerdusks, The

Ed Greenwood and Jeff Grubb

Wintersuns, the Wyvernspurs, the Indimbers . . . and House Indesm."

"Hmmm," the voice commented, "that certainly seems like a muster of all the far-flung and obscure household names among the nobility."

Immaril shrugged. "Many are country squires and come to the court once a year at most. Most of the city nobles, the true nobles of Cormyr, stand against Vangerdahast. As a group, they are greedy or stupid enough to think that they can trust each other and rule the realm better than an Obarskyr backed by all the war wizards. The recent and sudden demise of Ondrin Dracohorn should be proof enough to even the most stone-headed that they cannot, but a lot of us believe what we want to believe and not what the world shows us to be the truth." He raised his voice a trifle and said, "And I believe it's my turn to be shown some truth now. What are you?"

"A human woman skilled in magic."

"So much is obvious. I expected something more than what has already been established."

"Fair enough," the voice from the lights said. "Know, then, that I once shared King Azoun's bed, and—"

"Had a son by him," Immaril said calmly, "which is why you want all the Obarskyrs slain. Lady, so much is also already apparent. I trust you know that approximately half the Cormyrean noble sons of my age are reputed to have been fathered by our Purple Dragon?"

There was a little silence, and the voice was distinctly colder when it came back to him. "I have heard something of the sort. How many nobles will have to die, then?"

"Lady," Immaril said gravely, "you can't have enough rubies to manage all those killings. Besides, I myself am said to be Az—"

The bolt of roaring white death that snapped from the winking lights then left only drifting white ashes and a sharp burnt smell at the place where the two hallways met. An instant later, the little group of whirling lights flickered, faded, and was gone.

446

When the Purple Dragon sword captain Lareth Gulur came striding along a minute later, his sword half drawn and peering about for whatever might have caused the roaring sound, all that remained was the reek of fiery death. He stopped, sniffed, frowned, and shook his head. More magic. Someone—or two dueling combatants, perhaps—had died here.

He'd never thought the court in Suzail would become a more dangerous place than the battlefields of the Tuigan Horde. But it had. Perhaps it was time to retire and settle down in one of the quieter dales and brew beer. Gulur sighed and went back to his post. He knew he'd never leave this land, whatever happened. He just hoped his bones wouldn't soon be tossed into some pit in Cormyrean soil. He wanted to see the realm at peace again before he died.

* * * * *

Dauneth Marliir gasped and reeled as his descending sword suddenly came alive with sparks from end to end. He was still trembling helplessly when the young man with the glass in his hand set it down on a side table, loped to him, and removed his sword, then kicked the front door shut and took Dauneth's throat in the crook of one elbow.

Vangerdahast, smiling faintly, said, "Two daggers at his belt and one in his left boot."

Deft fingers plucked out the indicated weapons and tossed them away. They landed with steely slidings atop the discarded blade, and Giogi Wyvernspur said pleasantly to his prisoner, "Come and sit down. Cat'll—oh, have you met my wife, Lady Cat Wyvernspur? Sorry, should've introduced you straightaway—Cat'll be most upset if Vangey has to fry you with some spell or other. Tends to ruin the furniture and leave nasty stains and whatnot."

"Unhand me!" Dauneth snarled, struggling to get his breath. He drove a vicious elbow backward, but it seemed to strike some sort of tingling barrier.

"Ah, ah," Giogi reproved him. "Play nice."

"Wizard!" Dauneth roared, ignoring his captor and trembling with a rage that suddenly threatened to consume him, "You have betrayed your king, the crown, and Cormyr! You have brought the realm to the brink of war!"

The Royal Magician raised his eyebrows. "There is a fire in our young nobles that I sometimes wish could be kept alive as they grow older—and much wiser. Still, I'm pleased to see that you can distinguish between the differing calls of monarch, rulership, and realm. Very few of your fellow bluebloods can. I assure you, Dauneth Marliir—son of a family which has demonstrated expertise in determining loyalties, to be sure—that I am acting for the betterment of all three."

"Spare me your lies," Dauneth spat as Giogi sat him down in a chair, smiled like the gracious host he was, and wordlessly offered Dauneth a glass of wine.

The young noble struck it sharply upward, so that its contents splashed into Giogi's face. He then launched himself across the room, tearing out the dagger from its sheath in his sleeve, a dagger that Vangerdahast did not know of.

Lady Wyvernspur rose, lifting her hands and starting to mutter words, but Dauneth had already looped one long arm around the Royal Magician of Cormyr and brought his dagger to the old man's throat.

It struck some sort of barrier, and fire blazed from it. Dauneth ignored the sudden heat and pressed it in harder.

"Desist, young Marliir. I have no interest in slaying a loyal son of Cormyr."

The pain was excruciating now. Dauneth leaned into it with all the strength in his shoulders and snarled, "If such a great threat to the realm I love is destroyed, the loss of my own life will be worthwhile and gladly given!"

"Gods, I wish I heard such heartfelt words from more men of Cormyr!" said an admiring voice from somewhere off to the left. Dauneth raised his eyes from watching his dagger tip turn slowly red, inches from the wizard's hairy, scrawny old throat, and saw a single, shadowy form standing in an inner doorway. The watcher took a step forward and smiled, and as the lamplight fell across his face, Dauneth gasped and dropped his dagger. His hands slowly fell away from the wizard, who rubbed his nose, shook himself, and went straight to the wine bottle on the side table where Giogi—who was wiping at a nose that still dripped wine—had left it.

"You're getting old, Vangey," the man at the doorway said gravely.

"Old and forgetful," Vangerdahast replied, raising the bottle and not bothering with a glass. "Perhaps I should start considering my own replacement, eh?"

Dauneth was staring at the man by the door. When he could finally speak, he asked, "But—but—if you're here, then what's going on at the court? Who's trying to rule Cormyr?"

"A lot of folk, lad," the Royal Magician said with a smile. "A lot of folk. The reasons lie in the past, but to see the unfolding of their fruit, we must adjourn to the palace. Bring your sword. By now they'll all be waiting for us there."

32

Gondegal
The Year of the Dragon
(1352 DR)

he watch fires burned in a rough crescent along the hilltops south of Arabel. Each fire marked a thousand men, Purple Dragons, local militiamen, adventuring bands, and mercenaries. All were poised and ready for the assault on the rebellious city, come the dawn.

Arabel itself lay like a sparkling gem against a dark and dusty field of paddocks, tilled fields, and caravan grounds. Within its walls, the city blazed with light—the light of its own watch fires, of torches and lanterns, and of candles and magical radiances. Despite their shine, the surrounding watch fires would be visible in the city like a row of low, reddish stars. Neither the people in the city nor in the camps were getting much sleep this evening.

In the largest camp, the king's pavilion rose like a hulking purple mountain against the stars. Beneath its highest peak, the war leaders were gathered. Paunchy Baron Thomdor and balding Duke Bhereu anchored one end of the table, their faces hard twins of concern. Aside from a narrow aisle left bare along either side of the table, the room was crowded with chairs occupied by mercenary captains, militia leaders, and war wizards. Their attention was on the long, linen-covered table littered with papers, messages, reports, and diagrams. In the center of its clutter, wrought by magic but appearing as if sculpted of alabaster, was a three-dimensional model of Arabel itself.

At the table's head, in a low, carved throne of duskwood, sat King Azoun IV himself, seventy-first of the Obarskyr line, face furrowed, hand reflectively stroking his beard. The Royal Magician, Vangerdahast, stood to one side of his liege. He was the only one presently on his feet, and when he was addressing the gathered commanders, he would stalk the length of the table. For the moment, he stood bent over Azoun's right shoulder, looking every bit like the king's pet raven, perching.

"We know he's in there?" said the king, eyeing the sparkling white model of the caravan city.

"He, his men, and those who have flocked to his banner in the past three months," Thomdor replied grimly. His forces had spent those three months chasing the self-styled bandit king over most of northern Cormyr. Eight days ago their prey had alighted in Arabel, crowned himself Gondegal I with a crown snatched from a Sembian tomb, and dared any other man to take that crown from him.

No one knew Gondegal's origin, though he claimed the blood of kings ran in his veins. One thing was certain, as even Thomdor had to admit: He was a determined and charismatic leader of men. Time and again the baron had drawn up for an attack, only to have the forces he faced melt away into the fog and the forest. And with every near defeat, Gondegal's legend grew, and with those exciting tales had grown his supporters. On the first of the year, he was unknown. Now, three weeks after Midsummer Eve, he had encouraged Arabel to revolt once more and made it the seat of his own nascent empire.

In his declaration, Gondegal had laid out his new, nameless kingdom as running from the Wyvernwater northeast to Tilver's Gap, and from the desert of Anauroch southeast deep into Sembian territory. In reality, he ruled only as far as his sword would reach from the saddle of his ever-moving war-horse, but that did not lessen the effrontery of his demands. The Purple Dragon would not allow half its territory to suddenly cleave to a new ruler . . . even one as charismatic as Gondegal.

That declaration had been seven days ago, and for seven days, Arabel had held its breath as the "new king" readied his defenses. For seven days, the forces of loyal Cormyr, bolstered by allies who stood to lose land to Gondegal's kingdom, tightened the net around Arabel.

"Whoever he is, he's served in uniform somewhere," said Duke Bhereu, pointing to the alabaster model of the city. "He's worked wonders in a handful of days. All three gates have been fortified, and he's built outrider towers to cut off blind spots along the walls. Guard patrols have been doubled, water taken in from rivers in every jug and cask for miles around, and ballistae have been spotted in the major towers! This is no uprising of frustrated merchants; this foe knows his business."

"And all he need do is hang on to the city long enough to cement his hold on it, and he has us," added the baron grimly. "He literally only has to repel the initial assault. If we settle into a long siege, we'll be hurting Arabel itself."

"And what of the people of the city?" asked the king.

"Arabel has revolted so many times before that they have it down to an art form," said the duke bitterly. "The merchant livestock and caravans have been pulled north, and the paddocks are empty. Gondegal will likely have mages in the outbuildings, or missile-armed troops. Most of the townspeople have emptied their basements and are willing to wait out the duration there. The temples have been stockpiling food and water for a long time, it seems, and triple guards stand over all the wells."

One of the mercenary captains, a rough barbarian from the lands north of Phlan, broke in with a snarl.

"Bah! Then let us burn this ready fortress to the ground and slaughter all within its walls. Let their pyre be a warning to others who might think to thwart your king's will!"

A silence descended on the table as if a lid had banged closed. Vangerdahast broke away from the throne and drifted down along the table until he stood next to the barbarian captain. The mercenary looked to other faces for support but found none. All he saw was shock and indignation.

Vangerdahast put a heavy hand on the barbarian's shoulder. "The reason," he said, pressing down with a grip like the tightening gauntlet of an armored giant, "is that the folk in that city are Cormyreans, regardless of who leads them. They will be treated as loyal citizens of the realm until such time as they choose to actually raise arms against the Purple Dragon."

"But if they are in rebellion, haven't they . . . ?" asked the mercenary, wincing, his words cut short by the increasing pressure on his shoulder.

"They are our people," said the wizard through clenched teeth. "Half the army would desert if they had to fight their own brothers and cousins. We will treat them accordingly."

He released the mercenary captain, who exhaled and rubbed his shoulder. The mage had more power in his hands than mere wizardry.

"As has been said, Arabel rebels with astounding regularity," said the king softly. "Yet it has always returned to the shelter of the Purple Dragon's wings. One thing the long history of this land has taught my family is that creating grudges only perpetuates our difficulties."

He met the eyes of the mercenary captain and added, "Let me remind everyone present that this attack is no excuse for pillaging and looting. No one is to set any fires except by order. If the person fleeing from your sword is a civilian, he is a target you will not strike at, molest, or maim 'accidentally.' I'll consider that clearly understood by all of you; see that your men also clearly understand the punishment they'll face if they forget such things."

One of the militia leaders piped up. "Can't we convince just one of these loyal Arabellans to open the gates for us?"

The king shook his head. "They are cowed by Gondegal's swords and his popularity. Once battle is joined and we rout a few of his stalwart swords, the populace will rise on our side, but for the moment, all of them are lying low. The folk here are fickle, but dependably so."

One of the wizards asked, "What about the noble houses? Have they thrown in with Gondegal?"

Bhereu spoke up in reply. "A few of the minor houses have, the Immerdusks and Indesms being the most prominent. The Marliirs, the largest Arabellan house, have remained loyal. Most who bear that proud name are under house arrest now, keeping a few of Gondegal's troops busy guarding prisoners rather than manning the walls."

"Most of what we know about what's going inside has come from the Marliirs," added Thomdor. "Magical reconnaissance has been largely ineffective."

"On that note," said the king, "this is the battle plan for the morrow."

Vangerdahast nodded and waved his hands. A series of purplish blocks appeared on the table, outside the walls of the model city. As the wizard spoke, the blocks moved toward the walls.

"The militia will form on the left flank and mount a feint attack on the High Horn Gate and northwest wall, while the mercenaries will make a sally against the South Gate, more to draw fire and force a committal of defenders than to earnestly take the gate. The bulk of the army, on the right flank, will move along the long southern wall. The intent is to make Gondegal's forces think the bulk of our army is moving to the East Gate, to attack there. In fact, the forces under the duke will move farthest east, the forces under the king will stand to the center, and the forces commanded by the baron will assemble at the western end of the front."

Small blocks detached the from the larger ones and swept around the city to east and west. "Light cavalry will break off at this point and cut off both east and west gates, to provide an impediment should Gondegal's forces choose to bolt. They will include a few war wizards. Our main body of forces will hold the majority of our mages, the baron, the duke, and His Majesty."

A series of small flashes appeared along the southern wall, in front of the largest block. "The war wizards will bring down the wall in this area with lightning bolts and instruments of blasting. There is a potential for severe damage in the buildings immediately north of the wall, so while the first wave secures the area, the forces who are to penetrate the city must get past any ruin and move swiftly. Later we can examine the fallen buildings for survivors."

"Goodbye, Wink and Kiss," muttered Thomdor, thinking of his favorite tavern, located on the far side of the wall that was to be breached.

"With the walls blown," the wizard continued, "the main force will split up. Thomdor's men will take the South Gate and let the mercenaries in; together, they are to cleanse the breached area of hostile troops and hold it—in particular, holding any relatively unblocked streets and emptying the buildings along those streets, in case a route of retreat is needed. Bhereu's forces will enter the city and move to the East Gate, to take it—but even more importantly, to contain any enemy troops mustered there. The king will lead the main body across the city, to the Citadel of Arabel, to surround it and to try to force its gates. If we surprise them and move swiftly enough, it is likely we'll snare most of Gondegal's army in the city proper, before they can regroup at the Citadel."

"And if they do manage to gather at the Citadel?" asked the mercenary captain.

"Gondegal can hold out in Arabel indefinitely," said the king. "But unless he has substantially more food, plans, and men than we think he does, he cannot hold the Citadel for long if we hold the city around it. The signals you already know; pass on the orders to your subordinates and let all see to their weapons and prayers. We'll march before the sun crests the horizon and launch the attack at dawn."

A messenger in bright mail arrived to say the allied Sembian troops had arrived and were already complaining about their accommodations. The king smiled thinly and declared the meeting at an end. Chairs scraped and men rose, talk rising in the usual babble; the Purple Dragon pointed at his two cousins and at the wizard. They remained as the others went out.

"A solid plan," said the king.

"Working with your suggestions," the wizard said, "mated to the thinking written down in the court war files. There are table-sized piles of plans for attacking Arabel. Even during years of peace, it was a common practice for military scholars to attack a model Arabel with tin knights and dice."

Azoun glanced at the city model, then folded his hands before him and steepled his fingers. "The question is," he said slowly, "what happens afterward?"

"General amnesty," Thomdor replied.

"We get Gondegal and his chief subordinates and hang them for their crimes, then use the treasure he's looted for reparations," added Bhereu.

"Troops will remain in Arabel, ostensibly to repair the wall," said Vangerdahast, "but should remain thereafter in any case. Arabel is a frontier outpost. It should have sufficient protection."

"Agreed," said the king. "Cousin Thomdor, you will head up the Purple Dragon forces based here afterward, much as Bhereu controls the High Horn forces." Both cousins nodded.

"What of the nobles?" asked the wizard.

"What of them?" asked the king.

"The talk in the court lays the weakness in Arabel at the collective feet of the Marliirs," said the Royal Magician.

"All we know of Gondegal's preparations has come from the Marliirs," Thomdor said with a frown. "Old Jolithan Marliir risked a pair of daughters as messengers."

"The Marliirs are not to blame," said Azoun. "If anything, our own complacency brought us to this pass, wherein a charismatic imposter king can raise an army in a fortnight and seize a city in a season."

"True, but you know court politics," Vangerdahast replied. "Bleth, in particular, has reminded me of his contribution to this venture and of his great interest in seeing the Marliirs fail and a 'true' Cormyrean family have their seat in the city. Lord Bleth wants it badly."

"Lord Bleth will have to be disappointed, then," said the king. "My cousins are right. It would be unfair to punish the Marliirs after they risked so much for us. Besides, if I install a Bleth or anyone else who still thinks 'true Cormyreans' means born and raised in Suzail, I'll have another revolution on my hands before the decade is out. Anything else?"

There was nothing else, and the king retired to his personal tent while the two cousins peered at every detail of the white stone model, pointing and plotting. Vangerdahast left them to it and wandered to the southern edge of the camp, away from the city.

Here the posted guards were widely spaced and the shadows between the fires deeper and larger. Night held sway, however many swords were gathered under it. He waited, counting the stars in the southern sky.

After about ten minutes, a voice hissed from the darkness. "Black sword."

"Meets green shield," the wizard replied.

"To make red war," the darkness responded and broke away from the shadows to stand before the wizard. One of Vangerdahast's spies. Let the royal cousins depend on nobles for information. Any wizard worth his cantrips had his own methods and his own servants.

The spy was a young woman in dark cape and leathers. Nothing gleamed upon her save an oversized

Ed Greenwood and Jeff Grubb

golden ring on one hand. Her dagger sheaths, one on each hip, were wrapped in dark leather. Her face was soft and cherubic. "My lord wizard," she said, "I bear news."

"Speak," said Vangerdahast.

"Gondegal is gone," she replied, almost chirping.

"Gone? How so?"

"Vanished, faded away, evaporated with the summer dew," the spy said happily.

"How comes this to you?" asked Vangerdahast.

"Through one of his captains," said the girl, "or rather, one of the sword captains he left behind. Gondegal, a half dozen of his closest aides, and the treasure he's pillaged for the past three months, all have suddenly gone missing from the Citadel. The surviving captains have their collective undergarments in the proverbial knot over this, but for all their hunting about the city, uproof and downcellar, there is no sign of their heroic master."

"And what are their plans in the absence of their leader?" asked Vangerdahast, smiling in the darkness.

"The mages who allied themselves with Gondegal have already left the city by their own powers. The remaining leadership is split, but the larger faction supports freeing the Marliirs to plead for mercy with the king on their behalf."

Vangerdahast patted his wide belly with both hands. "Return to the city, then, and pass this message on to the Marliirs: There will be a general amnesty, provided the gates are thrown open to the king at the first approach of his forces. Gondegal's men should be waiting, unarmored and unarmed, at the base of the Citadel. The king will pardon all who are there but hunt down the rest to their deaths. Can you get that message back?"

"Without a doubt," said the spy. "I go."

"In good fortune," the wizard murmured and watched her fade back into the darkness. His eyes never could follow her far. Gazing into the night, Vangerdahast permitted himself a broad smile.

Then, mastering his face and emotions, he turned and

458

strode back to the king's pavilion.

As before, Gondegal had chosen to run rather than fight. But this time he'd left a city behind, a city that would laud the arriving king as a savior and forever crush the bandit king's hopes for an empire. Not a bad little war. Arabel regained and its loyalty ensured for the next generation, with not a drop of blood shed.

They'd have to check with the outriders, of course, but the wizard believed his spy. There would be no report of any horsemen fleeing the city, no signs of any foul play among Gondegal's supporters, no bodies turning up mysteriously. And in the morning, they'd form up as planned, in full array, and go ahead—but instead of death and falling walls, the gates to Arabel would be swung wide, and the city would be spared. The king would get flowers instead of swords.

But best to tell Azoun alone about this, the wizard reasoned. If a surrender did not occur, the army of Cormyr would have to proceed with the attack. Men braced to fight would respond well to celebration, but men expecting a surrender would not be ready for battle.

Vangerdahast's route took him through the wide circle of outward-facing Purple Dragons, who passed him through with silent nods of recognition. He proceeded around the pavilion and along the back of the king's private tent. The low light within cast the shadow of the royal occupant onto the canvas—no, two occupants' shadows, silhouettes moving and merging. Through the tent walls, he heard gasps, heavy breathing, and soft sighs.

The wizard cursed to himself. Even on the eve of battle, in the middle of an armed camp, Azoun could not keep his Obarskyr blood from boiling over. There had been enough misadventures over the years to teach any king a little prudence, but the hardheaded kings of Cormyr never seemed able to care about the danger inherent in trysts.

Vangerdahast circled the tent. A single guard was posted before the hoop-arch tunnel that led to its door.

The noise and shadows were not obvious from this side, facing the crowded camp, and the wizard thanked Tymora for the king's good sense—or blind luck—in choosing his bedroll spot. The guard was fresh-faced and young, a new conscript from some country town.

"Tell the king to contact me as soon as he is done," the Royal Magician said in a loud, brisk voice, then lowered his tones and added, "And see that the young woman is escorted quickly and quietly from the campground as well."

The youngster goggled at the elder wizard as if he had suddenly spoken of flying dogs.

"Done?" asked the youth, his voice cracking. "His Majesty was retiring for the evening and dismissed me from his quarters. There was no woman there then, and none have passed me since!"

Vangerdahast looked at the boy but could discern no lie on that set, firm, loyal face. He peered to the right, and the guard turned to look that way as well. With a snarl, the wizard brushed past the guard on his left, and the confused youngster snapped a quick protest and then trotted into the tent after the wizard's fast-moving back.

The king's personal sleeping quarters were at the back of the tent, behind a fabric screen that muffled both sound and light. The wizard burst through these and cursed at the sight.

King Azoun was lying on the raised divan he always used on campaign, his armor and robes both set aside. Astride him was a woman who wore an open red gown and not much else. She had one hand raised—and that hand bore a bone dagger, ready to plunge into the king's chest.

Vangerdahast's curse slid into a snapped spell—simple magic, quickly effected. A gust of air filled the tent, booming its sides outward and hurling the red wizardess from her perch.

The wizardess was on her feet in a moment with the grace of a panther, backing away from the divan toward the edges of the tent, keeping Azoun between herself and the wizard. The young guard had the presence of mind to snatch at his belt whistle and sound an alert.

"A murder is foiled," said the wizardess, "but a greater theft has been made." She put her hands on her hips and smiled at Vangerdahast. "Tell your king that Thay thanks him for his *gift*."

Vangerdahast pointed at the woman, and spears of blue fire lanced out at her. She shouted some brief words, then became a swirling, fading mist. The magical missiles scorched tent fabric or seared grass, and shouts arose from the guards.

Suddenly angry Purple Dragons with swords in their hands were running into the tent from all directions, shouting, "The king! The king!"

A sudden, silent flash of light made them halt and blink. Its source was the belt of the Royal Magician.

"Men of Cormyr!" he snapped. "I order you, in the name of Azoun, to stop trampling the king's gear and forthwith search the camp and the grounds around, moving out as far and as fast as your legs can carry you. Look for a sorceress in a red gown; bring her back alive if you can, but bring her back. A Thayvian—tall, barefoot, long black hair! Take custody of any woman in camp that you do not recognize as one of this company; bring all such to the pavilion. *Go!*"

They'd find nothing, Vangerdahast knew, but at least their departure would let him get a look at Azoun before it might be too late. Men in armor streamed around the wizard for a moment, and then he was alone with the king.

Azoun seemed unharmed, but mazed in his mind, not seeing the wizard bent over him and mumbling when shaken. The effects of a magical charm.

Vangerdahast touched the brow of his sovereign with his fingertips and muttered words that should unwind any spell in the Thayvian arsenal.

King Azoun IV grunted, grimaced, and grabbed at his forehead. The shattering of his thrall apparently bestowed a cranial punishment akin to a hangover.

"What—what happened?" the king muttered, blinking in the lantern light.

"A Thayvian assassin," Vangerdahast announced. "She's been driven off."

"She?" asked the king, frowning. Then, slowly, he nodded. "She. Yes! She appeared out of nowhere, all shimmering robes and soft scents. She had a name. Brandy? Brannon? I thought she was a dream."

"A nightmare," Vangerdahast replied softly.

The king shook his head firmly. "I hate assassins. Apparently clearing out the Fire Knives was not enough. When we are done here, we're going to have to outlaw assassins. And Red Wizards to boot!"

"But we're not done here," said the wizard softly, spreading a blanket over the tired monarch and calling to mind a spell of magical purification and another of shielding. "First Gondegal and Arabel. Then we'll take on Red Wizards and assassins. We'll take on anything that threatens the crown or Cormyr, whatever its origin. Trust me on this."

The king smiled sleepily. "Good old Vangey. Trust me. . . ."

"Trust me on this," said the fat wizard, his voice carrying the strength of iron. "As always."

33

At The Brink
Year of the Gauntlet
(1369 DR)

The Hall of the Dragon Throne was one of the oldest parts of the court; Obarskyrs had walked here for more than a thousand years. Tall, fluted pillars ran down both sides of the lofty chamber, supporting a wooden gallery added by Palaghard II in one of many renovations performed on the site over the years.

Between the lines of columns, in the open area that was usually crowded with murmuring courtiers, stood the great sealed stone tomb of Baerauble the Mage, its surface worn smooth by the touch of a million hands over the countless years. Facing it was the lowest step of the short, curving flight that led to the high dais.

On that bright-polished height stood two arch-backed chairs of state for the princesses of Cormyr, and between them the filigreed Throne of the Dragon Queen and the taller, simpler, far older Dragon Throne itself. All of them were empty.

"Why are we here, love?" Crown Princess Tanalasta asked, nestling against Aunadar's shoulder. Something about their lovers' stroll felt wrong. They had never come near the throne room before.

Ed Greenwood and Jeff Grubb

"Some folk are going to meet us here, and if all goes well, something important is going to happen," Aunadar Bleth murmured. The dark-paneled doors partway down the room opened, and a group of young nobles strode in. Gaspar Cormaeril led them, and behind him, Tanalasta recognized Martin Illance, Morgaego Dauntinghorn, Reth Crownsilver, Cordryn Huntsilver, Braegor Truesilver, and others.

Tanalasta stood very still. "This has the look of a meeting of state," she said and stepped quickly to a bellpull to summon guards. The cord came away in her hand and fell to the floor. It had been cut through with a sword. No alarm sounded.

"This is not right," Tanalasta said, and three quick strides took her back to Aunadar, to pluck at his sleeve. "Aunadar! What's happened? Why are we gathered here?"

"The road ahead for Cormyr must be chosen," Aunadar said, turning to face the high dais, as if he expected more figures to suddenly appear there. "Your father has died," he added shortly. "We think he died some time ago—and that foul wizard, our Royal Magician, hid that fact from us all, hoping to take the throne before you could be crowned."

Tanalasta reeled and then clung to him, fighting down sudden tears. Azoun! Papa! Oh, merciless gods! Her mind flooded with memories of a smiling bearded face, hands gently helping her to toddle her first few steps, or sweeping her up onto a saddle so high that she shrieked in fear, or . . .

Aunadar must have known that the wizard was going to appear by the throne. He was watching, hard-faced, as the air shimmered and glowed on the broad step below the thrones where men knelt to be knighted and envoys to plead. When the light died away, three men stood on that step: the fat old Royal Magician of Cormyr, and on either side of him a grim noble holding a drawn sword. Lord Giogi Wyvernspur was on the wizard's right, and young Dauneth Marliir on his left.

Tanalasta stared up at them through helpless tears.

What was going to happen? Was there going to be a fight?

She turned to ask Aunadar, only to discover that she stood alone. Her lover had walked back to stand with Gaspar Cormaeril and the other young nobles.

The crown princess looked from the trio by the throne to the confident line of nobility, and a sudden chill shook her. Father! she cried silently, come back! Cormyr needs you! *I* need you.

A voice cut through her anguish, a crisp, measured voice that struck her like ice water.

"The fates of our king and his two cousins have left a perilous lack of authority in Cormyr," said the wizard Vangerdahast, "particularly in light of the current dispositions of Princess Alusair and Queen Filfaeril. The whereabouts of both remain unknown; we can only presume they are in hiding. Moreover, Crown Princess Tanalasta is, by her own words, unwilling to take up the crown at this time."

His words echoed around the room. One of the nobles stepped forward and raised his head to speak, but the Royal Magician went on. "I will act as regent until the princess is willing to assume the throne. If, at the end of five years, she has not done so, we shall meet again—the wizards, high clergy, and nobles of the realm, all together in council, to debate the future of the realm. Until that time, there will be no council of nobles or anyone else in Cormyr. I shall assist the princess in making ready to ascend the Dragon Throne, and she shall marry her fiancé Aunadar Bleth during this time if she desires to do so. I hold here"—the mage raised a piece of parchment over his head—"a writ of regency, signed by Queen Filfaeril. It names me rightfully what I now claim myself: Regent of Cormyr."

Tanalasta stared up at the wizard, torn between grief and loneliness . . . and now, in the midst of that loss, a rising rage. The old wizard was seizing Cormyr as his own! And it was all her fault! She could have stood strong against him. She could have insisted on his kneeling to her . . . but she had not. And now it was too late.

But why had Father left her so unprepared? And where was Alusair? Where was Mama? Stolen away—as if by magic. Magic. Of course. In the face of such dark power, how could she hope to lead the realm?

Eyes swimming with tears, Tanalasta turned to face the line of nobles again. The next words would surely be theirs.

"You are sadly mistaken, Lord High Wizard," Aunadar Bleth said coldly into the waiting room, "and as usual, you sadly overreach yourself."

On their slow, numb way down the room to look at the nobles, Tanalasta's eyes fell across the doors the nobles had come in by, and there she saw a shadowy figure step forward and wave to her.

Tanalasta almost fainted. There was no mistaking that face, those gestures—and now a finger going to lips to counsel silence, and a grim motion to hold on. Tanalasta bit her lip hard enough to draw blood. The figure was already drawing back into the shadows beyond the doorway when she managed to marshal enough control to manage a careful, regal nod.

"Look at yourself now," Aunadar Bleth was saying, "as we do: alone save for a few misguided lackeys of minor houses. Yet you stand making demands and issuing orders with only your own pride to give them any authority. Wizard, you remain in Cormyr only at our sufferance, and you will be allowed to stay only if you accede to our rightful demands. We need no skulking, manipulating regent, but our proper *queen!*"

His shout rang back echoes from the high ceiling of the chamber and was answered by a second roar of approval from the nobles who stood with him. "The inexperience of the princess will be addressed by a guiding council of nobles, whose deliberations will be open for all the folk of Cormyr to hear. My dear Tanalasta and I will be wed forthwith, and as consort to our queen, I shall chair the council and ensure that it acts in a just and honorable manner."

Aunadar stepped forward, eyes alight with excitement, and pressed on. "In return for your peaceful agreement to this, Lord Vangerdahast, you'll be permitted to keep your title and be awarded a seat on the council, though your secretive and disloyal war wizards must and shall be disbanded. The time of Obarskyr kings who rule without regard for the people, trusting in the murderous spells of their own private pet wizards to keep them in power over a populace that fears and hates them, is past, and such days will never return to Cormyr. The people shall be free at last."

As if they'd waited for his words as a cue, a rabble of other courtiers, joined by a few clergy and high-ranking court officials, burst through the double doors at the end of the hall and surged forward, their boots thunderous as they passed through the paneled doors. They surged forward, voices rising, and the nobles already in the room turned to see what this new disturbance was . . .

. . . in time to see a concealed door open in one of the pillars down the hall, and the sorceress Cat Wyvernspur step forth. Her hands were already raised, a wand clutched in one palm, and her mouth moving. She turned, faced the advancing throng, and suddenly waved her hands outward dismissively, and the foremost priests and courtiers ran into an invisible barrier. Said barrier did nothing to hamper sight or sound, but permitted nothing solid to pass through. Thrown caps and daggers tested it for a few moments, but Cat had already turned to calmly face Bleth's nobles already in the room, her arms crossed. One of said nobles, Martin Illance, clapped a hand to his sword hilt, looking meaningfully in her direction, but she caught his eyes and shook her head ever so slightly. Illance's hand fell away to his side once more.

"More foul magic," Morgaego Dauntinghorn snarled, and the words had scarcely left his mouth when another secret door opened in another pillar, and a grim line of Purple Dragons strode out to stand with drawn swords, barring the way of the conspirator nobles.

A grim Lareth Gulur led the soldiers, and the center

of their line was anchored by his superior, Hathlan Talar. Most were battle-scarred veterans, but at the end of the line stood a new recruit, uncomfortable in his stiff new uniform, but whose sword twitched with eagerness. All the Purple Dragons bent their burning eyes on the luxuriously dressed young nobles.

"More foul magic indeed," the Royal Magician said into the deep silence. "Think for a moment of just how well a hundred nobles would fare if they were ever sent against a hundred war wizards."

Aunadar Bleth smiled crookedly and said in silken tones, "I have done so—and have an answer: a blade that I am confident can cut down a hundred war wizards!" He raised his hand and made a quick, intricate gesture as he called, "Hear us, Lady Brantarra! Attend us, Red Wizardess of Murbant!"

A moment later, as everyone in the chamber watched in breathless silence, a cluster of moving, winking lights appeared at Bleth's shoulder, and a low, purring voice that carried from end to end of that hall spoke out of it.

"Greetings, Vangerdahast, Royal Magician of Cormyr. Call me Brantarra— call me your nemesis. Long have you wondered who it was who shielded rebels and contrary nobles and outlaws from your seeking spells, and who protected them against your magic of rulership and punishment. I stand ready now to shield all the other nobles of Cormyr who desire such protection—from you and your petty magelings. I am the bane of the war wizards. I am the one who has frustrated you for so long."

Vangerdahast shifted and stirred on the step where he stood but said nothing. The triumphant voice rolled on.

"You think these were your masterminds, these clever young nobles unable to see beyond the ends of their swords? Mine was the hand that stole the abraxus from your precious vaults. Mine was the hand that guided these pawns before you. Mine was the skill that took your king's will, on a night eighteen years ago, in the sight of the walls of Arabel. Mine was the body that bore the son who will be your next king!"

Aunadar Bleth's head snapped around in surprise. He gaped at the sparkling, circling lights as the voice from the heart of them added, "Know, nobles of Cormyr, that the war wizards you fear so much will be shattered within the season and gone utterly soon after—as I and those mages loyal to me ensure that each war wizard is hunted to extinction."

There was a brief but sharp chorus of gasps and murmurs from the courtiers crowded up against Cat's barrier. The next words spoken, though they were soft, cut that noise off as if a knife had fallen across their throats.

"And who will protect Cormyr against the Red Wizardess and *her* wizards then?" Vangerdahast asked mildly, taking another step down from the throne. Giogi and Dauneth moved with him, their eyes watchful.

"Protect Cormyr against me?" came the low, rich voice out of the lights. "Why? I know and love the realm well. I have borne a son by King Azoun to prove it. A future king . . ."

More murmurs, and even some laughter, came from the crowd of watching courtiers just inside the entrance to the hall. The gathering of lights hissed a deep curse and the laughter quieted, but the murmurs continued. Even the densest courtiers realized the minimal value of an unrecognized son of Azoun.

Tanalasta cast a look at the dark doorway where she'd seen the figure that counseled her to silence, and then looked away again.

"This land has had enough of kings," Aunadar Bleth said firmly, "and despite what you have just heard her say, this Red Wizardess and I have a solemn agreement on this point. I know not the measure of Thayvians, but noble families of Cormyr keep their word and expect others to do the same."

"Do they?" Vangerdahast's voice was as soft as silk, or the edge of an oversharpened dagger. "I am pleased to hear of this new shift in their natures."

Aunadar Bleth showed anger for the first time, tossing back his head to glare up at the old wizard. "Don't bandy words about falsehoods with me, wizard. For over a thousand years and more, the Bleths have served the crown of Cormyr well, fighting and dying for their country. Yet somehow the Obarskyrs they served so loyally managed to overlook the Bleths time and time again. One can grow used to being taken advantage of, but one need not grow to like it. Now the blood of the Obarskyrs has run weak indeed, and the Bleths shall be overlooked no longer. Now will come the ultimate service to the Obarskyrs and to Cormyr: the fusion of the proud lineage of Cormyr's two oldest families into one bloodline—a Bleth bloodline that shall not hold the Dragon Throne in a tight-taloned tyrant's grasp, but share rule over the Forest Country with all of its people." He turned to the crown princess and smiled coldly. "The power I have come to love."

Tanalasta's lips trembled for a moment as she struggled to find the words she wanted to say, but when she did speak, her voice was firm and high and clear.

"I am shocked, Aunadar Bleth, to learn that you love me only for my station and lineage and the power you can wield through me. Do you care so little for Tanalasta the woman?"

There was triumph in the young noble's eyes as he looked into hers and shrugged. "It matters little if I love you or you me," he said callously. "What matters is that the power of the Obarskyrs be dashed down, and the wheel of time move this land into brighter, fairer times that all citizens can agree with. The old Cormyr died with your father—its last king."

There was a gasp and stir that rose almost to a shriek as the figure that had skulked in the shadows of the doorway strode slowly and purposefully into the room. When the watching crowd saw the crown glittering on its head, their cries died into instant heavy silence.

"I find your presumptions a trifle premature, young Bleth," said a voice that everyone in the room knew, "and I order your surrender. Kneel to me, your true and rightful king, Azoun Obarskyr, a man who, despite your best efforts, is not dead just yet."

Aunadar Bleth turned white and swallowed. He looked quickly around the room, as if seeking ways to escape, and then drew himself up proudly, eyes blazing. "No. I am no lesser man than you. Why should I kneel to a man whose time is past and whose morals demean us all? Why should I kneel to a man who should be dead!"

"Why," the low voice from the lights at Bleth's shoulder purred, "should you kneel to a dead man?"

A coldly, darkly beautiful female face rose into view among the whirling radiances. It was a face Vangerdahast had seen before, the night before the fall of Arabel. From its eyes leapt two red, ravening beams of light.

The nobles standing with Gaspar Cormaeril screamed and ducked for cover as the magical beams cut through their ranks and stabbed at the king.

The rays burst into raging flames upon striking an unseen barrier. The eye beams clawed futilely at a barrier that shielded the grimly smiling Azoun and washed out along it, revealing the true dimensions of the barrier.

The barrier was anchored at three points. One point was the sorceress Cat, who held aloft a small white oval, a talisman of protective power. The other two points were in the hitherto empty minstrels' balcony, high above the king, where two people rose stiffly, holding similar talismans. One of the two in the balcony was a Harper with hair the color of honey and eyes like two dancing flames—Emthrara. The other was a bright-eyed, unshaven merchant dealer in turret tops and spires named Rhauligan.

Ripples of Brantarra's ruby-red radiance rushed across the barrier now, streaming toward the three ovals at its extremities, and then reflected back, like ripples in a small fountain, to its center. The flames meeting there flickered, pulsed, and burst forth as a great reaching tongue of fire, which roared back at the face in the light with frightening speed and fury.

The Red Wizardess screamed. Her features vanished under the onslaught of her own returned magic, and sobbing howls of pain echoed off the vaulted ceiling of the hall for a moment before the lights winked, flashed bright again—and the agonized face was gone.

In its place stood something gleaming and golden, something that stood like an upright, motionless bull.

"The abraxus!" a dozen voices exclaimed in horrified unison. Aunadar Bleth smiled tightly and said, "Thank you, wizardess, for restoring my clockwork toy. It needs a human soul to power its magical engine, and my lady Brantarra has thought even of that!" He placed his hand along the back of the golden beast. There was the sharp click of a switch being thrown, and Aunadar pointed at Gaspar Cormaeril. "I have need of your noble spirit, Gaspar!" shouted Aunadar.

Gaspar Cormaeril screamed. The noble allies who previously stood alongside him now scattered like frightened fowl in a barnyard. Gaspar pawed at his ornate vest and pulled forth a large ruby, given to him days earlier by his friend Aunadar Bleth. Green and crimson flames erupted from the gem, spreading along his chest and arms as if they were coated with oil. Gaspar writhed in helpless, rising agony as the mystic fire consumed him.

The green flickering flames grew into a green snake of crackling magical force, a twisting, questing rope of radiance that climbed over the heads of the nobles and then descended, like a vengeful arrow, to strike the abraxus.

Strike—and be absorbed. The golden bull pulsed with green light, and the flames left the tottering, shriveled body of the stricken noble, infusing the abraxus with life energy. Gaspar Cormaeril fluttered like a dry leaf caught on grass in a high wind, and then collapsed into dust. Not even his bones survived to hit the floor.

The abraxus rattled, shook, and moved, raising its head and shifting its shoulders with a heavy clank. Its head began to turn, and Aunadar, fairly leaping with glee, pointed and shouted to direct the automaton at the king. This time there would be no mistake.

Forgotten on the dais, the Royal Magician of Cormyr

quietly finished casting a spell and let his hands fall, a grim smile on his lips.

Suddenly the crown princess burst into motion in a swirl of robes, racing to stand in front of her father. "No! Aunadar, you must not do this!"

Aunadar's intent, ruthless expression did not change. "Join me, my love," he hissed between clenched teeth. "Throw off your heavy past and join me in a brighter future. I will comfort you, care for you, protect you, in a way that these others never will!"

Tanalasta recoiled from the look in Aunadar Bleth's eyes, but her gaze did not leave him. She looked neither at Vangerdahast nor at her father, nor at the assembled trembling nobles. Instead, her mouth formed a smooth, thin line. "No," she said simply. "I will not. Stop this madness now."

His glittering eyes shifted from her in an instant, dismissing her, and turned back to his quarry, Azoun, who stood calmly and quietly, watching the metallic doom come down upon him.

Tanalasta raised her hands, as if she could stop the steadily advancing abraxus, and shouted, "Aunadar! Stop this! Don't—"

Aunadar lifted his lips back from his teeth in a wolfish grin, and a hissing began. The poisonous breath of the abraxus rushed out, swirling like smoke, but did not reach the terrified princess. Instead, it struck something hard and hitherto unseen in the air before it—something large and curving. The smokelike breath of the beast stole outward along it, revealing the great curve of another barrier, this one a sphere that enclosed the abraxus—and with it, Aunadar Bleth.

On the steps below the throne, the wizard Vangerdahast's smile tightened. Giogi looked at him. Just for an instant, he saw the glittering stare of the ruthless hunter in the old mage's eyes, and from below them came the raw sound of Aunadar's disbelieving scream.

The abraxus breathed again, and the sphere could be seen clearly now as deadly vapors swirled within it. It

473

was moving with the clanking monster, proceeding slowly down the Hall of the Dragon Throne toward the king.

Tanalasta turned an instant before the magical shield would have touched her. She stepped backward one step, then a second, and rushed into her father's embrace. Azoun's arms went around her and held her firmly.

Behind her, Aunadar's scream broke off into choking, frantic hacking sounds that went on and on as the smoky sphere advanced. Tanalasta turned in the king's arms to stare at it in horrified fascination. Her treacherous fiancé was going to die, but would he be the only one? Were they going to be able to stop this golden clanking horror?

Was it her imagination, or was the sphere growing smaller?

The abraxus hissed again, and through the rising smoke of its breath, she dimly saw Aunadar bend double and blindly stagger away, only to strike the far side of the sphere. He clawed weakly at it, and then slid down into the swirling smoke. The sphere *was* drawing in around the golden monster!

Up on the dais, Giogi and Dauneth both caught sight of sudden sweat bursting into being on Vangerdahast's brow. They turned to the old wizard, opening their mouths in identical protests of concern. The sweat was running off his old nose and dripping from the Royal Magician's beard.

The sphere grew smaller, and the wizard began to tremble. The two men caught hold of Vangerdahast's shoulders and elbows gently and held him up, even when his body began to shudder and spasm, folding up in violent, wrenching contortions.

"What can we do, sir wizard?" Dauneth hissed, but Vangerdahast set his teeth and made no reply. His eyes were steady on the sphere below him, the sphere that was dwindling rapidly now. It reached the edges of the abraxus itself, which stood hard and golden against it, though only for a moment. Then the golden automaton bent over sideways with a deafening crack of shattered metal. Tortured golden plates shrieked in protest as the sphere closed inward steadily. There was a splash of crimson as the body of Aunadar Bleth was broken along with the golden creature. Then there was another scream, the inhuman scream of crumpling metal.

Something tugged at Tanalasta's hands. It was Cat, placing the oval talisman into them. She closed the fingers of the crown princess around it, gave Tanalasta an encouraging smile, and stepped a pace away, raising her hands in a quick, deft spell-weaving.

On the dais, between Wyvernspur and Marliir, Tanalasta noticed Vangerdahast sagging like a man gravely wounded. Cat lifted her hands in shaping gestures, and Vangerdahast shouted a single tortured, almost unintelligible word.

The sphere vanished, consumed in a sudden ball of flames. Tanalasta flung a hand over her eyes an instant before the fire became blindingly bright.

Then the Hall of the Dragon Throne rocked under the force of a blast that hurled flames up in a roaring column to scorch the ceiling, but touched nothing else.

Cat Wyvernspur, whose spell had directed the flames harmlessly upward, reeled back into the Obarskyrs, father and daughter. Azoun's other arm found its way around her as well. The spent sorceress sagged against the king's shoulder briefly, then immediately disengaged. The ragged panting of the magess was suddenly loud in a chamber that had grown silent again. All within the Hall of the Dragon—royals, spell-casters, Purple Dragons, and nobles—were silent for a moment.

The sphere was gone, leaving only a scorched circle on the marble tiles. Aunadar Bleth was gone. The abraxus was gone.

And on the steps beside the throne, the old wizard rose unsteadily, his hands on the shoulders of two faithful nobles. Vangerdahast cleared his throat and roared, "The king is restored to us! Long live the king!" The ceiling echoed back the Royal Magician's words, and they rolled out and down the room.

Someone in the crowd of nobles cried, "Long live the king!"

Other voices joined in an instant later: "The king! The king! Long live the king!"

"Azoun!" roared the Purple Dragons, their swords flashing straight up in salute. "Azoun!"

"Long live the king!" The chant was spreading beyond the room now, resounding through the palace as wondering people flooded toward the Hall of the Dragon Throne.

"Long Live the king!" The roar echoed around the Hall like thunder, and then an old noble burst into tears and went to his knees. "Azoun—lead us!"

"Long live the king!" the chant came again, but it seemed to be coming almost entirely from outside the chamber now. Inside the Hall, man after man after highborn lady were going to their knees—another, and then another—until only the king, Tanalasta, and Vangerdahast remained on their feet. Dauneth dropped to one knee, but kept his sword ready and his wits sharp for one last attack.

Dauneth let his gaze drift to the face of Azoun—who was smiling quietly, and nodding to noble after noble, and to faces in the line of Purple Dragons—and then to the smiling face of the crown princess.

The heir to House Marliir looked at that face thoughtfully for a long time. He knew that both Lord Wyvernspur and Vangerdahast had noticed his intent gaze and followed it to its destination, and he did not care.

Gods, but she was fair. He could kneel to a woman like that. Dauneth drew in a deep breath, noting that Tanalasta had not wept for her lost love, Aunadar. Perhaps there was hope yet.

Dauneth Marliir, heir to a stained family name, sprang to his feet. "Long live the king!" he roared like a lion, raising his blade in flashing salute.

Azoun's head turned in time to see Giogi's blade flash up to join Dauneth's, and then the old man between them giggled like a schoolgirl. Sudden magefire shaped a sword in his hand, too. The three blades swung up together as Cat, Azoun, and Tanalasta laughed as one, and the three men on the steps thundered, "Long live the king! Long live Cormyr!"

The echoes of their shout were so thunderous that only Giogi and Dauneth heard the old wizard's muttered addition: "*This* ought to be worth a feast."

Epilogue

Year of the Gauntlet
(1369 DR)

he conspirators, real and incidental, were gathered in Gryphonsblade Hall. The king's sickbed had been removed and the original furnishings replaced. The windows that had been sealed for fear of contagion were now flung wide, and below them the city of Suzail was spread out like a blanket, leading downward to a cool, blue sea that mirrored the sky above. Somewhere down there a bell was tolling, long ringing peals that cascaded through the streets.

"The king lives," said Cat Wyvernspur, nodding her head towards the bell's joyous clangor. "Long live the king!"

The king in question was playing chess with Cat's husband, Lord Giogi. Giogi would stare intently at the board for many minutes, then carefully nudge a piece to its new location. Azoun would then stroke his beard twice, reach out, and make his move. Giogi would sink his chin into his hands and return to his intense concentration.

"How's the game going?" she asked, stroking Giogi's shoulders.

"Totally engrossing," her husband replied. "I've tried every variation in the book, but I can't crack his defenses. Worse, every time he repulses one of my assaults, I'm in a worse position. He's won three games so far, and in *this* little slaughter, I'm down two turrets and a Purple Dragon already."

Cat smiled fondly at the top of her lord's head, exchanged a solemn wink with the king, and took up a ewer of wine before sauntering over to where Vangerdahast, Dauneth Marliir, and Tanalasta were deep in conversation.

The Royal Magician looked over at the game in progress. "How is young Lord Wyvernspur doing?"

"Badly," said Cat, pouring herself a goblet of blood-red wine. "He's baffled by the king's masterful defenses."

"Should I let him in on the secret?" asked the mage, his eyes twinkling.

"Secret?"

"Azoun never plans out his moves in chess," said the wizard. "He just moves what catches his fancy at the moment. Thinks of a move, does it on the instant, and—bless my soul—it's usually right."

Cat chuckled. "Oh, don't tell Giogi. His Majesty beat him twenty-seven games straight when we were keeping him in the basement. My poor husband was up half the night memorizing *Chess Variations of the Masters of Old Impiltur* just on the chance of getting one more game in. I think he'd be crushed if you told him."

Giogi let out a curse, and the king answered it with a mighty laugh as he took the noble's queen and forced checkmate.

"Looks like he's crushed anyway," said the wizard, loudly enough for the two combatants to hear.

"It was a Theskan double-counter gambit," said Giogi mournfully. "I didn't stand a chance after the tenth move."

"One more noble crushed beneath the heel of the Purple Dragon," Azoun said, smiling.

"It's good to see you up and around again, Sire," said Dauneth. "But I'm puzzled as to how you were cured. It was my understanding that no magic worked against the venomous disease in your blood."

"Ah, but that's exactly the point," said Vangerdahast. "The blots of disease in the abraxus's venom were all enwrapped in their own dead-magic zones. Spells couldn't reach the disease itself through the zones, and so His Majesty could not be cured by magic. But those very zones held the key to defeating the disease."

Dauneth looked puzzled.

Warming to the task, Vangerdahast went on with the enthusiasm of a proud crafter of magic. "We bled His Majesty, then enchanted the blood we collected. A simple spell—Nystul's Magic Aura—that would just turn the blood magical. Except, of course, the parts of the blood surrounded by dead-magic zones."

"The disease."

"Precisely. Then we worked up a spell to teleport enchanted blood to another container. That left the diseased blood, with its tiny dead zones, back in the original container, since it could not be affected by the spell. Then we infused the king again with the purified, magic-free blood."

Dauneth shook his head. "But you couldn't do that with all the royal blood at once, or His Majesty would die. And such a process is like diluting wine—the taint grows thinner and thinner, but there will always be some scrap of disease left."

"Again correct," the wizard replied, "but eventually the healthy blood overwhelmed the tainted, and the body of the king began to heal naturally. We had to effectively replace all of the blood in the king's body twice before his natural resistance could deal with it."

Dauneth goggled. "But that must have taken days! I can't think of anything else so time-consuming . . ."

"*And* painful," added the king, taking a seat with the others around the table. Giogi, still shaking his head, moved to where Cat perched. She handed him a goblet of wine, and he held it in one hand, rubbing her bare shoulder absentmindedly with his other hand.

"It is not," Azoun said feelingly, "a process I care to repeat."

"Nor will it be," the Lord High Wizard responded. "Now that we know the process, we can craft a spell to duplicate its effects in manifestation. And as much as I want to take credit for the process, it is almost entirely the work of Dimswart and Alaphondar, our devoted sages. I'm afraid I was caught up in other things."

"No," said Tanalasta with a solemn smile. "You were too busy scheming and dreaming up plots against the crown."

"And successfully, I might add," said Cat.

"Don't blame our good wizard too much, child," said the king. "When I was a lad, one of the lessons he taught me was that things are not always what they seem, and that the most evil people can put on a good face if they are after something. While this blood process he's so gleeful about was going on, I was as weak as a kitten. So I gave Vangerdahast orders to keep everyone in the dark and let him spin out all the dark intrigues he could think of, so long as he didn't bring all-out war to Suzail or bring the palace down around our ears."

"Separating the wolves from the sheep," Giogi said brightly, "or the wheat from the chaff, or the mill from the floss . . . or whatever."

"Aye," said the king. "The power of the Cormaerils, the Bleths, and the others whose acts were treasonable is now broken. Their lands are seized, their titles are stripped from them, and some will be exiled. I'll not be slaying more folk than have already died, however. . . . That's one lesson I've learned from Vangerdahast and his forebears. The realm is stronger than any one man, and it's always best not to bleed away the best of its stock in wasteful executions."

"I've made it known," Vangerdahast added silkily, "that any interpretation of this clemency as a weakness of the monarch would be a mistake . . . almost certainly a *fatal* mistake."

"However, letting the *threat* of execution hang over a man seems quite a useful tactic," Azoun agreed. "Those who supported the traitors but were not immediately involved in the plot have either recanted or are heading for Sembia, Westgate, or Waterdeep with all the haste they can muster."

"And those who recanted or denied their allegiance to the conspiracy know they are being watched," Cat put in. "Knowing that, they are going to be on their best behavior trying to prove their loyalty like the youngest and most enthusiastic of knights for the next few years."

"And they will not be the only ones," Vangerdahast added slyly. "I made it a point to personally thank the families who sat on their hedges, blowing neither hot nor cold, as the realm almost pitched into the abyss around them. Particularly the supposedly loyal Huntsilvers, Crownsilvers, and Truesilvers. I'm sure they'll spend the next few years trying fervently to prove their loyalty to the crown as well."

"And what of those who passed your little test?" asked the crown princess, her eyes darting to meet those of the old wizard. "Those who risked life and limb when they were convinced Lord Vangerdahast was a traitor?" She lowered her gaze to the floor and added, "As I did."

One of Vangerdahast's large and hairy-backed hands closed over hers. "Lady Highness," he said gently, "how could you have thought otherwise?" The wizard rose and struck an actor's pose. "After all, I learned how to act from the best tavern dancers in Suzail! My performance, I'll have you know, was peerless . . . simply *peerless!*"

Tanalasta tried not to laugh, then snorted helplessly, and then roared. Vangerdahast blinked at her, affecting an air of innocence, and Azoun's rich mirth rolled out to join them.

When at last she could speak again, Tanalasta asked, "Seriously, Father, what about those who remained true, like Marliir and Giogi?"

"And Vangerdahast's mob of agents, including the Harper Emthrara, and that turret salesman—" the king snapped his fingers—"Rhauligan. A royal writ, absolving them from any charges, should do the trick. Particularly for the Harper and the merchant."

"And there are absences to be accounted for and holes to fill," continued the king. "For instance, with the passing of loyal Thomdor, I need a new military commander in Arabel. It strikes me that any candidate for such a post should be brave, loyal, and come from a local Arabellan family, so that the city will never go into rebellion again. Young Marliir, are you up to the task?"

"I?" asked Marliir, dumbfounded. "I—I—" He slid from his seat, dropping dazedly to one knee. "Are you sure, Sire?"

"We'll save the ceremony for later, in front of the full court," said Azoun with a smile, leaning froward to clap the young man on the shoulder, "but you'll be a good Warden of the Eastern Marches. It's good to see someone *care* so deeply about Cormyr. Moreover, your naming to that title will send a message to a number of people about their own place within my kingdom. And as for you, Lord Giogi . . ."

"Please, Sire," said the Wyvernspur lord, raising a restraining hand, "I'm quite content with my life in Immersea. I desire neither a military post nor a rank."

"Good to hear it, for I was going to offer neither," said the king heartily. "Bhereu's place at High Horn needs to go to someone with fighting blood. Perhaps that Bishop of the Black Blades, Gwennath. Don't take offense, young Wyvernspur, but I don't think even the most capable courtiers could survive you for long—or rather, your unique method of crashing head-on into problems and wrestling them into submission without ever understanding them!"

There was a general round of chuckles. Giogi reddened and ducked his head.

"By the gods, I wish half my nobles were as much fun as you provide," Azoun murmured, then straightened himself and boomed, "Nay, Wyvernspur, into your hands I give the Cormaeril lands, in toto, which should quintuple your income as well as your responsibilities. I hope you are up to it."

"He'll have a little help, Sire," said Cat, taking her

husband's hand. Giogi opened his mouth and then closed it again without saying anything. He tried the process over again, several times, and then helplessly poked Cat with a finger.

She looked down at him fondly and said, "Your Majesty, Lord Wyvernspur is so honored that he's speechless—for the moment."

There were chuckles all around once more. Azoun raised his glass in salute to his dumbstruck noble and added, "I look forward to playing chess with you again in the near future, too."

Even Giogi managed a chuckle—a rueful one—this time.

"I have one question," said Tanalasta, curling her feet up under her where she sat. "Once you knew you were going to live, did anyone else know about it?"

"Well, I had to tell your mother," said Azoun. "It wouldn't do to have her find out that I was alive through court gossips."

"And I sent word to Alusair," added Vangerdahast, "through my war wizards, so she'd not worry—and wouldn't come galloping home to defend the throne against the forty or so nobles who were already riding with her!"

"So what you're telling me," Tanalasta said to the wizard, her tone firm and her voice level, "is that I was the *only* one of the immediate royal family who did not know my own father was alive, and expected to remain so—and I wouldn't have to take the throne at all."

"Well, you might have told Aunadar, and, well . . ." said the wizard, before trailing off into silence. That silence suddenly held sway over the entire room. The crown princess leaned forward.

"Another of your little lessons, eh, mage?" Tanalasta pressed.

Vangerdahast cleared his throat. "Your Highness, as much as I respect your abilities, I have a duty to the crown, and as such must protect it as best as I can, whatever the personal cost."

"And I can't be the shy, dutiful daughter forever," said the princess quietly. She sighed and then lifted her chin and added, "I cannot afford the luxury of being a royal wallflower. I've decided I must develop my own self, my own strengths, and my own goals."

She stared into the old wizard's eyes and added, "If I do not, I'll always be a pawn, regardless of any apparent power I hold and no matter what crown I wear."

"Well, I wouldn't put it in quite so many words," Vangerdahast replied, reddening and pointedly ignoring the smile that was growing on Azoun's face.

"I would," said the princess, crossing her arms. "Since this whole matter began, I've felt unprepared and unready. Unprepared to deal with my father's illness, unready to deal with the vicious fights that promptly erupted among the nobles, and unwilling to take the throne on my own. That will have to change for Cormyr to continue. And you, wizard, will help."

Vangerdahast stood up and bowed low to her. "When the crown princess calls, I will do everything in my power to advise and to aid."

Tanalasta shook her head. "No. I'll not be your puppet any more than I should have been Bleth's. I want your real help. Long ago you and my father went traipsing all over the kingdom, did you not?"

"Ah, yes," said the wizard carefully. "It was necessary for a prince to truly know the realm and its people."

"And not a princess?" asked Tanalasta sharply.

Vangerdahast shrugged. "Well, I suppose we could make a few trips. You'll need some proper walking boots and warm, sensible clothing . . . and you should know the bath water in the wilderness will be colder than you're used to."

He seemed to remember something and added brightly, "There may be weretigers . . ."

Azoun looked at the ceiling, but Tanalasta thought she saw the beginnings of a smile at the corners of his mouth.

". . . but I'm told my snoring isn't all that bad," the old wizard continued, "and these old bones can still carry me a little way. But you already know most of what I could teach you: history, accounts, genealogy, and the like. . . ."

"You can teach me magic," said Tanalasta flatly.

In all his years with Vangerdahast, Azoun had never seen him stammer. The Royal Magician's eyes opened very wide, and he stammered now, his mouth flapping as he tried to get out the words, "Oh! Ah! Oh— W-Well . . . there's never been an Obarskyr mage before. . . ."

"Then it is seriously overdue," said the princess, "and you're the one who said that the kingdom needs both spells and swords to keep afloat! So what say you, mage?"

The wizard looked rather helplessly at the others. Dauneth Marliir stared at him intently, face carefully expressionless but eyes leaping with excitement, urging him to say yes. *That* one was going to be a diplomat, the wizard thought, and looked elsewhere.

Giogi patted Cat's hand and raised a goblet in toast to the idea.

Azoun spread his hands and said, "It is your decision, Royal Magician. Of course, I can refuse my eldest daughter nothing."

Vangerdahast let out a deep sigh, one that seemed to come from the core of his being. He blinked once, then smiled faintly.

"Very well," he said raising his own goblet. "Once more into the breach, for crown and for country, for king *and* for queen, and most of all . . . for Cormyr."